Hilda Hall

I Love Forever
July 1945 -

SIX OF THEM

AUTHOR OF:

- The Patriot (1928)
- The Devil (1928)
- The Rebels (1929)
- Guerra (1930)
- King Haber (1930)
- The Hero (1931)
- Mirror of Fools (1933)
- Another Caesar (1935)
- The Gaudy Empire (1937)
- The Friends of the People (1942)

SIX OF THEM

BY

ALFRED NEUMANN

Translated from the German by

Anatol Murad

THE MACMILLAN COMPANY · NEW YORK

1945

First Printing

A WARTIME BOOK
THIS COMPLETE EDITION IS PRODUCED IN FULL COMPLIANCE WITH THE GOVERNMENT'S REGULATIONS FOR CONSERVING PAPER AND OTHER ESSENTIAL MATERIALS.

MANUFACTURED IN THE UNITED STATES OF AMERICA
BY THE VAIL-BALLOU PRESS, INC., BINGHAMTON, N. Y.

TO

STUART AND ELIZABETH CHEVALIER

The writing of the book occupied the author from September, 1943, to June, 1944.

CONTENTS

The manifesto, printed in italics on pp. 116–117, is a free translation of the text of the handbill distributed by students of the University of Munich in the spring of 1943 and transmitted by the European underground organization.

Chapter One

DAWN

I

The beam of a flashlight stabs through the grated peephole in the iron door of the solitary confinement cell.

Sophia starts and awakens, torn out of a dream bathed in a bright sun and drenched in a happiness she had never known in all her twenty years. To dream it on the threshold of this very day! The world was changed under the new sun, though it was Munich, her own familiar city, through which the dreaming girl walked, her arm in Christopher's. "Now we are alone in the world," Christopher declared joyously. It was supreme happiness, the girl felt, to be alone in the world with her beloved Christopher.

And now the flashlight, yellow and piercing, has dissolved the blissful dream. The light-beam withdraws from the cell. Sophia lies there in icy fear.

During yesterday's long examination—or rather, during the many examinations—she never found time to be afraid; and when finally they let her alone, sometime in the night, she fell asleep, numb and apathetic. Unless her memory tricks her, she had also been asleep earlier, while still sitting under the Jupiter light, between question and answer or during question and answer. She can no longer remember very clearly the end of the examination; but this she can still recall: how her thick curly hair shielded her from the cruelty of the light and fell over her eyes, obeying every thrust of the head; how they wanted to tie her hair with a piece of string and it would not let itself be caught, obeying every twitch of the scalp. She remembers a voice saying, "We should have shorn off her blond halo;" and another voice, "The shearing will come anyway and radically."

Now that she has tumbled out of the good dream, she congeals from fear. It is fear proper, a physical condition, a hurt, which at the moment permits no reflection. The cell is ice-cold, and this icy cold is fear—fear coming from without, doing violence to the body which, from within, is turned to ice through fear. If this should go on, this breaking in and breaking out of fear, and if the two mighty forces should join together to crush her, then there would no longer be any hope for escape. Escape from what? The girl strives to find a name for the nameless fear. There are left in her head or in her ears only the two voices threatening her with a radical shearing. She puts her hands protectingly upon the hair which had shielded her from the glare of the inquisition, and presses it against her face. Look! It gives warmth, too, the dear hair. With quaking body, she weeps into her hair. And then she becomes calmer.

Was Christopher arrested too? she asks herself, as she had asked herself all day yesterday. It had been an endless litany of a question, humming in her brain throughout the examinations, obstreperously and unsuccessfully bucking the inquisitor's smooth reserve and dialectical superiority. Also when the girl was not under fire of examination, the question kept restlessly ringing in her ears and finally led, unanswered and unsatisfied, into the delusion and the fool's gold of the dream. It is withal an incomplete and improper question; for it should also include the others who belong to the "group," and whose fate is unknown: brother Hans and Alexander Welte, the professor and his wife. And if at least it were only love —the forgivable and ruthless fear for the beloved! But when the lightning struck and her quaking heart tossed up the question, the question about Christopher, it was not a thought of love, but a feverous grimace of a thought or a fright psychosis or simply hysteria. I should be ashamed of myself! Sophia had reproved herself that same instant, and had valiantly tried to forget the vile flashing image. But it came again.

2

In this land fate hovers in the doorbell. The period of anguish runs from eleven in the evening to eight in the morning. When the bell rings around midnight, it may be a friend who for good reason seeks refuge for the night. When it rings between seven and eight in the morning, it may be the telegraph messenger, that harbinger of heroes' deaths, of the deaths of husbands, brothers, sons. But woe unto the home where it rings in the gray of dawn, in the dreadful hour between five and six.

In this land no one has a good conscience when the bell shrills between five and six. Every one is guilty before this loudly pointed finger of omnipotence, in this hour of the catch. Many of the guilty must first be told their guilt, others not—Sophia not.

When the doorbell rang yesterday morning between five and six in Widow Brenner's small top-floor apartment in Martiusstrasse (one of the better residential sections in northern Munich), Sophia started from her sleep with an entirely clear and, as it were, rational mental exclamation: That was fast! Mrs. Brenner's old Dachshund bitch Lumpi, fat and weak in the hindlegs, barked furiously. Lumpi played a great role in Mrs. Brenner's life, so great a role that, when the air-raid alarm sounded, the well-rounded, dynamic, and fiftyish lady never and under no circumstances went to the air-raid shelter, as a protest against the order not to take pets along.

The bell rang incessantly. Sophia jumped out of bed, flung her bathrobe over her shoulders, and ran to the little hallway. Standing at the door to the apartment was Mrs. Brenner in a kimono of faded red silk, Lumpi barking between her legs. She looked at Sophia with a strangely quiet and vacant smile. Then she pushed the electric button to open the door downstairs. The ringing stopped, Lumpi quieted down. Light went up on the stairway.

"Now the game's up," said Mrs. Brenner with somewhat fluttering voice, the smile arrested on her full, still pretty face. "Now they come to get me. My son-in-law must have told these swine the truth over the British radio."

The Jewish son-in-law, an historian of some renown, played an even greater role in Mrs. Brenner's life than did Lumpi, though for ten years now he had lived in exile. For his sake she hated the Nazis. For his sake she aspired to three ideals: not to say, "Heil Hitler," not to display the swastika flag from her window, and not to donate a single penny to the Winterhilfe. She rented the room which once belonged to her daughter, a strikingly good-looking, dark-haired woman whose photographs adorned the living room, but who was mentioned less frequently than the son-in-law despite the fact that she shared his exile. Mrs. Brenner took only girl students or secretaries as tenants; and before showing an applicant the friendly room with its white furniture she would say aggressively: "I have a Jewish son-in-law, now in England." Two years ago Sophia had responded to this test question, "I wish you had him back in Germany." She was given the daughter's room and was treated like a daughter.

It took time to climb the four flights. The ascending footsteps were in no hurry; with heavy soles, evidently hobnailed, they crashed up the stairway. It sounded like hammer blows; the women's hearts hammered too.

"Now they come to get me," Mrs. Brenner whispered again, and stared at the brightly polished brown wood of the apartment door. Her chin hung loose, as if she continued to speak soundlessly.

Sophia is twenty years old; Mrs. Brenner to her is Mother Brenner, an authority, different, to be sure, from the professor, yet no less convincing in her unshakable faithfulness to herself and to the clear division of her sentiments into love and hate. Mother Brenner had said that it was she who would be taken away, and with the last remnant of her courageous smile she awaited the fate which happens to be the consequence of such devoted love and hate. Sophia wanted to believe her, and gave precedence to Mother Brenner's fate, out of respect, if nothing else; for it would have been precocious to shake her head and say, No, it's me they are coming to get. The girl hid behind the broad, motherly back and wanted to believe that it was not she, but the other, who would be taken—at least during the long, anxious ascent from the bell-ringing to the fourth floor and to the rhythm of the ever louder hammer blows of steps and hearts.

Now there was a snorting outside, in front of the entrance door, with "Phew!" and "Damn!" in tribute to the four steep flights of stairs. Lumpi growled threateningly. Mrs. Brenner took the dog in her arms to make it feel secure. Lumpi does not bark or growl in the arm of her mistress. There was a knock on the door—just one rap. "Open up!" came the command. "Secret State Police."

"Anyone can say that!" Mrs. Brenner exclaimed in sheer defiance. "That's the same story quite ordinary burglars have told us, too!"

"This is the residence of law student Sophia Moeller," it came back—and it was as though Mother Brenner had not uttered her impudent suspicion at all. It was as though she weren't there any more, no longer Sophia's authority and no longer her refuge.

3

Sophia ran back to her room, as if she were safer there. She could still hear Mrs. Brenner ask with choking voice, "But what is it you want from my young lady?" Sophia quickly and noiselessly closed the door and leaned against it with stiff body, stiff arms, stiffly stretched-out fingers. How could it happen so fast? Only last night Christopher had been here, had sat at the white table, with white face, yes, with white face, and had to whisper because Mother Brenner had rolled the anthracite wheel-stove from the living room into the open door of Sophia's room, the wheel-stove whose chief virtue was not that it furnished heat, but that it was a present from the Jewish son-in-law.

So far all was going well, Christopher had whispered. The first hundred had already been distributed when he had last talked with Hans and Alexander, shortly before seven o'clock. It was going too well to end well . . . Yes, that's what he had said; and yet right away he had turned to raving again as usual, and the wild look had come into his eyes, and his hair had fallen over his forehead and been thrown back, again and again. And then he had slipped into his raincoat, his only overcoat, a ridiculously thin coat for Munich in February, and had already left the room to run to the university once more to ask how things went—and then had come back once more as far as the wheel-stove in the doorway and had drawn the girl to himself, taking her head between his hands, his eyes wild, delirious big black eyes in a white face, and had said this, his lips pressed upon her mouth—had said this: "Perhaps it's unforgivable."

Thus her heart tossed up the question about Christopher, when the two plain-clothes officers opened the door, and, holding it, also held the girl as she stumbled backward, and thus her heart was struck by a flash of heinous doubt. Then immediately she thought, I should be ashamed of myself!

Perhaps it was shame that quieted her, or the terseness of the official proceedings. Only one officer spoke. He said, in all, three sentences. "You are the law student Sophia Moeller?" She nodded. He confronted her with a printed warrant filled in with neat typing, and spoke the second sentence: "Get dressed." The other officer said nothing and busied himself about the room. Sophia dressed behind the screen which stood in front of the washstand. She dressed quickly and mechanically, the presence of the men did not disturb her; she didn't even know what their faces were like—she hadn't looked at them.

Mother Brenner had not been allowed to enter the room and kept on talking outside in the hallway, incessantly. It was a sort of soliloquy meant for the ears of the officers, a eulogy—studded with moderate indignation and rhetorical questions—of Sophia's National Socialist virtues. It pained her to use the hated words; one could tell from her voice and her tortured High German.

But no one paid any attention to her gallant intercession, not even Sophia. She stepped from behind the screen, wearing the old dark-blue knit dress made of prewar wool, which made her look fuller. She saw that all the drawers were open; on the table lay, neatly piled, her college notebooks, letters, one stack each of unused typewriter paper and carbon paper, and the old Remington portable typewriter. The second officer, the wholly mute one, stood at her bed and tore off the bed cover. It was a coarse and brazen motion, the girl turned her back to him. The first officer stood at the bookcase running his finger over the backs of the books, as if he sensed with his fingertips which book was to be confiscated and which wasn't, then he turned around without pulling out a book. He spoke his third sentence: "You may take along necessary toilet articles and some underwear."

As they left the room she would have liked to look back once more; she was so fond of the room with its white girlish furniture. But behind her were the two officers; so she decided against it. At the door to the apartment stood Mother Brenner, dog in arm.

"A clear-cut mistake, Sophy," she said throatily. "You'll be back here soon, Sophy." She avoided looking at the small overnight case Sophia carried, and again had that halfway smile on her face, that fragment of a smile.

"Good-by, Mother Brenner. Good-by, Lumpi," said Sophia.

4

Night still covered the street, the war night without light and without life. Sophia climbed into a roomy limousine standing in front of the house, and was directed to sit down on one of the collapsible seats. In the back of the car sat the two officers; beside her on the other collapsible seat lay her typewriter and the confiscated papers, bound with a leather strap. The curtains had been lowered over the side windows, a superfluous precaution, since the eye could not recognize anything in the darkness. In front, separated by the glass partition, the girl saw the outlines of two uniformed men, the chauffeur and a police official, who paid no attention to the passengers. The car moved rapidly, despite the restricted visibility afforded by the short blue beam of the headlights. The sharp curve to the left told Sophia that they were turning from Martiusstrasse into Leopoldstrasse, heading downtown.

Will they take me to the Gestapohaus? she asked herself.

The car roared through the mighty center arch of the Siegestor where ordinarily automobiles were not permitted to pass and raced down black and empty Ludwigstrasse. To the right, in the void, was the university. As they passed it, Sophia instantly thought of lecture room number 77 and the small seminar room obliquely across. In her mind she saw Professor von Hennings' narrow, bald, hawklike head and Dora von Hennings' madonna hair and Alexander Welte's Swabian round head and her brother Hans' grave, tight-lipped, deliberate, yet bold Hanseatic face and Christopher's dark-eyed handsomeness like that of a Bavarian hunter. She thought of them all, in appropriate order; she left Christopher in his proper place and did not give him precedence. But the visions vanished the instant the car had passed the university, and Sophia had no time to take them along on her dark journey.

For near and ever nearer was the decision, which way she would have to go—she was all alone, rapidly nearing her fate; she had thrown out of the car, not herself and not the typewriter, that dangerous neighbor, but only the thought of her comrades, and the thought now lay behind her in the night. By now the car had reached and passed Ludwigskirche. Shivering, she crept deeper inside her soft camel's hair coat and awaited the near and ever nearer judgment of Odeonplatz. Were the car there to turn to the right, into Briennerstrasse, then it would take her to the Gestapohaus, halfway between Odeonplatz and Karolinenplatz, to the dreadful baked brick Gothic of the Wittelsbach Palace, the nightmare of the city. With her teeth Sophia plucked small shreds of skin from her chapped lower lip. Am I so cowardly, she thought, and wanted to feel ashamed again. Am I so cowardly, because I'm alone, the only one . . .

The car did not slow down on Odeonplatz, but drove straight ahead into the narrow black gorge of Theatinerstrasse. "Thank God!" breathed the girl with relief. The thankfulness was for Munich police headquarters, now revealed as the destination.

5

The examination did not begin until about ten o'clock in the morning. Registrations, complicated as they were, getting acquainted with the solitary confinement cell, and breakfast—a tin cup of, at any rate, hot Ersatz coffee and a piece of bread—took up only one of the four hours which she had to wait. She had time enough to think, to question and examine herself. She believed no longer that she alone had been arrested. Perhaps brother Hans or Alexander Welte, perhaps both of them, had been seized last night while distributing the handbills, despite the subtly planned distribution technique, despite uniform, war decoration, and war mutilation. That she is Hans' sister may be sufficient reason for her arrest. But why then immediate arrest and imprisonment, and the significant seizure of the typewriter; why not first a simple examination — Hans and Alexander surely would not betray her?

Topping the Perhaps and Why like a bell jar, was the question about Christopher. Had he been arrested too? Was she about to become hysterical and vile again? What did she want anyhow? What was it she wished? Answer! "Yes, yes," she whimpered, crouching on the cot, head between fists, "I wish he were arrested too . . ."

She rose and walked back and forth, coat collar turned up, hands in pockets. Her breath came from the nose, visible like cigarette smoke. A cigarette would help, she thought. Between the cot, the tin stand with pitcher and washbowl and the excrement bucket along one wall, and the folding table and stool along the other wall, there was room for three steps. Lengthwise there was room for four steps. She snapped the table open and shut. It had a mechanism like the collapsible tables by the window seats of through-train compartments. They had window seats, Sophia and Christopher, when they went to Salzburg a year ago. Oh, the beautiful journey into the enchanted world of that holiday week without war and uniform and swastika! Sophia walked back and forth in the lengthwise direction. Her heels rapped on the stone floor, and the rhythm of wheels rolling on rails rapped in her ears. Travel, travel, over boundaries, without boundaries . . . She stood still, a trifle dizzy, and her ears buzzed. I'll get it out of them, who was arrested, she exclaimed to herself, and they shall get nothing out of me!

She felt suddenly enterprising. She felt somewhat in a mood for traveling.

The two officers who had brought her in and had not been seen since, reappeared toward ten o'clock behind the old, walrus-mustached police sergeant who opened the cell, and motioned to the girl to follow them. Since they were already old acquaintances by now, and since, after all, Sophia was an attractive young girl, she ventured a faint smile and asked, "Really, now, what are you two up to with me?" Saying this, she looked at them for the first time. They had closely shut faces, carved of the same wood, so to speak, the one with a small blond mustache, the other with a small dark mustache, the one more round, the other more oval; one could exchange eyes, nose, mouth, and the coarse chin between them and the outcome would be just about the same. They did not answer.

Sophia turned her eyes away and had forgotten them. They walked up some steps and along a long corridor. They encountered several black SS uniforms who gave them never a look. They stopped at a door whose grooved opal glass pane bore the black-lettered inscription: SECRET STATE POLICE—COMMISSIONER NEGELE.

The fairly large room, in which no window was to be seen, was illuminated by artificial light—a bright, hard, very white light from the spherical ceiling fixture. At the double desk sat an older man in civilian clothes and a young Gestapo clerk in black uniform. In front of the desk stood a chair and a little table with Sophia's portable Remington and the confiscated typewriter paper. The man in civilian clothes, apparently Commissioner Negele, raised his head, lifted the red pencil in his hand in a sort of salute, and said, "Be seated." He had a chubby colorless face, a shorn head tolerating a few inches of sticky colorless hair parted in the middle over the forehead, colorless eyebrows, a colorless Hitler mustache, and colorless, strangely amused, little pig's eyes. The two officers, the old acquaintances, posted themselves against the wall at right and left of the door, incarnations of taciturnity. The young SS man did not look up and arranged neatly sharpened pencils beside a shorthand notebook. His appearance was like that of all SS men: handsome, lean, short blond hair parted on the left, professional determination expressed by a protruding chin—the "trained" chin, as the professor would say—and in the eyes the drilled-in, the terrible coldness. The professor called it: the artificially frozen soul. Brother Hans had looked just the same, earlier, in the days before the artificial leg, Sophia thought.

"Well, now we are all together," the commissioner started off cordially, twirling the red pencil between his fingers. "I suppose you know why—or don't you know, Miss Moeller?" The commissioner had the surprising gift of being able to speak several dialects; he spoke Bavarian, Swabian, and High German. He mixed the idioms according to his mood or his plan. The SS man acting as stenographer whisked the first pothooks across the pad and looked frozen-face at his fingernails.

"I don't know why," Sophia replied.

"Go on," Negele doubted amicably. "Let's begin differently—perhaps we'd better begin with this, Miss Moeller." His hand circled slowly over the papers on top of the desk, as though there were a considerable choice with what to begin. Then, with seemingly disgusted fingers, he lifted a sheet of very thin and much folded onionskin paper and stood up. He was not much taller standing than sitting, so short were his legs. He walked toward the small table where the girl sat, not knowing whether her face was putting on color or turning even paler than it was. The commissioner held the onionskin paper by its outermost edge with an almost horizontally outstretched arm, as one would carry a poisoned rat by the tail in order to throw it on a garbage heap.

"Do you recognize this?" he asked and held the unfolding, closely typed handbill before her eyes. Sophia saw at a glance that it was one of the set of one hundred handbills which she had typed, not one of that other one hundred prepared by Dora Hennings.

"No," she answered. "What is it?" If I only knew how my voice sounds, she thought, and coughed from excitement.

The commissioner looked at her with an amused twinkle and pointed to the Remington typewriter. "Then you don't know the machine either?"

"Certainly, that's my typewriter."

"And the paper?"

"It's my paper."

Negele took a blank sheet of paper from the table and held it next to the handbill. "Well?" he asked.

"I don't understand."

"Don't you think these two sheets are little brothers or sisters?"

"But, I beg your pardon, onionskin is standardized! You know quite well it comes in only two kinds, a heavier quality and this thin one. You can get them in any stationery store and find them next to every typewriter!" That was well done, she praised herself.

"Now, now, don't bite me," the commissioner said in Bavarian, and continued without a pause in High German: "How many legible carbon copies can you make on your machine?"

"Four," Sophia lied.

"Wrong. Six," Herr Negele said. "Kindly insert seven sheets with six carbons."

Sophia obeyed; not being sure of her hands and not wanting to betray any nervousness, she went about it with great deliberation. The commissioner showed no impatience, the SS man waited indifferently, looking at his shorthand pad, the two against the wall stood there unsympathetically and timelessly.

"All right," said the commissioner, when the girl had at last adjusted the papers in the machine, "now write . . ." He held the handbill with both hands, then stretched it lightly to smooth out the creases, seeming to have lost his loathing for the rat. He dictated: " 'Fellow Students! Freedom and honor! For ten years now these two fair German words have been misused, twisted, and degraded by Hitler and his clique . . ."

He stopped. She did not write. He stood behind her back and saw her blond hair undulating over her bent nape. "Well?" he asked.

"Why should I write that?" she returned in a low voice, and her narrow shoulders heaved up and down. "I mean, why don't you dictate something else to me, if you only want to know . . ." Her voice choked off.

"Do you refuse to write that?" the commissioner asked.

"Yes," she nodded.

"Even if your refusal should be proof to us that you wrote the handbill?"

Her shoulders stirred. "I beg of you . . ." she whispered after a long silence.

"I beg of you," Negele said, "to write what I dictated to you."

Sophia began to write. Only after the first five words the warning flashed through her brain: Don't betray that you know the text! She stopped typing and looked up in the air: "How does it go on, please? And is the beginning correct? It's impossible to memorize all this at once . . ."

Amused, Negele blinked at her back and repeated the words. She wrote with halting touch. He bent over her shoulders and said: "You purposely tap the keys too lightly and purposely make errors. Why do you want to incriminate yourself on purpose? Leave a space of two lines and begin again."

She obeyed and fluently wrote the intimately familiar words from the second half of the manifesto, the great, the heroic, the torchbearing words; and over the commissioner's colorless cold voice came the professor's impassioned whisper as he dictated the text of the handbill . . .

Commissioner Negele stopped and quickly bent over her shoulders: "Well, what do you know about that?" he mused in astonishment. "There we are, writing faster than we dictate! There are words here that I haven't spoken—and the right words at that! How do we explain that, young lady?"

Sophia had to swallow repeatedly, she had water in her mouth all of a sudden. "That follows from the sentence," she gulped.

"Excuse me, lady. I dictated: 'They are still doing it, day after day, and have . . .' That was all I said. And you already put down what I hadn't said yet. You wrote: '. . . shame and dishonor.' Why, if you please, does that follow from the sentence?"

"It follows from what has gone before and from the whole contents . . ."

"Why?" the commissioner shouted suddenly, and it was astonishing how his watery voice could shout. "The preceding sentence read: 'Even the simplest of all Germans must have had his eyes opened by this terrible carnage in the name of "liberty and honor" in which they drenched all Europe.' Why does 'shame and dishonor' follow from this—as it does in this infamous sheet?"

Sophia did not answer. Out of the corner of her eye she looked to the right: the young SS man had already finished recording the shouted words, the fingers of his left hand lightly tapping the tabletop, indifferently waiting, eyes on the note pad. The girl quickly glanced to the left: the two against the wall looked as if they slept standing up and with eyes open.

"I observe," the commissioner said in his usual voice, "that you have given no answer to my question. Is this to say that you have put down the correct words prematurely because you are familiar with the text?"

"No," Sophia answered.

The commissioner returned to his desk. "That's enough for the present," he said motioning with his hand toward the door. "You shall be called again."

Sophia rose, the two against the wall came back to life, led her out of the room, and silently marched her back to the cell.

Sophia squatted on the cot and tried to collect her thoughts. Had she comported herself well or badly up to now?

The professor had said: "Each one of us is responsible for the other. We are all responsible for our action. Our action is revolutionary, therefore responsible to the future. If one of us is arrested he must act in a manner to permit the other five to continue their work. If five of us are arrested, the five must act in a manner to enable the sixth to carry on. If all six of us are arrested, then we must act as if we were not six, but sixty or sixty thousand or six million—then we must act as the spokesmen of a power which has sent us out ahead into the present, and which loses in us only six voices, six out of six million . . ."

They were words of such luminous strength that they seemed to become visible when one thought of them. Sophia thought of them and saw them; but they were entirely out of proportion to her examination, they were too great and too beautiful and too weighty for bickering over carbon copies and for Negele's screaming about "shame and dishonor." Yet those words which she had written down because she knew them like the words of the Lord's Prayer, these words of mission, the core and substance of it all, these words which set Negele off screaming like the Devil when he sees the cross, these words she had denied with the next word she spoke. Was this right or was it wrong? Did the responsibility which she bore demand confession or denial? "If one of us is arrested . . ." she whispered helplessly to herself, "one of us, I, the one, I all alone . . . and what about Christopher . . ."

She did not know how much time had passed, when the two officers reappeared and again led her before the commissioner. The small table with Sophia's typewriter and typewriter paper had disappeared, the chair stood no longer at an oblique angle to the double desk, but faced it directly. With his red pencil the commissioner motioned her to be seated and said without his customary dialectical prelude: "Our typewriting expert has established two things with absolute certainty: first, that this handbill was written on your typewriter, and second, that the handbill was typed by the same person who typed the paragraph which I dictated from the handbill—in other words, by yourself." His red pencil pointed at the girl.

"But typing is not like handwriting," Sophia objected, pleased because she remained calm.

"Miss Moeller," said the commissioner, holding his head somewhat askew, "there are wrongdoers to whom one cannot deny respect. You, however, are beginning to make yourself contemptible."

"Why?" Sophia asked as her forehead got red. "Because I cannot comprehend that the identity of the person who used the typewriter is deducible from the typescript?"

"Because you want to make me believe that someone else has written the leaflet on your typewriter."

"But I have no such thought at all!" she exclaimed.

"Someone else . . ." Negele resumed, pursing his lips gloatingly. "Leaving aside the contemptibleness, this would lead to quite interesting and even clearly delineated perspectives."

"I don't understand at all what you mean . . ."

"You will understand presently," the commissioner said. "Here you have, for instance, living right here in the city of Munich, a relation by blood, Sergeant Hans Moeller, honorably discharged from the army for disability suffered in the war, now a student of law— Is that correct?"

"Yes—but my brother has nothing to do with this, nothing at all!"

"But you are implicating him just the same!"

"No!" Sophia cried and dug her fingernails into the palms of her hands.

"Well?" Negele asked, twirling the red pencil.

As though seeking help she looked across to the young SS man whose icy eyes were frozen fast to the shorthand pad and whose pencil drew languidly hurried signs over the paper. She glanced at the shorthand pad, she saw that far more than half of the thick pad had been covered with writing and the pages turned over backwards. When she had been sent out of the room after the first examination, only a few pages of the pad had been turned over—she remembered distinctly. The new examination could not have covered many pages up to now. In the intervening time, therefore, the SS man must have recorded something else—possibly the typewriting expert's testimony, or possibly also the examination of another apprehended person. Perhaps brother Hans had sat in this chair in the meantime and had looked at the commissioner with his deliberate brave eyes and had declared in his precise voice what he had to answer for, in the name of the six or the six million. "There are wrongdoers to whom one cannot deny respect," the inquisitor had said.

"Well?" Negele asked a second time.

"I wrote the handbill," Sophia said.

"Well, there we are." The commissioner used his good-natured Munich patois. He leaned back, his eyes closed for a few seconds. "And how long did it take you to write one page?" he asked unexpectedly.

"I don't know exactly," she answered in order to gain time; for she did not perceive as yet what was concealed behind the new question.

"Let's see, now," Negele spoke patiently, like an adult helping a child with its lessons. "The handbill, as I have already calculated, contains about 670 words, written in sixty single-spaced lines, without paragraphs and almost without any margin, a very economical exploitation of the space available on the sheet. Considering that you have only average typing skill and do not use the touch system, and taking account of delays made necessary by reading from the original copy . . . No doubt you had an original copy, a draft, didn't you?" he interrupted himself.

Perhaps he asks me all that only in order to throw in this last question, she thought in feverish exertion; but how can I say I had no original draft . . . "Yes," she nodded.

"And undoubtedly you had no help—I mean: no one who dictated to you?"

She shook her head impetuously: "No!"

"Considering all these delaying conditions," Negele continued reflectively, "it should have taken you at least twenty minutes to type one page, according to my calculation, perhaps even twenty-five minutes. Could that be approximately correct?"

"Yes," Sophia nodded.

"You see!" Negele rejoiced. "And when did you write the handbill?"

When . . . Sophia thought, that's what he is after: when . . . But I don't know whether telling the truth or lying will protect the others, so I'll tell the truth . . . "Day before yesterday," she said.

"When day before yesterday?"

"In the evening."

"When in the evening, day before yesterday?"

"From nine o'clock on."

Oh, that evening, the night before last! They cleared the table after supper, Sophia and Christopher, and it had been a delicious supper, a supper worthy of their work—hard sausage and smoked meat, non-rationed gifts from Christopher's people in the Oberland. In the open door stood the wheel-stove, dispensing warmth. A mixture of rain and snow dribbled against the closed shutters of the windows. "No disturbance to be feared tonight on the part of the honorable RAF," Christopher had said, and had sat down beside her. The alarm clock on the bedside table showed five minutes to nine when he began dictating. He dictated in a whisper because the door was open; but Mother Brenner, by nature not inquisitive, had already gone to her bedroom and was by now probably enjoying the first sleep of the night, which she was in the habit of praising for its depth and its health-promoting significance. Christopher dictated in a whisper, near Sophia's ear, and whisperingly came into pathos, kindled by the torch of the words. Fifteen times he dictated the manifesto and fifteen times he became impassioned, always by the selfsame words. When she had pulled the finished page out of the machine and had inserted fresh paper, she looked at him, and his fiery wild-hunter's face came near, with mute laughter, with flashing white teeth and flashing black eyes. Each time he rewarded her with a kiss—fifteen times.

"From nine o'clock on," the Commissioner resumed. "And when did you finish?"

"Toward two o'clock in the morning," answered Sophia, and saw the poacher slip out with the booty of one hundred leaflets under his raincoat, and then she still had to burn the used carbon paper in the wheel-stove.

"From nine till two," the commissioner repeated slowly. "And how many had you written in all?"

"How many?" Sophia asked back and felt her temples throbbing.

"How many copies of the leaflet had you prepared altogether?"

A trap! she thought in despair. He can figure out that it was one hundred—but Mrs. von Hennings typed the other hundred, and perhaps he knows that there are more than one hundred, and I endanger Dora . . . "Did I say until two o'clock?" she whispered in agitation. "That's a mistake, I worked much longer . . ."

"How many copies in all?"

"I worked at least until four, five . . ."

"I ask you for the third time: How many copies did you prepare?"

"Roughly two hundred."

"Hm," Negele grunted and wrinkled his brow, calculating, "one original plus six carbon copies or seven leaflets in twenty minutes, 105 leaflets in 300 minutes or five hours, that would be two o'clock in the morning. To prepare 210 copies you must, therefore, have worked until seven o'clock in the morning; quite an achievement for a girl apparently not endowed with a robust constitution."

"Oh, I am sure it didn't take that long!" she exclaimed throatily, and her hands fluttered up from her lap. "Certainly not longer than five—after all, the typing went faster as I got on, you understand—Why, I finally knew it by heart . . ."

The commissioner contemplated her with amused eyes, his left hand circled over the tabletop, reached, and held a thin closely typed sheet of tissue paper between the fingers. "Incidentally," he said, "we have here in our possession still another specimen of the handbill, though astonishingly one written on a different typewriter and by a different person, namely on a non-portable Continental typewriter, and by a person practiced in the touch system. Can you explain that to yourself?"

"No," she said, shaking her head.

"No?"

"It is inexplicable to me," she whispered almost inaudibly.

"That will be all for the moment, you shall be called again," the commissioner spoke, his red pencil pointing to the door.

6

On the way back to the cell Sophia said: "I am hungry."

The two officers disregarded the words.

Sophia said to the police sergeant who performed something like special duty at her cell door—opening up, locking up, opening up, locking up, "I am hungry." The walrus raised his shoulders, even the walrus mustache went up and down, his good-natured brown eyes showed embarrassment. But he said nothing and brought nothing to eat.

Perhaps it was hunger, then, that brought a certain spiritual disorder over the girl—hunger together with the diabolical rhythm of the intermittent examinations. Back to Negele, back to the cell, back to Negele: only the commissioner could see the pattern of the inquisitorial fragments, he who had invented the game and who put together the pieces of the mosaic. He put together the bits of testimony furnished to him from different sides—there could no longer be any doubt about that. But who besides Sophia contributed a part, who else sat in the chair before and after, that chair which, from a certain session onward, stood directly under the cascade of the Jupiter light? No answer was given her, and the answers she gave to herself were contradictory, automatically canceling each other out. Yes, they have Hans! her heart would hammer out suddenly, Hans and Welte! Dora—they have Dora! And sometimes the realization engulfed her like liquid fire: they have us all, also Christopher!

She fell into disorder. She forgot from one examination to the next what she had testified, and could not remember all the shreds of questions and answers heaped together by now. The commissioner would spear the contradictions with his irritating red pencil or, in amusement, let them run along, as it suited his rules of the game.

She could no longer fathom the complicated computation of 105 copies in 300 minutes and the circling of time around the critical hour of two. The commissioner set great store by this arithmetic and reverted to it, continually.

The alarm clock on the bedside table ticked in the back of her head and the "I'm alone, the only one"—and Christopher was much too near to this computation business, dangerously near—and the light overhead was like a shower of burning benzine—yes, it reeked of burned hair—my hair! she thought and put her hands upon her hair.

It was possible that she admitted the 300 minutes and the 105 copies—"Yes! Yes! 105 copies!"

But then, when the cycle was repeated—back to the cell, an indefinite time, twilight time, with raging hunger and raging headache, back to the blazing chair—then she no longer knew whether she had admitted it or whether only her thoughts had cried out: Yes! Yes! 105 copies!

However, this was no longer under discussion. It was the original, the draft, that was under discussion. An innocent question, once again a technical question: whether the draft had been typed or written out in longhand? In shorthand, was her answer. There followed a little examination in stenography which Sophia passed without difficulty. Then came the question about authorship. Sophia had long expected it and testified that it was she who had composed the manifesto. The commissioner made no ado about the confession, but remarked in a watery voice that as a rule stenography was not used to record one's own thoughts, but someone else's dictation. Sophia contested this. The commissioner pointed out to her that none of her college notebooks and none of the drafts of her seminar papers had been written in shorthand. Sophia countered that she had drafted the manifesto in shorthand in order to protect it from intrusive eyes. The commissioner called attention to the contradiction between this and her last answer, and he evinced great interest in the intrusive eyes and in the place and time of the drafting. He began to enmesh her again with the shuttle of his crisscross questions and with the blaze of the light. At last, in great exhaustion, she fell silent and had tears in her eyes for the first time.

The commissioner looked at her, got up and switched off the Jupiter light. "Miss Moeller," he asked, stopping beside her, "can you make something of the idea of the People's Information Service?"

Sophia quickly raised her head, had forgotten exhaustion and tears, and no longer felt the blessing of being free from the flood of light. Everybody in Germany knew what to make of the idea of the People's Information Service; for this ghastly undertaking of the regime was to make every one turn Judas to every one else. "I know about it," said Sophia, her eyes on the commissioner.

"The People's Information Service," Negele said, "is the honor service of the people's community. It is not yet too late for you to remember the duty imposed upon you by the nation's honor."

Sophia looked up at him and said nothing.

"We are sensitive to the subject of honor," Negele's eyes showed amusement, "and could understand that, considering the advanced state of your case, you might regard it as dishonorable and indecent to report—well, say, your accomplices, in case you should have accomplices—although it would be perfectly possible, purely theoretically speaking, that one or the other of your possible accomplices should belong to the People's Information Service without your having the faintest suspicion of it . . ."

He paused and pursed his lips gloatingly. Sophia looked up at him and said nothing.

"We should even consider you as fulfilling your People's Information duties," Negele continued, "if you would inform us regarding the moods and opinions within the student body and would in the future keep us informed about them. We could then regard the incriminating leaflet retroactively, as it were, as a technical auxiliary device in connection with your work for the Service, so that your next task would consist in watching the reaction of the student body to the handbill."

Sophia looked up at him and said nothing.

"The immediate consequence of your—shall we say—reactivation would be that your file would not be turned over to the Reichs Attorney's Office for prosecution in the People's Court on a charge of high treason. A collateral consequence could be that persons incriminated by their close connection with you, if by nothing else—I am thinking here of your brother—remain untouched."

Sophia looked up at him and said nothing.

"You wish to express yourself, Miss Moeller."

"You may switch that light on again, Commissioner."

The commissioner switched on the Jupiter light, returned to the desk and again picked up the red pencil. The SS man acting as stenographer looked up for the first time; but he looked at the commissioner, not at the girl, and his young eyes were like artificial ice.

7

Thus it went on, back and forth between the hot, blinding chair of the inquisition and the foul freezing air of the cell, alternating ordeals of unbearable pain. But the vacuous intermissions in the cell were now filled out with a thought more painful than hunger. It was a barbed hook of a thought, torn back and forth through her by the words, "People's Information Service," pronounced in Negele's chubby-faced manner, and by Christopher's last pale-faced whisper, "Perhaps it is unforgivable . . ."

Mercilessly the hook tore hither and yon, ripping and gashing in ever new ramifications, like the cobweb of cracks around an injured spot on shatterproof glass. Deeper and deeper it scraped, each new rent bringing new doubts and questions, driving new vein-like cracks into her memories—finally coming to press on the time when she had not yet known Christopher, a time of which he had only told her, strange, sinister, terrifying tales: the time he spent in the psychiatric hospital, his time of insanity which yet was not insanity, but an unbelievable struggle for freedom. Unbelievable—that's what she thought now; for earlier it had been believable, because he said it, believable and admirable. Now suddenly viewed in perspective it was a disreputable and deeply suspicious time, a black curtain hiding wild and at once mysterious goings on and releasing, as it is suddenly lifted, a free Christopher, an untouched . . .

"Untouched" was again a word to be put into quotation marks, a word of new meaning, a heinous word born in the mouth of Negele. Untouched Christopher suddenly had Negele's devilish claws on his shoulders like quotation marks and was a Negele quotation.

At this Sophia laughed out, horrified by the image of the devil's claws; she shuddered with disgust at her spidery thought. She shook her head and shoulders and her whole body; bitter bile rose high and she vomited.

It was night by now, unless everything deceived her. Shuttling between cell and examination she no longer encountered a single soul. Sophia was empty and numb, burned out by the blaze of the light, riddled by the rapid-fire of the questions.

Now the other names were in the debate too—brother Hans and the professor and Dora and Alexander Welte—they had slipped from the commissioner's lips as if casually and incidentally, and did not excite the girl any more. It may be that Christopher had also been mentioned, but perhaps he was present only in her thoughts and was not quoted by Negele because he was already branded as a Negele quotation, the untouched one. Sophia crept deeper into herself and closed her eyes, and must have fallen asleep again.

"Tie her mane together," the commissioner said in the direction of the door.

The grip on her hair awakened her and she screamed because she thought a knife was at her neck—so cold was the hand that tried, not roughly but unsuccessfully, to shackle the obstreperous locks with a piece of string. "What do you want of me!" she whimpered in a very high voice, leaning forward, shielding her face with her hands.

"My last question was," the commissioner said, "who sat next to you in the auditorium of the university on January 18, at the celebration of the founding of the Reich?"

"My brother."

"And on the other side?"

On the other side Christopher had sat. How could she pronounce his name when she was not certain whether his name had already been mentioned?

Christopher sits next to her in the university auditorium, his wild eyes shoot daggers at the putty-faced Gauleiter delivering his speech from the lectern in front. Christopher hisses through bared teeth: "Son of a bitch! Dirty dog! Filthy swine!" He throws a glance, a signaling glance, across to Hans whose nose has become pointed with rage and whose eyelids nod agreement. Yes, Christopher is the first to shuffle, the first to hiss, the first to shout, "Enough!" He leads the chorus shouting, "Enough!" And then begins the commotion, the exhilarating, the inspiring commotion . . .

Sophia sat stooped, hands on her nape, elbows on her knees, her hair obeying every twitch of the scalp, falling over her eyes again. Smiling, she floated with the commotion from the auditorium into sleep or, if it was not sleep, into a softly humming and buzzing twilight.

She started because someone shook her by the shoulders. One of the two officers, the one who had spoken three sentences in Mother Brenner's apartment, bent into the light cascade and spoke his fourth sentence: "You are through."

Sophia rose. Commissioner Negele fidgeted in his desk chair, his mouth wide open in a gaping yawn. This was the last picture of him she took with her, though not his last word. As she went toward the door already held open by the other, the completely silent officer, Negele said, still yawning, "We should have shorn off her blond halo."

The SS stenographer said in the precise accents of the North German, "The shearing will come anyway and radically." These were his first words. Sophia wanted to look back from the door, just to find out if the young man looked at her as he spoke them, at least looked at her. But she was too tired.

In the cell she wanted to slip off her shoes; but she had strength enough for but one shoe, then she fell face forward on the hard kapok pillow which smelled not disagreeably of some disinfectant.

The police sergeant arrived with a big tureen of hot vegetable soup and three pieces of bread. It had not been easy to obtain hot soup from the prison kitchen at this hour. It had required a mighty blowup. The walrus was inclined to blowups on this day. Through the grated window in the iron door he saw the sleeping girl. His walrus mustache went up and down, he switched off the light in the cell and turned around again, steaming tureen in one hand, tin plate with the pieces of bread in the other.

Toward morning, no longer in profound sleep, but not yet on the surface of consciousness, Sophia slipped off the other shoe. With the pressure relieved, a feeling of well-being came over her and then the dream, such a dream . . .

Chapter Two

THE ARTIFICIAL LEG

I

The beam of the flashlight beats through the window flap of the iron door into the double cell. Hans Moeller lies on his left side, a habit he has acquired since the amputation of his right leg. Even when the stump of the thigh had ceased to be sensitive to pressure, Hans had avoided lying on the right side, so that his left leg would not have to rest on the empty space where once his right leg had been. It was a peculiar sort of sensibility to pressure or, rather, it was a refusal to recognize and accept the empty leg-space, a refusal which he carried so far that in happier moments, such as the moments before falling asleep, he felt as if his right leg were resting on his left leg as it always had been.

Hans has been lying with his eyes open a long time, but he does not turn his head to the door; he submits to the exploring touch of the light until it glides to the cot against the opposite wall. There Alexander Welte lies peacefully on his back; his mouth is open and he snores, not too loudly. Now he closes his mouth, or the light closes it, and his breath comes more softly. The light-beam ambles back and halts, as if shocked, at Hans' bedstead. There, against the foot of the bed, leans the artificial leg.

It stands within Hans' vision as he lies on his left side, and he is glad to see it in the startled lightcone. There it stands in all its splendor. It is Hans who uses the word, an expression not of bitterness, but of his sincere feeling of admiration. He thinks: there it stands in all its splendor, in its slender perfection, in its faultless beauty of form—my leg.

The light withdraws from the cell, narrows and slips away through the peephole.

In the darkness Hans smiles at his leg, he loves it tenderly. He has had it only six weeks, the amputation occurred five months ago.

In-between was the time of terrible emptiness, the time when his trouser leg was cut off and pinned up, the time when he was a cripple at first sight, the time when, suspended on crutches, he had to hobble the gauntlet of condoling glances. Oh, those mournfully respectful looks wandering back and forth between the emptiness under the pinned-up trouser leg and the Iron Cross, first class, on his tunic—those piteous looks of misery with no fury behind them!

The artificial leg had been delivered before he was allowed to put it on. Every day he went to the surgical clinic to visit his new leg, to study the ingenious mechanism of knee- and foot-joints turning on ball bearings, to put it on stealthily, to try it out under pain and yet at the same time to delight in the joy of standing on two legs again. When the doctors finally declared the stump healed and capable of sustaining the pressure, when they attached the artificial leg and wanted to start training him to walk with it, he got up and walked, with correct posture and weight distribution, with the proper swing of the hips—an artificial leg virtuoso. And the rubber cushion in the heel dampened the metallic rustle of his step to a fine silvery tinkle as of knightly spurs.

Hans raises himself, gropes for the artificial leg and takes it into the cot with him. The leg is not heavy, it may even be astonishingly light, if only there were a standard for comparison. But how do I know how heavy my leg is? Hans asks himself, smiling. When I am tired or have a hang-over it's heavy as lead; when I feel brisk and gay, it is of the lightest fiber . . .

This is again praise for the artificial leg which is made of fiber, finished with soft rubber flesh here and there or with fine leather skin, and with hose covering foot and calf in roguish respectability. If it amuses you, you can even use a garter, just as on the left leg.

Hans moves the foot joint with his hand; its leather-clothed oil-pressure spring permits the free, nimble and nearly noiseless action which makes the step pliant and almost natural. He thinks of the night he just passed so badly, sleepless and pitifully legless even when lying on the left side—because he was afraid, of course he was afraid. He is not ashamed of his fear. That fear is a disgrace was one of the many stupidities he had once been taught. At the front he learned that fear is part of the trade and an elemental force in combat. Those who learn to manage fear as the sailor manages the wind, are driven forward rather than backward and earn their medal of valor honestly.

Now, with the fear-tortured night in his thoughts and with the artificial leg in his hands, he arrives at a logical conclusion which surprises even himself. If it is true, as he knows it is, that he spent a bad, sleepless and fearful night because he lay on the cot a helpless and pitifully one-legged cripple, just as he had been in the horrible days when he hobbled around on crutches, then it must be equally and incontestably true that the artificial leg should serve not only for standing and walking, but also for lying down. What a magnificent thought: to sleep with two legs! Why had he never tried it? Why not try it now?

He unhinges the thigh socket from the artificial leg and puts it on, the ingeniously constructed stump socket which is made of the softest, rubber-padded leather and which must be tied like a corset. He attaches the fiber leg, tilts it over the socket and fastens it with expert motions. He slips the supporting leather strap around his hips, pulls overcoat and wool blanket over himself again, lies down, somewhat overconfidently, on his right side and feels leg resting on leg.

2

"What are you doing over there?" Alexander Welte asks wide-awake out of the dark.

"I am copulating with my new leg," Hans answers. "It is a sort of emergency wedding."

"What do you mean? Do you want to get up already?"

"On the contrary, I want to sleep. I want to sleep with two legs because it didn't work with one."

"Pain?"

"No." Hans turns on his back, locking his hands under his head. "Alex, aren't you a miracle man when it comes to telling time? What time do you think it is?"

"Quarter of five," comes the prompt reply.

"Then I suppose we had better not sleep, but take some advantage of the opportunity, our first opportunity, perhaps our last . . ."

"Considerate of our hosts to let us stay together this time for the night." Alexander whistles through his teeth and adds: "I am sure they know why . . .

"We, too, know why," Hans suggests.

"To be sure," says Alexander.

Both think: there is either a listening device in this cell or a sound channel to the adjoining cell.

"Well, then," Hans begins, "let's keep shoulder to shoulder, so to speak. Understand?"

"Yes," Alexander answers, "shoot."

"We are in the Mensa," Hans speaks with deliberation. "We are sitting at the table, Alexander, we are sitting at the table. The Mensa is the starting point—or the table is. Perhaps our thoughts, or our concluding thought, must return to the Mensa—or to the table. Are we together?"

"Yes," Alexander rejoins in a drawl and his sonorous voice grows deeper yet, "certainly, since with the table goes the tablecloth."

"Excellent, you mind reader!" Hans rejoices.

Alexander Welte and Hans Moeller sat in the Mensa, the university restaurant. It was near ten o'clock in the evening and they had finished distributing the second hundred. The distribution technique was simple, though carefully thought out, and exposed the two as little as possible. The leaflet was meant for the students who had participated in the commotion in the university auditorium in January—medical students primarily, a few law students, chemists and philologists. For a whole week the two distributors had been after these students like detectives or pickpockets, had learned their daily schedules, their lecture rooms, their seats, the hooks on which they kept their overcoats, and then they had slipped the tightly folded tissue papers into overcoat pockets, desks, notebooks and textbooks. A small number of leaflets had been inserted in a double-paged party appeal (to house bombed-out Rhinelanders) and their distribution left to chance. Alexander had spirited the printed matter out of the head gatekeeper's office and smuggled it back again. The whole business had gone off without a hitch and without dramatic moments.

The two friends reviewed their success with satisfaction on meeting in the Mensa. They ate the standard potato soup with pieces of toast swimming on top. Then Christopher appeared, as had been arranged, and joined them at the table without taking off his wet raincoat. He was bare-headed as always, his dripping hair curling into stiff, jet-black ringlets. It was the second time he met with them that evening. The two friends reported the smooth distribution of the second hundred.

"Now all depends on whether they will swallow the medicine or spit it out," Hans commented.

Christopher stared at the table absently. He was very taciturn. Alexander surveyed him and jested: "Oh, Chris, you Bavarian prize product of blood and soil, even you are as white as the tablecloth which according to legend is supposed to have covered this table in time immemorial!"

"I am still in the Mensa," reports Hans to the other cot. "The tablecloth is worth lingering over."

"Is it really ready for the wash?" Alexander growls back. "After all, we must be economical . . ."

"Very economical," Hans stresses.

Christopher was remarkably white for a man of his dark type and with so brownish a skin that the professor called him the "wild hunter." It was a good name for him and suggested not only his audacious appearance, but also his inner being, which was irritable, undisciplined, capable of great enthusiasm and at the same time strongly introverted, lovable yet haunting—in short: devilish, in the real folklore sense of the word. Occasionally he even asserted that he possessed second sight.

As he rose, he said with his black look, "It will not end well."

"Is this your whole contribution this evening?" Alexander asked angrily. Christopher looked at him and shrugged his shoulders in silence.

"Are you going home now, Christopher?" asked Hans.

"Yes. Why?"

"I thought you would see Sophia first."

"I have just seen her."

"Is she as nervous as you are?"

Christopher again shrugged his shoulders. "If she is nervous, it's on your account. If I am nervous, it's on her account. But, leaving Sophia out of the picture, I am happy. Since even if things should go badly for us, they will go worse yet for the others. So long!"

He threw his hair back from his forehead with a jerk of the head, turned up the collar of his raincoat, and left.

"Second sight," Hans says to his cell companion.

"Or a second face, that is the question," Alexander returns and mutters on: "Strange, how love chooses . . ."

He thinks of Sophia, Hans smiles to himself, it is the old jealousy, even here and now. He says quickly, "Let's get out of the Mensa, Alex!" Welte murmurs something incomprehensible.

3

Then they had left the restaurant and were on their way to the faculty room where they were to meet Professor von Hennings at a quarter past ten. They felt some doubt regarding the advisability of keeping the rendezvous; tomorrow morning would afford an easy and unobtrusive opportunity to see the professor in the seminar and to speak with him. Perhaps Christopher's gloominess affected them and perhaps they would have done better to leave the university together with Christopher.

"I am still on the way," Hans reports, "and thinking back I ask myself two questions: first, did Second Sight purposely not invite us to leave with him; second, did he leave at all."

"Alas, we just do not possess second sight," says Alexander.

In the corridor leading to the faculty room they had met a group of postgraduate medical students, Alexander's classmates, who came from their evening lecture and had already put on their overcoats. The leaflets should now be in those hands stuck in overcoat pockets—if they had not been able to find them earlier, on their seats in the lecture room. They said hello to Alexander and went on their way silently; yes, they spoke never a word to one another. A young man wearing an assistant field surgeon's uniform brought up the rear. Alexander remembered very clearly the long double-breasted military coat and knew in which pocket he had slipped the handbill—and he looked at that pocket. The assistant field surgeon followed his glance, moved his hand in the pocket and said in passing, "Right you are!"

Alexander squeezed Hans' arm with joy. Christopher's pessimism was forgotten. They stood before the faculty room and knocked. Should von Hennings not be alone, but in the company of Councilor Seitz, the old dean of the faculty, then it would not be difficult to weave their report into a harmless conversation about seminar matters. The dean was a thoroughly good man and basically unhappy, not so much over the Third Reich, as over the neglect of Roman law, which was his special field. Moreover, he was shortly to be retired. On the other hand, should the young penal lawyer Vierck be present, the SS professor as Hennings called him because he lectured in his black uniform and made no effort to conceal the fact that he represented the Gestapo within the law faculty, then they were only to ask Hennings: "Any further wishes, professor?" That would mean the distribution had been successful. (Had it not succeeded, or succeeded only in part, the question was to be: "You have no further wishes, professor?")

Professor von Hennings was alone. He sat on the leather sofa, one long leg slung over the other, and read the *Voelkischer Beobachter*. Apparently he was as composed as he looked; for the newspaper in his hands did not quiver. He went on reading until the two had closed the door, then pushed the rimless glasses over his forehead—he used them only for reading and writing—and looked up as if haphazardly to determine whether the interruption was meant for him. Hans smiled at this subtle show of unconcern, typical of the mimic banter the professor loved.

"All goes well, Herr Professor," Alexander reported.

"So far, at least," Hans qualified.

"Fact is, the merchandise has been marketed," Alexander emphasized and seemed eager to go into details. The incident with the assistant field surgeon itched on his tongue. With steel-gray eyes set deep beneath gray, bushy eyebrows, Professor von Hennings looked from the one to the other; and that, at the least, was not an injunction to say no more.

"Right you are!" Alexander joyfully launched his account of the meeting with the assistant field surgeon, though he did not identify him. He spoke of a medical student. He also spoke of how completely the leaflets had been absorbed.

"So far, at least," Hans remarked again.

"Oh, you are still bothered by that wild hunter!" Alexander protested.

Professor von Hennings took off his spectacles. "What about him?" he asked.

"He was in his Cassandra mood again," Alexander answered.

"Perhaps he was depressed again today," Hans said appeasingly.

"I shall speak with him tomorrow," said the professor, "and meanwhile we'll await the reaction to the merchandise or, more correctly, its absorption. In two or three days we shall arrange a new and improved edition. Then, God willing, we can start in with individual therapy."

"Any further wishes, professor?" Alexander chuckled the code sentence in youthful elation. Hennings turned his narrow, hairless head with the aquiline nose toward the desk of the absent SS professor. "I believe we have no further wishes, Herr Kollege Vierck," he said to the empty desk, speaking through his nose, exactly as the professor of penal law was in the habit of speaking.

"In retrospect," says Hans across the cell to the other cot, "the jest about Vierck appears like a challenge to fate."

"In retrospect one is always wiser," replies Alexander.

"Not I," sighs Hans. "I only want to get wiser now, with your help."

"Let's get on," Alexander murmurs.

"One moment, Alex—since we just happen to be where we are and since we don't know anything about what went on there after all this jesting, tell me, Alex, did they pester you too . . . Did they ask you with such persistent inquisitiveness, where we spent the time between the Mensa and our arrest?"

"Yes," returns Alexander, "and this in spite of the fact that I told them from the beginning where I had been, and necessarily alone, to wit: in the toilet. And you?"

"I said nothing whatever."

"How tactful!"

"Many times I said nothing at all."

"Let's get on," Alexander says after a short pause.

4

The two friends usually left the university through the rear exit to Amalienstrasse. From there they only had to cross the street diagonally, to reach the house near Akademiestrasse where they shared a room. But the exit to Amalienstrasse was closed. That was unusual. The two looked at each other, Alexander whistled through his teeth.

They turned around and walked to the main exit on Ludwigstrasse. Standing in the entrance hall between staircase and portal were some scattered groups of students, looking into space as the two friends walked past them. The head gatekeeper leaned against the oak door and said brusquely, "Wait here, please."

"What's up?" asked Hans.

The gatekeeper raised a blue handkerchief to his gray sea-dog's mustache, blinked at Hans' uniform with cold-reddened eyes and snarled: "Don't ask me, mister; 'cause I don't know nothin', I never know nothin'. Just wait and see." He gave a loud and brusque snort into the blue handkerchief.

There may have been some fifty students, almost all of them medical students, and among them the postgraduates who had come from the evening lecture. Alexander walked up to the assistant field surgeon who leaned against a pillar and stared into the air. "Tell me, what is the matter here, doctor?"

"Right you are!" the surgeon answered without looking at him, his shoulders slightly hunched up, hands sticking in the pockets of his overcoat.

Alexander leaned next to him against the pillar, Hans leaned next to Alexander against the pillar. Each looked in a different direction, though their shoulders nearly touched. None of the waiting students spoke with another, none looked at another, each was for himself, his thoughts walled in behind an apathetic face.

This is the new academic silence, thought Hans.

"The new German silence," Hans speaks into the dark of the cell, to let his companion know where he stood with his thoughts.

"Is that all?" inquires Alexander.

"Why?"

"Well, I just thought of the old German saying about silence before the storm."

"Silence!" commands Hans, frightened by his friend's temerity.

The students did not have to wait long in the hall. Three SS uniforms bounded down the main stairway, an officer of the so-called Security Department with two subordinates. All three wore the notorious, silver-embroidered SD on the sleeve. Hans saw the SD and Alexander saw it, certainly the assistant field surgeon and all the others saw it too; yet none showed that he had noticed the appearance of the SD's.

The officer was an elegant, incredibly thin-waisted man, so enamored of his own elasticity that he never stopped swaying and rocking on his toes, even now when he stopped on the last step of the stair. With jerking movements of his head he looked over the scattered group of waiting students and snarled, "Attention, please!" As the students gave no indication of attentiveness he took a few more steps toward them, balanced on his toes and snarled again, "Come nearer, please!" His white-gloved hand described a semicircle.

Slowly the students came nearer. Hans, Alexander and the assistant field surgeon were hindmost in the group, because they were the slowest.

"Gentlemen," said the officer, trained chin protruding, arms akimbo and rocking on the balls of his feet, "cause of this little unpleasantness: distribution of enemy propaganda in form of leaflets among student body. In case not news to you, gentlemen, ask for your collaboration. That is: communication of your observations concerning leaflet, and delivery of same, if in your possession." He stopped, looked from one face to the other with jerking head, balancing on his toes. The faces remained blank walls. No one stepped forward. "Understand perfectly," the officer nodded, "embarrassing affair, myself feel like puking. Attention, gentlemen. Each one now proceeds separately to the head gatekeeper's office, which is unoccupied, unloads what he has to unload, and reappears unburdened. Discreet, what? Well now, please form single file and—march!"

Hans was the last in line, Alexander in front of him, the assistant field surgeon in front of Alexander. Step by step they approached the gatekeeper's office. The door was continually opened and shut and opened again after a short interval. The students who came out of the room—with the same impassive faces with which they had stood in line and had advanced toward the office—ranged themselves in formation again, without prompting, and in such a way that the man who had led the march to the gatekeeper's office posted himself next to the door and each following man came to stand to the right of the one who had previously stood in front of him.

Which will be the stronger in us now, Hans wondered as he advanced toward the door, the last in the single file— Which will be stronger, our ten years—half our lifetime—of standing in formation, or our new silence which is, after all, a silent refutation of that decade . . .

Standing behind the assistant field surgeon, who was taller than he, Alexander looked at the left overcoat pocket which hid the surgeon's hand. He was very curious. The field surgeon now stood right in front of the door, his rigid back did not budge. The man ahead of him came out of the room and closed the door behind him, looking into space. The assistant field surgeon went in and closed the door. Alexander had taken two breaths when the door opened and the surgeon came out again, left hand in his overcoat pocket.

Alexander entered the room. He saw an empty table, two empty chairs, an empty wooden bench. For the short space of two breaths he smiled. Then he left the room, closed the door behind him and did not look at Hans; but his hand still rested on the doorknob when Hans' hand seized it to open the door—and thus he could just quickly squeeze his friend's palm in a signal of triumph. When Hans came out of the room, the springy SD officer already stood in front of the door. Hans left it open and walked to his place at the end of the line, with swinging step and softly tinkling artificial leg, and with the feeling that the officer's eyes followed him for a moment.

"Alex," Hans speaks across the cell, "when I came out of the gatekeeper's office as the last one, the charming gentleman of the SD already stood at the door—remember?"

"Yes."

"Did he look at me then, as I walked to the end of the line? Try to remember."

"Yes, he did."

"I wonder why?"

"Because he noticed your walk, for no other reason. He looked at your legs or at the leg."

"Haha!" Hans laughs scornfully, "the mitigating circumstance!"

The officer had glanced into the room without entering it, and turned around. "Gratifying," he snarled, "very gratifying that none of you gentlemen needed to delouse himself discreetly. In conclusion, just one further little formality, quick look at identification cards, possibly spiced with few questions. Naturally reserve right to more thorough random test. Or does any of the gentlemen desire quickly to disappear in the enclosure once more? We all look away, and for my part I shall stroll, deeply understanding, as far as the stair and back." He was off with springy step and creaking leather gear. The students did not look after him and did not budge. He came back and with the other two SD men went into the head gatekeeper's office. One of the SD men immediately reappeared at the door and said: "Please enter one at a time. After identifying yourselves, you may go home." He stayed in front of the door.

The student who stood first in line disappeared in the room, came out again after a short while and walked toward the exit with buttoned-up face. No one turned his head to look at him, every one heard the heavy portal closing behind him with a dull thud. The students dropped in and out, the thud of the portal was the voucher of their freedom. Hans figured out that since, on the average, each one stayed one minute in the gatekeeper's office, their pockets could not have been searched. The tenth man stayed somewhat longer, as did the seventeenth and the twenty-third. Perhaps these were the random examinations. They came out with faces which told nothing, and were permitted to go home like their predecessors.

Out of the corner of his eye Alexander observed the man at his left, the assistant field surgeon, who, hands in his overcoat pockets, and betraying no anxiety, took a step to the left about once every minute, moving up toward the door with the dwindling row whenever the next man entered the room. The surgeon had a handsome, smooth profile and his eyelids with their blond lashes glided in regular intervals over the sea-blue eyes which looked at once patient and bored. Has he really still got the leaflet in his left pocket? Alexander racked his brains about it and was very curious.

Now the last three stood before the door, the surgeon, Alexander and Hans, and looked in the air, past the SD man who stood on the other side, also looking in the air. The man in front of the surgeon left the room, breathed out of his nose and went on his way. The assistant field surgeon entered, left hand in his overcoat pocket. Alexander stared at the brown wood of the door. Hans silently counted to sixty. He had not come to forty when the door opened again; the assistant field surgeon reappeared, left hand in his overcoat pocket, his gaze already fixed on the portal, and went on his way.

Alexander wanted to cast a look of triumph at his friend; but he refrained from doing so, in view of the SD man standing on the opposite side. He stepped into the room and thought: we too can go home.

We too can go home, thought Hans and advanced to the door.

The officer sat at the empty table, his SD assistant stood next to him. They don't even take our names, Alexander thought.

"Did you see the leaflet?" asked the officer.

"No," answered Alexander.

"Did you see anyone or did you hear of anyone who has seen it?"

"No."

"You understand that you are liable to punishment if you keep a product of enemy propaganda?"

"Yes."

"Your identification card, please."

Alexander handed him his student identification card. The officer read it and said, "Welte Alexander." Alexander thought that in pronouncing the name the officer expected a further corroboration from him and said politely, "Yes, sir." However, the corroboration was not demanded from him, but from the SD man who pulled a red, perforated index card from his breast pocket, also said, "Yes, sir!" and put the card down on the table. The officer looked from one card to the other with jerking movements of his head and handed Alexander's identification card to his subordinate. "Follow the man," he said to Alexander.

"Why, if you please?" asked Alexander.

The officer looked at him. You shall not glean anything from my expression, not you! thought Alexander, and in sudden anger a vein protruded from his forehead under his cap.

Hans stood before the door, looked at the brown wood and silently counted. He came to sixty and thought: perhaps they chose him for one of the random examinations—let them! The door was opened, the officer stood in the doorway—the officer, not Alexander.

"In conclusion, the Iron Cross, first class," the SD officer said and smiled invitingly.

Hans entered and felt the blood receding from his face. Alexander was no longer in the room. Hans looked back at the door in the foolish hope that his friend might have been dismissed through the adjoining room and that he might yet have a glimpse of him outside as he walked to the portal. He saw that the SD man who had hitherto waited outside the door had followed him into the room and had closed the door.

Hans made a hasty and clumsy movement, as if trying to go back to the door. It had been a false move for balancing technique, too, and the artificial leg slipped off to the side. He had to shift his weight to his sound leg in order to draw the artificial one back to him.

The officer leaned against the table on which lay a perforated red card and looked at Hans' right leg.

"Deplorable misfortune, Kamerad," he snarled. "Eastern front?"

Hans' nose became pointed, his right hand pushed the artificial leg still closer to the other. He said sharply, "I request information regarding the whereabouts of my friend."

"Which friend?" the officer asked slowly and pushed himself clear of the table.

"The non-commissioned medical officer who preceded me into this room."

"Oh, I see, Herr Welte, Alexander Welte?"

"Yes."

The officer picked up the red card. "Your identification card, please."

"My name is Hans Moeller."

"Moeller Hans," the officer read from the red card, "born July 14, 1920, at Bremen?"

"Yes."

"Your identification card, please."

Hans handed him his student identification card. The officer compared it carefully with the red card and turned it over to the SD man. "Artificial leg possibly mitigating circumstance, together with Iron Cross, first class," he snarled, balancing on his toes.

5

"Alex," Hans asks across the cell, "where was the car parked, in which you were taken away?"

"In front, in the circular driveway, near the south wing—the first of five cars that were parked there."

"Mine was in back, in Amalienstrasse— What a key to their distribution system!" Hans marvels. "And as I got in, another car just started off, the car in front of ours . . ."

"But my car drove down Ludwigstrasse," said Alexander, "and I wondered if it would turn right on Odeonplatz or keep on straight ahead. In your case the decision may have come as early as Theresienstrasse. Did you wonder too?"

"Wonder . . ." Hans takes up somewhat absently; for he thinks of the car that left just before his and was not Alexander's car. "No, not about this, Alex, frankly speaking I didn't think of the parting of the ways at all. I thought of you."

"Nice of you, Hans, especially since of course I had forgotten you completely . . ."

"Don't be silly, fellow. After all I had counted on being hauled off together with you."

"What good would it have done you, pal, sitting between those dear chaperons with the SD on the sleeve and the Mauser pistol in the holster?"

"I would have said one word to you in getting off, Alex, only one word—and for that they can't shoot a man dead, try as they will. I would have said to you: 'halves.' " Alexander is silent. "Bad conduction," Hans jeers, "and the candidate just about to take his physics examination . . ."

"Halves," Alexander speaks slowly, "connotes two persons honestly dividing a sum or a task or a responsibility."

"Exactly that," Hans corroborates.

"This presupposes that one partner can count on the other."

"To be sure."

"You could count on me, Hans; but I could not count on you . . ."

"Are you suffering a relapse into your typhus, my dear Alex?"

"No, but I could not know whether you had been arrested, too."

"Poor demented one . . ."

"Not with absolute certainty, Hans! The suspicion or the denunciation—or whatever it was—could have concerned me alone—and if not, it was still within the realm of possibility that we should have been accorded different treatment . . ."

"Oh, you mitigating circumstance!" Hans groans. "Go on! What are you hobbling up to with my artificial leg?"

"You know it anyway, Hans. I had to take over the responsibility for your share."

"Good God, my dear Alex, didn't you sense the terrible improbability of it?"

"Certainly, Hans. I seemed to be a source of quite extraordinary amusement to the gentleman who took me in hand here."

"Herr Negele—we need not hesitate to pronounce his name here."

"Yes, Herr Negele. He spoke German in three editions, from sheer pleasure."

"When were you examined for the first time, Alex?"

"Immediately after I was booked. I was not taken to the cell until after my first examination."

"How long did your first examination last?"

"Perhaps half an hour."

"Yes," said Hans, "my turn did not come until long after midnight." He ponders. "Alex," he asks, "when did you admit the whole business?"

"Immediately, of course, when they first asked me if I had anything to do with the leaflet."

"Why so quickly, why immediately? Why make matters still easier for Herr Negele?"

"The objection is silly, Hans. I have neither forged checks nor operated in the black market."

"Nor have I," says Hans. "Nevertheless I kept quiet for a pretty long time."

"I, on the other hand, spoke up," Alexander retorts impetuously, "because it was my firm resolve, from the moment of my arrest, to take the whole thing upon myself. Because it was my responsibility. Because my nerves demanded it. Because otherwise the ground would have slipped from under my feet and I would have gotten all muddied and muddled and dislodged from my responsibility and would necessarily have implicated someone else, God knows whom!"

"All right, all right, old man," says Hans soothingly. "And how long did you amuse Herr Negele with your solo number?"

"Until he told me that you had been arrested, too."

"When was that?"

"It was far along in the game, Hans, in the third session. I was dog-tired by that time and my scalp itched unmercifully under that Jupiter light—it has been ticklish anyway ever since I got typhus and lost my hair."

"Why for God's sake didn't you scratch, just scratch and scratch and keep your mouth shut," says Hans, and reflects about the Jupiter light never having been turned on for him. "But you did not keep your mouth shut, Alex. You even shouted, Alex. To Herr Negele's boundless joy you shouted at him that I had been arrested unjustly, since I had not the remotest connection with the whole leaflet affair."

Alexander whistles through his teeth. "How do you know this?" he asks somewhat chokingly.

"Herr Negele read it to me from the transcript at the beginning of my third session and gave a jolly good imitation of you. And he had his devilish joy not only in you, but also in me."

"Why also in you, Hans?"

"Because through this he got me to talk, entirely without Jupiter light. Because I had to give the lie to you and confess the truth—that it was I who was the *spiritus rector* of the enterprise and that you acted under my instructions."

Alexander is silent for a while. Then he asks: "Did Herr Negele have his devilish joy also in you because he got you to confess, or because he did not value your confession more than mine?"

"Only his eyes were amused," Hans reflects, "and perhaps that wasn't very significant. But it seemed to me that my confession amused him only in so far as it counterpointed yours."

"Could he possibly have doubted your ability to compose the leaflet, Hans?"

"The gentleman has a vexatious manner of dealing with confessions. He greeted mine with a hearty Bavarian exclamation, tabled it, so to speak, and dismissed me from further examination for the night."

"I was not recalled either during the night after the outburst he cited to you, or in other words after my third examination," says Alexander.

"You three times, I three times," Hans murmurs. "In-between there is no time gap, and it may have been toward half-past one when I was dismissed—no late hour for Herr Negele . . ." He thinks about the car which left before his and which was not Alexander's car. He thinks about Negele's insistent questions concerning the time between the Mensa and the gatekeeper's office. He thinks about his own persevering silence, which wasn't heroism, since his artificial leg protected him from more disagreeable degrees of examination, even from as much as the Jupiter light, and which did not even attain its purpose of leaving the inquisitor in uncertainty; for the amused eyes seemed to look through the silence as through a window. Why didn't he catch me the way he caught Alexander—why didn't he tell me that the professor had also been arrested? Hans thinks and groans.

"Don't go lacerating your breast like a pelican," Alexander consoles. "Herr Negele also showed some weak spots at times and, believe me, at such occasions it was a pleasure for me to give or to refuse an answer, depending on the situation: and because he still does not know what he wants to know so badly, he put us together for the night and planted his ears somewhere around here . . ."

"Alex, if you please . . ." Hans warns.

"No reason for fearing the weak spot, Hans! We can put our finger right on it! Admitted, that I distributed the leaflets. But how I distributed them—that remains an official secret!"

"Why?" Hans asks and laughs a little. "I said they were snatched from my hands, in front of the building on the circular driveway near the fountain, dark though it was . . ."

"Good!" Alexander laughs. "As the responsible editor you can say that. I, acting as a deputy, am bound to official secrecy."

"And he accepted that?"

"Not at all! That was where Jupiter came into action. Besides, they threatened me with other devices, but did not apply them—now I know why."

"Why?"

"Because I am to retain a presentable appearance, for the trial."

"I am quite sure no press photographers will attend," Hans declares. "But when was it disclosed to you that there will be a trial?"

"Last night, at the end. But to get back to the weak point. I finally told Herr Negele, as politely as Jupiter permitted, that no illumination or even any other means could induce me to talk, if I didn't want to talk. He realized it, intelligent as he is, changed the subject and came to his weakest point, to the most ticklish point . . ."

"How many copies," says Hans.

"Yes, after the How the How Many. I said I had distributed five hundred leaflets."

Hans laughed softly. "There is nothing like telling the truth, Alex! I said the same."

"I only wonder why the number angered him so!" Alexander affected astonishment. "Presumably because only up to four hundred copies had been delivered to the gentlemen of the SD . . ."

"Don't get cocky!" Hans cautions. "Being intelligent, Herr Negele is interested, not only in how many copies were distributed, but also in how many copies were prepared, and from this he construes rather clever causal connections . . ."

"If I distributed five hundred, I also wrote five hundred," Alexander declares categorically.

"Oh, God, Alex . . ."

"Stop groaning! I had spent fourteen days or nights preparing them!"

"And what did Herr Negele say to that?"

"So far as I remember, not much."

"And the next day, when were you recalled for further examination?"

"Not until yesterday afternoon. My importance apparently dwindled since you established your spiritual command, Hans."

"My turn, on the other hand," Hans speaks slowly, "came again as early as yesterday morning, at about half-past ten—and there was a little table in front of the double desk, and on the little table there was the typewriter . . ."

"Which typewriter?" Alexander exclaims somewhat hoarsely.

"The small Remington."

Alexander is as silent as if he weren't there any more. Now he is thinking of Sophia again, at last, Hans says to himself.

6

There was a little table in front of the double desk, and on the little table was the typewriter. "Good morning, Herr Moeller." The commissioner greeted the prisoner with studied amiability and immediately intercepted his look; but Hans' eyes did not rest on the typewriter. He had recognized it at the first glance and was prepared. The young stenographer in SS uniform who never looked up—from shame, Hans assumed in his favor—said "good morning" as if he were reading it off from his shorthand pad—yes, he too said good morning. Hans nodded silently; he disregarded their greeting which craftily glossed over the ugly fact of the typewriter.

"Please be seated," said Herr Negele, pointing with his red pencil to the chair which stood sideways to the desk, in front of the little table with the typewriter. Hans lifted the chair away from the little table and placed it so that it faced the inquisitor.

It is more difficult to sit down with an artificial leg than it is to walk or stand with it; for at first it remains stiffly stretched out like a wooden leg and one must either sit far forward on the edge of the chair, so that the heel can rest on the floor, or cross his legs and use the sound leg to press down the artificial leg, so that it folds up in the ball-bearing knee joint. Since Herr Negele looked on very attentively, Hans did both and, being nervous, did both badly.

"Do you still suffer pain, for instance now, when seating yourself?" inquired the commissioner.

"No."

"Can you handle the thing at all without help; put it on and take it off?"

"Yes."

"I could imagine, Herr Moeller, that there might be something like an artificial limb psychosis leading to a pathological resentment against all who stand on two legs . . ."

"Please come to the point, commissioner."

"To the point," repeated Negele, showing no trace of irritation. "This is the point." His red pencil indicated the Remington typewriter. Hans shrugged his shoulders. "Is this the machine on which you claim to have typed the leaflets, Herr Moeller?"

"Possibly."

"I can assure you that it is the machine, according to expert testimony. And you stick to the story that you rented it from a firm whose name you refuse to divulge?"

"Yes."

"Don't you realize that it would be a simple matter for me to make inquiries at all typewriter rental firms in Munich and to establish the falsity of your contention?" Hans did not answer. "I cannot understand in the least, Herr Moeller, why you did not say that you borrowed the machine from your sister without disclosing to her for what purpose! Wouldn't that have been entirely believable?" Hans did not answer. "Very well, Herr Moeller, you did not wish your sister's name to be thrown into the debate at all. But the way things have shaped up now . . . You see, I can drive you into a corner now. If I choose to do so, I could question and examine you to see if you can type at all, and I could prove to you, again on the strength of expert testimony . . ."

"Well?" Hans broke in.

"Well, therefore I myself introduce your sister's name into the debate."

"Explain yourself more clearly, if you please, commissioner."

"More clearly still? Very well, I shall be entirely clear. I place your sister's fate into your hands."

"Blackmail in other words," said Hans, and his nose was white and pointed.

"Herr Moeller," the commissioner spoke quietly, "now you violate also the law of causality. Let me assure you that it is because you are under suspicion, and shall soon be under accusation, of endangering the security of the Reich, that we have every legal right to subject you to 'blackmail.' This is only by the way."

"All right," said Hans, "I retract the word 'blackmail' and await your offer."

"Here it is. Your sister remains outside the danger zone if, first, you help us localize the—shall we say—infected portion of the student body, and, second, tell us truthfully how many leaflets were circulated."

"I am ready to answer," Hans said unhesitatingly. "Concerning the first point: since the leaflets were not distributed individually, but collectively, it is absolutely impossible to identify the recipients. As for infection—to use your term—the entire student body is more or less susceptible to infection. Concerning the second point: the original edition, as I have stated before, comprised five hundred leaflets, but could easily reach uncontrollable proportions through spontaneous growth from within itself, in accordance with the snowball system."

Herr Negele looked at him and said nothing. His little eyes blinked in amusement; moreover, his ugly, flabby mouth did what it was not supposed to do: it smiled. Even the young stenographer looked up and gazed at Hans with a frozen look, in frozen bewilderment—and Hans hated him with the hate of the front soldier for the "unexpendables" of the Gestapo, that most disgraceful and disgraced species of shirkers, yet he hated him also with the hate of the brother, of the twin, which is affection in reverse and which reviles resemblance because it cannot escape it. Thus Hans thought two thoughts at once as he stared back at the youth. He thought: you must be killed; and he thought: susceptible to infection. The other quickly lowered his eyes.

Herr Negele eventually resumed the discussion. "Set a rogue to catch a rogue, Herr Moeller. I expand my offer as follows: One: you and your adjutant Welte shall be set free at once. Two: your files shall not be turned over to the Reichs Attorney's Office for prosecution in the People's Court on charges of high treason. Three: your sister and any other persons possibly involved in the case go scot free. Four: distribution of the leaflets is to be regarded as having been the responsibility of the Security Department. In return you continue with your activity, enabling the Security Department to observe the student body's reaction to this leaflet in particular and to subversive whisperings in general."

"In return," Hans answered with equally sober tone of voice and without hesitation, "I shall relate the two versions of your offer at the trial."

"That will not be necessary, Herr Moeller," the commissioner enlightened him pleasantly, "because each of the five judges of the People's Court will have read the transcript of the preliminary examination. However, if you doubt the completeness of the transcript, go ahead and tell your story anyway." He looked reflectively at the red pencil in his hand. "Interesting!" he continued. "Your lack of family spirit as well as your callousness toward your companion are typically National Socialist. You sacrifice your sister, you sacrifice your friend or your friends, but not that filthy leaflet of an idea. Really, you can't be offended at all by my attempt to rehire you for the idea in which you grew up and which has formed you."

Hans felt himself reddening, from rage, from confusion, from a constriction in his throat as if tears were coming into his eyes. The commissioner watched him attentively. "But let's drop it," he said lightly. "The subject is closed. However, before I dismiss you this time, I should like to call your attention to your ignorance, Herr Moeller. Don't take this as a criticism of your intelligence, most certainly not, but only as a sober reference to all that which you simply cannot know and which has undoubtedly troubled you ever since your arrest. Now, it just so happens that you cannot know what we know or how we came to know it. How we came to know, Herr Moeller! My statement about the rehiring for the idea is perhaps a devastating statement, if you care to think about it. Remember, you are not the first with whom it has been tried, but perhaps only the first with whom it has not succeeded. Don't be angry because I speak so badly of people, especially of your friends; but at bottom you really don't treat them any better, you sacrifice them; I only slander them—and possibly just to pour poison in your cup. Now you may go."

7

Alexander is as silent as if he weren't there any more.

"Alex," Hans speaks across the cell.

"Yes," reports Alexander in a weak and narrow voice.

"Did they want to rehire you, too?"

"Rehire? What does it mean?"

"If the word is not something like a cue for you, they did not try it with you. Forget it . . ."

"We got to the small Remington typewriter," Alexander urges, distressed.

"Yes, my dear Alex, that's the way it is. Assume the worst. What is that line toward the end of 'Fiesco'? 'If the purple falls, the duke must after it.' "

"You mean by that," Alexander whispers, "if the typewriter is here, then also . . ."

"Yes, that is what I mean," Hans interrupts.

Alexander clears his throat; but he cannot get it clear and speaks with a thick voice: "Look here, Hans, this matter has also an entirely personal significance for me . . . I suppose now I can tell you, God knows I may not have another opportunity . . ."

"Oh, Alex, in such cases one always believes to have hidden his feelings in a deep dark well—and yet other people have noticed it long ago."

"Who has noticed it?"

"I have, for instance, and certainly she has noticed it herself."

"She has?" Alexander exclaims in amazement. "And she did not let on that she knew what was the matter with me? How could she? Of course she could!" he answers his own question bitterly. "After all, I am not so attractive, a thickset lug with a pie face, yes, I know, and since I had typhus my hair shows damned little inclination to come back properly and grows only in tufts, and my scalp looks like a mangy cat's . . ."

"That's no news either, my poor tomcat," Hans breaks in, smiling.

"Of course not. But a fellow must put things right for himself and clarify things and call himself to order. I am simply no match for handsome outdoor youths with a tinge of hysteria . . . Some mixture, that!" He stops short, as if he listened to something. Hans is silent. "Rehire?" Alexander asks across the cell in a whisper, "Not you, surely . . ."

"I am not supposed to be the first with whom it has been tried," Hans answers, "but perhaps only the first with whom it has not succeeded. Of course that smells like a Negelian experiment in decomposition, he admitted as much by indirection."

"But it smells," Alexander grumbles. "And I didn't smell it for nothing just as I mentioned the mixture."

"But that is what bothers me," Hans demurs. "Jealousy does not make for a good nose, and I am terribly afraid of injustice, Alex, along with all my other fears . . ."

"I have no love for it either and feel my nose getting clear again," growls Alexander. "And what they didn't ask me, starting yesterday afternoon: Why do I, as a medical student, take a course in criminal psychology? An extremely stupid question to ask a prospective practitioner of psychiatry and forensic medicine! Do I know who is the owner of a certain Continental office typewriter? Next to whom did I sit in the university auditorium on January 18. What are my connections with this and that person—in short, every name was mentioned except one, Hans, except one!"

"Yes," says Hans, nothing more.

"It just occurs to me, Hans— Were you asked if we spoke to fellow students in the Mensa?"

"No."

"Nor was I," says Alexander. "And now we are again in the Mensa . . ."

But the conservation ends—and yet the two friends do not know, or have their doubts, whether they will ever again be able to speak with each other. The conversation ends because their thoughts do not stay in the Mensa.

Alexander sees Christopher's troubled face, white as a sheet; but now he sees Christopher's brown face with flashing eyes and flashing teeth and black curls, the gaudy picture of a wild hunter, and next to him is Sophia, quite as it should be; for nearly always he had seen the two faces together. They are of the same height and make a handsome pair, the blonde girl and the dark youth. From the beginning he had seen them together . . .

The train rolls into Munich's East Station; it is gray November and the people are gray, their clothes are patched, the houses along the right-of-way and the terminal building itself are boarded up significantly. All these, and much worse, are familiar sights for Alexander and he barely looks at them; he is past that stage, he with his double dismissal, discharged from the hospital for contagious diseases at Linz and temporarily dismissed from military duty for continuation of his studies—and here his friend awaits him. But also awaiting him are these two who are not gray, but brightened by their handsomeness and their affinity: the blonde girl and the dark youth, arm in arm. And next to them, Hans hangs on his crutch. —"Yes," says Hans with a proud smile, "this is my little sister." Alexander knows her face already; in the field hospital Hans had shown him her photograph, the only one he carried with him, and immediately Alexander had fallen in love a little; for out there one does fall in love with pictures. And he had converted a wooden box into a bedside table for his friend, so he could set up the photo on it, and Hans did it, too, and never saw through the little artifice.

When his amputation wound did not give him much pain, Hans would speak about his sister, but never about other girls. "We are not even on good terms," he confessed tenderly. "That is to say, we love each other dearly, but our opinions always differed. She is more intelligent than I, or rather, she has more feeling or more courage or more character, and from the first she refused to go along—yes, and I beat her, I was fourteen and she eleven, because she would not break off her friendship with a Jewish girl in the neighborhood . . ." When Hans told about his sister, Alexander would look at the picture.

Now she stands before him and pleases him much better still than in the horrid uniform of the Association of German Girls which she had worn in the photograph. Now she wears a light, belted raincoat and a red kerchief and some rouge on her lips, which is "strictly undesirable," and her blond hair undulates freely over her shoulders—yes, her forehead and narrow nose and capricious chin are a picture of Hans, though her eyes are not blue as her brother's, but greenish brown and farther apart, with a more oblong cut and charmingly shaded by long, dark lashes, and her smile, her smile of greeting, molds her cheeks in feminine loveliness.

"This is my friend Christopher Sauer," Sophia says for Hans who apparently forgot to make the introductions. The dark one flashes eyes and teeth at Alexander: "You will have to put up with our modest East Station, Herr Welte: for the moment the Main Station is not quite presentable, because of certain cataclysmic events."—"Suits me!" Alexander laughs and looks at Sophia. The girl smiles, not at him, but at the dark youth by her side. "Suits us!" she says to Christopher, not to Alexander, who after all, had given her the cue. —He is handsome, Alexander thinks, he is alive, he doesn't do things by halves, and seems to have used his time well. "Also on study leave?" he asks Christopher. —"Leave nothing, mister, I am a genuine, professional, unadulterated civilian student." —"Well, well!" Alexander wonders and measures the young man's strong body with the expert look of the medical-corps man. "You look to me very much like a 1-A—now don't tell me you've got athlete's heart!" —"Sorry I can't oblige with anything but an entirely normal heart, Herr Welte," says Christopher, casting an amused glance at Sophia, "with a simple heart." —"Tell me seriously, Herr Sauer, why weren't you drafted?" —"I tell you in all seriousness, Herr Welte, I did not want to be." —"But that's impossible!" —"Correct!" laughs Christopher. "It isn't normal, it's abnormal!"

He didn't want to, thinks Alexander; as if we had wanted to! Yes, we wanted to! And Sophia belongs to that fellow who did not want to go to war. How is this now? Does Alexander hate the shirker or the rival? Hate? That's just it, he likes him, he can't help it—they all like him: Hans, the professor, Frau Dora; for he is handsome and brisk and determined; yes, he is the life of the group, the rioter, the leader of the "Enough!" chorus on the eighteenth of January. Who mistrusted him? Who inquired into his past, into the enigma of his thoroughly civilian existence?

Surely this is impossible: not to want to be a soldier and therefore not to be one, when one is twenty-one and built like a tree! This cannot be possible anywhere, least of all in the Third Reich. But only in the Third Reich can one find a certain bartering of souls and transactions of highly Mephistophelian character, miraculous deliverances from concentration camps and resurrections in the subtlest form of Judas Iscariot. Such things one can find, and this devil's disciple from upper Bavaria may be one of those resurrected ones. There is something about him that savors of witches' Sabbath and of black magic—it is quite possible that we are, all of us, the doomed attendants at his Black Mass. When the professor was dictating the manifesto to the two women, Sophia raised that dear face of hers, that beloved face, after each sentence and looked, not at the dictating professor, not at her brother, and not at me, least of all at me, but at her dark bewitcher, and her eyes would be green and large and her mouth open part way and her cheeks hot—she looked as if she were receiving, not the professor's words, but Christopher's love, and that was the last time I saw her . . .

Hans, on the other cot, remembers: he had once asked his sister if she knew why Christopher had not been drafted. She had answered that she knew, but was not at liberty to talk about it. Christopher, she said, had obtained something like a hunting permit and was entirely free. "Hunting permit" is an expression for a certificate of mental illness, much sought after especially in time of war. The answer sufficed; for the question had been prompted by curiosity and Hans, not inclined to inquisitiveness, had immediately felt its impropriety. Any suspicion was far from his mind, suspicion would have been an insult to the professor; since, if there was any seniority in Professor Hennings' seminar, Christopher occupied first place, Sophia second, Hans third and Alexander, as the last arrival, fourth place. The suspicion arose only in prison and must be reeled off backwards, a nasty undertaking, a sordid and sorry task. Here, lying on the prison cot, the life of a comrade is reeled off, and all that is white becomes black, all that is unequivocal becomes ambiguous; for the reel is controlled by Herr Negele. "Rehire" and "How we came to know"! With that every thought is turned to poison. Christopher speaks, and his speech is lies. Christopher laughs, and his laughter is betrayal. Christopher shakes your hand, and his handshake is murder. No, he mustn't think such thoughts, Hans is not rehired, he is not the Jupiter light over Christopher's head! He is sitting in the Mensa again and Christopher leaves, white as a sheet, suspiciously white. But what was it he said as he left? That things would go worse yet for the others . . . Stop, use your head, stop and think: let us suppose Christopher has been rehired as an agent provocateur and stool pigeon: why then did he not denounce his friends earlier, why not twenty-four hours earlier, why not one hour before the distribution of the leaflets? Was it not the distribution that was to be prevented at any cost!

Hans raises himself. He wants to express his thought and communicate it to Alexander. But how formulate it so that it will be understood by his friend, yet not by the listener at the wall? And Alexander is as silent as if he weren't there. He must be thinking of Sophia, leave him in peace.

Hans lies down again, on his right side, and feels leg touching leg. Let us suppose then, he thinks, that Christopher has also been arrested. Let us suppose that the car which left just before ours and which had not been Alexander's car, had taken the professor away. Let's consider the small Remington typewriter as fatal for Sophia as the big Continental machine for Frau Dora. Then all the members are together, all members. And from now on I shall sleep with my artificial leg, he thinks and must quietly smile to himself, from now on!

CHAPTER THREE

WITHOUT FAREWELL

I

THE single cells, numbers 17 and 24, are on opposite sides of the corridor. Should the shutters of the peepholes be open on occasion, the inmates could see each other, providing number 17 as well as number 24 pressed their faces to the left edge of the peephole. The occasion, understandably enough, never arises. Nevertheless, the distance between the two cells is so short that the flashlight need not be switched off between inspections, even allowing for the most meticulous observance of regulations designed to lengthen the life of the batteries. Karl von Hennings in 17 and Dora von Hennings in 24 shield their eyes against the intruding light, and they do so with the same gesture: each lifts his hand to cover the eyes, palm turned outward.

They will soon have been married nineteen years, and they have assimilated many of each other's gestures, words and thoughts. He is fifty-five and fifteen years her senior; but the difference in their ages had gradually diminished and was finally lost in the coalescence of their lives. For eighteen years they have never been separated. But now they are separated. Only their gestures and their thoughts still hang together.

The man in cell 17 and the woman in cell 24 know everything about each other save their present. But the multitude of common experiences is so powerful, and their separation so unbelievable, that illusions are still possible, especially at night. Thus each hears the other breathe, if only for a few moments, perhaps the few moments before falling asleep. Then they awake, frightened, and each knows of the other only that he cannot sleep, wherever he may be. And then the search for the other starts again, through the labyrinth of their intimacy.

Not that the separation had fallen upon them from a clear sky.

Karl and Dora had not plunged into their undertaking with th eyes shut; they knew what they risked. They understood the selves and understood the rebelliousness which bred and grew within them, cherished and fostered and talked about for the last ten years, and which was bound eventually to burst out in the open under the compulsion of its own growth. Because they knew and understood this, it had not been necessary to discuss the risk. But was it really unnecessary? Before Karl dictated the manifesto he had laid down directions for their conduct in the event of partial or complete discovery of the plot. These directions were to guide the six participants. Dora being one of the six, any separate discussion of the matter between husband and wife was superfluous. But was it superfluous?

On that last evening, when Karl returned from the university to their precious little garden house on Georgenstrasse, originally a sculptor's studio, Dora was still working on her assignment of one hundred leaflets. To make the work proceed faster, he dictated the text to her into the machine; it wasn't much different from his customary dictation of a contribution to some professional journal. When they had finished he stacked the leaflets carefully, put them in an envelope and put the envelope in his brief case. Then they went to bed, talking of this and that, and soon Karl was asleep. He was one of those people who fall asleep within the first quarter hour or not at all. In the night he woke up because in his sleep he had sensed that Dora was not sleeping. This peculiar sense, reaching out from the subconscious like a periscope, was a gift they both possessed.

"Dora?" he said gently in her direction. "Yes," she answered in a sleepy voice which he knew she only affected. "Were you sleeping?"—"Wonderfully . . ." —"Then forgive me, Dora . . ." —"It's all right, dear, I'm asleep again . . ." she murmured vaguely, drawing audibly regular breaths. He let it go at that. And it was the last night they were together.

Karl, arrested and separated from Dora, clings desperately to the outermost fringe of their companionship, though he already knows that it is ended. She, however, does not yet know it and waits for him, and his deep awareness of her waiting is for him the last proof of her presence.

For, the day ending in his arrest, that day is still their common possession: she knows where he is, and he knows where she is. When he has an evening class, he gets home no later than half past ten; it takes five minutes to walk from the university past the Siegestor to Georgenstrasse. He knows that in the dining corner of the studio—the large room has many "corners" and combines a whole suite of rooms: dining room, Dora's living room, Karl's study and their library of five thousand volumes—on the dining table, he knows, the cold snack stands ready for him, and Dora sits in her reading chair and reads Thomas Mann's *The Beloved Returns*, the latest book heroically purveyed by that remarkable bookdealer in some town on the Lake of Constance, who for the last ten years has been smuggling in books by exiled authors from Switzerland and yet is still alive.

Until eleven o'clock he knows Dora is not nervous. Until eleven o'clock she reads, and then the turnpike of the hour falls between the book and her eyes. Suddenly she understands no longer what she is reading, she looks up and sees the clock on Karl's desk; she puts the book away. She sits very quietly in her reading chair and looks at the clock. Then comes the moment, Karl knows, when the clock is too far away from her; she rises from her chair and sits down at the desk; she looks at her picture which stands next to the clock, a photograph taken in 1924, the year they were married.

She sits and waits and the two hands of the clock meet in their midnight union, the bells of Ludwigskirche can be heard pealing softly, and still more softly those of Schwabinger Kirche in the North on Ungererstrasse. Then the world becomes so still that the ticking of the desk clock begins to resound in her head. And Karl knows that Dora is now suddenly aging. At first there are rings, then sacks, under her eyes, the skin wrinkles around the corners of her eyes, lines furrow across her forehead and vertically between her eyes and from her nose to her chin, past the corners of her mouth, and one furrow creeps along her jaw and bulges the flesh of the lower part of her cheek, and the neck, the beautiful neck withers.

She gets up; she walks back and forth, but her feet are cold with a cottony insensibility. He knows that she looks at the dead telephone on the little table in the living-room corner, desperately and embittered, but she does not call the university. He knows she would not make the silly mistake of going to Hans Moeller or to his sister or to Christopher Sauer. But she walks out into the night, around three o'clock, because she must do something—and if it is not stupid, it is at least pointless. She walks out into the blind, wet, war night, he knows it, because the moment has come when she can no longer breathe in the house. She feels her way to near-by Leopoldstrasse, turns into it and walks toward the Siegestor, walks ever faster, runs to the university or at least to a point from which she can see the shadowy façade of the university in back of the circular driveway. There is no light and no sign of life. She can stand there; for the night is a cloak of invisibility also for her. She stands there only until she feels that her face is wet, not only from the heavy mist,—yes, she weeps a little that night, in front of the university. She walks back. And now the studio house seems to her completely changed, strange, empty and pitilessly indifferent. She sits in her reading chair as if she had been bled white.

And here their companionship, their common life, has reached its outermost fringe. Karl's thoughts can go no farther with her.

2

When Hans Moeller and Alexander Welte had left the professor's office, Karl looked at his watch. It was twenty-five minutes of eleven. I'll tell Dora that I am coming home now, he thought, and went to the old-fashioned wall telephone. He lifted the receiver and waited some time before the university operator responded. "This is Mr. von Hennings," Karl said, "please connect me with thirty-four-o-forty-eight." —"Sorry, Professor von Hennings, we have been disconnected," was the reply. —"Didn't the university pay its telephone bill?" Karl joked—there was no one who saw that he said it with pale lips. —"The police have disconnected us, sir." —"That's another story," said Karl and hung up. He rested his hand on the receiver and closed his eyes for a few moments.

I should also have asked what is the matter, he thought. Then he went to the hat tree near the door, slowly got into his overcoat and put on his hat.

The telephone rang. He hesitated for a moment, then he unhooked the receiver and gave his name. —"Please do not leave the building until further notice," was the message; "the Secret State Police want the investigation to proceed without attracting any attention." —"What investigation?" asked Karl. —The voice at the switchboard did not answer his question, but continued: "The gentlemen of the faculty who happen to be in the building are requested to stay where they are until new instructions are issued." —"Very well," Karl said, "I have some work to do here, anyway."

He replaced the receiver, went to the hat tree and took off his overcoat and hat. He sat down on the leather sofa, crossed his long legs and picked up the *Voelkischer Beobachter* again. He listened intently behind the newspaper. Outside, in the hallway, everything was quiet. In the distance a few doors slammed.

Now a fast, strong step came along the hall, the door was thrown open, Karl let his newspaper slump down. In the door stood Dr. Vierck. The black-uniformed SS professor looked at him briefly, without a greeting, without a word, and left, letting the door swing shut behind him. Karl winced and twisted up his face; he hated to have doors slammed. "Boor!" he said aloud; but the step went away again.

Like a child's idea of the bogeyman, Karl thought, or more correctly: like an SS man and not like a professor, the gentleman is in his element . . . He returned to his newspaper, thumbed through the pages and forced himself to read the death notices. "For Führer and Reich the third of our sons made the supreme sacrifice . . ." —"For our Führer died . . ." —"For the Germany of the Führer . . . gave their lives . . ."

Outside a step came tripping along. The old man, Karl thought, as he looked up. The door opened and Councilor Seitz entered, books under both his arms, pushing the door shut softly with his back. A brown, fur-lined ulster was romantically thrown around his shoulders, and on his white locks he wore an extraordinarily peculiar, black, high-crowned hat, a hybrid of a high hat and a derby, a hat famed throughout the university for the last forty years.

"*Salve, Collega!*" he said, sitting down on the leather sofa and depositing the books and the peculiar hat between himself and Karl.

"Good evening, Councilor," said Karl, looking into his wise, venerable, rosy face.

The old gentleman raised his eyes in mock piety and looked at the ceiling: "Leaflets," he said.

"Oh," said Karl.

"German professors of older vintage, on the decline anyway, are known to possess umbrellas," the dean said to the ceiling. "Let it rain down what may."

"Has anyone been arrested?" Karl asked.

"I have my umbrella," the old man recited, obstinately looking at the ceiling.

"I haven't," said Karl.

The dean gave him a quick look. "*Suum cuique*, I don't lend mine, *Collega*, I am of retirement age, Emeritus, Emeritus . . ."

The door was thrown open; Professor Vierck stood in it, the bogeyman. "A word with you, Councilor," he said to Seitz and waved him out of the room without giving Karl a look. The old gentleman jumped up obediently and tripped toward the door.

"Herr Vierck," said Karl, "even if you should not slam the door now, your conduct remains loutish."

The SS professor started; but he controlled himself and did not as much as turn his face toward Karl. Councilor Seitz stumbled over Karl's objection as if a stick had been thrown between his legs. But he only pulled back the ulster which had slid from his shoulder and was already in the door, held open by Professor Vierck, who politely closed it behind him. The uneven steps receded, there was no stopping and no whispering behind the door.

He left a forfeit here, Karl thought as he looked at the peculiar hat beside him. He wanted his thoughts to stay with the hat and its owner, and somewhat spitefully he wanted to picture the dean's grief over the separation from his hat and his joy at being reunited with it. But his thoughts jumped away from him and were with Dora,—and time also made a jump. When he looked at his watch again, it was eleven. Karl rose; for Dora was getting nervous now. Rightly so, Karl said to himself, and looked at the peculiar hat which apparently had not been forgotten, but sacrificed—at least for as long as the unprotected colleague without umbrella sat next to it on the leather sofa.

Emeritus seems to know that time is limited, Karl thought as he went to the door and opened it. Well, there was no black-uniformed bogeyman standing there. He stepped out into the hallway. Uncertain noises, as of voices or of one voice, were coming from the staircase to the left; to the right, between closed doors, ran the broad corridor, poorly lighted and with not a soul in it.

Only at the end of the corridor, where it turned into the south wing, there was a light, apparently coming from an open door.

But there, opposite lecture room 77, was von Hennings' seminar room to which only Karl himself and his assistant Christopher Sauer had keys. Karl walked down the corridor until he was certain that the light came from his seminar room. He hesitated for a moment; even a brave man hesitates at the threshold of disaster. Karl was still free to return to his office, there to while away the limited time of uncertainty. He did not turn back—less because he craved certainty than because he felt that he had to appear in order to protect Christopher, in case the young man had been forced to open the room.

The door stood open halfway and Karl saw there was no key in the door lock; but it was undamaged. Karl entered. A man in civilian clothes sat at the big table, at which the members of the seminar used to work and debate, and superficially examined books, pamphlets, neatly bound manuscripts of seminar papers, the contents of index boxes—anything unloaded on the table by another man in civilian clothes who cleared the stuff out of the open bookcase, the open manuscript case, the filing cabinet and the drawers of the table. Both men had their hats on, identical green shooting-hats with upright brushes of chamois hair at the back of the hatband.

"What do you want here?" asked the man at the table.

"What do *you* want here?" asked Karl. He was irritated because he had a deep aversion to hats with chamois beards.

"We are here on official business," the man countered, as he made that most repulsive gesture with which the secret agent reveals his badge: the metal shield under the lapel.

"Oh, is that so," said Karl looking from one chamois brush to the other with wincing eyes. "And for that reason you must keep your hats on?"

The agent gestured to his hat in some embarrassment and declared, slightly offended: "Yes, to differentiate it from private business. Don't worry, I know what is proper. I want you to know that I am an inspector, first class. And who are you, anyway?"

Karl had to smile. "If you gentlemen didn't have your hats on," he said, "I could greet you as my guests. I happen to be the host in this room and I suppose I may ask . . ."

"Then you are Professor von Hennings?" the inspector broke in, rising.

"I am," answered Karl. "And it would have been more correct to inform me first, to tell me the reasons for your mission and to consult me in your proceedings. How did you get in here, anyway?"

"Through the door."

"I mean, who gave you the key?"

"Herr Professor," said the inspector, "it is not my business to examine you, but it is still less your business to examine me. I have orders to investigate your seminar room, your lecture room and your desk in the office, room number 61, and then to lead you before my superior officer."

"Does my presentation to your superior officer depend on the result of your search?"

"No, I have only given you the sequence of the proceedings."

"And now I have disrupted the sequence," Karl said; "but, after all, I can go back to my office and wait there for my time . . ."

"You can no longer do that, Herr Professor."

Karl was silent for a while. Then he asked, "Have you a warrant for my detention?"

"More than that, I have a warrant for your arrest, Herr Professor," said the inspector and, reaching in the inside pocket of his coat, he pulled out the form.

Karl saw that his name had not been typed, but had been written in with ink—and the ink was fresh. "Well, don't let me disturb you," he said, sitting down at the table, in the chair he always occupied during seminar meetings. And here Hans Moeller used to sit, here Welte, Sophia, and there, where the chamois beard now waved, there Christopher used to sit . . . And Karl began to occupy himself with Christopher; he thought more about him than about Dora.

The work of the inspector consisted in leafing through everything—books, journals, manuscripts. His assistant carried most of the items back to where they belonged, but a few remained on the table and were bound with leather straps. It was difficult to discover the criteria which determined the choice of materials to be confiscated. Then, looking around the room, the inspector asked: "Is there no typewriter, Herr Professor?" Karl was jolted out of his thoughts and answered with unnecessary sharpness: "No. The seminar has no typewriter."

They crossed the corridor into the lecture room. Karl was directed to sit on one of the benches in the section near the windows. The two agents went through the rows of benches, bending down and sticking their hands inside the open desk compartments, as if they dusted them. Then the inspector stepped up to the lectern on the platform. The chamois beard in the academic chair effected a sort of short circuit in Karl's loaded brain. He jumped up noisily and stretched out his right arm.

"What's the meaning of this?" the inspector asked, perplexed.

"Academic rules prescribe that on entering the dais, the German salute must be given in honor of the Führer," said Karl with raised arm. "I insist on it!"

Reluctantly the inspector raised his arm. "Heil Hitler!" he said; "but I shall report the incident to my superior officer. Investigation may disclose that it was an act of contemptuousness and as such subject to the Treachery Act."

"Heil Hitler!" Karl exclaimed and sat down. The inspector stopped only a short while on the dais and left it without booty.

When they entered the professor's office, the famous hat of Dean Seitz was still on the sofa. My exodus stands under the sign of peculiar hats, Karl thought as he put on his overcoat.

"One moment," said the inspector. "Unfortunately a short search of your person will be necessary."

"For weapons?" asked Karl and took his overcoat off again.

"Please take off your coat and vest also," the inspector requested.

"And my trousers?" Karl asked, taking off coat and vest.

"Just empty the side and rear pockets of your trousers and turn the lining inside out, Herr Professor."

And the dean's hat is looking on, thought Karl, following the inspector's instructions. The two agents searched the pockets of the clothes he had taken off, the inspector examined the contents of Karl's wallet with a show of discretion. "All done, Herr Professor," he said, and helped Karl into his vest and coat. The other agent held the overcoat. Karl let himself be attended by them.

"And now, a quick look in your desk," said the inspector. "Which is your desk, Herr Professor?"

Karl could not help himself: with a vague gesture he pointed to the desk of the SS professor. The agent tackled it, shaking the drawer. "Locked, Herr Professor. The key, please!"

"Good God!" Karl cried out. "This is Professor Vierck's desk—don't touch it! Spring gun! And this is Councilor Seitz' desk—and this is his hat—don't touch it! It would be the death of him! And here is my desk, as open as it is empty . . ."

The inspector shuddered away from Vierck's desk, but reached for the peculiar hat, lifted it from the sofa with discreet fingers, looked into it, reached into it, and brought to light something truly amazing: a diminutive flat brush, hidden in a daintily pleated pocket in the lining.

It was at this point that Karl laughed, for the last time. Throughout his life he had been much given to laughter. "Emeritus! Emeritus!" he laughed. "That is what I call a finale!"

Before they left, Karl looked at his watch. It was after half-past eleven. He thought: Dora is also looking at the clock now . . .

At the exit to Amalienstrasse an SS man stood guard and unlocked the door. On the street three heavy limousines were waiting, parked against the traffic. The two agents went with Karl to the first car, whose driver started the motor. Karl clambered into the back seat and saw through the rear window that the portal of the university was being opened again. The inspector quickly pulled the curtain and sat down beside him. The car drove very fast. Karl paid no attention to the route it took. Ten minutes later, when they turned into a rectangular court surrounded by buildings, Karl looked around and said, "But this is not your Wittelsbach Palace, is it?"—"No, Herr Professor, this is our Police Headquarters." —"No housing shortage for this enterprise," Karl commented and felt relieved.

3

The bells of near-by Frauenkirche struck midnight as Karl was led before Commissioner Negele after a hasty booking conducted by worn and weary officers who registered his academic titles respectfully. The bronze bells resounded as loudly as if they rang in the building. Now Dora hears the bells of Ludwigskirche, but not as loudly, thought Karl.

The commissioner looked at him very intently, his elbow resting on the tabletop, his thumb under his soft chin, index and middle finger against his temple, not saying a word. Karl, standing six foot one, looked down at the colorless man and his eyes narrowed with aversion.

Finally, without moving his hand from his face, Herr Negele looked at the file lying before him, and read: "Dr. juris, Dr. medicinae honoris causa Karl von Hennings, Professor of Criminal Psychology in the University of Munich." He read it with special emphasis on "honoris causa."

"Honoris causa," Karl observed, "means: for the sake of honor."

"Thank you, Herr Professor, I suspected it."

"I assumed from your strained enunciation," said Karl, "that the two foreign words caused you some difficulty."

Again the commissioner looked at him silently, his little eyes strangely amused, but his thumb sticking deeper yet in the fat of his chin. Then he said, "By the way, I, too, forgot to give the German salute; or don't you attach any importance to it here, Herr Professor?"

"I attach importance to it when people keep their hats on in an academic lecture room," Karl answered not unpleasantly. "To be sure, this is no lecture room and you are bareheaded—but I would have expected it nevertheless, here and of you."

"Got that?" Negele turned to the young SS man who sat on the other side of the double desk, taking stenographic notes. The young man gave his affirmation without looking up from his work.

A red light flashed on the signal board of the telephone desk near the commissioner. "Now take the gentleman to the waiting room, first class," he said, glancing toward the door where the inspector and his companion were standing; then turning back to Karl, he continued: "It is customary to fall asleep in waiting rooms, Herr Professor, but I recommend to you, in your interest as well as mine, to remain as wide awake as possible, because we shall unfortunately have to see each other once more before the night is over."

Now he is going to have them beat me, Karl thought as he was led from the office. They went only a few steps along the hall and stopped at the second door, which displayed neither a number nor an inscription and had no doorknob. The inspector unlocked it with a passkey and let Karl enter. The narrow room actually looked like a waiting room, with wooden benches along the walls and an empty table against the closed shutters of the window. The inspector invited Karl to sit down on one of the benches, while he and his companion took seats on the opposite side. No one talked. The inspector yawned and, as an afterthought, with a furtive look in the direction of the professor, he raised his hand to his mouth; apparently he remembered his contention that he knew what was proper. But Karl, his head leaning against the back of the bench, looked into space so as not to see the two chamois beards. High up on the grayish yellow wall he saw a circular opening protected by a fine wire mesh and asked himself what purpose it could serve. He closed his eyes because it seemed silly to him to look for implements of torture in this unimaginative room which appeared to have been reduced to idiocy through sheer ennui.

"Please don't go to sleep," the inspector requested in a sleepy voice.

Is that it? Karl asked himself. Instead of beating me they keep me from sleeping? "I'll tell you how it is," he held forth didactically while keeping his eyes maliciously closed, "I am in the habit of falling asleep unresistingly when the barber lathers my face. Thus it comes about that the shaving brush on your hat makes me dangerously sleepy . . ." He heard a slight movement and opened his eyes. Both agents had bared their short-cropped heads—the inspector's was already amply bald—and had hidden the shooting-hats under the bench. It could be called a victory. "Thank you very much," said Karl politely.

This was the moment when he learned with a start what was the purpose of the circular, wire-meshed opening in the wall. It was a loud-speaker, and from it came Alexander Welte's voice, sounding somewhat veiled and far away, as voices do when the microphone is at a considerable distance from the speaker.

"I repeat with all possible emphasis that, not only did I have something to do with the leaflets, but that I alone and on my own initiative composed and distributed the leaflets . . ."

The transmission broke off with a slight crackle and came back after a short time, again with Alexander's voice, again with his sonorous and somewhat irritated insistence on his undivided responsibility, then a crackle and dead silence. Thus it went on for some time; only fragments of Alexander's aggressive self-accusation could be heard, but never the voice of the inquisitor. Then the wall was silent for a long time.

Karl sat motionless, with completely composed face; for the inspector was watching him intently. What is happening now? Karl asked himself. What are they doing to him now? And what about Moeller? They can't have taken him, if Welte so valiantly makes himself the target . . . He looked at his watch, which showed ten minutes of one. Poor Dora, he thought.

It was ten minutes later—as if the shattering strike of the church bell sounded through the loud-speaker like a mighty announcement —that the broadcast started again. For immediately after the bell came Alexander's voice, changed, strained, breathing loudly between words and crying out as if from a nightmare: "This is an error, I tell you! This is a great wrong! This is . . . I have no words for it . . . this is a shameful lack of respect for an injured war veteran! Suspecting Herr Moeller only because he is my friend, my front companion? But I tell you again: he has nothing to do with the leaflet, nothing whatever . . ." Dead silence followed the crackle.

Karl pressed his hands together so that his finger-joints cracked. His gaze was fixed on the loud-speaker. He shook it with his eyes, that it would speak again. Hans must speak! Hans must speak! he shouted at it with his eyes. It took a brief eternity; but then Hans spoke from the wall in his measured, precise, deliberate, courageous voice:

". . . to give an explanation. Herr Welte's testimony was given in the spirit of comradeship, but not in accordance with the facts. It was I who composed the leaflet and organized its distribution. Herr Welte acted under my instructions and helped only with the distribution." Then the loud-speaker was disconnected again.

Karl crossed his arms and swung one long leg over the other. If only Christopher should also speak now . . . he thought and glared like a lion tamer at the wired circle. After a few minutes the commissioner's voice came from the wall: "Bring Professor von Hennings in here." His voice sounded nearer and more distinct than the others.

"Slept?" Herr Negele asked, as Karl stood before him.

"No."

"Heard voices?"

"Yes."

"Did you recognize the voices?"

"Yes."

"Could you or would you tell me whose voices they were?"

"Those of my students Welte and Moeller."

"Well, you are doing beautifully, Herr Professor," Negele rejoiced, leaning back in his chair. "Then you have witnessed the noble contest of the two youths, or at least some fragments of it. May I ask for an expression of your position with respect to it?"

"Naturally it is I who bear the responsibility," said Karl.

"You mean that in a sense, as a professor of the two students, you bear a spiritual responsibility for their so-called spirit of comradeship?"

"Don't make me and yourself ridiculous," Karl said rudely. "I bear the spiritual and the factual responsibility for the leaflet and, logically, also the legal responsibility for the manual services of the two students."

"Thank you," said the commissioner. "I have finished with you for today."

4

Dora sat in her reading chair as if she had been bled white. Her evening had passed as Karl had seen it in his mind; but it had begun differently, there had been no peaceful waiting which permitted her to read *The Beloved Returns* until eleven o'clock. She had read only until about ten o'clock. Then Christopher had dropped in for a short while.

This was not unusual: Christopher was a close friend and had always been Frau Dora's protégé, even in the beginning, when she had dissipated the professor's doubts about his new student; and in gratitude, Christopher was deeply attached to her. It was not his coming that had been unusual, but his pallor; and so Dora had jumped up when she saw him and had whispered, "Good Heavens . . ."—No, no! he had parried, gently forcing her back into the chair, so far all was going well, the second hundred had also been distributed and swallowed without any trouble, he had just come from the Mensa and from speaking there with Hans and Alexander, the latter triumphant and touchy as a prima donna, and now, he supposed, they must be with the professor, reporting to him. —"But why are you so pale, Christopher?" —"Because it will end badly, Frau Dora." —"I don't think it is at all right of you, Christopher, to come here only to make me nervous. Couldn't my husband have told me the story of the second hundred just as well, in another half-hour?" —"I really didn't want to come to see you anyway, Frau Dora, I wanted to go home. But a short time ago I saw Sophia. . . . —I think it is terrible that women are involved, and I had wanted to say something to her, but didn't say it because I am sure she wouldn't have heeded it anyway—and so, all of a sudden, I am here, to say it to you. . . ."—"And do you think that I would heed it, Christopher?"—"No, Frau Dora, and no harm meant, and good night!"

He had gone to the door and then had come back, delirious big black eyes in his white face, and had said this: "If you should know of any place where you could hide out for tonight, Frau Dora . . ."

"Are you ill, Christopher?"

"Yes," he had nodded and was gone.

No, it was impossible to read, with such a prelude of fear, and the time of waiting strikes other notes, it yells with fear. And anger smoldered in her heart against Christopher, a smoldering anger which rose to her head and settled in her legs like cheap gin. Already by eleven o'clock, she had lost her reason or her inner coherence with Karl and had done what he had not believed possible: she called the university. The number was always busy; and the malicious staccato of the busy signal enraged her beyond endurance. She called "Information," and an unsympathetic voice advised her in one breath, as if prepared for the question, that no information could be given. The voice had sobered her and made her conscious of her error. She could visualize the bridge of Karl's narrow nose becoming sharper still in silent censure. Only toward three o'clock in the morning, when she felt she could not breathe in the house any longer, had she committed the second folly, the one Karl had believed possible, and had run to the university. She had run her head against the wall of the night and had wept a little, too.

After she returned, a great apathy came over her. She did not even take off her heavy wool overcoat, but sat in her reading chair as in a sleeping bag, with her legs pulled up, though they did not get warmer that way. Yes, it was cold in the house, as cold as outside, or the night had broken down the walls and she was sitting in the open, defenseless, exposed to seizure from all sides, and waiting —oh, no longer for him. Waiting was not painful any more; for she had not much sensibility left. Only in her head, which felt as cottony as her feet, anxiety stirred: if I should wait in vain also for this, what then? what then?

The professor's little studio house stood in back of a three-family house which was built in the manner of a Florentine villa and had once been the residence of one of those artist magnates who flourished in Munich around the turn of the century. The two houses were connected by a broad gravel walk. Gravel creaks when stepped on. In thirteen years the ear learns to distinguish familiar steps from strange steps, it can even discern the degree of familiarity: whether it is the most familiar step of all, the giant stride of the long-legged master of the house, or perhaps Christopher's fleeting approach. Thanks to the gravel, Dora cannot be taken unawares.

The gravel creaked strangely in the black morning, under the unfamiliar steps of two men. Dora immediately rose and walked with hasty steps through the studio to the entrance door in the anteroom. She could get up and walk quickly, because her blood suddenly circulated faster, the numbness of her head cleared away, and even her feet got warmer at once.

The two search officers had an experience which later they used to tell their beer companions. For their myrmidons' existence, tied to the gray hour of the catch, was one of grizzly monotony: houses foolishly locked, feigning blindness and deafness, which yet had to obey the shrill of the doorbell, and then the loud or subdued despair of the victims. Here, however,—and this was the new experience, the variation worth telling about—they did not have to ring a doorbell, at a quarter past five in the morning; here the entrance door stood open and in the door, as if ready for her journey, stood the woman they had come to take away.

Dora sat between the two officers on the back seat of the limousine. Before them, on the floor of the car, was the Continental typewriter in its wooden case amidst a heap of papers, documents, periodicals and books, rather indiscriminately confiscated from Karl's desk and from Dora's living-room corner. Among the books was *The Beloved Returns*. The library itself, containing a lot of forbidden literature, had not been searched, probably because it would have taken too much time. But such a search could still be made later on; for over the lock of the entrance door there was now pasted the notorious seal of the Secret State Police.

The car moved fast, and Dora made herself very small in order to touch her taciturn neighbors as little as possible. It did not matter to her if the car turned to the right at a certain place or went straight ahead. Rightly or wrongly she thought that the car would take her where Karl was—and that was what she wanted.

I am being taken to the same place as my husband! It was a comforting and also a not unreasonable idea; for she did not think: I am being taken to my husband. Her reason observed the significant distinction. And yet, what was the basis of the comfort she anticipated; only the identity of their destinies? Or did she expect more from the power of their companionship, a new knowledge of each other and feeling of each other through the walls that separated them?

But this is what happened. Dora was led to cell 24 and walked past cell 17 and waited three steps away from cell 17 for the keeper to let her into cell 24: yet nothing in her heart, nothing in her thoughts, not a nerve in her body, revealed to her his breathing nearness. And Karl in cell 17? He was awake, he thought of her, he tormented himself at the outermost fringe of their joint existence, his thoughts circled around the wilted one in her reading chair and could not go on from there. He did not feel her passing, he did not hear her, and yet he heard steps outside. Although the walls were thick, although the iron door soundproof, and the linoleum floor of the corridor deadened the footfall, the silence of the cell was stronger still and captured every sound from the corridor. But Karl did not recognize Dora's step.

5

"It is pleasant to work with you, Frau von Hennings," Commissioner Negele said the next morning during her first examination. "You make no fuss, you say what you have to say, and you avoid the unbelievable."

"I avoid nothing," said Dora.

"If you please, madam, if for instance you had asserted—perhaps to exonerate your husband—that you had not only prepared the copies of the so-called manifesto, but also composed it, that would have been unbelievable."

"That would have been untrue," said Dora.

"Certainly: because what seems to us unbelievable, is in ninety-nine cases out of a hundred also untrue. So, please continue telling the truth. How many copies of the leaflet did you prepare?"

"That is difficult to say, because I didn't count them."

"Then give us an estimate, please."

"I would guess a thousand," said Dora in her quiet, deep, true-ringing voice.

"What?" Negele exclaimed. "A thousand? I suppose you mean a hundred . . ."

"I mean one thousand."

"That is not only unbelievable, but also impossible, Frau von Hennings. To prepare a thousand copies you would have had to work at least fifty hours."

"It may have been that many hours."

"The day has but twenty-four hours, dear madam!"

"I worked at the leaflets at most four hours a day."

"I see," drawled Negele. "And how many days before would you have me believe that you started with the typing?"

"On January 18," Dora answered without hesitation.

"How do you know the date so accurately?"

"Because it was a special day."

"Because of the incidents in the auditorium of the university in connection with the celebration of the Reich's foundation?"

"Yes."

"Very interesting," said the commissioner, leaning forward a little. "That would indicate, then, that your husband was a traitor as early as January 18." Dora was silent and gave her shoulders a slight shrug. "Are you fully aware," he continued, "how seriously, how positively terrifyingly, you incriminate your husband with this date and especially with the exorbitant number of leaflets?"

"No," Dora answered, "I am not at all aware of it. My husband's responsibility for the manifesto can be affected neither by the date nor by the size of the edition."

"Frau von Hennings, as a lawyer's wife you probably know the difference between—let us say—manslaughter and premeditated murder. But let us leave the date aside and concentrate on your one thousand. The number may be of vital significance for the fate of your husband. With a burden of one or two hundred attached to him, he might still keep his head above water. With one thousand he is hopelessly sunk. Is that a clear picture?"

"It is an unbelievable picture," Dora replied.

"It would be better for your husband, if you believed my picture," Negele said threateningly. "It would be better for your husband, if you revised your figure to fit the truth. I give you one last chance and repeat my question: How high do you estimate the number of leaflets prepared by you?"

"One thousand," replied Dora, looking at him with her truthful eyes.

In the year 1914, when the young doctor of laws, Karl von Hennings, having just received an appointment as a professor at the university, went to the front instead as a lieutenant in the Second Guard Regiment, he still had a thin growth of blond hair. In 1919, when Captain von Hennings brought the remnants of his machine-gun company back home from Mesopotamia, he was bald save for a wreath of sparse hair along the back of his head from ear to ear. Since these early Victorian relics did not harmonize with his lean woodcut face, he resolved to be completely bald and from then on he had his head shaved along with his face every day. Gray stubble now covered his cheeks, his chin, and the back of his head—but his naked skull burned terribly under the Jupiter light.

"It is no pleasure to work with you, Herr Professor," Commissioner Negele observed gloatingly, "and this again is probably because your profession lends itself better to questioning than to answering." Karl's thin lips were pressed together so that they were but a pale line, and he extended the wings of his nose peculiarly, as if to arrest the flow of sweat which ran down the sides of his nose. Herr Negele leaned back in his desk chair, hands crossed in back of his head, quite like a man who feels well and who has time. His eyes did not meet the professor's, but looked a little higher, at the head that was red as a lobster. He stretched himself and stretched the pauses between his words. Suddenly he let his hands fall on the table and said in a sharp voice, "Who, then, in the name of God, wrote on your Continental typewriter, if the two students are excluded and if you yourself are out of the question because we have proof that you don't know how to type?"

"That, in the name of the Devil, is irrelevant!" Karl growled exhausted, barely opening his teeth. "Before the law the editor, and not his secretary, is responsible for what he writes."

"Then why don't you say in the name of God and of the Devil, that your secretary used the Continental!"

"I have no secretary."

"I beg your pardon, Herr Professor; Miss Sophia Moeller is your secretary."

"How can you make such an assertion!" Karl exclaimed wiping his forehead with the back of his hand. "Miss Moeller is my student and a member of my seminar!"

"That does not exonerate the young lady as long as you refuse to tell who used the Continental typewriter for you, Herr Professor."

"Well, I have a hundred students in my class and a good dozen in the seminar . . ."

"Right, Herr Professor, and that should give you food for thought."

"Why?"

Herr Negele put thumb and index finger to the corners of his flabby mouth and looked at Karl's gleaming skull. "Well, it so happens that here I am the cat and you are the mouse. That means that sometimes I play with you, with all due respect. That means that frequently I ask you about things which I know as well or better than you. I do that by no means just to test your honesty, but to cause you distress, human distress, emotional distress, breathing distress, any distress whatever. There you have, then, the students in your seminar, all partisans, and each eligible and competent to play the part of confidential secretary at the Continental typewriter."

"Should you have arrested my wife," said Karl, suddenly entirely calm, "you will demoralize neither myself nor her with this measure, but the cause you serve and which you have already sufficiently perverted by your methods."

"But nobody is speaking of your wife!" the commissioner exclaimed, and smiled unbecomingly. "We spoke of the members of your seminar and about why the thought should give you pause. Or did you see no reason for thinking about the fact that you were arrested immediately, precisely you, the right one, and not Professor X or Professor Y? If I were a trained logician like yourself, I could draw only the following conclusion: there must have been a Judas among my disciples. Of course, I express it differently, perhaps like this: there must have been a representative of our Security Department in the seminar."

Karl put his hand to his glowing head and said, "Then you might take one further step with your logic or mine and finally turn off this light."

"At your service," said Negele, rose and switched off the Jupiter light. Karl sighed with relief and kept his hand on his head for a few seconds longer. The commissioner stopped beside him. "When did you compose the text of the leaflet?" he asked.

Karl kept his eyes closed and relished the coolness—and he saw himself and Dora going home after the fiasco of the Reichsgruendungs celebration, arm in arm like two lovers, and Dora stretching herself up as high as she could, the pretty woman, and himself stooping a little so she could kiss his ear and whisper to him, "Now the moment has come . . ." Karl looked up at the commissioner and said, "On January 18."

Herr Negele was silent for a while, his hands in his coat pockets, and looked across the table at the SS stenographer; but the young man did not raise his head. Then the commissioner asked without straining his voice, "And how many copies were typed on the Continental machine, approximately?"

Karl relished the calmness that had come over him, perhaps because his last answer had been inspired by Dora. He reflected—not about whether he should or should not answer the significant question; he thought of Dora's words as he put the little pile of leaflets in his brief case. "A hundred is nothing," she had said; "if we had a mimeograph, it would be a thousand!"

"Are you again unwilling to answer?" Negele asked, reaching for the light switch. "What is your estimate of the number of leaflets prepared on the Continental typewriter?"

"One thousand," answered Karl, looking him straight in the face.

6

Why was I angry with Christopher? Dora asked herself in the long night of the cell. Because he frightened me. But when it became evident so soon that he did not frighten me groundlessly, was it still anger then? Then it was still anger over his mad suggestion that I run away. And when did anger cease and give way to suspicion? My anger never quite ceased, really; since my anger turned against my suspicion and still is . . .

Dora wished that Karl could have witnessed his assistant's unexpected visit last night or that she could tell him about it. She desired his judgment, strictly speaking, his condemnation of her suspicion. But would he be just? Had he not been prejudiced when the young man registered with him for the winter semester 1940 with the aid of a questionable recommendation from the medical director of the psychiatric clinic, who was a friend of Karl's and who described the student as a "crazy fellow"? "The crazy fellow seems to me somewhat uncanny," Karl had said to his wife then, "for one thing, because he seems uncanny to himself." "Then you just send him to me," she had suggested to him.

And Christopher had appeared for tea at Dora's one Saturday afternoon—Karl had a faculty meeting—, had stopped in the doorway of the studio, turning his handsome head right and left, up and down, and had introduced himself with a strange—no, with an unforgettable statement: "Imagine, Frau von Hennings, it smells of happiness here."—"And how does happiness smell?" she had asked laughingly. —"It smells like an absolutely undefinable perfume which I herewith name: 'Here is good resting.' " —"A beautiful name," she nodded to him, "in Italian 'Bencistà,' and that is what some Florentine friends of ours named their villa." —"Bencistà," Christopher repeated and looked at her gravely. —"That is more modest than happiness, a terribly presumptuous word: happiness," she said and looked gravely at him. "How could we say that we are happy . . ." —"You mean, beyond 'Bencistà,' Frau von Hennings —you mean outside of this house . . ." And with that he had become her friend and her protégé.

"I have never told it to anyone," he had said later on, somewhat unexpectedly, and his pupils were suddenly immobile, "but shall I tell you, Frau von Hennings, how it happened that I am sitting here and not in Norway with some Bavarian mountaineer regiment?" —"No, Herr Sauer, you don't have to tell me about it." —"But how then can I win the professor's confidence?" —"What sort of confidence do you expect from my husband, Herr Sauer?" —"Exactly the sort of confidence you have bestowed on me here in 'Bencistà,' Frau von Hennings . . ."

I am no detective, thought Karl in the long night of the cell, although admittedly my field of study develops speculative propensities. While I am cognizant of the conspicuous paleness in the Mensa, I do not begin with the key to the seminar room. Even a locked room without a key is no problem for an inspector, first class, and as for paleness, anyone who goes into the firing line is entitled to it. And if there is a Judas among my disciples, he must be a poor devil of a Judas, a traitor who is torn hither and yon between two poles of treason, a slave of the SD in the very last moment and already too late, a fifth columnist of miserable quality: for he betrayed not the deed, but only its perpetrator—and that is not so important any more after the deed is done . . .

Now, it was precisely this consideration which led him back to Christopher. The fellow was not full of falsehood and deceit, he had not dissembled and lied for the two and a half years of their spiritual and physical proximity, he had not been waiting for his Judas hour—it would have been a wait of truly infernal patience. But perhaps he was a bartered soul, perhaps his decent heart trembled when he contemplated the day of reckoning, the day which he prepared with the fire of his youth and whose approach filled him at once with fervor and with horror—what agonizing torments they must have been! And finally he paid and saved his skin, as he must have saved it once before: by doing violence to himself.

What speaks against it? Everything that speaks against a speculative idea; the impossibility to prove the contention. Who speaks against it?

Dora, who knows human nature well, once spoke against the doubts he had harbored toward the "crazy fellow," and he had thrown them overboard, though not entirely without reinsurance. At the next opportunity he had confidentially asked Professor Ackermann, the psychiatrist who had given the questionable recommendation (and whom he could ask such questions point-blank), "Could this Sauer be a stool pigeon?" —"Then I could logically be supposed to be one also, since I sent him to you," Ackermann had said, "and if I examined both cases, his and mine, I should say that I could be one sooner than he."—"And why is he a 'crazy fellow'?" —"Because he did not give in; under prevailing conditions this is abnormal, it is madness." —"Was he ill, then?" — "I attested that he was ill," the psychiatrist had answered hesitatingly, and then had added: "Yes, he was ill."

"Had you been ill?" Karl later had asked Christopher himself.

"No," he had answered immediately and then added with hesitation: "That is, I don't know . . . after all, one stands so strangely at the borderline . . ."

"I am not inquisitive, Sauer, but I would like to come into the clear with you, out of the fog."

"Excuse me, Herr Professor, but has that anything to do with whether I was ill or not?"

"In a sense it does."

"Do you mean my intellectual capacity to follow your lectures?"

"No, I mean your moral capacity, Sauer."

"You wish to know why I am not a soldier, Herr Professor?"

"Yes."

"Because I don't want to be!"

"Millions have to be, whether they want to or not, Sauer."

"They must take their detour. I am already there where they will be when they croak or come hobbling home."

"Where are you?"

"So to speak between night and day—to use nothing but an image."

"For those who 'croak' out there, Christopher, we must turn the image around and say: between day and night."

"Oh, no, Herr Professor, for they die benighted, benighted by hate, the black hatred against that for which they die. And then death is brighter than dying, just a little brighter, as if tinged with the gray of dawn. And I have not the slightest fear of dying, I am a good Catholic, Herr Professor, perhaps everything is due to this, that I have a sacred recalcitrance in my blood, the recalcitrance of the saints at the stake. But I do not want to die benighted. If I must die, let it be between night and day, no sooner, to stay with my image."

At this Karl had silently shaken his head, not from doubt, but from wonderment, as one does when he stands before a crazy fellow. His doubts were thrown overboard. Dora had been right.

Were you right, Dora, and did you persist in being right when the venom of doubt seeped also into you, when you were gripped by the horror of the eternal evil of Judas among the disciples? Is the crazy fellow who claims to have not the slightest fear of dying, of dying between night and day . . . Do you speak against it, Dora, that he may have become the traitor between night and day?

Karl listened for her answer, not with his thoughts which after all could only hover in the past, but with his ears. The effort was great and loosened the connection between question and answer. All that still mattered to him now was this: to hear something from her; and he felt how, in the intentness of listening, he glided from consciousness. Thus he heard her breathe. It was, he recognized it at once, her breathing in feigned sleep, her tenderly lying breath —in back of it, however, her waking denial of his suspicion, her defense of Christopher.

"Don't you believe it?" he whispered cautiously into the emptiness.

He started from his doze, awakened by his own words, he felt the strange cold air of the cell and shivered in sudden despair. "Without farewell," he whispered, "without farewell . . ."

Dora had fallen asleep a little, from exhaustion. She awoke and felt as though she had heard Karl breathing next to her. She knew she had dreamed; but she had forgotten what she had dreamed. She lay there quietly and suddenly felt the comforting warmth in her breast, the deep joy of possession which she always felt when the gravel in front of the little studio house announced Karl's long strides. Perhaps this had been her dream. "How much better off I am than I was yesterday at this time," she whispered, and with some slight astonishment she listened to this, her own voice, in the strange room.

When the flashlight makes the inspection of the two cells in a single, uninterrupted sweep, Karl in number 17 and Dora in number 24 shield their eyes against the intruding light with the same gesture; each lifts his hand to cover the eyes, palm turned outward.

Chapter Four

THE FIVE AND THE SIXTH

I

The flashlight probing the cells and the five people was part of the night and does not herald a new day. Morning begins with the stroke of seven, when the bells of near-by Frauenkirche peal for the chosen souls and for the damned, when the fifteen watt, wire-screened light bulbs in the cells light up—a miserable light, to be sure, but nonetheless a light. *Fiat lux*, and here is the day, this day.

Here are these five people, already booked and charged as a bundle, as the treason case "Hennings and Associates," already on the conveyor belt of an inexorably speedy and precise machinery of justice: and yet they do not know whether they are to be dealt with as a bundle or are to be broken separately. At seven-thirty they get their breakfast, at seven-forty-five they are told that they are to be brought before their judge, from eight o'clock on they are led away. The authorities do not wish to waste time; but they can afford to sound off the common fate of "Hennings and Associates," not with the striking of one full chord, but with the arpeggio of a broken chord. In other words, they still don't bundle them together, but deliver them to the court one by one, though in rapid succession. It is useful to keep them as long as possible in tormenting doubt about all connecting links; and it is imperative to block even the least possible channel of communication among them.

Professor von Hennings heads the list and is the first to receive the news. Stroking his stubble with the back of his hand, he asks: "Where is the writ of complaint which, pursuant to Paragraph 20 of the Penal Code, must be submitted to the accused before the opening of the trial?" He asks for it because the writ of complaint must disclose the names of all the defendants. The clerk shrugs his shoulders and goes away; he can give no answer, least of all when paragraphs unknown to him are cited from memory; he was to make one and the same announcement in this order: to von Hennings Karl, von Hennings Dora, Moeller Hans, Moeller Sophia, Welte Alexander. He is gratified to find that, except for the queer professor, none of the several constituents of the bundle to be handed over to the People's Court fences with paragraphs of the penal code or says anything at all.

Since the journey from Police Headquarters to the Palace of Justice requires but a few minutes, one car takes care of transporting the five, shuttling back and forth, carrying only one passenger with three SS guards on each trip. Karl is the first to be taken away. The curtains are drawn over the side windows of the limousine; but during the short ride he sees a bit of everyday life through the windshield in the rapid succession of houses, streets, people, and again he strokes his stubbly cheek. He is not accustomed to leaving his house unshaved and the prickly skin gives him an unpleasant feeling of being unwashed. Forced to parade his two-day beard past the restaurant of the Kuenstlerhaus, where he used to dine with Dora occasionally and drink a good Moselle wine, he considers himself expelled from polite society and dispenses with bidding farewell to it in his thoughts. The three guards get out with him in the inner court of the Palace of Justice and do not leave him.

The car fetches Dora and then Hans, then Sophia, then Alexander—and each of the four has his escort of three black-uniformed men. Each of the four has to look out into the February morning, into a segment of city life which one would think enviably peaceful for a prisoner riding from Police Headquarters to the Palace of Justice surrounded by three armed men. But Dora, occupying the seat just vacated by Karl, still cherishes in her breast the warm feeling with which she awoke—she feels it still, especially now that she is following her beloved, for the second time and for a reunion free of every doubt and uncertainty. Yes, she can expect even more than the same fate which only yesterday was doubtful and questionable: for could not Karl and she be made to disappear without a trace, the one here, the other there, ending in mystery, stifled by the cloak of invisibility with which the regime treacherously covers its adversaries? The trial, however, even in its hastiest form, is a visible and audible scene, the confrontation of accusers and accused. Dora can expect to see Karl in the flesh—and this outlook is more overpowering than looking out at the everyday life of the city.

Hans, on the other hand, is annoyed on the short ride, because of a trifle. When his three myrmidons led him out of the double cell, he said to his comrade, "Good-by, Alexander." The other, however, said with special emphasis, "Auf Wiedersehen!" And Hans is angry with himself because he said 'Good-by,' and not 'Auf Wiedersehen.' It is a bagatelle; but it is enough to last for the whole short way and like blinkers it obstructs his view.

Sophia sees the Wittelsbach Fountain as the car passes it, crated in boards and protected with sandbags. But she continues to see it in her mind as the car is already driving along Karlsplatz, and the fountain, divested of its covering, stands under the early autumn sun, the water roars from its spouts, a gust blows through the transparent coat of water ringing the raised center basin, sending a spray over one of the two mythological figures on the outer rim of the fountain, and Christopher exclaims: "A rainbow!" squeezing the girl's arm, as if the rainbow or the playful fountain or the playful sun were a gift for his beloved. That was half a year ago—and now Sophia already drives into the courtyard of the Palace of Justice and does not see the fragment of everyday life, but Christopher's rainbow.

Alexander Welte, however, last because of the position of his name in the alphabet, because he is the most recent member of the seminar, and because of a certain philistine insignificance in life generally, smiles a wily smile during the ride and enjoys the distrustful glances of his three black jailers. For he is a remarkable fellow, he knows, and it matters little to him that he is the only one who knows it—a fellow with logical and extraordinary objective mental powers, a fellow who has discovered through the labor of his competent brain, what poor Hans, intelligent though he may be, just couldn't discover and what probably no one else would be capable of discovering: that Christopher could not be suspected because a denunciation would have made sense only if it had been made before the distribution of the leaflets. This penetrating insight came to Alexander at the moment when the light was turned on in the cell. There was no time left to think out ways and means of letting Hans share in the enjoyment of this extraordinary product of thought. It was no longer necessary, either; with their departure for the courthouse they embarked, so to speak, on the proof for the validity of this logical deduction. And so Alexander contented himself with the significant, the enlightened emphasis on the "Auf Wiedersehen!" a prophecy including also Christopher. But poor Hans did not understand . . . The fellow with the wily smile is very curious to see, not the bit of everyday life to which he pays no attention, but the reunion, the Wiedersehen.

2

Karl von Hennings is waiting with his three guards in a large, bare room with no facilities for sitting down. Between the two black-uniformed men he stands against the wall, which is covered up to two-thirds of its height with wooden paneling worn dull and dark. The third man stands in front of him, facing him.

"May I walk back and forth a little?" asks Karl who dislikes standing in one spot, especially when he is nervous.

"No," says the man in front of him, an athlete with a smashed nose.

"Are you a prize fighter?" Karl asks.

"You are not allowed to speak to me," says the prize fighter, somewhat flattered.

"That's just like the motorman on the streetcar," Karl observes. "Passengers are not allowed to speak to him, but everyone does it."

"Shut up," says the prize fighter.

At least, Karl reflects, they didn't make me stand facing the wall.

Opposite him is the double door, guarded by a police sergeant with a revolver in his belt. Karl forces his eyes away from the door and lets them wander over the rectangular room. He takes it to be a dismantled courtroom, perhaps a medium-sized room for jury trials; the parquetry of the floor, worn dull and dark like the wall paneling, is damaged along the main wall, indicating the place formerly occupied by the judges' dais. But immediately Karl's gaze is drawn back to the door again, and his anticipation is so great that he parts his lips a little and breathes through his mouth.

There is no experience comparable to such waiting. To stand in a railway station, testing with one's eyes, like a trackman, the glittering spurs of rails on which the train will come rolling in, is an experience of an entirely different sort. One is reasonably sure who it is that the train will bring and unload into one's arms. Karl, however, who has already gone through the bitterest experience known to a loving human—separation without farewell—does not know whom the door will admit to the bare room, and yet he expects, his mouth slightly ajar, that it will be Dora and the comrades. He awaits his reunion with Dora, as in a railway station, though he cannot even draw upon a memory of this kind in order to release the tension of his nerves; never having been separated from Dora he never waited for her in a railway station and does not know the serene happiness of having her again. And perhaps it is as well that he does not know it; he cannot lose himself in the memory of how he held the returned one and how he crushed and forgot the time of separation with his embrace and with those first words of concern for her well-being. For, separation without farewell cannot be undone, and even if the phantom train should come rolling in and unload her in the room where he stands and waits, he could not embrace her and could not even ask her the simple words of the eternal question: How are you? And yet this breath-taking, heart-shaking, wildly throbbing anticipation!

There is a short and forceful knock on the door, and Karl starts. The police sergeant opens the door part way, looks out, and then opens it wide. A black uniform appears. The prize fighter standing in front of Karl throws a quick look over his shoulder to inform himself, and says as if he had been coached: "I warn you that I am ordered to suppress ruthlessly any attempt to establish contact."

An ugly word: establish contact, Karl thinks mechanically and nods mechanically—and he is standing in the railway station and the train has come in . . .

Preceded by one SS guard and flanked by two others, Dora enters, small and pretty, and even the shortest of the three towers over her mightily. But also the biggest of the three is not big enough to cover her smile. She looks at Karl smilingly, on the way from the door to her place against the wall at his left. What is a long way, what is a short way? Here there are fifteen short light steps, a way which is both long and short as in a dream. She looks at Karl and with her look and her smile he receives everything which belongs to a reception and which he has never experienced, since he has never met her on her return from a voyage:

he receives her embrace and her "How are you?" and her "Now I am back again!" And he learns that she has been well during the conquered time of their separation, and he admits that she looks well, her cheeks sweetly flushed with happiness, her eyes moist and radiant. That is very much and little enough for fifteen steps, much and little as in a dream, and now it would be time to walk to the exit, arm in arm, the words choked off by the joy of being together again; and with the surrender of the used ticket at the gate, the last remnant of their separation would be forever put away. But should this picture be too extravagant, he would be content with this: to stand against the wall arm in arm and to be together—yes, with this he would be content . . .

God knows, they do not stand arm in arm. Between Karl's group and Dora's there is a space wide enough for three men to stand; and the woman is surrounded by her escort even as her husband is surrounded by his: one each on the right and left, the third standing in front, facing her. Karl cannot see her unless he were to bend forward and look sharply to the left, past the two men standing between him and her, and the empty space between them. But he does not bend forward to look, out of consideration for Dora. The prize fighter might regard it as an attempt to establish contact which must be ruthlessly suppressed. Karl makes himself as tall as possible, he stealthily lifts himself to his toes, towering over the two men in-between. He wants to stand like a tower for Dora to see whenever she might dare look over to his side. And should she not dare, or be too deeply stuck between SS pillars, it would not matter. At least they are standing against the same wall and are together—he is content with this.

The wall is long and offers room enough for many more, for how many? Karl and Dora are confident again because they are together once more, almost unchanged externally, without the ravages which their innermost knowledge of each other had visualized during the period of separation: the woman has not wilted, and he is merely unshaved. Now they both close the personal chapter, the strangely wonderful story of deathly separation and dreamlike reunion, and they know that they are not two, but six. But the fear they both harbored was that there might be five of them, five out of six. That old fear, however, which for days concerned itself with the sixth, belongs to the nightmare of their separation and not to the joy of their reunion. Now they both stand ready to receive.

Hans Moeller enters and stops, barely through the door, his three-man escort also stops and the one who walked in front steps aside a little, as if to give the prisoner a clear view. Hans looks at the professor and looks at Dora and then at the long, empty wall. He raises his hand to his cap twice, to salute Karl, to salute Dora. Karl returns the grave greeting with a grave nod, Dora with a smile, and Hans returns the smile with a smile. The guards do not disturb him, they do not regard the greeting as establishment of contact, they wait for him to proceed of his own accord—he remains privileged. He does not walk in step with his three escorts; and between the forceful treads of soldiers' boots there is the tinkling of the artificial leg, faint and knightly as of silver spurs. He does not look up on his way to the wall, but he feels his friends' eyes upon him. Then Hans' group stands against the wall, to the left of Dora, at a three-man distance.

Sophia comes in and stumbles at the door—so perplexing, relieving, surprising, deeply anticipated and disappointing, so unbalancing is the spectacle of the three standing along the wall. But she may not stop and collect herself; her three guards are not stopping and the one at her right grasps her arm, as if to warn her. She walks on and doesn't know at whom to look first, and her worried eyes jump back and forth between the professor and Frau Dora and brother Hans, and they also jump to the empty wall which shows clearly enough that there is no one else standing there . . . her eyes jump back and the hard lump in her throat softens and melts; for Frau Dora smiles at her and she smiles back, and already the professor and Hans respond with a smile. "Hans . . ." she speaks with closed lips, all to herself; it is audible like a faint sigh. Her brother looks at her until she vanishes in the clutches of black uniforms, to his left along the wall.

If it goes according to the alphabet, Karl thinks, then S comes before W.

Now Alexander and Christopher are still missing, Dora thinks and does not want to break up the twosome of the names: Alexander and Christopher . . .

If it goes alphabetically, Hans thinks, it wouldn't be so good should Alex come now . . .

But Welte is still missing, too, Sophia thinks, and in her thoughts does not even call him by his first name.

The door opens for Alexander Welte, who stands at the bottom of the list in the alphabet, in the seminar's seniority ranking, and in importance generally. Neither his wily smile nor the smart bearing with which, two fingers touching the vizor of his cap, he marches to the wall amidst his guard as if he were reviewing the parade of friends, earn fitting appreciation; one might say he was paid with ingratitude. The professor and Hans, his friend, look at him with profound gravity. Sophia even turns her eyes away from him, reproachfully, alas, as a demonstration of his insignificance for her, and fastens her wide-eyed look to the door again. Only Dora has a smile for him and perhaps it was she alone, the revered lady, who reached the same conclusion that he, ingenious Alexander, has reached, and who understood the meaning of his smile: that they will all be reunited, not five of them, but all six. Certainly Christopher is still missing, Alexander can see that as well as the others; but he is not frightened by it, not he, the logical thinker. For if his logic has taken him so far as to restore the wild hunter to the group with all honors, then it is only one step to the further conclusion that the SD catchpoles will not leave him out. You may rely on me, all of you! Alexander thinks and looks toward the door like the others. But he is the only one to lean back against the wall comfortably, with his arms crossed.

3

A gentleman appears, wearing the black attorney's robe, an elderly, slender gentleman with a grayish white, neatly trimmed goatee, a timid gentleman. But the effect of his appearance on the five against the wall, the five people surrounded by fifteen black uniforms, is out of every proportion to his unmenacing personality.

Here is someone in the robe of the court—whoever he may be, whatever he may want: he comes because those who are to be judged are assembled, and they are five, not six. Even Alexander drops his arms, conquered.

The gentleman senses the wall of disappointment, depression, bitterness and wrathful gravity rising before him, and he does not understand it: for he is no enemy, he is not even a judge. If these faces at least showed fear, fitting and comprehensible fear for which he could feel a profound sympathy—not because he himself lives in fear (that would be saying too much and, very wisely, he provides no occasion for it), but only in apprehension. Here, however, he encounters only increasing stiffening and repulsion, making his already delicate task still more difficult. Embarrassed, he fusses with the bows of his spectacles and speaks in a plaintive little voice: "Well, now—if you please—my name is Langbein, Dr. Heinrich Langbein, and I am the defense attorney officially appointed for the case Hennings and Associates— Well, that means your case . . ."

He pauses, although he can hardly expect any statement from Hennings and Associates in response to his meager revelation; and yet he seems sadly confused by the cold silence of those whom he addresses. He does not go on speaking, his face has a worried expression as if he had lost the thread of his thoughts, and then with a jerk and in great haste he gives himself two occupations at once which cannot be carried out simultaneously: he wants to put on a different pair of glasses and at the same time open his thick brief case. Evidently the gold-rimmed glasses he is wearing serve only for general use, and the manual complications in which he gets involved apparently are due to his intention of opening the brief case, while at the same time requiring his reading glasses to extricate certain documents from it. But since he acts too hastily, taking off his glasses with his left hand, and using his right hand to open the catch of the brief case, with only his drawn-up right leg to aid him, he gets himself in a rather hopeless situation. Sightless and balancing unsteadily, he has no other recourse but to put the gold-rimmed spectacles back on again, and even this is no easy undertaking for one shaky hand. Now he can at least hold the gaping brief case with both hands and is standing on two feet again; but he is unable to single out what he needs at the moment from among the contents of his stuffed brief case, notwithstanding his arduous efforts. He looks up, shaking his head as if perplexed. Not a sound issues from the wall, not to speak of help.

He clasps the brief case between his knees with determination, taps his breast in hot anger, extracts a glasses case from under his robe, exchanges his gold-rimmed glasses for horn-rimmed ones with a show of steadiness in his grip, pulls a number of documents from his brief case which he then deposits on the floor beside him, and says in his plaintive little voice: "Well, now—yes, if you please—the accelerated proceedings of the People's Court, which according to Article III, Paragraph 3, of the law of April 24, 1934, has taken over jurisdiction from the Reichs Supreme Court, bring it about that various . . . Well, briefly put, here is the writ of complaint which . . ."

Here he gets stuck again, raising his eyes from the documents, the worried expression again comes over his face—yes, he actually changes his glasses again, depositing the documents on top of the brief case on the floor. Through his gold-rimmed glasses he surveys the five accused along the wall, motionless faces all, and murmurs in great embarrassment, with a puzzled shaking of his head, "Well, now, just one moment, if you please . . ." He gathers up brief case and documents, walks to the door with swishing robe, whispers something to the police sergeant who only shrugs his shoulders, and finally leaves the room.

What, now, does the prize fighter see who stands facing Karl, and what does each of the other four group leaders see who stand facing their prisoners? They see nothing extraordinary, nothing worth noticing. Karl only lifts his head and also raises his thick eyebrows; Dora opens her eyes wide and her lips a little, as if she were listening to a very faint tone; Hans Moeller, controlling his excitement, only exercises the muscles of his lean jaws; Sophia intertwines her fingers, very firmly, and pinches the ball of her hand with her thumbnail; Alexander again crosses his arms and the wiliness returns to his face, if not his smile. And they all look toward the door—no, not all, not Sophia. She looks at her entwined hands, still afraid of her new hope.

Sophia is inclined to believe that there can be no feeling of happiness without anxiety and painful distress; her love for Christopher is her only experience, and one that caused her anxiety and distress from the start. So she heeds the call of hope while her chest is choking with anxiety. She raises her face slowly, releases her wet hands from their entwinement, only pressing her arms against her body, and sees that the police sergeant is opening the door a little and then opens it wide.

An SS man shoves himself through the door sideways, right shoulder first, as if the dimensions of his body did not allow him to enter like a normal person. He is no giant, however, but only a human tractor; leashed to his left arm another arm appears, in the sleeve of a raincoat. Christopher shoves himself through the door, he, too, sideways, or is being dragged in—and now they stand in the room side by side, the prisoner's right wrist shackled to the guard's left wrist. They walk to the wall, followed by two SS men; they do not walk side by side, however, but the one following the other sideways on the shaft of the coupled arms, as though Christopher were calling attention to the fact that he is handcuffed.

And each of the friends against the wall feels his heart swell with the thought that none of them had been handcuffed; but that is perhaps only the most concrete and obvious in the rush of their thoughts, and their hearts beat because Christopher looks at no one and because nonetheless it seems strangely understandable that he should look at no one. His face taciturn and hostile, he follows his steely leading strings like a stubborn child; but he walks also like a sinister dreamer, oblivious of the world around him, albeit his eyes are open.

And each of the friends thinks of some excuse for his aloofness: perhaps he was beaten—though his gray, unshaved face does not show any traces of mistreatment—, perhaps he is drugged. Who knows to what devilish means these devils resorted in order to break his resistance? Only the two women, Dora and Sophia, think further, more boldly, yet in a way more naïvely; for is he not the wild hunter who possesses second sight? They think: he doesn't look at the one who suspected him; and since he looks at none of us, we have all suspected him . . .

Sophia clings to his face with her eyes pleading: please, look at me! But he has already passed her, with stony profile. And then she speaks the words—she meant only to whisper them, but it was a faint cry:

"Please, look at me!"

Christopher stops, strokes his forehead with his free hand and covers his eyes for a moment, quite like someone regaining consciousness.

"You are not allowed to speak with your fellow prisoners," says the SS man standing in front of Sophia somewhat belatedly and rather mildly.

"Come on! Don't start acting up again!" says the SS man to whom Christopher is handcuffed.

Christopher stops and looks at the girl, serious and sad. "Forgive me, Sophia," he says softly. He looks toward Dora. "Forgive me, Frau Dora." To Karl: "Forgive me, Herr Professor." To Hans: "Forgive me, Hans." To Alexander, the last one, always the last one: "Forgive me, Welte." Only Dora nods to him and attempts a smile, and only Alexander turns his whole face into a grin; he, after all, is the fellow with the logical mind and now he thinks: *Quod erat demonstrandum;* though unfortunately he may not say it. But the others receive the strangely monotonous and pedantic apology with startled expressions on their faces, and Sophia shrugs her shoulders helplessly.

Christopher's SS man yanks him by the shackled arm. "When you shouldn't talk, you talk," he snarls, "and when you're s'posed to talk you got a cramp in the chin. Now stand up against the wall here! Or are yer stuck to the ground again?"

"I demand," Christopher speaks louder than before and doesn't move from the spot, "that my shackles be removed."

"Not until we are in the courtroom," his handcuff partner counters, "and if you're stuck to the ground again, we'll dig you loose once again . . ." He gives Christopher's arm a sharp thrust forward and pulls like a draught animal in harness; his men grab the reeling Christopher by his legs, the one to the right, the other to the left, lift him and deposit him in front of the wall, at the proper distance to Alexander's left. Alexander, no longer grinning, but pale with anger, leans forward to see what is happening to Christopher.

Welte's watchman, as though infected by Christopher's uprooter, grabs him by the chin and pushes him back into the prescribed position, shouting: "Stand still!" The leadmen of the other groups likewise call: "Stand still!" For all the prisoners are bent forward: Sophia, Hans, Dora and Karl.

The timid gentleman in the attorney's robe stands in the middle of the room; no one had noticed him coming in. He wears his horn-rimmed reading glasses, probably so as not to see what is happening along the wall, and thumbs through his papers.

"Mister Defense Attorney," Karl now addresses him, "kindly see to it that either Herr Sauer's handcuffs are removed or that we are all handcuffed. There are no grounds for discriminatory treatment!"

"Well, now . . ." laments the gentleman and looks blind into the world.

"Plenty grounds!" the SS tractor calls from the other side of the wall. "This fellow is a maniac, a dangerous one, and there is no telling what he'll do!"

"Well, if you please . . ." the gentleman whines.

"Mister Defense Attorney," asks Karl, "are you apprised of any occurrences which may have occasioned the man's remark about Herr Sauer?"

"In a way I am informed about the accused Sauer's possibly pathological behavior during the preliminary investigation," the gentleman laments into space.

"What do you mean: possibly pathological?" Karl asks severely. "If Herr Sauer is ill, he is not capable of standing trial, and it is your duty . . ."

"I am capable of standing trial!" Christopher's voice comes from the other end of the wall, clear, incisive, and tolerating no contradiction.

A short silence ensues. Then Karl's SS prize fighter, apparently in charge of all the guards present, takes a few steps backwards and calls an order to Christopher's group at the other end: "Squad leader, unshackle the man!" The friends along the wall hear the click of the opening steel spring.

"Well, now if you please," the gentleman in the attorney's robe speaks in a plaintive little voice, "my name is Langbein, Dr. Heinrich Langbein, and I am the defense attorney officially appointed by the People's Court. We have just about half an hour until the opening of the trial"—shaking back the wide sleeve of the robe he lifts his wrist watch to his eyes. "To be exact, twenty-four minutes. You will want to use the time to familiarize yourselves with the writ of complaint and to give me such information as you may consider pertinent to your defense. The way matters stand, I, as officially appointed defense attorney, can only try for mitigating circumstances, and your information would therefore have to relate to such mitigating circumstances . . ."

"The case is called: Hennings and Associates," Karl breaks in, "and that automatically points to mitigating circumstances for the

Associates, since the principal defendant has established his total responsibility from the start. Consequently you may dispense with any efforts in my behalf."

"Mister Defense Attorney," Christopher speaks from the other end, clear, incisive, tolerating no contradiction, "I must ask you to limit your intercession in my behalf to the barest minimum, or to run the risk of being disavowed by me. I shall speak for myself."

"Mister Defense Attorney," says Hans Moeller, "I wish to inform you that I shall not tolerate any attempt to capitalize on any pity evoked by my invalidity."

"Mister Defense Attorney," Alexander Welte says in his sonorous voice, "if you wish to gather information referring exclusively to mitigating circumstances, I hereby declare emphatically that you shall not obtain any information from me and that, consequently, you are under no obligation to speak for me—a simple, logical conclusion!"

"Confine your activities, then, to defending the interests of the two accused ladies," Christopher speaks again, though more softly.

"I cannot see," says Dora gently and firmly, "how it is possible to protect my interests and not those of my husband and my friends—I would even very decidedly object to any special consideration!"

"So would I," Sophia comes in impetuously, almost uncontrolled. "I won't have any exceptions made for me—*that* would be unforgivable!" It is meant for Christopher and spoken in his direction, too. He quietly shakes his head as over an unfortunate misunderstanding, rubs his right wrist and moves his fingers, as though they had gone to sleep. The guards do not notice the establishment of contact.

Moving his head ever so slightly, the official defense attorney, like a frightened bird, turned to look every time in the direction from which a protesting voice pressed upon him, but he could see only blurred, dim splotches instead of faces. "Well, now, yes . . ." he breathes plaintively, goes through the ritual of changing his eye glasses and distributes the six copies of the writ of complaint.

Chapter Five

THE STORY OF THE STUPOR

It happened almost three years ago, on March 15, 1940, in the courtyard of the Munich Bodyguard Infantry barracks in Türkenstrasse, that Private Christopher Sauer, who had been inducted that very day and had not yet been put into uniform, "turned to wood" to use the company sergeant's expression. Since the man stood in the crowd of new inductees, his rigidity was not noticed immediately, not even by his fellow recruits who, at the command of a corporal, had to line up in the order of their height. That was great fun for the twenty-year-old lads, all the more so as military discipline did not start in earnest until after the uniforms were issued. The "Bodies"—as the regiment was popularly called in Munich—had always been the elite regiment of Bavaria; it claimed the hardiest human material, mostly peasant boys from the Bavarian Highlands, and required a minimum height of five foot ten and a half. Inductee Sauer, of strong and slender build, just reached the minimum height. He did not join in the game of "who is taller," and unresistingly let himself be crowded further and further to the right by the competitors in his height group, until finally he was the last man in the row.

The sergeant then called out the names in alphabetical order, and all went well from A to R: as each name was called someone in the formation claimed it and answered "Present!"

"Sauer Christopher!" the sergeant called next, and there followed no "Present!" —"Sauer Christopher!" a second time, still louder, and then a third time, as loud as only a company sergeant can roar. But there was no answer. The sergeant disconcertedly looked up and down the row of young men; for here something was going on that could not be. The list of names had been compiled from the order which each reporting inductee had handed in. Every one whose name appeared on the list must therefore have handed in his orders, and was bound to be present—there couldn't be a simpler calculation. Shaking his head, the sergeant read off the rest of the names and then ordered all those who had answered "Present!" when their names were called, to raise their right arms. The whole row responded—except the last man.

A sergeant facing his lined-up company has a positively theatrical technique for pouncing on a culpable individual in the formation. Merely by relinquishing his place far out in front of the line-up in order to swoop down on a particular man, he fatally shatters the anonymity of the group and suddenly becomes terribly personal. His approach is silent, slow, long-strided, his threateningly flushed head shoved forward like a Gorgon's shield—all this for purposes of intimidation. Then, when the culprit is reached, the storm breaks.

But here the storm did not break. Already as the sergeant advanced, Gorgon-like, toward the man at the end, he became aware that his efforts were directed to a vacuum and were bound to be ineffectual. Neither the breathless silence of the scene nor the ominous approach of the actor-sergeant had induced the intended victim to turn his glance to the right, whence disaster was coming upon him: he looked straight ahead with immobile eyes. Hence the sergeant himself had to maneuver to the right in order to put his own person, as well as the necessary intimidation, within the obstinate man's field of vision. Now he looked straight into his eyes, came nearer and still nearer, as near as sergeants' technique prescribed, to land his roar—in place of his fist—in the delinquent's face.

Just then he discovered three things in rapid succession in the eyes of the recruit: that they did not perceive him, even though they seemed to look at him; that the pupils were rigidly fixed; that the lids did not flicker over the eyes. This immobility of the eyelids, in particular, seemed odd, and made the sergeant more uneasy with every breath.

"Is your name Sauer Christopher?" he said in a near whisper, instead of roaring, and shook his head, not expecting an answer. "Are you sick?" he whispered.

"Prob'ly has a fit," diagnosed the man standing next in line, a lad wearing the brown shirt of the Hitler Youth with a squad leader's insignia, and immediately went on to recommend the proper therapy: "Cold water over his head will work wonders . . ."

"Shut your trap!" the sergeant bellowed at him and, with a nasty look at the insignia on the boy's shirt, gave vent to his stowed-up roars. "Even if you was a general in your damned kindergarten, here you just answer when you're asked!" He turned again to the man at the end, who had not reacted to the noisy incident with the slightest quiver of his pupils, and grasped his sleeve gingerly. Through the cloth he felt an arm as hard as wood. He tried to move it, to lift it sideways a little, to push it forward or backward. But the arm was immovable, as if it were not hinged to the shoulder joint, but grown fast to the body like a branch to a tree.

The sergeant let the man stand, went back to face the formation and told the recruits that the corporal would now take them to the supply sergeant to get their uniforms. He commanded, "Dismissed!" and hoped that the man at the end would be sucked in, so to speak, by the whirl of general departure, that even with the last glimmer of awareness he would avoid letting himself be isolated. But Sauer Christopher remained standing as though rammed to the ground.

The sergeant waited until the noisy horde had disappeared into the barracks. Then he approached the solitary man again.

"Now we are alone, Sauer," he said as winningly as he could with his voice that had shouted itself hoarse in the barracks courtyard, "now be reasonable, son, and don't get yourself in no trouble. Or I have to report you, don't you understand that?" He scratched his head, contemplating the motionless figure. "Why don't you say 'Yeah' at least, or just nod your head a little," he continued imploringly. "Is your name Sauer Christopher? Yes? Come on, nod your head. —See? Almost you done it now . . ." Christopher didn't nod.

"Look here," the sergeant now grumbled, "you want I should report you for insubordination? You want I should have you court-martialed?" Even this fateful word brought no life into the jet-black luster of the man's eyes. "Okay," said the sergeant. "Now you watch me go straight to the commanding officer of the regiment." He departed, taking perhaps twenty steadily slower steps, stopped, turned about, saw the man standing there like a ram, and returned. "Perhaps you're sick just the same," he suggested, stroking the recruit's cheek paternally. The skin felt as if it had been stretched over wood. The sergeant withdrew his hand. "Hey, listen, come on, Sauer, I take you to the hospital. You are unfit for service, any child can see that. The medical officer is sure to see that right away and discharge you. Come along, Sauer."

Neither the whip nor the sugar was of any use: Christopher did not budge. "Now I got enough, now you come along!" the sergeant finally shouted after all, forcing his hand between the recruit's arm and body to move him from the spot, though he did not apply too much strength. A strange feeling like horror forbade him to use force. And the lad seemed as firmly rooted as a tree. Not only his arm, but also his body was hard as wood. The sergeant let go of him, from horror or whatever it was, and now really went to the barracks without looking back.

He entered the office of the infirmary which was ruled by medical sergeant Mayr. The company sergeant's name was also Mayr, and they resembled each other, although they were not related. Since the medical sergeant had been in the service a little longer, he was called Mayr I, while the other was Mayr II; among themselves they called each other One and Two, for fate had willed that both should have the first name Franz and the middle name Xavier. The visitor did not stop at the desk of his namesake, but stepped to the window overlooking the courtyard. Below, the recruit stood silent and motionless, rooted to the ground.

"What's the matter, Two?" the medical sergeant asked, looking up from his papers.

"Come over here," Two requested, without turning around; and there was something in his voice that made Mayr I, a man somewhat inclined to laziness, get up and go to the window at once.

"Take a look at that fellow," Two requested, pointing to the man in the courtyard.

"Yeah," One nodded, and his eyes narrowed. "What's the matter with the guy?"

"Turned to wood," Two answered.

"Aw, go on," said One, glancing sideways at the other man.

"One of my new ones," Two explained. "Brung in fresh today—and don't hear, don't see; just stands there and don't move or budge. Yeah, and his whole body is like it was wood."

"I'll fix that guy in a hurry," One assured, stepped from the window and put on his cap. "I know how to handle them hard-boiled ones . . ."

The two sergeants walked across the courtyard toward the motionless man; Mayr I kept increasing his speed, Mayr II kept slowing down.

"Hey, you! Wake up!" the medical sergeant shouted in the recruit's ear, and beat the air with his fist in front of the man's nose. The company sergeant had stopped at some distance and shook his head; but he raised no objection. Mayr I circled around the immovable lad, stopped behind him and suddenly pinched his ear. "Two!" he announced. "That ear ain't made of wood!"

"But he don't budge!" the company sergeant observed, still shaking his head.

"Attention!" called Mayr I. "Now that block of wood is coming alive!" and he took a run like a football player at the kick-off. The company sergeant shook his head; but he raised no objection and watched very attentively.

Not a muscle quivered in the young face when Mayr I landed the kick in his rear. Sauer Christopher fell over forwards with not the slightest movement or the slightest twitch of a gesture to protect his face, and he lay on the ground, stiff as a block of wood. The impact had sounded at once hard and dull, and the company sergeant shuddered. The lad did not even bleed from his nose; when the medical sergeant rolled him over on his back, his eyes were open and his eyelids never moved.

Even the medical sergeant seemed alarmed; but he would not admit it. He only said: "Let's take him to the infirmary. Two, take hold of him!"

Mayr I grasped him under the arms, Mayr II under the legs; then they lifted him. He was much heavier than his slender build would have led one to suspect. His middle did not cave in as that of an unconscious person always does when carried, but stayed rigid. It was as if the two carried a board between them. They dragged him into the building and up the stairway to the hospital division. Soldiers who encountered them gave way silently and looked after them silently. The company sergeant felt sweat dripping from his armpits, from exertion as much as from horror; for the legs he had to hold were hard as wood.

In the infirmary they put him on a bed. Mayr I got busy taking off one of the man's shoes, because it was forbidden to lie down with boots on; Mayr II loosened the other shoe. It was hard work to pull them off, for the toes seemed to be firmly braced against the soles from within, but it was only that the toes were stiff and spread a little, as it turned out.

"That'll be all as far as you're concerned," said One to Two. "You put down the man's sick—best if you say he fainted—and send the report book over to me so as I can countersign; then everything'll be in order. And forget about that kick in the ass."

The company sergeant did not seem to be listening properly; he stood before the figure stretched out on the bed and whispered: "The way he's laying there! Nobody can be laying that way! Look!" He shoved his hand carefully under the young man's hollow back. "I can close my fist," he added, "and just the same I don't touch him."

"Yeah," said the medical sergeant impatiently, "that's going to pass. And now, scram."

"That's not going to pass," the company sergeant said, shaking his head and departing reluctantly.

"Hm," grunted the medical officer on duty, as he looked at the patient. "How did he get these bloodshot spots on his forehead, nose and chin?"

"From when he fell on his face, sir," the medical sergeant replied.

"And he fell flat on his face, just like that?" asked the doctor.

"Just like that, like a board," the medical sergeant answered.

The doctor, who had the rank of a first lieutenant, made a cursory examination of the pulse and of the reflexes, pressed on the drawn-in abdomen, the muscles of which were so taut that they felt like tightened straps of upholstery, and gave up. "Hm," he puzzled. "Could be shock, could be a gold-bricker— What's your opinion, sergeant?"

"I don't know, sir."

"Then we'll just let him lie here," said the doctor as he turned to the next patient. "Perhaps he will have made himself more comfortable by the time we make the evening round."

Meanwhile Mayr II, the company sergeant, could not rid himself of the man who had turned to wood. The healthy human, especially if he is a professional non-commissioned officer, does not, as a rule, run after horrifying things. The second Mayr, however, did so, and gave himself no accounting for his reasons. He went to the infirmary an hour later and saw that the recruit was still there, exactly as he had left him: completely dressed, except for his shoes, motionless on his back, with open eyes and hollow back. Only the bruises on his face had turned darker. The company sergeant bent over him, opened the collar of his red-checked sport shirt, though without touching the skin of the man's neck, and went away again.

He came back two hours later, pushed his hand exploringly under the rigid curvature of Christopher's back, and then went to look for the medical sergeant who received him ungraciously. For, between sergeants, spheres of influence are as rigidly divided and as jealously defended as between generals.

"You can still push your fist under his back," he reported, and there was reproach in his voice.

"That's none o' your damn business, or is he a bastard of yours?" the other retorted with excessive rudeness.

"If the man isn't looked after immediately, I'll report it to the captain!" the company sergeant threatened, confident of his own sphere of power.

"The man was examined a long time ago," said Mayr II deprecatingly.

"By the chief medical officer?"

"By the assistant medical officer."

"This is a case for the chief medical officer!"

"Sergeant," Mayr I cried out in somewhat formal wrath, "it is definitely not up to you to decide this matter! It is entirely a matter for the medical department and will be decided at the time of the evening round!"

The evening round was made at four o'clock and was, strictly speaking, an afternoon round. When Mayr II appeared in the infirmary at five o'clock, he saw his man lying in unchanged position on the bed and learned from the three other patients who were put up in the same room that again the assistant medical officer had made the round alone and that his effort in behalf of Sauer Christopher had consisted in feeling his pulse and saying "Hm!"

For the first time in fifteen years of military service Mayr II violated regulations and entered the chief medical officer's room from the corridor in order to avoid having to walk through the medical sergeant's office. In the name of the commanding officer of his company he requested the red-faced and rather formidable man to look at a recruit afflicted with a mysterious illness. The reference to the captain was not in keeping with the truth; but Mayr knew that his chief would back him up. No commander will fall out with his sergeant, if he wishes to continue a tolerable existence.

"What's wrong with the man?" the chief medical officer inquired somewhat brusquely; it happened that he had just been in the process of winding up his activities for the day.

"In a way, sir, he is not alive; he turned to wood, sir."

"Oak or mahogany?" the doctor asked, and enjoyed his joke with a hearty laugh which completely restored his good humor. "Well, let's have a look at the carving," he added getting up and reaching for his cap. But then he called in his booming voice: "Mayr!" And so the medical sergeant reentered the stage and shot a devastating look at the other Mayr, the illegal intruder. But Mayr II stood fast and immediately parried: "Captain von Kirschbaum requests the chief medical officer to examine the inductee Sauer Christopher."

"What's the matter with the man?" the doctor asked the medical sergeant.

"He is in the infirmary, sir. The assistant medical officer is not quite certain yet if the man is a faker, and wanted to report to you about the case tomorrow after the morning round."

"I see!" said the doctor, and went to the infirmary with the two Mayrs. He observed the motionless man attentively, opened the red-checked shirt and put his ear to the hairless, tanned chest. "I wish I had a heart like that," he announced and, as he straightened up again, his face was redder even than usual.

"Would you please look, sir," the company sergeant begged and pushed his hand under Christopher's hollow back. "That's the way the man has been lying ever since he was brought in here this morning."

"As impressive as it is uncomfortable," observed the doctor. "Let's change his position. Put him on his feet."

Mayr I promptly stepped to the bed and grasped Christopher's shoulders. The company sergeant, however, hesitated. "How do you mean, sir?" he asked in order to gain time.

"You are to lift the man out of the bed and stand him on his feet, sergeant!" This, now, was an official order. The two Mayrs lifted the recruit from the bed just as they had lifted him into it: One by the shoulders, Two by the legs. Then they put him upright like a board, and he stood. "Two steps from the wall and one step from the bed!" the chief medical officer commanded. The medical sergeant clasped the recruit around the middle and lifted him like a dressmaker's dummy to the prescribed spot. "So," said the doctor by way of settling the matter as he turned to leave, "when he gets tired of standing he can lie down again; when he gets hungry, he can open his mouth; and you may tell your captain that he will soon have his block of wood back again and that he need not congratulate himself on this new acquisition."

He left the infirmary. The medical sergeant waited somberly at the door until his rival had also gone through it, closed it emphatically and snarled in a carefully subdued voice, since his superior was still within earshot: "From now on you are forbidden to enter the infirmary."

"Aw, go . . . yourself." Mayr II whispered a favorite Bavarian oath in reply. But it was a defeat—and one brought about by his own fault, to boot. Without his intervention and without the unfortunate experiment with his hand under the hollow of the back, Sauer Christopher would at least be lying down, stiff back or no stiff back. But now the poor devil had to stand. And Mayr could not get the standing man out of his head.

Christopher stood two steps away from the wall, one step from the bed, in stocking feet. His six roommates—three more men had been brought in during the day, following a march with full pack—gave him diverse bits of advice and finally ceased bothering about him when they realized that they were preaching to the wind. The center of general interest then shifted to the supper. The supper tray that had been brought in for Christopher stood next to him on the bed cover, untouched for twenty minutes, until it was taken away again by the infirmary corporal. This gave the others some new occasion to concern themselves with Christopher; it was the clinching proof for them that there was something radically wrong with the man. Then some obscene stories were told, but they sounded forced and had no zip. The man standing there motionless bothered them.

When the lights were turned out at nine o'clock and only the bluish night light shone from its opalescent glass globe on the ceiling, the restlessness started. Each of the men had turned his back to the figure standing there. One after the other they turned about again to face him and to stare at the rigid figure outlined in the bluish light.

"I can't stand it!" someone called suddenly, and everybody knew what it was he couldn't stand.

"Lie down!" they called. "Lie down, man!" And suddenly they got to shouting senselessly as if it were their only weapon against the lifelessness standing among them in the room.

The non-com on night duty rushed in, turned on the lights and let loose a storm of abuse into which he managed to squeeze a question about the gang having gone insane. It was not his appearance, however, that brought the men back to reason, but the bright lights. They demanded that the "civilian creature" be put to bed or removed. The non-com declared tartly that the man could lie down whenever he wished, but that explicit orders had been issued not to touch him. The fellows should close their eyes and sleep, then they wouldn't see him; and if further disturbances occurred they would all be liable to arrest. With that he turned the lights out and went away.

The threat was effective for half an hour; then the restlessness started again. But this time it took the form of a conspiracy with the objective of putting the standing man to bed. They whispered back and forth, but no one could be found who was willing to perform the deed. Finally a man with an injured foot got up and hobbled toward the rigid man.

"Give him a push, and he'll flop on the bed by himself," they counseled him in whispers.

"Then he'll lie crosswise," someone warned.

"At least he'd be lying down," another said.

"That fellow will stand even when he's lying down, and won't let us sleep!" whispered a skeptic.

The foot patient stood before Christopher and did not touch him, only stared at the lifeless mask of his face which seemed to be phosphorescent in the bluish light. "That fellow is dead!" he exclaimed backing away. For a while there was deathly silence.

Then someone whispered: "I know that infirmary room 3 is unoccupied." This was the signal for the soundless exodus of the six, three with injured feet, one with stomach pains, one with mastoiditis, and one, the skeptic who wasn't ill at all.

Company Sergeant Mayr II woke up in the night at an entirely unaccustomed hour, turned on the light and looked at his watch. It was twenty minutes past two. He stayed in bed a few moments longer and looked into space; then he got up. The floor creaked under his heavy bulk.

His wife started from her sleep and asked: "Six already?"

"Nonsense!" he growled. "Go back to sleep!"

"Why are you getting up then?"

"I've got a sick man there," he grumbled, putting on his trousers and tunic, but not his boots. He went in his felt slippers because he wanted to walk softly. All married, professional, non-commissioned officers lived on the same floor of the main building of the barracks, fronting Türkenstrasse. Mayr I lived in the apartment next to that of Mayr II. There was no danger that the medical sergeant might not be asleep at this hour; but the company sergeant did not want to risk waking him and sneaked soundlessly past his neighbor's door, in his felt slippers.

He sneaked soundlessly to the infirmary and listened at the door. He heard nothing and entered. It took his eyes a little while to get accustomed to the dusk of the bluish light: he saw first the man who was standing, and then the six deserted beds, and then again the man who was standing, two steps away from the wall and one step from the bed, in terrifying solitude. The sergeant sneaked noiselessly up to him. He can't hear me coming, he thought, and if he is startled now, I'm not going to tell a soul . . .

But Christopher was not startled and did not look at the sergeant as he stood before him; his wide open eyes stared unseeing through the visitor, and the eyelids never moved. Mayr sat down on the bed and scrutinized the standing figure. The shadow of a beard covered chin and cheeks, the eyes rested in their deep shadowy hollows, the face seemed to have grown smaller, smaller and harder still; but the chest moved up and down, breathing. Mayr bent down and put his hands on Christopher's stocking feet. They were ice-cold. He kept his hands on the feet for a fairly long time; but the feet did not get warmer and Mayr's hands got colder and colder. He straightened up and reflected, his eyes fixed on the lad.

The sergeant got up from the bed, stepped in back of Christopher, put his arms firmly around the recruit's shoulders and chest, just below the neck, and slowly walked backward, pressing the young man's body to himself. As Christopher's body leaned against him obliquely and stiffly, he let the upper part of the lad's body glide gently to the bed and then lifted his legs to the bed, rubbed his feet, wrapped them in the bed cover, took another blanket from an adjoining bed and spread it over the rigid man, covering him up to the neck. Then he removed the identification card from the foot end of the bed, stepped under the night light and wrote in overly legible print on the back of the card: "At 2:30 o'clock in the morning, while making inspection, the undersigned found the man described on the reverse side of this card standing motionless next to his bed, and conformable to duty, put him on the bed assigned to him. Signed, Mayr II, Sergeant, Company 5." He deposited the card on the recruit's chest, well knowing that the man who had "turned to wood" could not shake it off.

The following morning witnessed two offensives whose central objective was the recruit Sauer—the one staged by Mayr I, the other by Mayr II. This time, however, the company sergeant proved the better and swifter strategist. For when the medical sergeant reported the events of the night to the chief medical officer who usually put in a late appearance, Captain von Kirschbaum of Company 5 was already reporting to the regimental commander. That gentleman immediately ordered the doctor—who, after all, ranked no higher than a captain—to appear before him. The commander was highly displeased. One hour later a military ambulance delivered the recruit Sauer Christopher, though still in civilian clothes, to the psychiatric hospital.

There the patient, or sham patient, was at first treated according to the laundry-bundle theory, meaning he was let alone; for time is of no moment in the lazaret for sick souls. But as the patient's rapid and almost eager deterioration necessitated recourse to artificial feeding, Professor Ackermann, who was the medical director of the hospital and a well-known psychiatrist, personally took charge of the observation.

This rather unusual interest had been evoked, in addition, by still another circumstance: the astonishing obstinacy of a sergeant in the "Bodies" forcing his way into the presence of the busy doctor to arouse his interest in the case,—sergeants, after all, are the reverse of prophets, who are not honored in their own land: sergeants are honored only in their own barracks—and the somewhat extravagant manner in which this apparently simple soul described the first twenty-four hours of the man who "turned to wood" (without forgetting the kick in the rear).

The professor saw Christopher for the first time when he was asleep, and his attention was immediately riveted to the sleeper's face which, covered by black stubble, no longer betrayed its youth. He saw in that face such fanatical defensiveness and enmity and such determination to persist in this defensiveness and enmity, as even sleep could not assuage. The professor regarded sleep as an important witness, a soul mirror, which was much more clear and honest than the nebulous and contorted symptoms of the waking psychopathic. Christopher's sleep was no relaxation and loosening of body and spirit, it did not relieve the tension of the organism, but maintained or even increased it—sleeping seemed to be a tragic and mysteriously sad chore. The doctor would have designated it as a perfect example of stupor sleep had he not doubted whether the man was sleeping at all any more. And now, without any physical contact or any noise occasioning it, Christopher slowly opened his eyes, as if his eyelids were lifting a great weight.

"Did I wake you up?" the professor asked casually.

Christopher did not answer, and his look froze. Dr. Ackermann gave him a very extended examination of tormenting thoroughness, with many painful and startling reaction tests; he suffered them as though it were not his own body. The professor left without a word either of encouragement or of suspicion.

Christopher was put on a wheel-bed and wheeled to a bathroom. There the head end of the bed was cranked up so that the tub, filled with water and heavily padded with rubber, came within his field of vision. From the outside came screams that could have emanated from a donkey; the dreadful sound not only issued from a chest breathing out, but also roared back into the chest with the intake of breath, uninterruptedly. Three attendants brought in a muscular man with tufts of hair on his chest. He acted somewhat like one afflicted with St. Vitus' dance who, in the harried rhythm of his convulsion, brays like a donkey.

It took long and horrible minutes for the attendants to get the jerking and tossing body into the tub and to spread over him the rubber sheet which had a slit for the neck and held the head above water. Only the head protruded, with its thick mat of hair growing deep down the forehead; and as the man, looking like nothing but a mouth torn wide open, brayed like a drowning donkey with ever shorter and more harassed cries, he beat against the tub with crazed limbs under water.

The tepid bath, added to the excessive strain on the body motor, had a fairly quick effect which set in with strange suddenness. The drumming and screaming ceased as on a signal, the head, standing on the rubber mat as if severed from the body, kept swaying back and forth for a short while with open mouth. The screams gave way to a throaty rattle. Then also these sounds died out and a melancholy settled over the bather's worn face, inexpressibly dull and resigned, the very prototype of sadness, so to speak. And only now he noticed the guest on the cranked-up bed, stared at him with his protruding eyes, stretched his head forward on the rubber surface as far as the neck slit permitted, his look clinging like a leech to the stranger, and softly, slowly and hopelessly put together the syllables, "An-ne-ma-rie . . ." Then he wept quietly to himself.

Dr. Ackermann had been sitting behind a screen in the background of the bathroom as Christopher was wheeled in and had watched him throughout the scene. He observed that the catatoniac in the bath made no impression whatsoever on him. Stiff and motionless, Christopher looked over and past the scene and did not even seem aware of it. But the professor asked himself whether this steely indifference in the presence of such a ghastly performance might not be a matter of will power. He decided on the tearing-up test. Christopher was wheeled out of the room.

At the next round Dr. Ackermann said: "The patient is to be put among the restless ones. He may become restless himself any moment."

Christopher was taken to the "hell," where humanity is turned upside down. The big hall with doors which never open and with ingenious devices for the prevention of accident, escape and vandalism, was dominated by a permanent rebellion against the world of reason, of morals and of balance. Unrest is a moderate and human word. These restless ones, however, were inhuman, because they knew no restraint and had no objective; and inhuman was what they produced by way of unrest, of screams and of commotion. The insane restlessness—whether it was noisy or, more horribly yet, a speechless asthmatic to-do—never stopped; but it had its periods, a unison of ebb and tide, and a mystifying power of infection over the collective excitement. High tide came at night between twelve and three: that was witches' Sabbath and dance of the mad dervishes and a hysterical game of cops and robbers with guards and doctors—and then, with the sureness of experience, the ringleaders among the patients were fished out of the horde, put on the bed, kicking, and held down until they received the injection. And when they faded out, the excitement of the hall ebbed away too.

Christopher lay quietly in this hell of unrest, a strange saint of quiescence. On the third day Professor Ackermann asked him if he had any desires and, when Christopher did not take notice of the question, he asked him if he wished to get out of the unrest department. Christopher took no notice of this question either. Every third day the doctor asked him the same question and Christopher gave no answer. He stayed two weeks among the restless ones, let himself be nourished intravenously, had a thick, black beard around his bony face and something like an isolating wall around him that kept him from seeing or hearing anything. Then Dr. Ackermann capitulated, had him taken out of the unrest department and put in a single room.

It was a week later that Professor Ackermann came into Christopher's room accompanied by a strange gentleman who did not wear a surgeon's gown.

"This is the poor devil," he said, pointing to the motionless figure on the bed.

"What did you say his name was?" whispered the gentleman as he produced a document stamped with many seals.

"Christopher Sauer," said the doctor. "And you need not whisper, Commissioner; his sensory apparatus is not functioning."

"Christopher Sauer," the gentleman repeated in a normal tone of voice, looking at his document, "incurable."

"That is what I reported to the Commission for the Elimination of the Mentally Ill," Dr. Ackermann confirmed. "It is one of the worst cases I have encountered in my practice—in short, the perfect case for a mercy death." As he spoke these words in a dry, didactic manner, he looked at Christopher and could detect no reaction.

"Quite so. The Commission has already decided upon elimination," said the gentleman, pointing to a paragraph in the document.

"Where is he to be taken?" the doctor asked. "To Castle Grafeneck, or to Hartheim? As it is, we happen to be just halfway between the two places of mercy . . ."

"To Grafeneck," said the gentleman. "Hartheim is not thoroughly organized as yet."

"And when is he to be taken there?"

"Immediately, of course. After all, that is why I am here."

"Of course," the professor nodded, keeping his eyes fixed on Christopher. "And when will the operation be performed?"

"According to regulations it is to be performed immediately after the patient's arrival, in other words, sometime tonight."

"I would call that a very humane provision," the doctor nodded. "Just one other thing—and I trust you will not regard this as an attempt to interfere with official procedure, nor as sentimentality or anything of that sort, but merely as a medical recommendation—in brief, then: I plead for a strychnine injection followed by a heart puncture, and against experimental asphyxiation."

The gentleman pulled out his fountain pen and wrote a few words on the document. "Made a note of it," he said. "Naturally the decision on this purely technical question rests with the commandant of Grafeneck. Anything else, Herr Professor?"

"That is all, Commissioner."

"Then may I ask you to sign the transfer of the man. Sign here, please." He handed him the fountain pen and document. The doctor signed. "Thank you," said the gentleman. "My men will be here in five minutes."

"The man is ready," said Dr. Ackermann, as he accompanied the visitor to the door. "The poor devil is always ready." He closed the door after the gentleman and turned around.

He saw that Christopher had closed his eyes. He stepped to the foot end of the bed and leaned forward. Not a muscle moved in Christopher's face and it was dry; his eyes remained closed. The minutes crawled through the leaden silence. The doctor never turned his eyes from the quiet, hostile countenance.

There was a knock. Dr. Ackermann said, "Come in!" and posted himself at the head end of the bed. Two attendants entered with a stretcher.

"This is the man," said the doctor.

Christopher did not open his eyes, and his eyelids did not flicker, as he was lifted from the bed, stiff as a board, and put on the stretcher. The bearers lifted the stretcher. The doctor walked alongside the stretcher from the bed to the door, watching Christopher's face.

"Stop!" he said, and the bearers put down their burden.

The doctor bent over Christopher. On his forehead he saw tiny drops of sweat.

"Put him back to bed," he ordered. The attendants complied and, at a sign from the professor, left the room with the empty stretcher.

Ackermann sat down on Christopher's bed, pushed the lad's hair back from his forehead and let his hand rest just above the closed eyes. "Herr Sauer," he said, "the gentleman who was here a while ago and whom I addressed as 'Commissioner' is our head bookkeeper, a harmless and reliable man who has been with us many years. He played his part quite well. You play your part here better, you play unbelievably well, Herr Sauer, almost perfectly—almost, my friend. The fraction which makes your portrayal short of perfect is beyond the control of your will. The sweat of fear is autonomic, like death sweat."

He stopped, and Christopher did not move.

"At that," the professor spoke again, "your almost perfect portrayal is a scientifically impossible one. For the stupor which you are exhibiting, Herr Sauer, is too static to be real. It should have eased up by now, and should have given way to sustained excitement. But you were very smart, my dear fellow, not to have anything to do with that. Not even you could have stood such exaltation for as much as two hours."

He stopped, and Christopher did not move.

"Herr Sauer," the doctor spoke again, "we know that you belonged neither to the Hitler Youth nor to the National Socialist Students' Union, and that you did not complete your labor service nor your one year's agricultural service. On the other hand, we know that you were a member of the dissolved Catholic Youth Movement of Chaplain Rossaint, whose trial came off a few years ago. In brief, we know all about you."

He stopped, and Christopher did not move. But his forehead was dry again, Ackermann could feel it.

And he continued, more softly: "When I say: 'we know,' I do not mean to use the editorial 'We,' my friend. I could also have said: 'they know.' Only in the last sentence I could not have said it, since knowing all about you refers also to the stupor. And as for that, only I know all about you."

He stopped, and this time he waited a long while. But Christopher did not move. Only a muscle near the corner of his bearded mouth began to quiver.

"I am sending a recommendation to the Army District Command today," Professor Ackermann said, "that you be permanently discharged from the Army as unfit for service because of schizoid attacks. And, also today, I am sending you to the Army Convalescence Home at Oberstdorf in Allgäu. In six weeks you will have overcome the shock you have inflicted on yourself. Of course, you won't have overcome it completely; for you are a psychopathic, and as for the difference between Healed and Well, you will have to settle that by yourself—even as many of us who are well and yet painfully await a healing, some faithfully, some skeptically, and only a few as fanatically as you. And when you are ready to register for another semester, come to see me; perhaps I know of a good teacher for you, possibly a better teacher than I have been a doctor for you. And now open your eyes, Christopher."

Christopher opened his eyes and looked at him, silent.

An orderly from the regimental office handed Company Sergeant Mayr II a copy of the Army District Command's order discharging inductee Sauer Christopher from the Army as unfit for military service on the recommendation of the psychiatric hospital. The sergeant smiled quietly at the document for a while and then took it personally to the infirmary office. In silent triumph he stuck it in Mayr I's face. The medical sergeant rudely tore it from his hand and without a word put it in the folder to be submitted to the chief medical officer. That same evening, however, they made up in the canteen, with the aid of some coarse, hearty words and an exchange of backslapping. After all, the incident was closed and at bottom both Mayrs were really good-natured fellows.

Chapter Six

SEMINAR OF REBELLION

I

The courtroom of the People's Court is a mighty and noble room, toned in two colors, red and gray, blood-red and misty gray. Blood-red are the curtains of the five large windows, a velvet drapery of the gallery above the main wall where the judges' tribune stands, the velvet background of the tribune's center which like a stage curtain separates the judges' chamber from the courtroom, the upholstery of the high-backed judges' chairs and the robes of the president, of the Court's second law member at his left, and of the prosecutor. Misty gray are the high walls in their classical simplicity, the heavy stuccoed ceiling and the thick floor covering which also extends over the three low steps leading to the judges' tribune on either side.

The five judges sit elevated and stately and far apart on their majestic chairs in back of the gigantic and richly carved judges' bench. The president's throne is crowned by the Reichs Eagle and over it on the wall, above the velvet curtain concealing the judges' chamber, hovers the symbol of the Third Reich's majesty, the bronze eagle with spread wings and swastika. The two red robes of the president and his associate judge are surrounded by uniforms, by judges in uniform, gray, brown, black. To the president's right sit an army officer and an SA officer, to the legal adviser's left an SS officer. They sit bareheaded. They are five. On one side, however, where the judges' tribune turns at a right angle to the courtroom, there sits another blood-red robe, the Reich's Attorney at the People's Court, the prosecutor. Thus there are six on the dais.

The box enclosing the prisoners' bench of dark, brightly polished wood, stands sideways to the judges' tribune, facing the window wall. The bench is so long that all the accused can sit in a row, with one SS man on either end and one SS man separating each of the prisoners from the next. Karl is the first at the left. Then they sit in alphabetical order. Alexander Welte is the last, always the last. When they look straight ahead they see an empty box, perhaps for witnesses; for here there is no public. And they see, reaching down to the wooden paneling of the central heating radiators, the high opaque window, partitioned into small, lead-framed panes, and bearing the Reichs Eagle in red glass painting. The windows do not reveal whether the sun is shining outside, but the light of day, refracted through the facets of the eagle, is reddened as by sunlight, even if it should rain outside. And in the hall all five electric ceiling chandeliers are lighted, oblivious of the day streaming through the windows with five eagle suns, and on the judges' tribune three desk lamps are turned on, one each in front of a red robe.

Below the judges' tribune, exactly opposite the president's throne, stands a small naked table. In front of the prisoners' bench there is a whole row of small tables, at the first of which sits Dr. Langbein, the official defense attorney. He wears his reading glasses, since there is nothing for him to see. No court stenographer is in evidence; what is spoken in this secret court apparently may not be recorded.

The noble hall is far too mighty for the few people; for, strictly speaking, they are six against six.

2

The president speaks in a languid tone of voice: "I open the session."

He straightens up and sits very erect, not touching the back of his chair. He is a broad-shouldered man in his early fifties, with a broad, firm, beardless face covered with weals left by sabre cuts, and topped by sparse, grayish blond hair. His name is Dr. Fritz Behn. In 1932 he was only a small district judge, but by 1933 he had already become presiding judge of a superior court. It had paid him, who had carried the party badge in his pocket ever since 1925, to find the SA rowdies led before his bench "not guilty" by reason of having acted in self-defense; for that they called him "Self-Defense" Behn in his district. It had paid him to have faith in Hitler or, more correctly, in Hitler's success. And a faith that pays is, he believes, a good faith. And a believer who climbs ever higher becomes a firm believer, a severe believer.

President Behn looks sideways at the prisoners' bench and sees that none of the prisoners is facing the judges' tribune. He speaks, and his voice is no longer languid. "The People's Court is not bound to the procedure prescribed by the penal code. It is responsible only to the Führer, is guided by, and renders its judgment in accordance with, the principle on which he has founded this court, to wit: A man is to be judged guilty or innocent according to whether or not he constitutes a danger to the security of the State. The procedure of the People's Court serves solely to render this decision; it is not impeded by any formality nor constrained to any legalistic cliché. The Court may even revoke its admittance of the officially appointed counsel for the defense if it should consider his activities injurious to or interfering with the judgment of the Court."

President Behn sees Dr. Langbein lowering his head to his chest at these words, and he expected this expression of humility; the official defense counsel always lowers his head at these introductory words, as a confirmation of his well-known and esteemed subservience to the judgment of the Court. Behind the defense attorney, the president sees the profiles of the defendants, and perhaps it is only the professional humility of their counsel which makes the faces of the six appear so steadfast, nay, so haughty: none of them looks at the man who sits in the seat of judgment and who speaks of the one and only decision. Dr. Fritz Behn narrows his eyes a little, not the better to see—for his eyesight is excellent—, but to ponder the procedure he should follow. He is something like a procedure artist, and in each case he determines his methods by inspiration which, in turn, is nurtured by the fount of his pragmatic experience and by psychology. And now he already perceives it in broad outlines.

The president's voice is languid again: "Hennings and Associates are accused of having composed, prepared and multigraphed a leaflet, and of having distributed the same among the students of the University of Munich. The contents of the leaflet shall be read in full by the court reporter." He leans forward and fingers the papers lying before him. It is uncertain whether he is reading his papers or listening to the reporter's reading. His face retains the appearance of deafness.

The court reporter is the red robe at his left, the other lifelong member of the People's Court, the second highest member of the tribunal. He is the oldest of them, a man in his sixties with snow-white hair and a yellowish gray mustache, but with surprisingly dark eyebrows, so that one would think they were dyed. But any-one who knows the magistrate, or only looks into his honest, at times vacant face, knows that the thought of artificially rejuvenating himself could not possibly occur to this man. Nor did the thought occur to him to stir about among the sharks and the pikes when the new flood broke down the old dams, and yet he swam along and did not quite know what had befallen him. His name is Walter Lucius and he has long been a high judge, one of the highest judges, a Reichsgerichtsrat, and a nationalistically minded man. And the new flood carries the nationalistically minded, tears them forward, whirls them through fresh water and brackish water and swampy water and deadens the good old sense of distinctions. But it does not deaden the feeling of being unbalanced, of having no ground beneath one's feet, of being irresolute. For ten years now Lucius doesn't know what has befallen him; and what is most up-setting is this: the confusion which surged in from without, now hovers within him and distressingly tries to fight its way out, to find an escape. In brief, he is distressed by his heart which seems to be ill, or at any rate no longer sound.

The court reporter does not find the text of the leaflet at once. Perhaps it is due to the fact that the president, in his intuitive determination of a procedure requiring the reading of the incriminating document, calls for an upbeat which the orthodox jurist did not expect; for, so far there was not even any discussion of the defendants' personal data. Or perhaps it is due to the fact that his inner confusion, in other words, his heart, causes the Reichsgerichtsrat unusual trouble today, ever since he woke up, and incidentally for inexplicable reasons, and thus promotes a slight mental and physical inexactness. And so he twice fails to locate the leaflet while thumbing through the file which had been handed to him at seven o'clock that morning and with which he had immediately familiarized himself despite a certain indisposition. At last, his hand sure and his eye clear again, he finds it.

He clears his throat and reads. His pleasing voice has that moderate solemnity and sobriety tempered with mildness, often possessed by Protestant clergymen—and Lucius, scion of a family of pastors from Tübingen, had also studied theology before he changed over to the study of law for reasons no longer quite clear to him. He reads, and his voice keeps a moderately solemn, mildly sober distance from that which he reads:

"Fellow Students! The defeat of our soldiers at Stalingrad has deeply shaken our country. Senselessly and irresponsibly, 330,000 German men have been led into death and destruction by the strategy of a corporal. Our Führer, we thank thee!

"The people of Germany grow restive. Shall we continue to entrust the fate of our armies to a charlatan? Shall we sacrifice the remnants of German youth to the low instinct of a power greedy party clique? Never!

"The day of revenge has come. It is time for our German youth to settle accounts with the most hated tyranny our people ever had to endure. In the name of all German people we demand the restoration of personal liberty, our most treasured possession, which has been filched from us through base treachery.

"We have grown up in a state which ruthlessly muzzled every free expression of opinion. The Hitler Youth, the SA and the SS have resorted to the most criminal means to regiment and to drug us in the most impressionable years of our lives. 'Ideological education' is what they call their contemptible method of drowning every attempt to think independently in a deluge of empty phraseology. In its Teutonic castles a devilish and narrow-minded 'Führer Selection' is raising a generation of unscrupulous exploiters and murderers, as godless as they are shameless and brainless, to be the party leaders of the future. They would like to have us 'brain-workers' become the lackeys of this new super class. Front soldiers are being treated like schoolboys by so-called student leaders and by other arrogant Nazi youths. Women students are being offended by the lewd 'jokes' of party leaders. German women studying at the University of Munich have given an unequivocal answer to such filthy defilement of their honor. German students have stood up for their women colleagues. That is a beginning in the struggle for our right of self-determination, without which any really creative work is impossible. We all owe gratitude to those brave comrades, young men and young women, who have set a shining example for us.

"For us there is only one rallying cry: Fight against the party!

Renounce your membership in party organizations which hope to strangle us politically. Walk out of the lectures of those professors who in reality are nothing but SS leaders and party stool pigeons. We struggle for a genuine academic and intellectual freedom. They cannot frighten us with any threat, nor by closing the universities. Each and every one of us must struggle for our future, our freedom and honor as members of a morally responsible nation.

"Freedom and honor! For ten years now these two fair German words have been misused, twisted and degraded by Hitler and his clique, who, devoid of all conscience, drag the Nation's highest goods into the mire. They have given more than ample proof of what liberty and honor really mean to them by destroying in this one decade every trace of personal and spiritual freedom and every moral substance of the German people. Even the simplest of all Germans must have had his eyes opened by this terrible carnage in the name of 'liberty and honor' in which they drenched all Europe. They are still doing it, day after day, and have heaped shame and dishonor upon Germany—lasting shame and dishonor, unless German youth finally rallies to annihilate its destroyers and to help build a new Europe.

"Fellow Students! The German people look to us, they expect us to emulate the example set by academic youth in 1813 and to destroy the terrorism of 1943 with the might of the spirit. Beresina and Stalingrad are the torches that have flared up in the East; the dead of Stalingrad call to us: 'Forward, my countrymen, the signal fires blaze!'

"The people of Germany are ready to end Europe's enslavement by Nazism and to fight for a true and rejuvenated faith in freedom and honor!"

Judge Lucius stops, coughing a little; his throat is scratchy from the rebellious words, however cautiously and soothingly he spoke them. But his heart is beating and drumming in a positively absurd tempo—and that is annoying, nothing but annoying, since there is no reason for it, not even the obvious reason of indignation at the leaflet. His heart does not beat in indignation, but in dismay, groundless dismay; that is precisely what is absurd about it, and at the same time serious. Today seems to be a bad day, as far as the heart is concerned.

Walter Lucius dabs the corners of his mouth with a handkerchief and looks to the left because he feels himself besieged by a pair of eyes from that direction. He looks into the handsome, deeply outraged face of his neighbor, SS Sturmbannführer Baldur Uhle who, at thirty-six, is the youngest member of the tribunal, just one year above the minimum age for an honorary judge of the People's Court. "Outrageous!" Uhle murmurs and his burning indignation shows that he has not yet read the file which lies before him and which contains a copy of the leaflet. Lucius undoubtedly observes this neglect of duty, a neglect unfortunately not infrequent with the honorary members of the Court. But at the moment, this is not what matters, it is the heart that matters and he envies his young colleague for his untroubled heart; for Uhle shows sincere indignation, not groundless dismay. The permanent member of the Court replies with a tired nod.

Yes, also Baron von Freyberg, the army officer at the opposite end of the judges' tribune, has not yet touched the file, because of a deep-rooted aversion to reading; consequently he too is unacquainted with the leaflet, and during the reading of the text he lifted his emaciated, yellow, sleepy face. He is not outraged, but interested in his own way, and that means he feels pleasantly titillated. He feels this titillation at horse races, prize fights and pornography on the one hand, and on the other hand he feels it when confronted with brazen acts of opposition to the state and the social order. That had also been the nature of his sympathy for the Nazis when they made their first noisy and plebeian appearance, although it was not sufficient reason for him to join the party. After all, he did not become a jockey or a boxer either, and even with respect to women he had maintained a titillated passivity. At bottom he loves neither the state, nor society, nor people in general, nor himself in particular. He had come out of the first World War a first lieutenant with the Iron Cross, first class, and with stomach ulcers. Now he is fifty and a captain—no great difference. During the interim he had sold second-hand automobiles and let himself be titillated by the national revolution, by the reconstruction, by the new war and the magnificently brazen claim to world domination. For him personally the difference is small, except for the stomach ulcers. These have grown bigger, made him unfit for field duty, caused him to be appointed a department head in the War Clothing Office and to be elected an honorary member of the People's Court for five years. Whether he will still be alive in five years, is another question. But he is of the opinion that for himself there is no great difference between living and not living. He does not love life, and he has his reasons. He, Baron Freyberg, is condemned to being nauseated by his own breath. When he doesn't smoke he munches peppermint tablets. But this leaflet is titillating. He clamps his monocle into place and surveys the prisoners' bench as though it were a starting place for a horse race or a boxing ring.

But to his left on the judges' tribune, between him and the president, there sits a man who represents the extreme opposite of the baron, not to say a mockery of him. The man is puffed up, abounding and overflowing with flesh; he has a stomach capable of digesting anything; he is a man who is pleased with himself and his world, a man deeply satiated, a man voluptuously greased with the fat of triumph. This man is the representative of the party, powerful like the party, excessively powerful, his body bloated with the might of his flesh, his uniform bloated with the might of his body, rich in blood and honors: Alois Schneidhammer, flag leader of the SA, staff director of the Reich Food Estate, Cattle Department, leader of the Group South of N.S.C.U., the National Socialist Cattle Dealers Union—once himself one of those cattle dealers and so unsuccessful in the struggle against his Jewish competitors that his party membership book bears the venerably low number 333. Honorary Judge Schneidhammer has not read the file bearing the title "Hennings and Associates," or has he listened to the reading of the leaflet. He is otherwise and fully occupied, despite the satiety of his flushed face, buried in the multiple chin and in the fleshy weals of neck and jaws: in his mind he composes the speech he is to deliver a week from today at the national convention of the N.S.C.U.

President Behn speaks in a languid tone and seems to continue reading his file; though speaking, he doesn't lift his eyes from his papers and even makes occasional red-pencil marks on them: "So much for the leaflet. The existence of the leaflet justifies the presumption of high treason in the sense of Paragraph 83, Section 3, of the penal code. The Reichs attorney at the People's Court has accordingly brought a charge of high treason against Hennings and Associates."

He pauses without looking up, as if to give the motionless prosecutor an opportunity to show some sign of life. Reichs Attorney Tischler does so with a cursory bow in the direction of the president's chair. He has no love for the procedure-virtuoso Behn, who deals not much more gently with the prosecutor than with the official defense counsel. But Ulrich Tischler is not humble, he has two obstinate protuberances on his receding forehead which is framed by steel-gray, bristly hair. He is a prosecutor by nature and oratorical passion—the best mixture for an extraordinary career. The new trends favor the prosecutor as never before; but this rapturous lust for punishment is hampered by its formlessness, its laconism and its eagerness for execution, as well as by autocratic soloists, illusionists, and all-round athletes like this Herr Behn. Ulrich Tischler wants to accuse until the walls tremble; he has the rhetorical temperament and the voice necessary for it. And he has no opportunity to do it any more; he only stands on the assembly line of the judicial machinery, he, a public prosecutor, Reichs Attorney Tischler, who even as state prosecutor at Leipzig was known as "Der Sargtischler"—the coffinmaker. But he is still called that, although now he is but one of six coffinmakers.

President Behn continues languidly: "In the preliminary examination all of the defendants have made confessions, however provocative, contradictory and overlapping. Five have given verbal declarations, duly recorded in official transcripts. The sixth, defendant Christopher Sauer who represented a special case in the preliminary examination, made a written deposition. In anticipating the result of the preliminary examination, I set it aside, since the Court will know how to achieve an independent view of the case."

The president raises his head. "The Court sees itself confronted with a twofold task: it shall have to reach a decision about the defendants' (a) subjective, (b) objective dangerousness to the state. For this purpose the procedure with respect to (a) will be designed to reveal any subversive features in the lives and characters of the defendants. This the Court wishes to achieve by having the defendants themselves discuss their personal circumstances and by regarding such discussion as a part, a principal part even, of the evidence."

Here the president raises his voice. "Furthermore, I give defendants complete freedom of speech. They are to tell who they are, when and why they declared themselves against the Führer's Germany, and how it happened that they became what they are and think as they do. They may speak the truth and they may lie. They may defend themselves and they may accuse. They may also remain silent if they lack the courage to speak. For their cowardice, too, will be a useful part of the evidence which we are now to hear."

Even as he raised his voice, he saw that the defendants had turned their faces to him—no, not all of them, not the last but one, who, according to the alphabetical seating order as well as to his strange behavior, could be none other than Sauer Christopher, the special case of the preliminary examination. Also now, after the emphasized words, the last but one is the only one who does not turn his eyes away from the wall and the windows with their eagle suns. President Behn narrows his eyes and thinks for a moment what a truly audacious turn of procedure it would be to start with this strange outsider. But he rejects it immediately; his almost musical feeling for the structure of his judicial fugue makes him counterpoint the first idea with the decision to let Christopher be the last to testify.

Then he lets his eyes wander over his own world, the judges' tribune, to determine the effect of his undeniably original program of procedure; for he is vain and loves applause, especially from the law members of the Court—the honorary members, after all, are less capable of appreciating piquant deviations from procedural orthodoxy. He looks first to the left. Prosecutor Tischler arches his eyebrows, gray and bristly as the hair on his head, and confines himself to a silent, furtive bow, as he did earlier when the president referred to him without, however, looking at him; Tischler's response may be taken as rather ironical approval. Baldur Uhle sits like an archangel, handsome and threatening, until the eyes of the president, leaning forward, remind him of his laudatory duty. He clicks his heels under the table and says, "Extraordinary!"

Judge Lucius does not meet the demanding eyes of his neighbor to the right, but persistently looks at his hands—old hands, he thinks, much too old for sixty-three years, hands with the dark spots of age and with horny yellow fingernails. . . . "This may possibly turn out to be much more than taking evidence, Herr Präsident," he whispers obstinately like an old man. "It may be like taking X-ray pictures—mutually."

President Behn looks at him somewhat bewildered; it is not the sort of compliment he expected. But Lucius has a bad day today. He is growing old, Behn thinks, and had he the time at the moment he would think of a successor to the old judge. But he turns to the right. There sits Judge Schneidhammer, the party magnate, mightily resting in himself, in sated fullness, in sated emptiness, dozing with his eyes open; he does not see, does not feel, does not fathom the demands of decorum. As stupid, lazy and voracious as he looks, Behn thinks, let's disregard him. Certainly, one may disregard him, be contemptuous of him, though, advisedly, only in one's thoughts—and yet the president is mistaken; the honorary member representing the Party, notwithstanding his Falstaffian appearance, is thinking, though not about the matter at hand.

Baron Freyberg, however, meeting the president's look with an animated expression, makes a strange grinding motion with his lower jaw—due to his effort to keep the peppermint tablet from interfering with his speech—whispers in his terse manner, "Most promising!" and means it honestly.

President Behn straightens up and sits stiffly, not touching the back of his chair: "Defendant Karl von Hennings," he says in a changed voice, very clearly and slowly.

"Present," Karl responds.

"Arise." Karl rises.

"I suppose that as a teacher of law you are disposed to favor the old procedures prescribed by the penal code and therefore to be prejudiced against the new methods of taking evidence, as practiced by me."

"No," says Karl, "that is a misapprehension."

"You are ready to speak, then, without wasting our time with professional discourses about technical peculiarities of the law or with other shop talk?"

"Yes," says Karl, "I am ready to do so."

"Then come forward," the president commands. "Step to this table here."

Between the first row and the railing of the prisoners' box there is a narrow passage, just wide enough for a person to pass through it without brushing against the knees of those who sit on the bench. Karl does not brush against the SS man who sits on his left, the first in the row, and who opens the gate for him. Karl does not turn to look at Dora and the comrades; but he feels their eyes clinging to him.

Well, well, thinks President Behn, viewing Christopher, and how the fellow can turn his eyes when it comes to looking at his gang leader!

Karl stands facing the president's throne, at the bare table beneath the judges' tribune; he stands six foot one, and his head reaches well above the carved judges' bench on the dais, three steps above the floor. Behn must even look up at him and thinks: that is the biggest man I have had at the sinners' table to date.

Karl waits a few moments more, thinking that perhaps a question, an order, an invitation to begin would be given to him. He looks only at the president, not at the other judges on the right and left. Dora's and the comrades' eyes are fixed on his back. An almost sacred silence pervades the hall. The president looks at him, calmly, as one experienced and long practiced in looking at defendants with judicial unconcern and lack of feeling; and occasionally he looks past him at the next to last of the accused who now stares at the man in front of the judges' tribune as insistently as he previously stared at the eagle suns of the window.

The president utters not a word. It is for Karl to speak.

3

"In the year 1904, at the age of sixteen, I, the son of the Royal Prussian Minister of State, Karl Heinrich von Hennings, deserted from the military academy at Grosslichterfelde. My desertion was an act of rebellion not only against the educational prison, but against my Royal Prussian patrimony in general.

"This is not an unnatural, but an entirely natural reaction. All youth carries a revolutionary potential within itself. I wish to stress this emphatically, as a fundamental principle.

"Well over one-half of my classmates in their sophomore year at the military academy felt the same hatred and the same urge to rebellion. I differed from them only to the extent that I gave in to my lust and hatred and ran away. The courage I displayed in the venture may have been questionable; after all, I was the son of a Minister of State. Consequently nothing happened to me, either by my father's command or out of deference to him. My father proved astonishingly amenable to my rather passionate arguments, acceded to my request without any ado and sent me to the Gymnasium at Rostock from which I graduated two years later.

"This, however, was bad for the development of my rebellious propensities; the spirit of rebelliousness can grow strong only when confronted with opposition.

"I was a normal graduating student, a normal law student, a normal doctor of law, magna cum laude, a normal, war-spirited reserve lieutenant in August, 1914. But I returned from the war a changed man, externally and internally, shaken loose from normal life and almost as rebellious as at sixteen.

"For war is the foster father of rebellion, and defeat is the mother of revolution.

"But my body was utterly exhausted, my starved spirit was skeptical of any spiritual exaltation, my methodical intellect wanted nothing but order and thus the revolution turned out to be a tired, skeptical and orderly one, if it was one at all. However, I was satisfied with it and with myself, as I had been satisfied with Rostock after Grosslichterfelde, and arrived at my second period of normality—an academic career. The new state with its humanistic orientation let me work and teach, gave me rank and honor and professorial chairs at Kiel and Marburg and Bonn and finally at Munich, and at first I repaid its favors well or badly by not being and not wanting to be anything but an unpolitical professor.

" 'Professor,' however, is derived from *profiteri*, and this means: to avow something, and this means: to stand for something, and that is the political postulate for the defense of a conviction and for the courage to defend it.

"To be sure, courage of one's conviction in this humanistic sense may remain academic in a free republic—and Weimar Germany was a free republic which tolerated even anti-humanistic, anti-Christian, and nihilistic convictions. But had there been enough professors at that time in Germany who were professors for the sake of the sacred *profiteri*, then the danger to the new state would have remained academic too, and the students of the

Weimar Republic would not have become the shock troops of its stranglers and flayers.

"Youth is subject to leadership and is continuously remolded into new shapes; consequently it cannot be subjected to any political immutability. This, too, is connected with its explosive potential, its urge to rebellion and its mutinous tendency, which I claim to be fundamental.

"Now, I myself did not belong to the handful of professors who fought for a conviction; but neither did I dwell for long in the ivory tower of research. In 1924, when I became a full professor at the University of Marburg, I married the woman who now sits with me in the prisoners' box, and it was due in no small measure to her live sensitiveness, to her feeling for the living, that I did not stick to the norms and grooves of the teaching profession. I entered upon the third rebellious outbreak of my life, not thereby abandoning my scientific activities, but on the contrary using my science, criminal psychology, as my weapon.

"Armed with my new understanding of crime and criminals, I attacked the social order, its legal and political institutions, and its moral traditions. I hammered away at society's enormous responsibility to seek and to find the causes of antisocial behavior. For only if the causes of crime have been discovered is it possible to break the chain of causes in time to forestall the criminal result. Only through such decisive knowledge and through conscious righting of antisocial attitudes can society hope to reduce criminal activity. And from this I formulated new methods of prevention, improvement, protection and discouragement. And from this I developed the following criticism of our prevailing methods of fighting crime: that their severity and inelasticity are rooted in society's fear, that its fear, in turn, is based on deliberate ignorance, its deliberate ignorance again on fear—fear of recognizing in the criminal deed its own defects, the flaws in the structure and operation of the social organism. I hammered away at the contention that primitive and brutal methods of repression cause crimes and produce criminals.

"I do not wish to dwell on the question whether my work for human society was successful or in vain; for the State I served, even though I rebelled against it, perished.

"But I do wish to affirm that the downfall of the State did not destroy my doctrine: it was there, in me and through me, to recognize the nature of the newly risen power.

"Humanism, the close companion and fount of strength of the inquisitive spirit—as the earth was the fount of the giant Antaeus' strength—was declared an enemy of the State; anti-humanism in all the forms I denounced, intolerance, primitiveness, irresponsibility, want of dignity and conscience, brutality, avarice, power lust and murder lust, paganism, Satanism, megalomania, hysteria, psychopathy, sexual pathology—in short, all criminally antisocial tendencies were officially recognized by the State. The sum of all the rotten, corrupt, depraved and wretched impulses—crime—proclaimed: *l'état c'est moi.*

"I myself was not destroyed either; for I measured up to those troglodytic concepts of racial purity, and I was protected against any interference with my person or my teaching activities by the appalling ignorance of the new Minister of Education, who saw in me a nonpolitical professor with a title of nobility, a former army officer and—once again—the son of a Royal Prussian Minister of State. I was left undisturbed, but I wanted to leave the country. I did not shun the thought of emigration, which has become the title of nobility of the best among our countrymen, although I am inclined to doubt today whether the title shall ever be recognized. I would have been among the few who did not depart into misery; I had in my pocket an offer to teach at one of the great American universities.

"But I stayed, perhaps because my wife fell gravely ill at that time, probably because of that time, as if her sense for the living had been run over and crushed by the terribly loud and broad-gauged new life all around her, like a meadow path by a tank—and yet it did not result in a mental or emotional illness, but in nephritis. Perhaps I stayed because I recognized very soon that my position with the students was not weakened, but rather strengthened; in any case even then the more serious students—and it was mostly these who came to me—showed greater interest in the scientist than in the many young, green, amusingly costumed party professors or in the few older turncoats. But perhaps I stayed because it was a profound and, once again, a rebellious challenge to be a criminal psychologist in the Third Reich, certainly no longer a penal reformer, but an observer of a state psychology which belonged in my own field of investigation. In grim silence I conferred upon myself the title of a criminal-state psychologist, and I should like to call attention to the fact that this new word should be written with a hyphen between criminal and state.

"I spoke of rebellious challenge and grim silence; they belonged together, they even were one and the same. The criminal-state psychology was locked up within myself, I alone and all by myself relished its rebellious challenge and enjoined myself from spreading it abroad. My classes, which confined themselves to the straightforward analysis of famous criminal cases of the past or roamed about innocently in the borderlands of forensic medicine and criminal pathology, received only the most infinitesimal doses of subversive poison in the first few years, if they received any at all. As for the prescribed Hitler salute, I had my own manner of dealing with it; on my way from the door to the lectern, while the students rose to acknowledge my entrance, I would make a short, sharp downward movement with my arm. Until a much later incident, this was accepted as a sufficient compliance with the ceremonial.

"I even enjoined myself from thinking of anything more than immanent rebellion; as a criminal-state psychologist I recognized very soon the sinister significance of the ingenious trick of the National Socialists not to permit any martyrs to arise. This stroke of genius immediately was turned into the principle of the emasculation of martyrdom through secret strangling of life, into the principle of concentration camps—medieval oubliettes, abodes of oblivion, refurbished with a new and cheaper name and colossally intensified in number of occupants as well as concentration of effect: mass production of oblivion. And the consequence of this principle is the emasculation of the dispensation of justice, of the speaking, hearing, audible and visible court of justice. It is the strangulation of justice through the restoration of the Vehmic courts of the Middle Ages under the cheaper, though mendaciously blasphemous name of the People's Court as the highest tribunal of judicial secrecy and secret strangulation, with judges and judged swathed in invisibility and with the noiseless punching machine stamping out the inevitable double sentence: death and oblivion.

"No, I wanted to preserve myself, I wanted to preserve myself for the sake of the rebellious challenge of my new researches—but at the same time I did not want to despise myself. So I spun a theory to justify my silence in my own eyes—and there we have again the German professor with his equivocal attitude toward *profiteri* —a thesis on the meaning and significance of passivity, a doctrine concerning the tactic of playing dead. Its basic proposition is that omnipotence, unobstructed power, contains the seeds of its own destruction. Omnipotence deteriorates through the absence of opposition. I have always found the degenerating influence of non-resistance to be the most deleterious factor in the development of Caesars, prison wardens, slaveholders, sergeants and dictators; it is their ruin. They succumb to the devastating effects of omnipotence as to a narcotic. Dictatorships should therefore crave resistance in order to maintain and aggrandize themselves and their deeds; they should create and nurture opposition instead of cutting off its head.

"My theory, then, may be summed up in the paradox: complete self-effacement, silence, passivity, and playing dead are the quickest means of ruining the dictator. This involves self-deception, and as for myself I could not endure my theory because I could not endure self-deception, not because the theory itself proved false. For, after only six years, the German people's cringing self-effacement and the world's passivity led to the crisis of omnipotence, to an uncannily rapid freezing of Nazism into an icily rigid bureaucracy, to a varnish-like, airtight cellophane wrapper for the gigantic boxwork of co-ordinated national life. And yet the only purpose of a criminal state is to throw out waves, ever higher waves of all the rotten, corrupt, dangerous and wretched impulses. Thus, after a handful of years, the criminal state, already grown sclerotic and apoplectic through the lack of opposition, created the movement vital to its existence, the opposition, the *ultima ratio* of all dictatorships: war.

"With the war I came out from within myself and entered upon the fourth rebellious period of my life, upon my first truly systematic work for rebellion. In the winter semester 1939–40 I began to teach my secret doctrine of Criminal-State Psychology. For war is the foster father of rebellion and defeat is the mother of revolution . . ."

4

"Stop," the president interrupts in his languid voice. "This leads us to the other chapter, to the objective danger; we leave that until later. You may return to your seat."

President Behn lets his eyes wander over his own world, the judges' tribune; he looks to the left and to the right, this time not to demand approval, but to crush the seeds of a possible palace revolution with a mere look. For he may judge by himself. The principal defendant's autobiography, which he, the magician of unheard-of procedures, had conjured up, contained passages, numerous passages, that turned his stomach and almost lifted him out of his chair, and he had to cry out to himself: let him speak! let him expose! he is worth more to us than the whole Security Department!

Reichs Prosecutor Tischler furiously takes notes and does not look up; he has already piled up a whole stack of notes. The fool is building up his case, Behn thinks, as if this were a sensational trial in the confounded period of orderly justice and not the tribunal of secret strangulation. The president narrows his eyes, partly from contempt for the prosecutor, partly because he has caught himself thinking in terms of some of the autobiographer's concepts.

Sturmbannführer Uhle looks at him, yes, his eyes cling to the president, as one who is seasick clings to the railing; his light eyes with their long lashes have a greenish tinge, but the color of his skin is greenish too, and it doesn't look like anger, but like physical sickness; the man, endowed with a boyish prettiness, now looks like a schoolboy who has smoked his first cigar. Fritz Behn quite openly smiles at his youngest, who is not yet used to strong tobacco and for whom it is a good thing that his stomach turns; for even such convulsions of the resisting organism promote the vital movement recommended by the autobiographer.

Judge Lucius, too, his forehead propped on his hand, does not give the impression of protest and murmurs unasked, probably only to himself, "Most distressing!" He finally utters the word that issues from the heart, and perhaps he refers only to the behavior of his heart, not to the conduct of the principal defendant.

"It is precisely what I want!" the president says unpleasantly and loud enough for the whole assembly to hear.

Remarkable! Even the gorged flag leader and Party dignitary to the right seems to be enlivened and to have used his time in a manner very like the frustrated coffinmaker on the other side, on the left wing: he made notes on his writing pad, though so far only two words.

Casually, President Behn leans over the table toward the right, curious to find out what thought pictures of Schneidhammer's were precipitated in the two words; and there, not without astonishment, he reads from the note pad: 'Fellow Germans!' Are these words the marginalia of indignation at the defendant, or nothing but stupid distraction with the pencil? Behn is inclined to the latter view. Yet they are neither; they are the visible beginning of the future speech which in Judge Schneidhammer's bravely laboring brain has already made considerable progress.

Captain von Freyberg holds a beautiful baroque silver snuffbox in his long, ring-bedecked fingers, takes a peppermint tablet from it, puts it in his mouth with epicurean enjoyment and shuts the heirloom with a small, pert, good-natured snap.

Karl returns from the sinners' table to the prisoners' bench. Oh, the gift of this short way, the look at his wife and friends, the look that says: This is how we must act, as if we were not six, but sixty or sixty thousand or six million; we must act as the spokesmen of a power which has sent us out ahead into the present and which loses in us only six voices, six out of six million . . . And with their eyes the friends promise him that this is how they will act, and they thank him for the guidance he has given them, the example he has set for them, and they are proud of him and love him. That is their answering choir.

But how, in the short space of five steps, can his eyes encompass each single face, how exchange question and answer, give counsel, help and confidence, how resist the temptation of giving more attention to the most and to the least intimate among them than to others, to the nearest and to the farthest, Dora and Christopher?

Dora smiles to him, even as he turns around and before he takes his first step, he smiles back and then to Hans, Sophia, Christopher, Alexander; it is like lighting the lights of a Christmas tree—no, only Christopher does not light up.

There is black fire in his eyes, live embers of determination, certainly no fear of his fate, no protest against Karl's example—But why this gloom and seclusion amidst the answering choir of the others' eyes to whose solemn promise he surely joins his own? Why this renunciation of his customary enthusiasm so well befitting him with his flashing eyes and flashing teeth? Why does his wild hunter's face, his bony, pale, stubbly, wholly unyouthful face, express such fanatical defensiveness and enmity and such determination to persist in this defensiveness and enmity when he looks at him, Karl, the helper and foreman? Or is he, the special case in the preliminary examination, the only one who did not testify but only made a written declaration, who was delivered to the court dramatically, the last of the six, and demonstratively chained to his keeper—is he the poor devil of a Judas after all, who by some agreement, inconceivably devilish and conceivable only by the criminal state, sits on the prisoners' bench playing the disciple until the crucifixion? Or is he the boldest of us all, the demon among the six out of six million who runs amuck between night and day?

But as Karl now passes through the gate into the prisoners' box, he devotes himself only to his wife, whose face is turned to him. It is only two steps more to his place, separated from hers by the black pillar of an SS man, and Karl has the right and the duty to use the rest of the way for the private relation between husband and wife. For her look expresses understanding not only for what he said, but also for what he did not say; and this is a private matter between husband and wife which does not concern the friends.

He looks at her intently and gravely: you heard, Dora, that I omitted every allusion to your role during the period of my silence, of my sham death and my self-deception, and you know why—you must not add anything or expose yourself and must let it go as your nephritis; for, just as you were subjected to your illness and had no choice but to be ill, so the appearance must be preserved that you were also subjected to silence, sham death, self-deception, and finally rebellion, subjected to it by me of course, with no choice but to do what I did—perhaps it will save you, Dora . . .

All this is in the look exchanged between man and wife during his two steps from the gate to his place, and she reads it off as from a scroll and smiles in deep understanding—for he is grave, and she nods to him, yes, she dares to nod. Then he sits down and is swallowed by the black SS canyon, and has vanished for her and for the friends.

Already her name is called from the throne of justice, in a voice at once languid and pompous: "Defendant Dorothea called Dora von Hennings, née Roemer."

Man and wife, separated only a moment ago, see each other again. Dora rises from her submersion and has to walk past Karl. She looks at him and is different— Oh, he knows her gentle face when it is colored most charmingly by the courage of her convictions and her eagerness to fight for them. He smiles up to her, imploring and soothing: you know why, Dora . . .

She looks down to him, full of love and very grave— He knows what it means, he reads it off as from a scroll, and now she is so near him, so unbelievably near, as in a dream, that he could grasp her hand, her dear left hand, and could press his fear into it and his request, which she reads from his eyes anyway: don't do it, Dora, don't do it!

His SS neighbor at the left, the prize fighter, the gate opener, intently looks at Karl's hands which are way in front on his knees, and watches for any possible establishment of contact. Karl does not need his hands; Dora brushes against his knees, and that says clearly and distinctly once and for all: don't worry, I love you . . . And now she has passed him.

Dora stands at the sinners' table. She is so small that her head barely reaches over the carved edge of the judges' bench. Karl sees her narrow back, and he holds her with his eyes and supports her and warms her and caresses her hair and slender neck. But how can he protect her, how can he prevent it?

Now your hair is on fire again, Dora . . .

5

Perhaps also Dora had acquired her sense for the living through rebellion against her parental home. Her father was a marine painter and her youth was surrounded and hemmed in by naval paintings, of battleships, cruisers and torpedo boats, of fleet maneuvers, of naval battles and all conceivable variations in the sign of "full steam ahead." Professor Roemer wore the beard and the mentality of Grand Admiral Tirpitz; for he too was a creator of the Imperial Navy. But he suffered no defeat, he painted no defeat, he did not scuttle the fleet at Scapa Flow, and for him November 9, 1918, was a sufficient occasion to launch a fantastic superdreadnought which, in bearded solemnity, he christened "Deutschland über alles." Fifteen-year-old Dora was called to the studio to witness the baptismal act and saw her father smash a bottle of German champagne against the stone floor between the legs of the easel, and was ashamed for him; it looked foolish. She was also ashamed for her mother who dabbed her eyes with her lace handkerchief and wept.

Her father continued to paint, enlarged the Imperial Navy and sold his paintings faster than ever. But he did not part with the superdreadnought "Deutschland über alles," in spite of tempting offers; that one painting he kept for himself, for sinister celebrations at the altar of the ship's name. Whenever a significant political murder occurred in the Weimar Republic, the baptism was reenacted and a bottle of champagne was smashed between the legs of the easel: for Eisner, for Karl Liebknecht and Rosa Luxemburg —and since these two had been slain and drowned together, a debate arose between father and mother to determine whether they should rate one or two bottles, and the frugal mother won out —for Erzberger and Rathenau, as a special tribute also for the Kapp putsch and for Hitler's beer-hall putsch.

The daughter always had to attend these celebrations; she was no longer ashamed for her father, but became estranged from him and his world, occupied her mind with the various victims responsible for the celebrations, established a life-long connection between "Deutschland über alles" and murder, developed an allergic aversion to nationalism as a sacrament, to tradition as a strait-jacket of the present, and came to the youthfully devout conviction that life was meant to be different and better and that being alive imposed the duty to make it different and better.

Again with bearded solemnity, she was expelled from the parental home when her father discovered that her room contained election propaganda material of the Independent Socialists. She went to Kiel to study medicine, or to find out if the practice of medicine would enable her to realize her still somewhat nebulous conception of being alive, wandered off into the subject of forensic pathology which stands on the borderline between medicine and law, and was attracted to Professor von Hennings' lectures because the name of his course, whether by chance or by augury, was "Nationalism and Political Murder." She felt as if he lectured just for her and her youthful, courageous rebellion against the paternal superdreadnought. She sensed how rebelliously alive and manfully sure the bald professor was. She followed him to Marburg, studied under his guidance for her doctorate in law, but only passed the examination given by her beloved, much older and more skeptical than she, to test the qualifications of her feelings. She graduated as his wife. Immediately she had to fight against the marine painter's readiness to bless that titled daughter-in-law of a Royal Prussian Minister of State, now however deceased.

She also had to fight, though in all love, against a certain academic self-sufficiency and ironic lassitude in her husband whom the rare bliss of this marriage had lured to contemplativeness, to the abandonment of his rebel's duty to make the world different and better. And while she quickly attained emotional and spiritual maturity through him and through his work against the social body's pathological criminality, while she rapturously learned that her girlish babbling about duties imposed by being alive had become clear and true beyond all measure, she crowded him out of research into attack, into penal reform. So happy was she with him and through him, that she thought being alive meant humane reform, and that Karl's fight for crime prevention was the means of preventing her father's superdreadnought "Deutschland über alles" from ever again having murder for a godfather.

Perhaps a woman like Dora, outwardly so delicate and inwardly so strong, so full of sincere zeal and of pragmatic courage, can enter into a secret pact even with illness, perhaps she could fall ill purposefully. Her illness came on April 1, 1933, or Dora was bold enough to say that she let it come on that day which the National Revolution had proclaimed as the day for the boycott of the Jews, the rehearsal for the pogrom. A foolish tradition is linked to this day, and to many people it did indeed seem like an April fool's prank, only drenched in the brutish brown of the new national color and heightened to a sort of popular lynch justice. But Jew-hating had slipped from the memory, and even from the temper of the people of Munich, and while they received the hate injections of the new state propaganda, they did not feel them. The people did not really enjoy all the merrymaking and did not even pretend to make the best of a bad bargain. It was no fun for them, it was just another SA maneuver.

Ever since the announcement of the boycott, Dora had saved all essential and unessential purchases for that day. She went to the shopping center to make her well-planned round of Jewish stores and wanted to be among the few nonuniformed people to enjoy this first of April. The high color of her cheeks, however, was not due solely to the joy of breaking the boycott; already while getting up in the morning she had noticed that the pressure she had felt for some time in the region of her left kidney had thickened to a slight pain. The sight of swastika banners and brown shirts, which she had previously managed to avoid, and which now overwhelmed her with their massed official pomp, may have been partly responsible for the sharpening of the slight pain to increasingly violent stitches. For the blood-red flags flaming in the wind enlivened their crippled black crosses, their broken and running crosses, made them into gigantic tarantulas vampirically thirsting for blood; and the brownshirts, the leather-belted shirts of brown murder, had nothing human above them, between themselves and the chin-strapped caps, no divine stamp, no distinguishable faces, but only a leathery base, war elephantiasis of the legs in their black top boots, straining for something to trample under foot.

It aggravated Dora's illness; perhaps the burning vehemence of her revulsion was a manifestation of the fever she was running already. And thus she did not derive the pleasure she had anticipated from forcing her way into Jewish shops through the stereotyped barrage of posters and through oral SA warnings that German women had no business trading with Jews, and from leaving them again with the visible booty under her arm, with the neatly wrapped racial stigma, tilting her Aryan nose at the fuming brownshirts and exalted by the realization that she was by no means the only blockade runner.

On the main square of the inner city she then saw a short scene from the time of the witch trials, a young girl with her hair cut off and a slightly Jewish-looking gentleman in drawers, both carrying, suspended from their necks, placards proclaiming race defiling self-accusations, and both escorted by brownshirts in stately pomposity. It was also like a scene from the era of silent moving pictures, strangely noiseless, shadowy and badly directed; the public participated neither as extras nor as onlookers, showing no interest whatever in the performance. The girl's face, pretty and haughty to the point of laughter, was remarkable, Dora thought; and the man's eyes, God-forsaken eyes with a plaintive, distant look, lamented that God had forsaken humanity. Perhaps it was this that gave her a deep stab in the kidney, so that all of a sudden she could not walk erect.

It would have been time to take a taxi to go home. But she passed a small boycotted haberdasher's shop and entered it because the two coarse SA youths were so provokingly out of proportion to the modesty of the little show window. The shop was empty. Behind the cash register sat an old man who did not move, did not raise his heavy reddened eyelids, but merely asked, "Why today?"

"I would like to have some white and some black darning cotton," Dora whispered, taken aback.

"Are you Jewish?" asked the old man.

"No; but I need darning cotton . . ."

"Why do you say No?" asked the old man and shook his head.

"But why do you think that I am Jewish?" Dora asked back softly.

"Because you are so stooped."

"Oh, that," Dora whispered and swallowed because tears were coming to her eyes from the pain in her kidney or from the misery of her heart. "And what about the darning cotton . . ."

"Go home and have a good cry and come back tomorrow for the darning cotton," the old man decided with an almost severe farewell gesture of his hand.

Dora went home, but did not go to bed. She sat and waited for Karl. She did not want to receive him as a patient, possibly a gravely ill woman; but she did not know as yet for what purpose she held her illness in reserve. She only felt that in spite of her excruciating pain and of this lamentable first of April she was not without energy and a certain curiosity about herself. When Karl came she knew at once that his profound exasperation and his preoccupation with his own problems made him unseeing and incapable of recognizing her condition.

"Well," he said, walking past her with long steps, bent forward a little, and sitting down at his desk, "now we have a new professor of penal law. And guess whom—Professor Vierck."

"Vierck?" said Dora in astonishment. "But isn't he the foster child, the protégé, the creature of Professor Bruch?"

"Exactly—and now the successor to the same Professor Bruch who discovered the gifted but indigent young Vierck among his students, financed the continuation of his studies and prevailed under great difficulties to have the young man admitted to the faculty despite his reputation as a communist."

"And what happened to Professor Bruch?"

"Dismissed, because he had two Jewish grandparents and because his library contained Marxist literature. Possibly he also had the impertinence to use Marxist phrases during the search of his house. At present he is in the concentration camp at Dachau." Dora said nothing. "And do you know," Karl continued, "who was in charge of the SA men who searched the house and took Bruch away?"

"I can imagine who it was," Dora said.

"Yes, Professor Vierck, in old devotion, even if he was not in brown but in black; you see, he has been an SS man, too, approximately since the creation of that elite guard—in short, some creature!" Dora said nothing and still waited and writhed with bated breath, crouched in the reading chair. "I am fed up!" Karl exclaimed and opened the portfolio on his desk.

And then Dora could not wait any longer, and it was as if she had opened the sluice gates and let the stored-up illness break forth: she turned a yellowish gray, her face was wet with perspiration, and her teeth chattered from the fever-chills.

"Here is my cable to Harvard accepting their offer," Karl said and pounded a piece of paper with the flat of his hand, and then, pounding another piece of paper; "here is my resignation from the faculty. If you say Yes, I'll send them both off immediately. You know you haven't said Yes as yet, Dora . . ." He started and jumped up; Dora whimpered and writhed in pain.

She was in bed almost three months and required another six weeks to convalesce. She dared to say that she got well only when Karl had buried and forgotten the thought of emigrating. As a sort of equivalent he went under cover or, deeper still, into his scientific concrete underground fortification, and to the outer world he showed nothing but the harmlessly attractive disguise of his academic teaching routine. Dora apparently approved of it, seemed to understand the theory of nonresistance endangering dictatorship and secretly to enjoy the glittering steel thrusts of his newly revised art of fencing against the criminal state. Thus grew up the new, deeply conspiratorial companionship of these two, the new rebellious secret of their married life.

On the evening of June 30, 1934, when the rumors of Hitler's bloody cleansing bath filled the air like the croaking of ravens from Tegernsee to Munich, and the birds of death ominously darkened the skies, Karl was alone in his quiet study, blood-drunk and craving drunkenness. He had never experienced such a state, and there was something like the beardiness of Tirpitz in the solemnity with which he brought forth and opened a sacredly guarded bottle of Bernkastler Doktor, vintage 1921, to drink to the first success of his theory of murderous nonresistance.

"No German champagne?" asked Dora, not even smiling. She hurt him terribly with her allusion to her father's baptismal acts at the superdreadnought "Deutschland über alles." He pushed the bottle away, got up, walked back and forth, and the narrow bridge of his nose became sharper still in silent censure.

Karl stopped in front of her. "Dora, why are you so cutting? Because I don't run and sacrifice myself to the State monster?"

She shook her head and drew him down to herself. "Because I don't know, Karl, where devastation begins and where self-deception starts."

Yes, it was Dora who first spoke the word self-deception, a pointed word, a needle of a word, and then she left him in peace, in a needle-pricked peace. He took the pricking without wincing, he was too honest a man to contest the incontestable. It worked in him and she could wait. She could listen in tender patience to the reports of his small acts of sedition, his disparagement of the Hitler salute and his homeopathic poison doses to his classes. It worked in him and he became self-critical. He began to complain about the disguise of his work as a teacher, he called himself a disguise, no longer a provocative rebel playing dead. She saw that he suffered.

During one of Hitler's annual March outbreaks—Dora could not remember at the moment whether it was the re-introduction of compulsory military service or the occupation of the demilitarized zone of the Rhineland—Karl also broke out: "I can't bear it any longer, Dora!"

"What can't you bear any longer?"

"The self-deception!"

There it was out, the word and the needle; and it was not Dora, it was Karl who found the new technique for swimming on, between Scylla and Charybdis, without self-deception and without having to sacrifice himself to the monster.

There began, in the stillness of his study, the most peculiar method of rebellion or of incitement to rebellion which a professor with a conviction, one who derives from *profiteri*, could apply as a spiritual lever of revolution. If Karl had ironically imagined himself as a criminal-state psychologist, he now stripped off the irony and prepared in holy earnest to spread his doctrine of Crime as State. He wrote his future lectures about the Dictatorship of Crime, in logical sequence of development. It was a labor of unsparing precision, a dissection with the sharpest knife and the surest hand. Nowhere was it stated that under the massing of crime forms sat the compulsory state, the Nazi state. As layer after layer was peeled away, the naked and indignant eye, the eye of rebellion, finally had to see that anti-socialism had turned into the form of government of the Third Reich, to the point of so complete a reversion of all concepts of justice and freedom that Crime as State had come to be the walls of a monstrous prison for justice and freedom.

Since it was not enough, however, to write the lectures, not enough preparation and not enough proof as to how the students would react to them, they also had to be delivered, in careful and critical rehearsal. And this idea of practical exercise, of turning their married life into a seminar of rebellion, came from Dora. He was the professor, she the student body, and she was inexhaustible and incorruptible in her living and varied representation of a youth grazed by crime, repelled or attracted by it. He fashioned his lectures into fine sieves, ingeniously graded to sift out the receptive students from the unreceptive; and all this took time.

But Karl and Dora made good use of their time, and perhaps these were the most beautiful days of their married life. When they worked on the already far advanced lecture which bore the well-sieved, deeply revolutionary title: "The Limitations of Penal Rule," and when Dora—the student body—conceded that something could now be done with the siftings, that there was a sifted residue, the sediment of rebellious youth, when they had reached that stage the time had come once again for one of Hitler's March outbreaks, and Austria was incorporated in the Reich.

War was Karl's deadline for the transition from rehearsal to performance, for the transfer of rebellion from the quiet study into the lecture room. After March, 1938, he believed that war would break out in the same year and worked feverishly on his "virulence" lectures, as he called the more advanced stages of clarification to distinguish them from the intermediate "infection" lectures. Dora did not believe in the imminence of war, just as the people in general, and saw no reason to doubt that the State would be successful in its criminal policy of creating Greater Germany with no other means than blackmail. Thus it came about that it was not Dora but Karl who fell from the clouds when the city, the city in which they lived, became a ghastly concept, when Munich became "Munich" and the bloodthirsty tarantula flags arrayed in mighty solemnity received the bloodless and anemic capitulation of the Western powers: with two all too human signatories facing two supermen, the obesely Roman chin and the nostrils overshadowing the little mustache.

"With Munich," Dora said, "the fear of war ends and the hope for war begins."

But Karl only shook his head and persisted in his gloom. He did not work with her any more, the "seminar" was closed, for days, for weeks. She waited in cheerful patience, she knew him and the automatic safety devices and compensations of his temperament.

The shooting of a secretary of the German embassy in Paris by a certain Grynspan set off an unseasonal November outbreak of the regime, a horror ballad of a faked popular wrath. Now, this was a peculiar and instructive way of staging the hatred against the Jews: since it had to come from below, no official dignity could be lavished on it, and the symbols of sovereignty, the tarantulas, could not be unfurled. Mob played mob, the officially licensed mob masqueraded as the nameless elemental mob. For the SA did not wear its uniform as it set fire to synagogues and Jewish business establishments, as it cut the fire hoses, as it squirted ink on the window curtains in stormed and trampled Jewish apartments before it tore them down and threw them into the street through shattered windows; and the SA men considered themselves safely disguised because they did not wear their brown shirts and top boots, and yet they wore them, even had they raged with naked chests and bare feet; for this uniform grows into flesh and bones, and even the raging is executed with exactitude, in uniform step, in the much practised step of the storm battalions. And in addition to the trucks carrying haphazard collections of Jews to Dachau, there were other carloads headed for the same destination and filled with people who had recognized the "popular" wrath and who had been courageous enough, or stupid or careless enough, not to keep this knowledge to themselves, as did all the others who were there to see it.

It was on that November day in 1938, that Karl, without further explanation, resumed work on his "virulence" lecture, entitled: "The Limitations of Penal Rule," with Dora as a well-sieved student body.

"How high would you estimate the percentage of receptivity in the upper classes at the moment?" he asked her in the peculiarly academic conspiratorial jargon which they had developed.

"Five per cent virulent and twenty-five per cent infected, conservatively calculated," Dora replied factually, like a statistician.

"With the 'Limits of Penal Rule' we must raise it to ten and fifty," Karl said severely.

"And in time we'll come to calculate less conservatively," she added smilingly and stroked his hand.

The time which was still left to them for the incubation of the seeds of rebellion, comprised approximately the span of human pregnancy—and that was also the time needed by the criminal state to give birth to its war. The hour came at dawn, September 1, 1939, and there followed forty-eight long, paralyzing hours for man and wife, hours of doubt that shook the very marrow and purpose of their lives. Will it be a new Super-Munich? Finally, on September 3, came the NO of humanity's deeply mournful voice, first from London, then from Paris.

Karl and Dora listened to the radio and did not speak for a long time. Then they spoke.

Dora: "And if they win?"

Karl: "They will have victories, but not victory."

Dora: "And if they have victories and final victory?"

Karl: "It cannot be, because it is against the right faith. And it is a war of faiths. There can be no religion where Evil is victorious."

Dora: "Has Evil never had victory?"

Karl: "Only victories, but not victory."

Dora: "And if nonetheless they are victorious unto victory, what will you do then?"

Karl: "I can safely say that I would then take my life. The hypothesis does not cost much, since I know that it will not be necessary for me to take my life."

Dora: "And what is this Evil that cannot be victorious?"

Karl: "Crime as State."

Dora: "And what is the name of the State?"

Karl: "Germany."

Dora: "And who are the criminals?"

Karl: "Germans."

Dora: "And what are we?"

Karl: "Germans."

Dora: "And can there ever be a distinction between Germans who are guilty, partly guilty, and not guilty?"

Karl: "How can that concern us, Dora? We are not building the party of those who are not guilty, but of those who have faith again, the right faith. And those who are in exile and in concentration camps and the nameless three-man cells of underground workers' organizations, they are not guiltless, but derive from *profiteri:* the faithful and the fighters. And as a professor I begin my work of faith on my students, the guilty, the partly guilty, and the not guilty."

Dora: "And many, many will die a false death, in a false faith, in the service of Evil, and will not even have wondered whether they are guilty, partly guilty or not guilty, and the blood that is being shed comes from human beings, on this side and on the other."

Karl: "And may the bloodshed fall upon the head of the evil one, Amen!"

Chapter Seven

BY GOD YES! BY GOD NO!

I

Friedrich Moeller, Judge of the Juvenile Court in Bremen, was arrested during the terror wave launched with the aid of the Reichstag fire, for no other reason than that he had been a local director of the democratic "State Party." Only six weeks later he was released again, thanks to the intervention of his thirteen-year-old son Hans. The boy's influence had traveled over a devious and somewhat obscure road—through classmates who already were enrolled in the Hitler Youth to a Bannführer who was apparently induced by Hans' blond handsomeness to bring into play his connections with equally blond and handsome party magnates.

On his return, Dr. Moeller looked changed, probably because his head had been shaved or because he had grown very thin or because his eyes had acquired a frightened look and a tic, too, a peculiar sort of fluttering of his eyelids, coming at irregular intervals. But the Hanseatic strictness, which regulates the emotions, forbade any expression of exaltation at the reunion of man and wife. Although Frau Frederike's heart ached when she saw him, she forced herself to transpose her feelings into a somewhat embarrassed, restrained yet tender phraseology which would not have sounded very different had he been returning from a prolonged journey.

Also the joy of Sophia, his ten-year-old daughter, his favorite, was regulated, though in a different way. She said almost nothing and never ceased looking at her father until she felt that his eyelids fluttered and flickered because she looked at him; then she did not look at his face any more, but at his hand that rested on her shoulder and she saw that his hand had dirty fingernails and swollen, skinned knuckles and blackish tears and blisters and weals, and she took his hand from her shoulder into both her hands and would not let go of it.

Hans was not back from school yet. Frau Moeller amplified this information with a slightly drawled "Incidentally, Friedrich, perhaps you already know . . ."; and then, in vivid and exceptionally colorful words, but with anxious eyes, she told about their son's gallant and ultimately successful efforts for the liberation of his father. Dr. Moeller had not known about it at all and believed that he was free because it was just about time for even the most arbitrary authorities to realize that his detention was unjustified; he did not consider himself an exception, but only the fortunate first among many who were about to be returned to civil life by a discerning justice. No, he had not known about it and did not understand; but since he had just come out of the bog of terror, and since he who has been stuck in it up to his neck has no mouth left to question, he only shook his head, with fluttering eyelids.

"Here he comes now," Frau Moeller said, with an uneasy look, and there was something in her announcement that seemed to beg for indulgence as well as for respect.

A key had been pushed impetuously into the lock of the apartment door: and it was against the rules of the house, established, not without a touch of pedantry, by the Judge of the Juvenile Court, for the boy to carry the key with him. Noisy, apparently hobnailed and so to speak autocratic soles came crashing in; and it had been a softly treading boy, cautious and reserved, like still water, whom the father had left not long ago. The door was thrown open—Hans wore the brown shirt of the Jungvolk, the organization preparatory to the Hitler Youth, stuck out his arm upward and sideways, but transmuted the salute after all to a neutral gesture of welcome, waved with loose fingers, and found the smart and scanty greeting: "Well, old man!"

The father stared at him and had neither hand free to greet him; his left hand was held tightly by Sophia, more tightly still since Hans had come in, and his right hand stuck fast in the pocket of his gray jacket; he found no word either, because he had forgotten how to speak in the presence of a brown shirt.

Frau Moeller quickly took possession of Hans' arm, to forestall a regressive development into the Hitler salute and also to act as a sort of deputy for her husband in shaking the son's hand indulgently and respectfully. "There, you see . . ." she said with an uncertain smile into space, and thus the fragment of a sentence could be meant for the father or for the son as well.

"There, you see," Sophia took up, snuggling up to her father and looking at her brother in pure maliciousness, "Papa also thinks you are disgusting in your brown outfit!"

"Shut up!" Hans snapped in military fashion and in a falsetto tone, because his voice was breaking.

"Don't be so saucy!" Frau Moeller chided her daughter, and then looked at her husband imploringly. "I don't find it at all unbecoming, Friedrich . . ."

"I am only asking myself," Dr. Moeller said softly, "who has given the boy permission to join this organization—or does such a thing no longer require permission?"

"It does," Hans smiled, deeply amused.

"Of course it was I who gave it," Frau Moeller said, "since you weren't here . . ."

No, the father had not been here, he had been away; the remark proved to be embarrassing, and not only the man's but also the woman's eyelids now fluttered.

"And already as good as dead, is that right?" the father murmured with barely opened lips.

"Friedrich!" the mother lamented, "now that you know how matters stand! You know whom you have to thank . . ."

"Oh, yes," the father nodded, "now I know how matters stand . . ."

"Well, then everything is all right," said Hans, slightly impatient. "That is, there is just one more thing to be settled, Father, preferably at once and between you and me— Mother, please take the child out with you."

She is actually leaving! thought the Juvenile Judge, and saw how his wife motioned to their daughter. Sophia stretched to reach his ear: "Don't give him a hiding, Papa," she whispered, "though he surely deserves one . . ." Then she made a face at her brother and preceded her mother out of the room. Frau Moeller, however, between door and doorpost, sought her husband's eyes and implored him silently and urgently to proceed with reason as well as caution.

"I guess we might as well sit down," Hans suggested.

"No," said the father.

"As you wish," said Hans, spreading his legs apart and hooking his thumbs in his leather belt on the right and left. The father had never yet seen him in this landser's posture; but he knew it from the camp. "Well, Father," said Hans and tilted his head to one side, "you need not bother thanking me, I did it as a matter of course and it really wasn't so difficult after all. You see, there is a terribly nice Bannführer, only nineteen years old and already ranks as a regimental commander so to speak, a fine fellow and really terribly nice to me, and he will also be my official leader when I am fourteen and transfer from the Jungvolk to the Hitler Youth. Well, I told him that you are a decent sort fundamentally, Father, only a little off beam like most old gents, and he understood at once and even said that he preferred someone like you to those March casualties. I suppose you know, they are the turncoats who switched horses in March and suddenly became 150 per cent National Socialist—anyway, he did some telephoning here and there and the matter was fixed."

"Fixed," repeated the father. "How simple!"

"Incidentally," said the son, "did you catch an eye inflammation or something like that in your health resort?"

"Why?" asked the father in return. "Are my eyes watering?"

"No, only you have a funny way of blinking sometimes."

"That's funny," said the father and, as if to convince himself, he grazed his eyelid with the tip of his finger.

"And now as to you," said the son, "you will have to be thinking of your future now."

"That's funny," said the father again, probably still referring to his blinking.

"I could be of further help to you in this matter," said the son, "on the supposition, of course, that you have come out of Papenburg a changed man."

"I have," said the father almost inaudibly.

Hans raised his chin, and the Juvenile Judge discovered that the boy's chin also had changed and had already become a small edition of that dominant facial characteristic which had made the masters and the guards of the camp resemble one another. "Look here, Father—and let's keep this between ourselves, even mother needn't know about it—the thing is, the matter had been fixed at least three weeks ago, in other words, you could have been home three weeks ago. But for a man like you the concentration camp isn't punishment, it's an education, and that is why they did not release you until now, out of consideration for your future."

At this point the father's right hand, still stuck in the pocket of the jacket, burst forth, ready to strike; but the son, instead of drawing back, took a step forward, as if in curiosity, thumbs hooked in his belt, and the father's hand returned to its pocket.

"There is nothing you can do about it, Father," Hans said; "your future depends on the success of your education. Now, if you were in a position to affirm the National Socialist faith—I am sure you'll find the right way of doing it—then I could arrange to have you meet the Herr Bannführer tomorrow and he can do some telephoning here and there and you are back in office."

"I am not in a position to do so," said the father.

"Well, then, let's wait another week or two."

"I shall not be in a position to do so even then," said the father.

"All right," said Hans and he had a crease between his eyes, "in that case you will have to be pensioned."

"Yes," said the father, "that is what I want."

"Out of the concentration camp and pensioned, at barely forty-five . . ." Hans grumbled.

"You mean that under the circumstances the whole business wasn't worth while, my son? Then you must send me back to the concentration camp, and the matter is fixed again."

"But, Papa, what are you taking me for!" Hans flew up, and for the first time addressed his father again in his customary manner. "I only mean that this is not exactly a brilliant educational result!"

"You are my educational result, my son, and to justify my retirement I shall be as ill as your thirteen-year-old National Socialist faith requires—out of sheer gratitude."

Hans looked at him sheepishly, his ears were red and even his chin receded a little.

2

If Dr. Moeller's presumption in choosing this sort of future for himself could be interpreted as opposition to his son, it was also his last act of resistance and did not abridge the hegemony which Hans had established over the family. The pensioned father sneaked around shamefacedly, the mark of superfluousness on his forehead, grew increasingly silent and more cautious even in his thoughts, so to speak; he even dropped his correspondence with Karl von Hennings who had been his deeply admired friend since student days, because the Munich professor couched his letters in a reserve that might possibly be called suspicious.

On Frau Moeller's part there was no hostility to his renunciation of his career, possibly because in her heart she had feared a much more serious clash between father and son. She was by nature inclined to compromise and possessed a talent for seeing the silver lining in every cloud. For the sake of her dearly loved son she found the new order of state and family which he so emphatically represented not unworthy of love and adjusted herself uncomplainingly and even with a quiet contentment to her husband's retirement and retirement pay.

Hans, on the other hand, no longer got red ears but instead—in the course of time which was increasingly devoted to a service shrouded in a sacred veil—he won ever new braids and insignia, the sense and significance of which remained as incomprehensible to the father as the jagged double-talk now sported by his son. The only opposition to Hans within the family came from his little sister; it was a childish opposition, but it was rooted in sacrilege, as it turned out later.

Sophia refused to see, for instance, why she should curtail her relations with Hilde Wolff. For the moment nothing more was being demanded from her by the anxiously conciliating mother, and brother Hans did not yet appear in the role of highest authority. But even this insecurely imposed halfway measure collided with the absoluteness of the two young girls' friendship. Hilde Wolff was her best friend, and that implied a somehow moral position, protected by its own laws and conventions which could not be changed or shaken. In her frequent stock-taking of her sentiments, Sophia ranked Hilde Wolff as number three, because father and mother just simply had to occupy first and second places; but in the secret, so to speak illegal, balloting in which the girl indulged now and then, Hilde Wolff stood in second place, between father and mother. How then could it be conceivable to think the mere thought of no longer walking together to the same school and walking back together to the same house—and that was what her mother demanded as a first and clearest mark of the curtailment of her friendship—how could it be conceivable, when they had lived the same life as long as she could remember, lived in the same house in adjoining apartments on the second floor, were of the same age, had gone together for their first day at school, sat next to each other at the girls' high school, with Hilde Wolff persistently occupying first place among the girls of their class and Sophia second place, obstinately determined not to lose her place next to Hilde.

"But, don't you see, they are Jews!" her mother lamented.

Yes, the Wolffs were Jews; Sophia knew it ever since they started going to school, because Hilde did not attend Pastor Wurm's boring lessons in religion. Sophia had nothing against the Wolffs being Jews, she even liked it. For Hilde's father ran a small chocolate factory, and sample packages of every conceivable variety of sweets flowed through the Wolffs' household in a never ending stream, and Sophia loved pralines and hated religious instruction. Thus it came about that as a child she associated all things Jewish with a mixture of chocolate and release from religious instruction, and even as a half-grown girl being Jewish had a pleasant flavor for her. But had "Uncle Wolff," as she called the widowed neighbor, produced cod-liver oil, he would still have retained his high rank in the list of her affections, because he was gentle and amiable and because he was Hilde's father.

It turned out, however, that the attack on Hilde, which meant an attack on the fortress of her friendship, did not emanate from the parental home alone. At school the so-called Jew-bench was established, a distinctly isolating place for Hilde Wolff and the other Jewish girls in the class, and it had grave consequences. Since the occupants of the Jew-bench were not included in the general ranking of the class, the honor of leading her class fell to Sophia. This promotion at the expense of her friend, separated from her and heartbreakingly degraded, constituted the most revolting of crimes against friendship which in the honor jargon of the girls passed under the name of "colossal meanness."

Consequently Sophia considered it necessary to take a seat on the Jew-bench the following day, as the second, next to Hilde Wolff who began to cry. This natural act of loyalty threw the class in a tremendous turmoil and divided it into two parties: those who considered it "colossally decent," and those who denounced it as "Jew coddling." The old teacher, himself a novice in the new practices, was much embarrassed by this demonstration on the part of his second-best in favor of his best student, in his heart he was even deeply moved by it. He recognized Sophia's motive for what it was: an act of loyalty. For this reason, and also for the sake of keeping his own balance, he parried the obstinate act not with severity but with pedagogy in the new sense, with a discourse about race theory. Picturing lovely, blonde, blue-eyed Sophia Moeller as the personification of the Nordic race, he hoped to evoke her vanity and uncontained delight in her race superiority and thus to help her surmount the cliffs of a now obsolete decency.

Now it so happened that Hilde Wolff, too, was blonde and blue-eyed, though a shade darker than Sophia; she even had a more pronounced and finished prettiness than her friend who resembled her strikingly—for one thing because she wanted to resemble her and also because her youth had been formed in the same mold. Sophia therefore exclaimed in sisterly joy: "Exactly like Hilde Wolff!" and this remark, meant not as an ironical sneer but as a simple statement of fact, caused an outburst of laughter most derogatory to the race theory. The practical demonstration of race superiority was at an end, but the incident gave the teacher an opportunity to settle the matter along disciplinary lines. Sophia had to stay over for an hour and received a demerit for bad behavior, lost her place as leader of the class, was demoted to seventeenth place and requested to take the penalty seat immediately, which meant that she had to leave the Jew-bench. Sophia obeyed, in the sweet consciousness of suffering for her friend. But there was a difference between her sweet and Hilde's bitter suffering, she had to learn that, too.

Brother Hans went into action. The incident had been serious enough for the teacher of the class to ask Sophia's parents for an interview. It was not clear whether Hans had been instructed by his mother to represent her—the father had renounced any claim to acting as the head of the family—or whether he had appointed himself. Sophia had kept the matter to herself, not from fear of her brother but from consideration for her father, and had explained the visible consequences—the notice of censure and her demotion —with a superficial confession to a naughty school girl's prank. She did not suspect that the attack on Hilde was now carried forward by an alliance between school and home—no, that the school had allied itself with the party uniform in the home.

On the afternoon of one of the ensuing days, as Sophia was leaving school, her arm linked to Hilde Wolff's in sweet provocation, Hans stood in front of the entrance, uniformed and mighty, and pounced on her with the face of a policeman who has recognized a fugitive from justice and proceeds to make the arrest. Sophia pressed Hilde's arm to her and stared pugnaciously at her brother—but just then something unexpected and deeply disturbing happened: Hilde tore loose from her and ran away. And somewhere girls were laughing. Hans grabbed his sister's thin wrist with a painful grip, a well-taught and expert grip which was meant to cause pain. But since she had just suffered a great hurt, she could bear it quite easily, as a sort of counter-pain.

"Haven't you any decency left in you?" he said through his teeth, and pulled her to the other side of the street.

"No," she answered.

He tightened his grip. "After all this you dare go out on the street arm in arm with that Jew girl?"

"Ouch!" she tried to suppress the cry. "And I suppose that's all you learn in the Hitler Youth! Jujitsu tactics against girls!"

He let go of her. "I just saw Dr. Gruber," he said. That was the old teacher of Sophia's class.

"Is he entering the Hitler Youth now?" she inquired.

"Insolent as snot, too!" he observed. "And just now Gruber told me the whole story, and it's so insane, so . . . so . . . or perhaps you don't know what it's all about?"

"Of course, it's all about blonde girls like myself or Hilde Wolff who show all the characteristics of the Nordic race."

"You are just plain stupid," said Hans and shook his head. "You are so abysmally stupid that one can't even be angry with you. I guess that's why that spineless Gruber said that you should be treated gently. Gently!"

"And that's why you use jujitsu?"

"Good God, I was simply furious when I saw you coming out of there hanging on to that Jew girl—I could have put you down . . ."

"What do you mean, put me down?"

"Well, that means . . . Well, I could have killed you."

"I see; 'putting down' means killing— What you boys don't learn!"

"Now kindly shut your impudent trap and listen to me, Sophia. How does it go, somewhere in that pious moth-eaten thing? 'Lord, forgive them, for they know not what they do'—or something like that . . ."

"Whom should the Lord forgive," Sophia interrupted; "you Nazis? But you do know what you do to the Jews!"

"Yes, we know," Hans said heatedly and his head turned red. "We also know why; but you don't know it and that's why the Lord should forgive you, or rather we should forgive you and teach you and develop some race consciousness in you, which should be quite simple since, after all, as my own sister you are a German race companion; or, the other way around, since you are of German blood you are my sister."

"I think, Hans," said Sophia, "that now you are talking terrible nonsense."

Hans stopped, turned to her and not ungently took her by the shoulders. His clear blue boy's eyes looked at her big and solemn. "It is not a matter of blond hair," he said, "but of blood. Sis, we both have German blood, your Jew girl hasn't. To have German blood means to be race-conscious. That is the duty and responsibility of German youth. The old generation has tired blood and must abdicate anyway—just think of Papa as an example! It is our duty and responsibility to fight and to defend the purity of the Aryan race. The Jew is the enemy of our race. The Jew is the enemy of our blood. That's why we must exterminate him like a disease. Is that so hard to understand?"

"That's quite easy to understand," Sophia answered.

"Of course, quite easy, more than easy, even if you are only saying it now. At first I also just said it, and then I suddenly noticed that my blood had absorbed it before my reason had. But it's not a question of reason, it's a question of blood. And there is a compulsion about it because it's a property of your blood, you can't get around it; and then you too will feel this natural defense of the blood against the racially foreign, and you'll be able to smell out the Jew no matter how he disguises himself and you'll repulse him and expel him as a foreign body, and you will be as you must be and as

I am and as we all are. You can't get around it and I really don't need to threaten you any more now or to exact your word of honor and such nonsense—your blood knows all about it now and it'll do things right."

Sophia was silent and frightened.

Yes, Sophia was frightened and confused. It was not only her home and the school and her brother, and back of him the whole Hitler Youth, who combined for the attack on Hilde, on the stronghold of her friendship, it was also the German blood in herself, in the little girl Sophia. How was this and how could she bear it: not to have the same blood as Hilde, to be drenched in blood that possessed the despicable property of repulsing Hilde and of expelling her as a foreign body—how could she be Hilde's bosom friend and at the same time her mortal enemy? But, thinking of the hurt Hilde had inflicted on her, of Hilde's most damnable act of cowardice in tearing herself loose and running away—how did it happen that all of a sudden Sophia breathed in one of those vapory words that hung in the air like exhaust gases, that she had it within herself, that word that the Jews are cowards? Did it happen because her blood knew all about it now?

Hans took her home and behaved decently, as Sophia had to admit, even though in his somewhat autocratic manner. He reported to his mother that Sophia's teacher had discussed ways and means with him to make the brat—that was how he referred to his sister who was present—more familiar with the National Socialist point of view, that he, Hans, had talked with her on the way home, seriously and not without success, as he felt justified in assuming. He said all this during the evening meal which had to be served as early as six o'clock because Hans had to leave the house again at six-twenty to attend to one of his official duties. Sophia looked gravely at her plate, and the mother, smiling and relieved, spoke one of her vague and appeasing sentences which could be taken as expressing praise for the pedagogical son as well as for the obedient daughter. The father, to whom the report was not addressed and who lived apart from his family even when he sat at table with them, looked at his daughter in lost silence. Sophia felt his look.

When Hans had left the apartment, she said, "I'll drop in on Hilde for a moment."

That was the way she always said it; it was the accustomed sentence announcing the accustomed visit to her friend. But today it took her mother so unawares that she shook her head with astonished eyes and didn't know what to say except a subdued, "But . . ."

The father spoke as from far away, looking over his raised teacup, "Go right ahead, my child."

If only I were as old as dear Papa, and my blood as tired as his! Sophia thought as she walked across the hall to the Wolff's apartment and gave three short rings, her customary bell signal for Hilde. She heard her friend dash from her room and to the door and she was glad that Hilde came running to answer the bell signal and she smiled happily. Hilde tore the door open, pulled Sophia inside, closed the door again quickly and threw herself into her friend's arms, sobbing a little. Sophia couldn't sob, since she was smiling happily; but seeing that Hilde did it, she sobbed a little too, for Hilde's sake, and she didn't even have to pretend, she simply gave a sound to her smile.

And then . . . well, it was a dramatic and glorious embrace after all that had happened, a victory of friendship and not the slightest resistance of the blood; now one could well make a further test of the sample—Sophia sniffed around a bit on Hilde's cheeks and neck and hair and she smelled the delicate scent of the young girl's skin, washed with gardenia soap and dabbed with Cologne water; and since the laws of friendship set up by the two girls prescribed the use of gardenia soap and Cologne water, Hilde smelled exactly like Sophia and no race distinction could be sniffed out.

Not until they had gotten to her room did Hilde, sitting close to Sophia on the Victorian sofa with her arm around her friend's shoulder, ask: "Did he do anything to you?"

"You mean Hans? He didn't dare! But can you tell me, or rather can you justify yourself for having torn loose and run away from me—you know, that was mean of you, Hilde."

"Mean?" Hilde exclaimed, deeply shocked, and her hand fell from Sophia's shoulder. "But for Heaven's sake, I did that only on your account!"

To lie to each other was one of the gravest crimes against the law of their friendship, and Hilde was not even one of those mild liars, one of those who occasionally lied to their father or teacher or to girls with whom they were not friends. What she said, therefore, was the truth, however startling and as yet unexplained. Now Sophia in her turn put her arm around Hilde's shoulder and asked: "Then it wasn't cowardice, just a little bit of cowardice?"

"Cowardice?" Hilde was stunned again. "But excuse me, how could this question possibly come up . . . I mean, how could I possibly have the choice of being cowardly or not cowardly—it's only you who have that choice!"

"I?" Sophia exclaimed.

"Please understand me, Sophia. I am Jewish and you are not. I have to suffer because I am Jewish, and no matter how cowardly or how courageous I may be, I have to suffer because I am Jewish. You don't, you could choose to be cowardly and not to have anything to do with me any more because I am Jewish. But you aren't cowardly, you are not mean like the others, you are decent and that's grand of you."

"I beg your pardon," Sophia protested, "I haven't any choice either. Am I not your best friend? And you had no business running away, not even for my sake!"

"If I had stayed with you, Sophia, he would have beaten you; I could tell from the way he looked. And I don't want you to get beaten up on my account, I simply don't want it! I happen to know exactly when it gets to be too much, what you have to suffer because I am Jewish—too much for me, since after all it's I who have to suffer when you are in trouble because I am Jewish, and in the end I'll break down under it and then it will make no difference if you are decent or as mean as the others . . ."

Here she broke out sobbing again. But Sophia did not sob with her; her young brain had to work powerfully, the problems accumulated, the terrible alliance against their friendship took hold even of Hilde, and perhaps it was really due to the properties of the blood, though they could not be felt or smelled . . .

"Is it enough to make you break down when we walk arm in arm to school and from school?"

"Yes," Hilde whispered, "yes, yes, yes! Because today it's your brother who beats you for it and tomorrow the whole class!"

"But I'll hit back!" Sophia exclaimed in sudden wrath. "What's it to you if I choose to get into fights with everybody—you don't have to join in!"

"Whether you hit back or not," Hilde whispered, "whether I join in or not—I'll break down under it . . ."

"And tomorrow, Hilde, are you going to school arm in arm with me tomorrow morning, or aren't you?"

"I am not going to school tomorrow," Hilde said very softly, turning her face away.

"That's very sensible," Sophia assented. "Why shouldn't you play hooky for once, you have never done it yet and you can afford it now that you are no longer at the head of the class. But what about day after tomorrow?"

"I am not going to school at all any more," Hilde said very softly, turning her face away. "Papa has decided today that I am to go to a private Jewish school, Papa says that I would be chased out of the public high school anyway sooner or later, because I am Jewish . . ."

There was a long silence. The little girl Sophia saw with horror how her little world proceeded to change maliciously, building a wall between her and Hilde before her very eyes, as though in peaceful unconcern. Oh, she knew, it was the wall of blood, the detestable separation and rejection which Hans had prophesied; and should she not fight against it, should she not do anything about it now, then the tyrannical blood would do things right and she would be as she must be and as Hans is, as they all are, and she would smell the enemy of her blood in Hilde and would hate her and exterminate her like a disease. But how could she fight against her own blood; what was the one and only and extreme step she could take against it to protect her friendship, the one and only and extreme step?

"And what of our sworn friendship?" she asked throatily and pale from determination.

Hilde slowly turned her face to her. "You don't think I am swearing off our friendship because I am changing schools, do you?" she said.

"No, but we are going to be separated; and before we part we must seal our friendship anew—you know that's agreed between us, Hilde!"

"But only in case we shouldn't be able to see each other at all any more—in case one of us should have to go to Berlin or to America —but we shall be separated only during school hours . . ."

"No, I want to seal our friendship anew, I want to do it, I must do it!" Sophia whispered, beside herself, and her little face was wild and pale at the same time.

"Yes." Hilde nodded, paling in her turn and suddenly under Sophia's spell. "I also want to do it . . ."

"Have you courage?" Sophia whispered, very close to Hilde's face.

"Yes," Hilde nodded.

"You know what is the supreme seal," Sophia whispered almost into Hilde's lips, "the seal by blood . . ."

She held her breath; it could be, oh, God, it could be that Hilde now saw through the pious deception, because she also had learned about the decree of blood properties and participated in the blood horror and put the new law of blood enmity above the old one of blood friendship . . .

But Hilde already nodded: "Yes," and sobbed a little again.

There was a table in front of the sofa on which they were sitting, and on the table stood Hilde's sewing kit; and in the sewing kit there was a used razor blade which Herr Wolff had given his daughter to rip seams. Sophia took the razor blade, cut herself in the ball of her left thumb without turning a hair, and handed the blade to her friend; and Hilde likewise cut herself in the ball of her left thumb, but she had to shut her eyes tight and press her lips together. Then they joined their thumbs, cut to cut, and pressed them together in the rhythm of their loud heartbeats to pump the blood out of their joined wounds and let it flow into the other's body.

After ten minutes—they had heard that a blood transfusion takes approximately that long—Sophia ordered their hands held still and close together until the bleeding would stop. Then they separated the sticky thumbs, and the delicious pain caused by severing the cuts was like the fulfillment and consummation of their childishly mystical marriage. They sat side by side, silently and without looking at each other. Hilde sobbed a little now and then, but Sophia smiled, mysteriously triumphant. Then, their eyes meeting in silent agreement, they rose, went to the bathroom, washed their hands and put sticking plaster over the wounds. Sophia's enthusiastic suggestion that they continue wearing a sticking plaster over the cuts even after they had healed, as a memento of the supreme seal, was rejected by Hilde as impracticable. They did however inscribe the date of the sealing ceremony on each other's plasters, not with blood as Sophia had requested—Hilde rejected also this request because it would have necessitated another injury—but with red ink.

The one and only and extreme step had been taken, and the little girl Sophia was now pervaded by the strangely floating and proud sensation of having done something that in her mind reached the limits of the conceivable, consequently the limits of human capacity. But the deed also reached the limits which separated the good from the wicked—no, it was at once divinely good and devilishly wicked, depending on whether one looked at it from the point of view of blood friendship or blood enmity; and yet it was calming, reassuring, it produced that floating pride that was well-nigh invulnerable, that could not be shaken by the school-day separation from Hilde, nor by the school's adherence to the enemy camp, nor by the uncheerful parental home with Hans as commandant. Not even her brother terrified her, although the deed had been directed most passionately against him and was too extreme, too mighty in itself, for her not to reveal it to him during their next quarrel.

When, not many days later, on a warm June evening after supper Hans ordered her to his room for a confidential talk, she knew at once that now the time had come.

"If you want something from me, I'm afraid you'll have to take the trouble to come to my room," she said, walking out of the room ahead of him, calmly and with floating pride. Dr. Moeller looked at his wife, and his eyelids began to flutter.

"What I was going to tell you"—Frau Moeller hastily began telling a story whose liveliness and length were not proportionate to its insignificant contents.

Entering Sophia's small room, Hans first looked at the bedside table between the door and the bed. Hilde's photograph was still standing there. With lightning speed he threw it on the floor, crushed glass and frame with his boot, picked up the picture and tore it to pieces. "So," he said, and was amazed that she did not intervene with howls and lamentations, "that's that."

"There are other and better pictures of her," she said calmly; but her eyes were green with hatred.

"Now it's getting serious," he announced.

"I can see what you mean by getting serious," she said.

"I have been informed," he said, "that you went swimming today with the Jew girl in the Jewish swimming pool."

"That happens to be exactly correct," she said, "and it wasn't the first time, either; you know very well that the Jews are not allowed to bathe where Aryans get rid of their filth."

"It's immaterial where the Jews get rid of their filth," he said. "The point is that you had the cheek to go swimming in the Jewish pool."

"And, pray, where should I go swimming?" she asked.

"Where you belong!" he shouted.

"Ha!" she exclaimed, "will you tell me where I do belong?"

"Have you lost your reason completely?" he asked in the falsetto of his breaking voice.

"I thought you said that one doesn't need his reason, and besides I didn't lose my reason, I didn't lose much at all—but you lost me, you and your gang, and that's what I wanted!"

Hans opened his mouth, but he couldn't utter a sound.

"Yes," she said, "there's nothing you can do about it; you can go to the devil with your blood properties. I can do as I please now and I belong in the Jewish swimming pool because I have Hilde Wolff's blood in me now and she has mine, and you will say I defiled my blood, but I wanted to defile it and it makes me feel fine . . ."

She smiled proudly and raised her hand to show him the sticking plaster with the red inscription, the memento of the supreme seal. "What you see written there on the plaster is the date," she explained. "And it is written with her blood," she lied.

Never before had she seen her brother so pale or his nose so pointed. The boy did not say a word, but his chin grew bigger and bigger, he was nothing but chin, pointed nose and icy blue eyes; he detached his shoulder belt without haste.

"Oh, I see. Now the 'putting down' starts . . ." Sophia whispered and looked around for a weapon. But she found none. She found only a cambric handkerchief with a lace border and her name embroidered on it; it happened to be a handmade present from Hilde, and she stuffed the dainty material between her teeth, protecting her face with her arm.

"What was that?" the father asked in the dining room and put down his teacup.

"There's nothing the matter," said the mother and continued talking, with restless eyes.

"What was that?" the father asked a second time, more softly; he got up and went to the door.

Frau Moeller interrupted herself and said slowly, "Don't interfere, Friedrich."

He stood before the door and his head was lowered. From Sophia's room came the boisterous step of his son.

"Don't interfere!" Frau Moeller warned.

The hobnailed boots crashed along the hall to the door of the apartment, past the dining room. The door slammed shut, the father started. Outside, the boots crashed down the stairs.

The father went into the hall and softly knocked on Sophia's door.

"Little one . . ." he said half-asking, half-entreating.

"I am already in bed, Papa," Sophia answered, and she struggled bravely for a voice which would not give her away.

"Sleep well," whispered the father and went back. But before he entered the dining room again, he stopped and pressed his fists against his fluttering eyelids, and he shuddered.

3

And yet, the chin of Hans, the Hitler youth, receded again. He was a squad leader now, endowed with a strictly circumscribed power domain, subjected to strictly echeloned superior powers; he kicked those below him and was kicked from above, it had to be so and it was good and just. It was an extensive war game, so serious that one had to set one's teeth and pull one's bones together when the body threatened to give out; one had to take oneself by the collar and buck up when occasionally nauseated or when the slightest misgivings arose about the increasingly lopsided relation of the primary play service to the secondary school work which accommodated itself most obligingly to the various ranks of the play service. All in all it was the best and simplest of all possible worlds, perspicuously put together; it was a mighty flight of steps, inexorably leading higher and higher to the highest, the Führer, the god who was always visible and audible through his likeness and his written and spoken word, and not infrequently in his own sacredly sullen and hoarsely exploding person, amidst the storming Heils.

And yet, even this clear order of his world, cleansed of any question and doubt, could not relieve the boy of certain experiences and anxieties with which he was not able to cope because they fell outside the catechism of his service religion and, therefore, in a sense were not of this world at all. They eluded him in this pathless and uncharted Beyond because they surged up from within himself, from his innermost self, where apparently his rank of squad leader no longer counted. This increased his helplessness and drove his chin back—drove him to the father, the helper in need who himself stood beyond, and not in, this world.

His sister's deadly sin, incidentally, was not among the experiences and anxieties that, so to speak, made him eat humble pie. In that matter he had known how to help himself, not by administering, in his first wrath, the severe beating she so well deserved, but by getting to the bottom of the thing once he had calmed down and regained his reason, and by determining the extent of the damage inflicted on Sophia's blood. He submitted the case to the race hygienist or "eugenist" on the staff of the Hitler Youth, though he did so in an impersonal way, posing the question as a hypothetical problem. The expert's unseemly amusement over the question immediately made Hans suspect what he then finally learned: that the act of blood mixing was objectively harmless "romantic nonsense" which could neither alter nor corrupt nor even taint the racial qualities of the blood. This verdict was a relief for Hans, but it was also painful; for how could he explain to his sister that she had deserved the thrashing only subjectively and not objectively, without compromising himself and without relaxing the radicalism of his blood doctrine? Besides he could not banish the memory of her mysterious silence and of the moving gesture with which she rose uncomplainingly after he had let go of her, the way she showed him the handkerchief she had bitten to shreds as a sort of receipt, and hobbled to bed. In short, he shrank from bringing the embarrassing matter up again, postponed the explanation from one day to the next, until the summer vacation came along and Sophia, to his astonishment without protest, departed with her class for the Oldenburg country to help with the harvesting. And by then Hans had become fully preoccupied with his own troubles.

It seemed that the reference to deadly sin, which had been meant for his sister, could equally apply to himself. But for him there was no amused father confessor of the Party who was selling the indulgence of "romantic nonsense." Had not the Party itself suddenly declared as sinful what up to this moment had been the mystic consecration of the boys' organization, a sacred discipline of the body bound by the play service to the duty of obedience and surrender? Alas, the Party declared as sinful something that Hans, the Hitler Youth, had always considered as sinful in his clean and badgeless innermost self. And who was the visible expression of the Party, the competent highest authority that proclaimed the new law, the prohibition and the new directive which was again terrifying to the boy, sinful and repulsive? The Bannführer? Yes, the Bannführer; but not the same one, not the handsome, terribly nice, helpful and yet horrible young man who at the age of only nineteen already had the rank of a regimental commander and who suddenly disappeared, suddenly was on earth no more, whose name was accursed and no longer to be mentioned after June 30, 1934. Hans suffered great spiritual distress, he was helpless amidst his experiences and anxieties—and he asked the father who stood outside of this world for a confidential talk.

The former Juvenile Judge looked at his son and recognized that this time the boy who stood before him was not the protagonist of the new state-youth that put fathers under tutelage, but a bashful, fifteen-year old boy who didn't know where to turn— Yes, Dr. Moeller was vividly reminded of his former office which had daily confronted him with wayward or fallen adolescents. It did not frighten him that he faced a boy who was not only helpless but conscious of his guilt; it had been a source of deep chagrin to the father that his son, wrapped in the splendor of his uniformed mission, had so far shown no trace of repentance at his stupidly domineering, presumptuous behavior; and if the boy should now repent only his guilt toward the child Sophia, no matter for what stupidly autocratic reasons he may have beaten her, it would have been the first joy for the father in a long time.

Hans looked into space, his brow wrinkled by his mental effort; he didn't know how to begin. The burden which weighted him down was not easily put into words; but even without this intractability to expression, it was so intimately connected with the sacred and secret mystery of the service that it seemed hardly possible to separate the two. After all, he wanted to betray his inner feelings—not the Führer—to his father. He shook his head dejectedly.

"It is terribly difficult, Papa."

"How would it be," said the father, "if you put on another shirt, Hans. You still have your other shirts, haven't you?"

Hans looked up startled and saw the man who had turned gray early in life and from whom he had his eyes, his nose, ears lying close to the head, his narrow mouth, his spare facial structure; but instead of seeing that he was the son of his father, he saw a face wholly different from those he was wont to see in his world, a different love and a different wisdom.

That's very smart about the shirt, he thought, it might be easier to talk without this shirt.

He hurried out of the room and was back in an amazingly short time. He wore a white, short-sleeved sport shirt that was somewhat too tight but revealed his well-built chest and made him appear at once younger and lovelier. He was an ephebus in the first splendor of manhood and it was now that the father was frightened by a vague apprehension.

Hans did not stand in landser fashion with straddling legs, but leaned gracefully against his father's desk with an open and at the same time dejected smile. "Papa," he asked, "is it possible for one of my age to have suffered a crack?"

"I don't know what you mean by a crack," the father answered seriously, "but generally speaking it is precisely at your age that one is exposed to all sorts of strains and stresses which may be dangerous, though they will rarely cause irreparable damage."

"But a crack is when something has cracked inside one, when it's broken in two," said Hans.

"You fear, then, that you may have been damaged for life, my boy?"

"Sometimes, Papa."

"When for instance don't you fear it?"

"When I am on duty."

"On duty? You see, Hans, I don't quite know what that is, your duty. At times I believe that you are always on duty, even here at home. When, then, have you the time to fear that something may be awry in you?"

"For instance at night, Papa."

"But is it not as good as certain, my son, that you have suffered this supposed or real damage on duty or through your duty?"

"It is certain, Papa."

"Could you not, therefore, put matters right again by quitting the service which imposes these duties on you?"

Hans' back stiffened and he did not lean against the desk any more. "What does that mean, Father?"

"It means, Hans, that the damage may possibly disappear if you give up the service in which or through which you have been damaged. And it might mean still more—just let me finish, my boy—it may be that you have misjudged the real connection between service and damage and that the service itself is the damage, do you understand that?—That the idea you serve is your crack."

Hans had tried impetuously to interrupt, as if to prevent his father from finishing his sentence. Now he dropped his arms in deep disappointment. "Wrong, wrong, wrong, Father. Why do you have to start talking politics that belong to the ice age! You are on the wrong track . . ."

"My dear boy," said Dr. Moeller, and his eyes fluttered a little, "it is up to you to put me on the right track."

"Is it possible," Hans asked with haste and determination, and he looked like one who takes a start to jump off, "Father, is it possible to sin with one's body?"

"Most assuredly," Dr. Moeller answered. "And I am convinced that you have already given yourself the answer to that question. But there are so-called sins of youth which physiologically are not much more than developing puberty blowing off steam under excessive pressure and which lose their dangerous aspects the moment you recognize them as sinful. Is that what you mean?"

"No," said Hans and looked in his father's eyes, firmly and urgently.

Dr. Moeller did not speak for a while and lowered his eyes to his hands which he folded. Hans also looked at his father's folded hands and saw that the heads of the fingernails were bloodless, so firmly were they pressed against the knuckles.

"Yes, Hans," the father said softly, "that is indeed a sin, because it is a sin against nature. But since you have come to me and since you are in distress, in well justified distress, and since you call your sin a sin, all is not lost yet by any means and you can achieve what one can achieve only through sensibleness and self-criticism—you can achieve renunciation."

"Renunciation . . ." Hans repeated slowly; it might have been a question, too.

"May I ask you, Hans, how long you have already felt it to be a sin?"

"A long time already, ever since the beginning—but you see, it was regarded as a duty . . ."

"As a duty?" the father exclaimed.

"Obedience means: with body and soul!" the son exclaimed.

"Obedience to your superiors?"

"Of course!"

"And as a superior you yourself demanded the same obedience from your subordinates?"

"Of course!"

"And you knew that it was a sin?"

"No, I was only afraid it might be, and I saw it differently, and when I'm on duty I am not myself; that's the first thing one has to learn. And that's not the question, Father; we are getting into an argument again!"

"We are not getting into an argument, because it's a question of your sin!"

"No, Father, not sin, but suddenly my duty turned into a crack and was a sin and my superior to whom I owed obedience was a criminal—and now I ask you, Papa, what am I?"

"Not a criminal, my child," said the father leaning over the desk and taking his son's hand. "Formerly, at least, it was only the seducer who was punished, not the one who was seduced."

"That's different now," Hans said softly. "Now all get punished . . ."

"And what is the punishment, Hans?"

"You call it: renunciation," Hans said softly.

"Then you didn't understand what I meant by it, Hans. That could never be a punishment; it is the rational and moral solution of the problem, the human way back from aberration."

"But what then is this renunciation?" cried Hans in sheer despair.

"Renunciation of that which is against nature, is the acceptance of that which is natural—extremely simple, Hans."

"In other words, going with girls!" Hans said throatily.

"If you wish to call it that—yes."

Hans slowly raised his shoulders and the father saw to his astonishment that the boy's eyes were filled with tears. "That's what it is called, Papa," he whispered with a choked voice, "and if I had known that you are really saying exactly the same as the new law . . ."

"My dear lad," the father broke in smiling and firmly held his hand, "this law is as old as humanity and is in you because you are human and about to become a man . . ."

"You see, Papa, now we have come to the point," Hans whispered and blushed deeply. "The only thing that's in me is disgust—and that's just what I mean by the crack . . ."

"Why don't you give yourself time," the father pleaded. "Let time work for you, let time decide if there is a crack or not . . ."

"But they don't give you any time, Papa, they simply command!"

"That, too, would be a command contrary to nature and need not be obeyed—you have had your experience now with commands against nature and you must have gotten over them already, otherwise you would not have come to me."

"But what if I am simply unable to believe that time can help me, Papa?"

Now the father released his son's hand and gave judgment, stern like a judge: "Then you will have to live as if there were no help for you. Then you must renounce the sin which you recognize as such and keep away from the one you don't recognize. You will see that it is possible to live between renunciation and acceptance."

Hans slowly nodded assent. "What sort of life will that be for me," he asked pensively, "a hard life or a poor one?"

The Juvenile Judge was strangely moved by this question. "Why do you ask this?" he asked hesitantly.

"Because they tell us that we are leading a hard life, but a rich one."

"Do you believe that?"

The son said nothing, went up to his father and gave him a kiss on the forehead. He had not done that in a very long time. But then, with a subdued "Thank you, Papa!" he clicked his heels as always.

When the father was alone he did the same thing that he had

done recently in the hallway between Sophia's room and the dining room: he pressed his fists against his eyes and he shuddered.

4

The times also took hold of Sophia—how could it be otherwise. This partisan time was a mighty loudspeaker, its self-possessed pronouncements commanded all ears and penetrated all brains, whether they wanted it or not; and even if they only grew dull, only got used to the clamor of this time, they had already fallen victim to it. This time which did not stand still, but ran, identified itself for all ears with the new state power which, in deafening presumption, called itself "the movement." The listeners became bondsmen and moved along in the living compulsion of time: they grew older.

The children grew older, Sophia grew older and with the passing of time she learned what her brother had not dared disclose to her; that her supreme seal had been romantic nonsense, child's play deserving no more than a passing smile. She learned more still; she learned to accept what she could not refuse any more than the air she was breathing. At one time Hilde Wolff had been securely hers through the supreme seal, and she rather enjoyed going with her class to work merrily in the fields during vacations. She derived a roguish delight from her own, invisible, exceptional uncleanness and perhaps she already felt slightly bored with the sobbing grievousness of her bosom friend and blood companion. Gradually then and extremely painlessly the compulsion of time set in, the movement of life, the growing older; they saw each other less frequently and took it sensibly, after all they were children no longer. All at once the whole class was put in up-to-date uniforms and the leader of the class, Sophia Moeller, also was in uniform of course; she thought herself attractive in the uniform of the Association of German Girls because they all thought themselves attractive, and now she saw Hilde Wolff still more rarely, at first from an understandable and thoroughly tactful considerateness and then for the simple reason that she was at home ever more rarely. Certainly, she still loved Hilde Wolff, but already like a relic, always with girlish romanticism deserving no more than a passing smile, somewhat like a curl kept in a rarely opened case.

But it went beyond that, beyond the painless acceptance of the times, beyond the painless separation and estrangement from her childhood friend; for time runs and tolerates no lingering, and these times of movement made Sophia move on and drove her a long way, until she noticed that time had been running a circle and that as an adult she stood exactly where she had started from as a child: at the rebellious passion of the supreme seal. She had to start all over again and had to go through the school of this time until she graduated to hating this time.

The merry work in the fields became the Labor Service and that was as though a heavy door had fallen shut—all of a sudden the girls were stuck in the educational prison that was to turn them into the state youth. That displeased all of them, not only Sophia. But there was no opportunity left to express this displeasure; the supervision was complete, discontent was outlawed and already made senseless. For immediately there began the exorcism of the I and its replacement by the We. The I was punishable as such, a remnant of the Jewish democracy; the mere word was egotistical and the enemy of this time which made short shrift of its enemies. In the face of such a threat and of an organization possessing the power to turn each threat into action, none of the girls dared to cling to the I, all the more so because they had but scant acquaintance with it.

But the We—the new, sacred, glorious and victorious We—was the irresistible pronoun of the new time, of the new movement, of the people's community, and included even the Führer and the semi-goddess and woman leader, a lady who required violent adoration and whose name was Frau Scholz-Klinck. Yet, even as it was easy to pronounce the pronoun and to proclaim it often, in loud and shrill voices, so it was made hard for the girls to be the We, with such cleverly devised severity, trials and pressure as if the mass product to be obtained posed at the same time a packing problem—like that of a packing plant with a shortage of containers. It was part of their education for the girls never to be alone, never without supervision, without the stratifying, sorting and repressing hand; to make life oppressive, confining and compact was pedagogically necessary, as was the suppression of all individuality, of individual activity, individual speech and, as far as possible, individual thought. For individuality impinged on the mysteriously precious space belonging to collectivity; and even the rigorous exorcism of the spirit or of spiritual development and its replacement by the collective spirit, which made word and thought march in step, seemed to be first of all a packing method. Only one single individual right was left to the pupil and was at the same time declared a duty: the right and duty of every individual to spy on every other individual and to inform the authorities whenever there was anything to inform about, be it ever so paltry an act of wilfulness. Was this a decent thing to do? Well, it was logical and at the same time educational, furthering the interests and the glory of the great We. For, you see, children, if the last wretched remnants of the little I can still yield a complete Judas, how outrageously and abysmally indecent must be the whole, stuffed out I of which you have been freed!

Sophia suffered as silently and acutely as the others. The difference however was that she did not suffer without hope of escape. Young people living under such crafty repression cannot very well escape into thought because they have no experience in thinking and because their thoughts lie on their tongues which are tied. So they let it go and accept the injunction against thinking, because in its scope and effect it parallels the injunction against free speech. What would be the sense for them to build thoughts into empty space like a bridge having no bank on the other side, therefore having no support? But it did make sense to endure their sorrow, as prescribed; for, lo and behold, very soon they were no longer conscious of living in sorrow, repression and confinement, and they lost themselves in the mass because there was nothing else to do and it was decidedly best that way.

Sophia, however, had a hold on the other bank, and could at least build a thought bridge. She even had the choice of escaping in her thoughts to her father or to Hilde Wolff. Both had to suffer from this time, both were excluded from the compulsory collectivity, and she loved them both. She chose to build the thought bridge to her friend because it was a continuation of her defiance, a clandestine return to the secret pact in spite of all prohibitions, and because her dear, silent father had to be treated with consideration and could not even receive her thoughts without his eyelids beginning to flutter.

Even this mental return to Hilde Wolff was an escape. Oh, what a relief it was to close her eyes and ears at night in the dormitory, to coax a tired body to postpone its badly needed sleep for another quarter hour, to sit on the Victorian sofa with her friend and unload her heart of its troubles, to accuse, to sneer, to jeer, to foam, and to leave not a particle of good in the finished collective day—oh, what a relief! But Sophia soon observed that it was much more than relief, that it was resistance merely to collect her obstreperous thoughts, that there could be resistance against the irresistible, perhaps even immunity against the compulsory contagion. When she realized this, her thought bridge no longer sufficed.

She began to write to her friend and each letter was somewhat like a heroic deed, written in toilets without doors, at night under her bedcover with the aid of a diminutive flashlight attached to a pencil, or brazenly during study hours under the very eyes of the supervisor who believed that she was writing a composition in her notebook, and yet Sophia had in that notebook some loose, carefully inserted pages which alternated with the assigned theme in remarkable mental elasticity; one page each of glorification and of defamation of the movement. Each letter was contraband and excitingly smuggled out of the camp, and secretly transmitted through a reliable peasant girl who believed herself to be nothing more than a *postillon d'amour*. And each letter became a greater crime against the sacred collectivity; from accusation, mockery, and derision of her compulsory service, Sophia advanced to ever more penetrating criticism. She criticized the educational principle which emphasized the mass spirit and deliberately induced imbecility; she criticized her companions who let their souls be packaged and mutilated in the sole hope that some day they would no longer be clay but potters; she criticized the numberless species of Führers, special clay in the hands of competent superior potters, with no other feeling left in them but that of fear, with no other remnant of the I left in them but that of the Judas complex which faithfully climbed up the ladder with them. And from this criticism Sophia advanced to the outright attack on the principle of this time which was at once Pharaoh's pyramid and a penitentiary.

Hilde Wolff never answered. Well and good, it was smart and

prudent not to answer, it was easy to see that this correspondence necessarily had to be unilateral; just the same, Hilde's complete silence was a little offending and wasn't necessary either; it would have been enough to send a postal card now and then with whatever trite words of remembrance. It was not that her letters went out into emptiness—Hilde was still around, Sophia knew it from her father's letters which customarily ended with the stereotyped postcript: "The sad neighbors send you their greetings." At least her friend sent her greetings, and the father's monotonous refrain about the neighbors' sadness may have been an indirect excuse for Hilde's silence.

But one day a message arrived from Hilde, a miserable scrap of paper written in a disguised and harassed hand: "Please please please don't write any more!" And the threefold "Please" was written in ever larger letters, just as, in the days of the silent pictures, the tone volume of a scream was rendered by the size of the letters. The signature consisted of an oblique "H" that gave the impression of collapsing, and the whole thing was a riddle, though a frightening one. For the date of the postmark did not tell Sophia anything. November, 1938, was nothing unusual to her, she knew nothing, no, she knew nothing; time had built the enclosure of the collectivity around her, the deeply hated fence against which she stormed, bravely and expertly; she was taken aback and furious that Hilde should strike the letter weapon from her hand, and she suspected that the crying and collapsing "H" must have suffered a great hurt: but what happened outside did not penetrate to her. And her father's next letter ignored her cautious question about the neighbors, or answered it with the dubious postscript: "The sad neighbors send you their greetings."

To be sure, when she went home for the Christmas vacation she learned what had happened in November, and she also saw the gutted synagogues and Jewish business establishments, and she saw Uncle Wolff who had been released from the concentration camp only a few days before and who recognized her with difficulty and had no inclination at all to speak with her. He had grown old, bent, distrustful, and obstinate—very obstinate, Hilde whispered, for he would not emigrate, under any conditions, because he could not abandon his wife. His wife had died when Hilde was born, and had been lying in her grave alone for sixteen years now. But that was just the point: Daddy Wolff had visited her in the cemetery every Sunday morning for the last sixteen years, each time renewing his promise that she would not always lie there alone, and contemplating the marble tombstone on which he had carefully provided space for his own name.

Hilde was always whispering when she was with her friend, and rarely looked at her. There was something morose, not to say hostile, in her set and already somewhat hard face, that was reminiscent of her father; and after each sentence she looked over her shoulders to the right and left, although in back of her there was only the gracefully curved back of the Victorian sofa. And she didn't laugh when Sophia observed that this urge to glance over shoulders was not by any means a Jewish movement, but the new movement of the German people. Perhaps it wasn't such a good joke or a tactful one; Hilde stiffened her head, distended the nostrils of her thin, straight nose and closed her eyes for a moment as if she were about to swallow something distasteful.

Then she whispered on—how their apartment had been searched three times and how she had been afraid that another of Sophia's letters might have arrived and been intercepted; she told of the terrible moment when they had come to get her father in the gray of dawn, and how he had asked with persistent monotony: "Why please? Why please?" until he was struck in the face twice, once with the palm and once with the back of the hand, and how he had been silent with shame, with frightful shame, with a never to be forgotten expression of shame—not of anger or fear or pain.

Hilde whispered a motley and disorganized pellmell about the bad times in general: that they couldn't keep servants or a car or a telephone, that her father had long ago been forced to give up his chocolate factory, that they were not allowed to buy oranges and that when they got some anyway they stealthily put the peels in the Moellers' garbage can, that they rarely had milk or butter because the milk and butter were all gone when they lined up in front of the dairy at the prescribed hour, the Jew hour—yes, that they would soon have to wear the star of David on the street, the yellow star!

Again she fell silent with distended nostrils as if Sophia had cracked another tactless joke, closed her eyes, opened them wide and looked at her friend— What a look that was! And she whispered: "You are all so terribly mean to us!"

"We?" Sophia flared up, and immediately she was frightened by this "We" and hastily retreated from the collective word. "But not I, Hilde dear. I have to suffer in my way just like you, I am also in a sort of concentration camp, don't you know . . ."

"In your way!" cried Hilde; no, she whispered no longer and suddenly had hot cheeks. "How can you compare your way with my way! For you it's easy! You should talk!"

"For me it's easy?" Sophia asked in boundless astonishment. "But don't you know, didn't I write you everything? Surely you must have read my letters . . ."

"Partly."

"Partly . . ." Sophia repeated slowly. "What do you mean, partly?"

"I mean that I read your first letter entirely, only scanned the later ones, and at last burned the letters immediately without reading them."

"Hilde," Sophia whispered. "Hilde, why?"

"Why? Good God, there are so many reasons: first of all, of course, fear! Imagine what would happen to me and to poor papa or what would happen to you if one of these letters should be caught by the Gestapo or by your brother or only by the block warden! And mixed in with the fear, naturally, was my anger that you should endanger us so thoughtlessly— Yes, and in addition to that I had the feeling that I was nothing but your dumping ground, the only place where you could comfortably get rid of your stories. And finally, my dear, your stories really don't concern me at all, just as little as what I am telling you about myself concerns you—if you forgive me for saying it!"

Was that so wrong and unjust? Had it not been a consciously one-sided correspondence, unconscious only of the danger which it might bring to the recipient, the Jew girl holding in her hand the attack on the sacred collectivity of the people? And had not Sophia said to herself while Hilde was whispering about her woes: she talks only about herself, and what is there that's so bad about the butter and the orange peels; when I think of my penitentiary; and after all she isn't wearing the yellow star yet, but I have had to wear the collective dress for a long time; and even about the beating I could tell an entirely different tale if it hadn't happened to old Wolff, but to Hilde instead—the way it happens to the girls in camp whether they ask, "Why please?" or not . . .

How did matters stand with these two blood companions? Things were at an end between them, not because they had grown apart now, each harping on her own way of living and suffering and finally not understanding or listening to the other. No, there were declarations and protestations aplenty during the remaining days of vacation and finally a tacit agreement to refrain from any mention of the times and of the different sources of woe, and that was a somewhat melancholy tight-rope act of their friendship. But it was at an end between them because they were not to see each other again. It would be idle to ask whether it was fortunate or unfortunate for them not to have known it.

Sophia returned to the corral. There were no more contraband letters she could write and she asked herself if she hadn't exaggerated her father's need for consideration; it seemed to her in retrospect as if the silent man's eyes had rested on her with a certain expectation, as if they looked deep into her and only needed her affirmation that it was thus and that they had not been mistaken. Very well, she could do something with this appearance also in retrospect, and as a sort of substitute for letters she could mentally talk with her father as she would have liked to talk with him, though during vacations she neglected to do so or at best did so only in a lame and embarrassed manner. Now they both were more talkative and less considerate, and the father's colorless letters, punctually sent off every first of the month and containing the inevitable postscript, trailed limping and amusingly senseless behind the exchange of thoughts, and their dull cautiousness was not enlivening Sophia's knowledge of things which happened outside her enclosure.

She knew nothing, no, she knew nothing; and then war broke out. Very well and quite natural; war had arrived, the exultation of the collectivity was great or at least greatly displayed, the customary Siegheils were appropriately increased, everything ran smoothly, and the self-taught little "I," named Sophia, concentrated on hating the war because it became the piercing shriek of the collectivity: We and the war—We ride against England—And tomorrow the world! Not a thing was new for Sophia and for the state youth: not the time-possessed We, not the song that had to be bawled on each of the thousand marches, at least when passing through a village—and not the war. Now they were in it, it had gone so far. How could it be otherwise with this war game that had long since become a terribly serious play-service requiring obedience with body and soul! Only the older people outside, beyond the confines of the corral, had believed in the Führer's rantings about peace, had sworn by the magnificent, peaceful extortions of the war game, and were speechless with dreadful surprise. The young state mass, however, product of pressure and packing, had never heard the god and the gods ranting about peace. It had only heard them, and itself, shouting Siegheil, and was not speechless, but continued rhythmically to shout the same indifferent, meaningless word.

The war brought no changes for Sophia. To be sure, brother Hans volunteered for army service although at nineteen he could have stayed out of it another year, could have taken two more semesters in law school; he could even have finished his studies and gotten his doctor's degree before joining the army, if he had wanted to. But he didn't want to, and volunteered because he was a soldier after all, a graduate of the long war game that never stopped; for when at eighteen he outgrew the Hitler Youth, with honor and distinction, the doors to the two armed formations of the Party already stood open imperiously demanding his entry, and he had chosen or had been forced to choose the SS, on account of his honors and distinctions. However, the volunteer did not join one of the SS battle formations, but the Wehrmacht, and this new change of uniforms was the only surprise for Sophia in an otherwise quite natural course of events, a surprise which led to mental dialogues with her far-away father. Hans himself did not explain his choice, least of all to his sister whom he hardly ever saw any more and probably hardly knew.

Did the war bring no change for Sophia? Well, in her corral she had to live with extreme caution, self-restraint and dissemblance; for at the end of the state-youth manufacturing process she was promised freedom, or at least release from the inner to the outer world of compulsion. As an excellent student she was sure to pass the several subject examinations necessary for her graduation; but it was not so certain that she would also pass the political character test. This test, in the form of a rigorous communal work service, was a last hurdle for the chosen few who were otherwise qualified to enter a university. Sophia had to set her teeth and to keep under control every word, every move, even the rebelliousness of her thoughts; the goal justified her uncommon effort. The goal was the university—the word had not yet been done away with, and still contained the universe, the extreme, unbelievably rapturous antithesis of the corral. She too wanted to study law, she was drawn to it by her love for her father, by her love for justice which she did not know but surely had to be the antithesis of injustice and must be contained in law. And her father's monthly letters now seemed to bear the fruits of the mental dialogues; instead of saying nothing, they spoke of his daughter's goal, of his joy over her decision to study law, they spoke of Munich and of his old college friend there, a law teacher who was highly esteemed, both personally and professionally. Dear, quiet, sagacious father! Had he perhaps sent his son Hans to Munich, to his highly esteemed friend and professor? Oh, no, the SS man had begun to study law in Berlin . . .

How sordid a life was this, driving toward the goal with lies, hypocrisy and grotesque dissemblance! Sophia was steeped in all the mysteries of collective life. But so were her competitors, and besides, prize students of Judas lore that they were, they knew the useful effect of their first commandment which says: slay your neighbor. Thus there developed among the graduating girls, beneath orthodox observance of the rites of comradeship, a silently murderous struggle of each against all, a spying for the weak spots in the armor of faith, auscultation of every word, however harmless, the dagger ever ready for the death blow. Since Sophia was not out to slay her neighbor, she could concentrate on defense, and since she knew all the tricks and pitfalls and could rattle off the words of salvation in blameless, unshakable indifference and in the racial halo of her blondeness, she did in fact escape being slain. And during the dreaded recreation hour which was one of the most infamous character tests, with the camp goddess present in the role of comrade, Sophia would say something like this, holding her chin high and her shoulders straight: "Yes, I am happy and grateful that I am permitted to share in so valuable an experience of communal living and to look my leader straight in the eye."

When she said such things, she knew that the staff girl who sat next to the leader and kept her head steadily lowered to take down the whole conversation in shorthand under the table, was recording an expression which would be a credit to the character file "Moeller Sophia."

Did the war bring no change? But what about these doctrines of "womanhood" and "procreative duty"? It was horrible enough merely to rattle off such things, but now they suddenly closed in on the graduating girls with unconcealed demands. Only lasciviousness still wore a disguise: the old watchword of obedience with body and soul. There were also other well-known disguises: solstice celebrations with all the ceremonial of the new and the old mythology, with parades, addresses, raising of flags and Siegheils, with fire blessings, stuffy old dances that had to be danced with bare feet, flowers in the hair, the girls' bodies draped in mere veils, with swimming in the moonlight and with ceremonious to-do, mystic and lascivious. Such celebrations took place every year, and by and large they confined themselves to the erotic play of a state youth still in the fledgling stage. But this first war solstice celebration, under the sun of fabulous military triumphs and coinciding almost to the day with the capitulation of France, had been announced in the jargon of the preliminary instructions, as "mobilization of womanhood," as a state-sponsored, solemn orgy of hero worship and hero procreation. For this time it was not boys and girls of the state youth mystically playing with one another, but young men and young women, that male youth which was riding against England and tomorrow against the whole world, and these graduating girls who were to be submissive to them, as a character test, and who were to bear future world rulers to the world conquerors, as a triumph of breeding. And Sophia was on her guard. Her father had just written her that Hans was in Bremen on a short leave to say good-by to his parents before going into action with his Panzer regiment. "The farewell will not be hard for him," the father wrote, "for he is far away from us even when he is here." Sophia invited her brother to attend the solstice celebration and to say good-by to her. And he came, a taciturn future conqueror, a cool brother, but perhaps a protection.

He did not protect her or did not want to protect her or wanted to seek his own pleasure. He disappeared when it began to get dangerous. Nothing was easier than to disappear; the June night invited it and so did the park of the Oldenburg manorial castle which belonged to the Party and had become headquarters for the Girls' Labor Service, and so did the fields beyond under the silver moon. But it was baffling why Sophia believed that Hans wanted to surrender her to her fate and why she didn't realize that the girls were there also to serve Hans. Had she told him that she had invited him as a chaperon? She had not dared tell him that, and their conversation had been halting, as it would be between people who have nothing to say to each other. And why should the handsome young man sit with his sister and not choose a girl for himself? And how could she have thought that he had come for her sake and for her protection and not because of the girls? And yet, Sophia was disappointed, was angry with her brother and afraid without him.

Promptly a young man and future hero appeared, approached, clicked his heels and asked: "What do you say, sweetie?" There was something incongruous in the heel-clicking and the bold offer, and Sophia looked at her suitor, a mushy man who in his efforts to impart a military bearing to his long arms and legs achieved a storklike stiffness of movement. A similar effort could be detected in his face which was immature, loosely joined and droll like a young puppy's; struggling with droll embarrassment against the painful duty of having to be a bold suitor. Sophia lost her fear.

First of all she piloted her escort to the lawn below the terrace of the castle. The lawn was lighted by glaring searchlights, and on the terrace sat the staff which had established something like control stations there with those sharp-eyed staff girls who had their shorthand pads on their knees, but their eyes everywhere. And she said to the young puppy, "If you do insist on calling me sweetie, why for God's sake don't you put your arm around me!" And he did so, at once stiffly and mushily. Thus they walked across the lighted lawn into the dark park.

It was very dark; the suitor cautiously squeezed her arm and his fingers got restless, apparently from indecision whether to move up or down her arm. He decided to move downwards and seized her hand, and his hand was wet, and he didn't know at all what he should say. Sophia who had an unpleasant sensation from the wet hand, maneuvered her handkerchief in-between and asked: "Do you suffer from damp hands?"

"Unfortunately," he whispered, and one could hear from his voice how he blushed.

"Then please," she said and relinquished the handkerchief to him.

He dried his hands energetically, forgot to give the handkerchief back to her, hardly dared to touch her any more, and confessed: "Even in the plane my hands are wet, but then I wear gloves."

It turned out that he attended a school for pursuit pilots, and since Sophia displayed a lively interest in pursuit-pilot schools, he started off, deeply relieved, on a well-nigh fluent factual discussion of pursuit-pilot schools, pursuit flights and of the various types of pursuit planes. Thus they walked through the park into the blue-silver of the moon night above the fields, turned back as the shop talk petered out, plunged back into the darkness of the park and now, entirely silent again, they heard whisperings of another kind in the bushes.

"Rest a little?" he asked throatily.

"At your service," she said, and they lay down. That is, Sophia sat down with her back against a tree. "Now I am all agog," she said.

"About what?"

"About the pursuit flight."

"Pardon me; but what do you mean?" he asked with strange formality, military formality.

"I mean your power dive into a declaration of love. Why don't you get going?"

"Good God, sweetie . . ."

"Is that all?"

"Tell me. What's your name?" asked the suitor.

"Sweetie," said Sophia.

"Then I suppose you are not interested in my name either?"

"No, I am only interested to learn why we are lying here."

"Do you really want that?" he whispered, and one could hear from his voice how he blushed.

"What?" she asked and already sat carefully poised on her heels; he couldn't see it anyway.

He was silent; he cleared his throat. "But perhaps my hands are wet again . . ."

"Then why don't you keep my handkerchief," she said and disappeared. Nothing was easier than that.

Where the wide road leaves the park and turns toward the ramp of the castle, she found Hans. He sat alone on a stone bench covered with ivy. Sophia sat down next to him, he looked at her briefly and lighted a fresh cigarette with the one he was just finishing.

"Without a girl?" she asked.

"Yes," he said and inhaled the smoke deeply.

"Funny," she mused. "I thought that would happen."

"Why?" he asked with surprising sharpness and turned to look her full in the face.

"How do I know?" she returned, shrugging her shoulders. "I just thought so!"

"Well, and you?" he diverted. "Amused yourself?"

"What do you mean?"

"Don't act so innocent! Weren't you coming from the amusement park . . ."

"My dear Hans, I didn't come from any amusement park; I am not out for amusement— Use your brains!"

"Well, well."

"And do you know why I was in the park with no matter what stupid boy? So that the control would see me. Yes, comrade, one learns how to get around here! And then I lost track of the boy in the darkness."

"Well, well!"

"And you, dear little brother—you made yourself scarce earlier in the evening so as not to spoil my pleasure, isn't that so?"

"Maybe."

"Or perhaps you call it a duty?"

"Maybe."

"Then it would have been nice of you, Hans, really nice and impressive if you had reminded me of my womanly duty and sent me into the park!"

"Now will you please shut your mouth!"

"Oh, God, Hans, you haven't found many new answers for me in the course of the years. But at least you don't beat me any more with your shoulder belt—or was it your trouser belt?"

Hans lighted a fresh cigarette with the half-smoked one. "I have regretted it to this day," he said.

"To this day or beginning today?"

Hans did not answer. She looked from the side at his tight-lipped face which bore deep shadows under the dim light which reached them from the candelabra lining the ramp of the castle, and she discovered his marked resemblance to their father.

"And are you still with them today?" she asked softly and tenderly.

"With whom?"

"With them!"

"By God, yes," he said and looked at her. "I am with them!"

"But why did you join the Wehrmacht, Hans, and not one of the SS formations?"

"Why? Is the Wehrmacht perhaps not a part of them?" he asked back impetuously.

"But why then are you not with the girls; that's also part of it, isn't it?"

"That is not part of it for me—just as little as it is for you . . ."

"But there is something wrong, Hans. If I were with them, it would be a part of it for me!"

"Why do you have to torment me, child?" he implored softly.

"I really didn't want to torment you, Hans!" she exclaimed in consternation, took his hand and asked herself in vain what it was that tormented him so.

"I joined the Wehrmacht," he said hesitatingly after a pause, "because I wanted to get out of the SS . . ." She looked at him questioningly, but she did not dare to question. "I wanted to get out," he blurted out, "because I wanted to get well."

"But you aren't ill, are you?" she asked, taken aback.

"In a sense, I am," he murmured and got up. "Yes, little sister," he said in a changed voice, "I must start thinking about getting home . . ."

"Not yet, Hans, please."

"But it's getting late . . ."

"Not late enough for pleasure-loving comrades, Hans."

He smiled and sat by her side, until morning dawned.

5

Brother and sister did not see each other again until Christmas, 1941. The law student Sophia, member of Professor Hennings' seminar and initiate in Hennings' secret doctrine, traveled from Munich to Bremen because her brother was there on leave from the eastern front, because she wanted to see her parents again and of course also Hilde Wolff. Yes, Sophia had won her freedom and some insight into law and justice, an undreamed-of insight at that; but her accomplishments were of a nature requiring deep silence, she had become a taciturn girl and rather shy, no longer carrying her rebellious thoughts on her tongue or in her pen. She differed little from the others; for they had all grown taciturn, whether from insight or not. It was a taciturn, gloomy and uncomfortable voyage, with people closely packed together and yet timidly hiding behind their walls of silence, even though their arms and legs and shoulders touched, and it was a taciturn land, this victors' land. The Hanseatic city of her birth, nibbled by the first air attacks, had never been a talkative city and now it stood wholly silent and black, strangely forsaken and already a little shabby—like an unemployed man who has not yet lost his self-respect. Thus it stood by its broad river and by the one-time open sea, itself stopped up and without occupation.

The father, as silent and solitary as ever, now looked like one who, by a mysterious fate, had been driven to the Antipodes and had neglected to learn the strange language because he was homesick and tired. So he had acquired the face of a deaf-mute, kissed his daughter on the forehead with a distant smile, accepted the greetings from his old friend Hennings with a silent nod and asked nothing further. The mother, old, emaciated and long since relieved of her job as conciliator, said the words which one customarily said at reunions in the unemotional city, and added an unexpected and irrelevant accusation against the father who refused on principle to go to the air-raid shelter when the alarm sounded.

"On principle," Dr. Moeller confirmed with the uncertain smile of the deaf-mute.

"I can understand it," said Hans, a taciturn vacationist, already a sergeant according to his insignia and a hero, to judge by his decorations. Even the mother, the only one who wanted to know about it, had already given up every attempt to coax a single word out of her son about his promotion and his so signally rewarded war exploits. But the brother had a good smile for his sister, when he saw her again.

But what about Hilde Wolff?

Sophia had not expected her friend to meet her at the station, even if the train had not been hours late, arriving only shortly before midnight, and she had not asked about her, out of consideration for Hans and also because one had gotten out of the habit of asking about people's whereabouts. She had not even figured on seeing her that night, only tomorrow, early in the morning. But as she ascended the familiar stairs of the parental house to the second floor, she saw on the Wolffs' apartment door, in addition to the brass name-plate which was still there, a gray cardboard sign with red letters, and when she stood before it, she read: "Closed by order of the Housing Authority."

She stood there staring at the red words. Her father had already opened the opposite door to the Moeller's apartment. Her mother said somewhat uncertainly, "Welcome home, my dear!" as it is customary to say at such occasions and as she undoubtedly also said to the vacationist Hans, and her brother said nothing and was still standing behind her on the last step of the stair, holding her suitcase. It was her father—who else should it have been—who walked back the short way to the neighbors' door, stopped close by his daughter and in his quiet voice varied his erstwhile postscript: "The sad neighbors left recently."

"Where to?" Sophia asked hastily, as if still out of breath from climbing the stairs, but one doesn't ask such things. The time does not allow such questions, least of all regarding the whereabouts of Jews. And therefore there could be no answer.

It was half-past one before Sophia got to bed, and she was dead tired. But here was her old room, left unchanged as much as possible in honor of her visit, as if she should once again be the little girl she had been, and such a homecoming had something of excitement in it; one had to reorient oneself, find one's way back and at the same time discover that there was nothing left of the childlike magic, although even Hilde's photo stood in its original place on the bedside table between bed and door—it was different and better than the one Hans had trampled on, though long out of date. Wonder if father put it there or mother? she asked herself, looked at it and knew that now still other thoughts would come to keep her from sleeping. Then there was a soft knock at the door, and even from the knock she knew it was her father.

"Are you asleep, child?"

"No, Papa."

"Are you very tired?"

What a perplexing and sleep-chasing question at this hour and after thirty hours on the train!

"No, Papa."

"Then come to my study, child; but put on some warm things—you have a good ten minutes yet."

What an enigmatic, sinister, and penetratingly urgent invitation!

When she entered her father's study, again in travel costume and coat and with a bandanna around her head, the Juvenile Judge, fully dressed and wearing a gray wool scarf around his neck, looked at his watch. His face was calm as always; he said nothing and looked at his watch. Then he rose, turned off the desk lamp, groped his way to the window, pulled the curtains apart, opened the window and raised the Venetian blind halfway.

Father and daughter stood at the window and looked down the street, deserted and black with the war night. When they closed their eyes it was the same; it did not seem that the invitation was meant for eyes which could see nothing but black night. The piercing cold—perhaps not only the piercing cold—made them more wide-awake.

"I don't sleep much," the father said quietly. And after a while: "I am quite familiar with the nocturnal timetable." And after a while: "That has been going on for a week now, but only every other night." And after a while: "You know we are quite close to the freight depot here. But we not only are favorably located for the Jew transports which pass by every other night; we are also a good target for the aerial bombs which will come, perhaps every night. I spend much time here at night, thinking about the aerial bombs which will come. I don't sleep much." And after a while: "The Jew transport gets under way at two o'clock." And after a while: "It is not only sheer guesswork whether neighbor Wolff and Hilde are among tonight's contingent, but a matter of indifference; we can see nothing or almost nothing. But if you wish, my child, you may imagine them passing by." And after a while: "Now . . ."

Now there came a rustle out of the night, still rather far away, a dry rustle—it could have been almost anything—a rustle as when in autumn the wind blows into a pile of fallen leaves and sweeps them over the asphalt. No, it was not so soft and light, it was more like the rustle of those street-cleaning machines with thick cylindrical brushes in front and in back, which scrub dust and leaves and paper into the gutter. And then it was after all the rustle of walking, not of steps, not the hard, bony, hollow, dry and clear rhythm of soldiers marching in the night—never yet was the distinction between walking and stepping so clearly audible as here; for that which approached did not step, it only walked, swept and dragged over the asphalt in utmost marching disorder, in tottering disharmony.

And now three little blue stars came dancing side by side into the street below the window. They were the flashlights fastened to the uniformed chests of the escorting guards, properly colored and shaded in accordance with war regulations, and now one could see other little blue stars moving along in single file on either side of the street. Inside this frame of stars the main mass of the procession moved past, in its center blacker and more impenetrable than the night, but dissolving into human shadows along the sides, in the scanty blue light of the starry frame. There was a faint suggestion of heads and shoulders, even of the figures of men, women and children who all walked bent over, as if fighting against the wind. But it was only that they had all sorts of invisible burdens to bear, in their hands, on their shoulders or on their backs. The main mass was wordless, though not soundless, and moved along not only with the rustle of dragging feet but also to the accompaniment of the whining of sleepy children and of something else besides, of something that was hardly a sound and yet audible, something like a chorus of forcibly laboring lungs which yet did not produce a groaning nor even a panting, but only a strangely loud breathing. A little blue star closed the moving rectangle and in its light one could see a broad-shouldered man walking in front of it and carrying a child on his neck, and the child, wrapped in a blanket, laughed and cried, "Giddap!" and this Saint Christopher's back was the last and most clearly visible in the transport.

Then it was over; the shuffling of feet trickled away in the night, and Dr. Moeller lowered the Venetian blind. He did it softly, but still there was an echo—or perhaps a blind was lowered in the next room too. Adjoining the study was the dining room. While her father closed the window and the curtains, Sophia turned on the light and opened the door to the dining room. There was Hans, fully dressed, closing the window and the curtains. He walked up to his sister who stood in the door and looked at him.

"Funny," said Hans, clearing his throat and shaking his head, "when I am on leave I don't sleep much." He blinked in the dazzling light and rubbed his eyes.

"Incidentally," said the father, not taking any notice of Hans, "tomorrow morning there is an auction next door; but I am not going to it. I only look at the corpses at night, not at the vultures by day."

Next morning, at breakfast, Sophia said to Hans, "I am going to the auction next door." She looked at him.

"I'll go with you," he said.

There were people in the hallway between the two apartments, and on the stairs stood people, gloomy, silent and with hostile looks for one another. Preceded by a police officer who cleared the way for him, a short, fat, perspiring, yet agile man came up the stairs. Even as he climbed up he announced with a booming voice that he was the official auctioneer and that he was pressed for time because he had five more Jew auctions scheduled for the day. He called it that: "Jew auctions." He opened the door to the Wolffs' apartment, and the mob surged in after him.

Hans and Sophia were the last to enter, and everything was just as Sophia had known it many years ago. One could almost say that the apartment was still warm from its occupants, a pair of red-leather gloves of Hilde's lay on the dresser in the hallway, the dining-room table was set for two, on one of the plates was half a slice of bread, the two glasses were half filled with water, as if fate had overtaken father and daughter at mealtime or as if they had not been able to swallow their last meal.

The auction was as full of movement and haste as the auctioneer, who even carried around a portable auction table—a wooden stand like that of a street peddler containing his inventory lists and his hammer, with which he struck the three decisive blows each time, storming from object to object, from room to room, droning out figures, perspiring and alert. The mob, following close on his heels, was eager in its bidding, spiteful and greedy for the smallest tidbit; and there was a gaunt man with a red neck who at each bid crowed that he had a moral prerogative because the Housing Authority had awarded him the apartment. But no one recognized his moral prerogative, and the crow came out empty-handed, without any of the large or small tidbits—apparently not in a position to bid beyond the base price.

Sophia fled from the tumult into Hilde's room, and Hans followed her. That she would be in Hilde's room at this hour of the morning, she had known as early as yesterday on the train; but the circumstances were different, the auction raged two rooms away in the so-called library, Uncle Wolff's comfortable retreat, and next to Sophia on the Victorian sofa sat, not Hilde, but Hans—a truly unforeseeable change. She saw that her brother's eyes rested on her own photograph which stood on Hilde's bedside table, even as in the reciprocity of friendship Hilde's picture had to stand on Sophia's bedside table; it was an attractive vivid likeness from the year 1934, with a provocatively fervent dedication written in the big, stiff handwriting of a little girl. The picture and dedication dated from the time of the supreme seal and had been given in exchange for that other and better picture of her friend which had replaced the destroyed one. Sophia asked herself what her brother's prolonged look at the picture presaged. Would he now demand that she take it with her before the mob should discover it? But Hans said nothing.

"Do you think it still resembles me?" she asked provokingly.

"After a fashion," he said, and would not let himself be provoked.

"Are you by any chance going to bid for it?" she asked as if jesting.

"No," he answered gravely, "I am not going to bid for anything here."

"Well, I like that, coming from you."

"Why just from me?"

"Because you let my picture get into the Jew auction and don't even trample it under foot."

"Don't be so vindictive," he said.

Before them on the table stood Hilde's sewing kit. Sophia opened it and looked for something. And she did find a razor blade, but didn't know it was the same one.

"One doesn't rummage around in things that don't belong to one," Hans observed.

"Don't be so pedantic," she said; "besides, it is only since today that these things don't belong to me."

"That's enough," he said.

The auctioneer and the mob broke in. The fat man oriented himself with a deeply experienced, all-inclusive look around the room and had already torn open the door to Hilde's big wardrobe. The clothes were strange to Sophia, but not the delicate, clean smell of Cologne water and gardenia soap which wafted over to them and overcame the musty effluvium of the bidders. The auctioneer droned out figures, knocked on his portable stand with his wooden hammer, and threw the motley rags to the victors; it looked like the feeding of beasts of prey. Now little dresses from earlier times were coming forth, which Sophia knew or thought she knew; but the scene was too loud and too coarse to permit the return of memory to delicate things. Already the morally privileged new tenant fought, crowing but unsuccessful, for the wardrobe itself, and Hans, with a disgusted look, proposed that they leave.

"One moment longer," Sophia begged, and admitted to herself that she wished to stay for the sake of the sewing kit. Clamoring, hammering, and continual yelping raged on in Hilde's room, and the air grew steadily worse.

"One picture frame of wood with bronze corners and glass!" the auctioneer droned in front of the bedside table, and left out the photograph as worthless. "Opening bid 75 pfennigs!"

Hans and Sophia looked at each other and smiled. The picture or the frame of the picture brought 1 mark 75 pfennigs. And the hammer knocked down Hilde's bedside table to the highest bidder, then Hilde's bed and the Victorian sofa, from which Sophia and Hans obediently rose.

"One wooden sewing kit with contents, opening bid 25 pfennigs!"

Bid, bid! Sophia commanded herself, and suddenly her heart palpitated. But she couldn't open her mouth, perhaps because Hans was looking at the sewing kit with the disgusted look which he had for all the auctioned objects—perhaps because it was robbing the dead . . . The sewing kit was already gone, for 50 pfennigs.

When Hilde's room had been eaten bare and the swarm of bidders pushed after the auctioneer into the bathroom and Uncle Wolff's bedroom, Sophia looked at her brother and challenged him, suddenly impatient: "Say a word, at least!"

"What is there to say? It is disgusting."

"Not more than disgusting?"

"Maybe."

"And last night, at the window: Did you also say to yourself there that it was disgusting or maybe more?"

"I said to myself: They don't know where they will be taken—but I know."

"Was that all?"

"That was not precisely so little."

"But you are still with them, Hans?"

"With whom?"

"With them!"

"Yes," said Hans, and his eyes still looked disgusted.

"Recently—you know when, Hans—just outside the amusement park, you answered: 'By God, yes!' That is much more: 'By God, yes!' "

"Yes is enough," said Hans.

"Yes is enough!" she repeated and came very close to him—and her eyes were green (he knew those green eyes from before, from the scene with the shoulder belt). "But No is also enough! You understand? I want you to know that I am not with them! I am elsewhere!"

"That does not astonish me particularly," he said and even smiled a little. "I wish you luck just the same."

She did not reciprocate his wish, in this heated moment, and later she regretted that she had not wished him luck, too.

As they left Hilde's room, Sophia's photograph, removed from its frame, lay on the floor near the door to the hallway. They passed it as though they had not noticed it.

It was her last stay in the city of her fathers. A few months later —Sophia had long since returned to Munich, and Hans, in Kharkov, still had both his legs, even if his feet were full of chilblains— the former Juvenile Judge Friedrich Moeller lost his life in one of the first full-scale air attacks on Bremen. His wife, who had gone to the air-raid shelter in conformity with official orders, escaped unscathed. It was, so Hans and Sophia felt, at the same time the irony and the mercy of fate.

6

The field hospital at Rostov on the Don, where Hans had his right leg amputated toward the end of August, 1942, was quartered in the extensive cellar of a gutted city schoolhouse. One of the hospital attendants was Alexander Welte, a non-commissioned officer in the medical corps. Welte saw his future friend for the first time when he received him from the ambulance and wheeled him into the operating room as an emergency case, and he was impressed by the way the seriously injured man looked at him with a faint smile and whispered: "A stupid accident . . ." Generally the men brought to the hospital spoke in an entirely different way about their wounds, even when they were not so badly off and especially when they did not already possess the Iron Cross, first class, like this sergeant whose heroic aspirations seemed to be satiated. Alexander, who lived so to speak on the pitifully human reverse side of heroism and who, probably for that reason, had come to hold somewhat heretical views, distributed his favors—and in this cellar his favors were by no means unimportant—precisely according to the degree of heroic satiation, which meant that he favored those who were content with being simply poor devils.

His special affection for Hans Moeller began immediately after the cripple came out of his anesthesia; the man did not bewail the loss of his leg, which would have been understandable enough, or refuse to believe, in feverish obstinacy, that he had lost it—which was bound to lead to disagreeable scenes of explanation—but declared anew, in feverish obstinacy to be sure, that it was a question of a motorcycle accident resulting from a blood-colored oil puddle.

Alexander saw that he suffered great pain, and gave him his first morphine injection sooner than prescribed.

When Hans awoke from his twilight sleep, he said: "It was blood and oil, and I must have rocked the handlebar a little—I didn't want to stick my feet in the mess; and the hind wheel skidded, and there I was, flat on the road. Behind me came a flak truck from my own column, and that swine of a driver must have been dozing or looking in the air, where the boys were peppering their stuff, so that he didn't see that I was there . . ."

"Where did all this happen?" Alexander asked in order to find out if the man was delirious.

"On the East bank, after the cursed Don crossing of the 24th of August."

"Lively country," Alexander confirmed. "And if you ask me, sarge, I'd rather be here with one leg and be done with the shit than east of the Don with two legs and have the shit ahead of me, whether it's called Kotelnikovski or Stalingrad—and that's no joke, mister, that's logic."

The logician's affection for the man who had lost his leg through a traffic accident in lively country expressed itself first of all in his decision to put him "in first class." That was a closed off room with a mighty furnace, once the central heating plant, where formerly the coal had been stored. The chute under the high window hatch through which the coal was dumped into the room was still there, the walls and the brick floor were still black with coal dust; but Hans was alone: this was "first class" and an extraordinary privilege.

It soon turned out that the favor had not been awarded entirely without selfish motives; the logician, pervaded by a strong impulse for communication, took advantage of the likable one-legged man's privacy and talked, talked perhaps more than the patient's condition permitted. But that was not enough: a few days later he set up his field bed next to Hans in the coal cellar, in order to have the traffic accident case under control, as he expressed it. Hans was satisfied; the non-commissioned medical officer not only talked, but nursed him marvelously.

Yes, Hans liked his sonorous voice, even when he was still too weak to interrupt Alexander's monologues. It was good to hear him talk, it made sense, not yet a very clear sense—as nothing had as yet a clear, a new sense since he had walked back to consciousness through a strangely narrowed tunnel as through opera glasses turned the wrong way—no, not walked, but crawled back; for his leg was missing, that was the first and only clear thing, and his body terminated with such terrible and irrevocable impressiveness in the lower part of his thigh that he forgot the other leg and crawled into awakening on two stumps. It was good then, to see the solid, broad, reliable face of this non-commissioned officer, the first of all faces; it made sense, and above all he had to explain to the first of all faces that his leg had not fallen in combat, albeit in oil and blood.

But why did he have to explain this above all; what was the difference whether he had lost his leg in the hard-fought advance east of the Don, through an aerial bomb, a grenade splinter or an accident? Oh, there was a tremendous difference, and it could not be established quickly enough, and it made sense, though the sense was not yet very clear, that he had lost his leg not through the enemy, but through his own war machine.

It made sense to listen to his new friend and to look at him; Alexander Welte was of the same age, had the same experience and had started on the same road through life, the same product of the state-youth manufacturing process. The world around Hans had been called Bremen, Alexander's world was Ulm. His father, a veterinarian, was also a logician, though his was the logic of expediency. He differed from Hans Moeller's father in that he maintained, and even knew how to increase, his useful and necessary occupation by useful and necessary adaptations to the new times, and he differed from Hans' father most of all in that he was still alive. But Alexander had been forced to live, to speak, to think and to be obedient with body and soul, just as Hans. And Hans was very anxious to see what it had led to.

"I didn't have my stupid eyes opened until I got in the army," said Alexander; "that was a horse of a different color, and they ground away everything that smelled of Hitler Youth. The more insignia and conceit the state youth possessed, the more he was kicked around."

Hans nodded; it had been the same way with him. But he hadn't had stupid eyes any more, being the son of his father and the brother of his sister, and he hadn't minded being ground down and polished, because he had believed that it might make a new man out of him. Well, it hadn't made a new man out of him, only another mass product, a new minute part of the gigantic machine; as delivered semi-finished material he had had to be polished and reshaped somewhat, but was accepted and could be used admirably. Perhaps he would tell the other fellow about it, when he was stronger, or perhaps the other fellow would tell of his own accord where his opened eyes led him.

"To which I should add," Alexander observed, "that the military immediately restored stupidity to the eyes that had just been opened, so that now even my three semesters in the Munich medical school appear to me like a conglomerate of Hitler Youth, SA and army, plus occasional sitting at attention in the classroom."

"Oh, Munich," Hans whispered. "That's where my little sister is studying . . ." He looked around in his wallet and pulled out a snapshot of Sophia. It was, so it turned out, the only picture he had with him; he didn't seem to have a girl. That was none of Alexander's business; but on the following day he carpentered a bedside table for the patient: again for not entirely unselfish reasons, because he made the stand also for the photograph, to be put up and looked at—by the carpenter, too. And Hans told a few things about his little sister who had always disagreed with her big brother; it was the first time he had taken an active part in the conversation.

"If I had such a sister or such a girl," said Alexander, looking at the picture, "my eyes would have been opened long ago."

"What precisely do you mean, Welte, by eyes that are opened?"

"Opened so that I can see what it is."

"And what is it, as you see it?"

"Filth."

"And what do you do with the filth—clear it away?"

"What do you think I am, sarge? God Almighty? And even He lets it be. Perhaps it'll turn into good dung."

"Would it not be better then, if your eyes had not been opened? Only to look at filth and not let God Almighty be a good cleaner-upper?"

"With a little logic one can make something even out of filth, and at least one can learn to realize that life can't be other than filthy."

"And when did you have your eyes opened?" asked Hans, and he seemed exhausted.

"When we all had our eyes closed by the cold, mister, when we didn't take Moscow in our pretty, photogenic, mass Panzer excursion with 'strength through joy,' but when we were taken by winter instead, the Russian winter, the coldest Russian winter in one hundred and fifty years, a shooting winter that featured long destroyed armies of Russkies as snowstorms, and reminded us, those of us who were still alive, that we had unfortunately forgotten to take along our winter coats on our joyous, summerly 'Drang nach Osten'—and this again is only a polite paraphrase for the pigsty of an army command which hadn't provided at all for winter clothing!"

Hans closed his eyes, tired and disappointed. Grumbling! Grumbling! They all grumbled through the inconceivably dreadful winter, they grumbled until they froze to death, they obeyed grumbling and fought grumbling and fell grumbling, they stayed alive grumbling and stood the gaff, rested and began their summer offensive on June 10th. It didn't make any sense, here in the coal cellar, no new sense.

"Every logician," said Alexander, "necessarily becomes a heretic, and so I arrived at the heresy of the formula 10:1." His droll round eyes turned rounder still, so much was he pleased with his pretty, though obscure pronouncement. "The formula 10:1," he continued by way of explanation, "is our SA recipe dating from as long ago as the Weimar days. I have it from some of the old fighters, hall fighters and street fighters, who with the aid of 10:1 comfortably finished off the Red Front and the followers of the black, red and gold banner. Later the formula formed the basis of our peaceful conversion of Austria, the Sudeten country, Bohemia and Moravia. Our campaigns against Poland, Denmark, Norway, Belgium, Holland, France and the Balkans were built upon that formula. The heresy of the formula is that we are supermen only when we have a majority of 10:1. Do you follow me, mister?"

Hans nodded.

"Does the heretic make you shudder, mister?"

Hans shook his head.

"Good," Alexander commended. "And once you have come so far, it follows with startling simplicity that the tables can and must be turned, and the vaunted glory of invincibility must go in the ash can like an old newspaper when the formula doesn't fit any more and begins to waver, 8:2, 7:3, 6:4 . . . And when you have waded through this winter now, through the spring, through the summer, through snow and mud, through oil and blood, to quote you, mister—when you have duly realized that you have sought out Russia as your enemy, haha! One-fifth of the world, plus British world empire, plus USA, two-fifths, three-fifths, haha! The counter formula! Then you know, mister, why the heretic shudders. *Quod erat demonstrandum.*"

That was logic! That was a formulation, my likable one-legged fellow! Alexander looked at the patient with his round, happy eyes. Hans moved his head on the pillow and asked quietly: "Just what is it that makes you shudder, Welte?"

"What is it! What is it!" Alexander repeated vexedly and thought the objection not at all on the high level of his logical demonstration. "Insanity, of course, and most of all, what goes with it and what follows from it!"

"Why then don't you and I make you shudder?" asked Hans, and again moved his head on the pillow.

Alexander looked at him pensively and did not answer. But Hans' strange question seemed to preoccupy him; for on the following day he said to him: "Please let me develop my heresies in their proper sequence, Moeller, and don't confuse me with questions which may possibly tinkle somewhere at the end of the logical chain. But I haven't gotten that far yet."

"Nor have I," said Hans.

"I have only come to my second heresy," said Alexander, rubbing his hands, "causally deducible from the first. But since it is incidentally directed against the second commandment that sayeth: 'Thou shalt not take the name of the Lord thy God in vain,' I shall let caution prevail and shall circumscribe the name of our Lord with the military rank he achieved in the first World War. So when I speak of the 'Corporal' you will know whom I mean, Sergeant?"

Hans nodded.

"And it will not frighten you if I am heretical against the Corporal?"

Hans shook his head.

"Good," said Alexander. "Let us paraphrase the proverb, 'Man proposes, God disposes,' to fit the actual military situation. Then we could say, the General Staff proposes, the Corporal disposes. If we add to this the result we obtained from heresy number 1, we come to the qualifying extension: the General Staff proposes well, the Corporal disposes badly. That, reduced to the least common denominator, is the prevailing view held since last winter by everyone from the commanding general down to the last footslogger—and not only in our Sixth Army, as you will admit."

"Good God!" Hans sighed and closed his tired eyes; for the logician could not get away from his Russian winter, and now it was summer, and if they should take Stalingrad by fall and seal the Volga and get Baku, then it was the Führer after all who proposed, and the Führer who disposed, as the greatest military genius of all time . . .

"Don't get uppety, mister," Alexander reprimanded. "Up to this point I have at the most arrived at criticism—the generally prevailing criticism, which is of course subject to fluctuation because it originated in a state of depression, and even the smallest boost might cause it to vanish. But with me it does not fluctuate, because it is firmly linked to the causal chain, and I have not yet drawn my personal conclusions, have not yet arrived at heresy number 2—which I would not venture to call original. Listen to me, Moeller. With the experience of the badly leading Corporal I now let my logic dance backwards, into the past, into our youth, called Hitler Youth—Didn't we ardently adore him then, the Corporal, and didn't we often see him, the produced and much reproduced one! And now I ask you and myself, Who was it that we adored and saw? and I let you, and myself, look at through the spectacles of heresy? Haha!"

Hans opened his eyes wide and asked: "Whom did we adore?"

"A rather middle-sized, badly built man with drooping shoulders, broad hips and a soft belly, who doesn't know what to do with his hands and conveniently folds them over his private parts, probably because they seem to him to be safest there."

"Those are superficial characteristics."

"Those are intrinsic characteristics, Hans—please permit me to call you Hans—those are characteristics of so revealing a nature that I cannot suppress a mild pride at having brought them to light. Because now, when I look at his face, a face which is in itself neither handsome nor ugly but lukewarm with mediocrity, I see the bad build of his body repeated in it; I could attach the same adjectives to his face as to his body, bold and extravagant though it may sound, and they would fit. Yes sir, I say that his face has drooping shoulders, broad hips and a soft belly, and I go so far as to say that in the dark impulse of the little mustache to cover up something, I rediscover the folding of his embarrassed hands over his private parts."

"And the eyes, the famous eyes?"

"There isn't a part of his face that is not famous. And because there is something monstrous about this pouring out of fame over a bad build, because it is a highly dramatic burden, the eyes become melodramatic. They look out of the bad build—that is secret lamentation. They look into fame, no, into deification—that is monstrous, unbelievable, never comprehensible triumph. And between these two, between lamentation and triumph, there is no bridge, only the vacuum of spiritual embarrassment and physical callousness. That is why the eyes must become piercing and must draw courage and strength from the deification to break through the blockade of the body. Then he can finally outdo himself before the masses. After all, it is easier to be a roaring god than a mute one."

"And the result?"

"The result is heresy number 2: we adore a corporal."

"But with that you are surely not solving the problem; that is to say, the phenomenon of his success."

"Maybe I am, though, or at least very nearly, Hans. And couldn't we formulate it differently, too? For instance: our idol is inadequacy."

"If the idol of a nation is inadequacy," Hans said and seemed agitated, "then it is a question of national inadequacy."

"There is a certain logic to that," Alexander nodded.

"Then why don't we go a step further?" Hans pressed him.

"Further still?"

"Further still!" Hans exclaimed and sat up in bed, for the first time. "Haven't we swallowed him, day after day, in daily communion, like the Eucharist? I tell you, he has gotten into us, he is part of us, do you understand?"

Hans' face was greenish with pallor and his nose was pointed and waxen. Sitting up seemed to strain him considerably.

"Now don't *you* go outdoing yourself," Alexander said with concern, and made him lie down again.

From then on Alexander practiced restraint, in the interest of the convalescent and from a certain dread of the direction in which his friend seemed to be driving. He confined himself to comments about these murderous September days and used to interrupt himself with round eyes: "Did I say Verdun? I meant Stalingrad, of course . . ."

Hans, however, was content to go on alone in his direction, step by step, and the healing process of the amputation wound was not jeopardized by it.

At the end of September, the night before Hans was to be transferred from the overcrowded field hospital to the interior of the Reich, Alexander brought him a letter from Sophia and his crutches. "Damn," he said as he handed them over. "Now we have three more typhus cases that were smuggled in here somehow."

Hans wasn't listening; he sat on the edge of his bed and read the letter; then he raised his head and looked at the crutches.

"Brand new," said Alexander, slipping them under Hans' shoulders, "just because they are for you."

Hans was hanging between his crutches, with strangely high shoulders.

"How do you feel?" Alexander asked.

"Well," Hans observed, "I can't say that I feel exactly right."

"I don't either," said Alexander. "I have a headache, my belly is hard and itches, and my urine is discolored. But that's not exactly what I mean, I mean that all of us are not exactly right."

"That so?" said Hans somewhat absently, and his neck seemed as much shorter as his shoulders were higher.

"Remember, Hans, you said recently that we swallowed him. I thought about that. You are right."

"Yes," Hans nodded, hanging in his crutches high-shouldered and short-necked. "I am right."

"Do you want to jump around a bit, Hans, for practice?"

"Just let me stand; even that is something new and must be practiced."

"Hans, I feel as though I had the plague in me . . ."

"I suppose it's the national inadequacy," Hans interrupted.

"No matter; but now I make myself shudder— Didn't you ask me right in the beginning why I didn't shudder . . ."

"I asked you why you and I didn't make you shudder."

"You and I make me shudder," Alexander admitted softly and scratched his belly. "We die like flies for him . . ."

"That's passive insanity, but I suppose there is also an active variety, or isn't there?"

"Oh, yes, the Russians are croaking by the thousands too."

"And also the Poles and also the Jews; we don't just destroy warriors, we destroy entire races, or don't we?"

"Oh, yes, Hans, there is something wrong with me . . ."

"There are millions of soldiers, excellent, possessed soldiers—that's what we are on the battlefields—and there are hundreds of thousands of possessed or willing race butchers—that's what we are in the slaughterhouses. And so I ask you a terribly stupid, terribly significant question, Alex: Is an order to exterminate twenty-five men in an enemy machine-gun nest the same as an order to exterminate twenty-five people, men, women, children, Russians, Poles, Jews?"

"Orders are orders," Alexander whispered, and he seemed suddenly to feel hot; he opened his tunic.

"And then I ask you, Alex: Is the extermination of the twenty-five people an order carried out or a murder carried out?"

"An order . . ." Alexander whispered and moved his shoulders as if he had chills. "A murder . . ."

"And if I ask whether we are soldiers or murderers, and if I am no longer satisfied with the answer that orders are orders, and not even with the answer that we are soldiers *and* murderers, but if I ask you this, Alex: Why do we obey, all of us, all, all, *all?*"

"Haha!" Alexander laughed with chattering teeth. "How long you can stand on three legs!"

"We are all obeying blindly," said Hans, "because we don't come face to face with such stupid and significant questions, and it's easy for us; possessed people obey their own commands and therefore also command themselves . . ."

"Pleasant commanding to you!" Alexander riled. "But I've got the plague in me!"

Hans looked at him and hung motionless between his crutches, only the empty leg of the hospital pajamas swayed softly back and forth. "You are Catholic, aren't you?" he said after a while. "And you Catholics are supposed to know all about exorcising devils. How is it done?"

"So far as I can remember," Alexander answered and laughed again with a loose chin, "one has to work with prayer and incense and cross and *apage Satanas*—" His laughter broke off, he made round eyes, forced his hand between belt and tunic, groped along his hard, itching belly and felt eruptions. But he said nothing.

"You see," Hans smiled, "exorcise the devil! That could become the new sense for someone like you or me. Incidentally, I shall have myself discharged to Munich, to study. That's where my little sister is, you know."

"You lucky fellow with oil and blood . . ." Alexander murmured.

He was already in the typhus barracks when on the following morning Hans was lifted into the hospital train, together with his brand new crutches.

Two weeks later Hans arrived at Munich's main station and on his crutches swung himself down the three high steps of the Vienna through train. Under his long military coat one could not see the pinned-up right trouser leg. In the station Sophia was waiting. He let himself be embraced by her, what else could he do—he couldn't let go of the crutches. She bravely swallowed her tears, but she could not speak. He, however, did speak and he even smiled. He said something like a password, and she understood him—of all the people in the world his sister alone understood him.

He said, "By God, NO!"

Chapter Eight

THE OTHER LIFE

I

President Behn sits rigidly on his judge's throne without touching the back rest, as he had sat before, broad and firm of face. There is nothing in this room of sovereign decision that could touch him, that could as much as turn a hair on his head; there is no passion, no crime, no revelation, however overwhelming, but would not founder on his iron posture, on the rock of judgment that he is. And yet, much has happened; he does not deny it.

Before him at the sinners' table, before his judicially calm and unemotional eyes, five people have stood. They came and they went in the rhythmically natural sequence of the sexes: a man, a woman, a man, a woman, a man. They did not defend themselves, they accused, and above all they revealed themselves, exactly as the magician of procedure had intended. But to say that they had forfeited their heads by talking would be worthless rhetoric; for they would have lost their heads through silence as well. The procedure, however, is not worthless: it loosened their tongues. Only their heads were worthless, not their brains, as they demonstrated. They revealed not only an expanse of thought, an underworld, a no man's land of thought, but also the area of enmity within the one and only Reich, amidst the state youth, which is closest to the Führer's heart. The revelation speaks for itself and surely speaks convincingly enough also to the members of the tribunal, excepting, perhaps, Judge Schneidhammer. The president need no longer solicit praise nor suppress any possible palace revolution with a mere look.

President Behn not only had looked at the man or woman standing before him, staring into his face or through him or past him, but also had kept his eye on the prisoners' bench, beyond the speaker, and he had learned all sorts of things. He had noticed, for instance, that during the testimony of defendant Dora von Hennings the principal defendant obviously suffered, that he lost his erect posture, that his brows were wincing and his hands restless,—and President Behn had drawn his conclusions from this and from the attentiveness of the other defendants who apparently had not known the woman's life history.

He had further observed that Hans Moeller's account had electrified his sister, a heretofore rather lethargic person, and had made her visibly impatient for her own turn to speak. And the unusual vividness of her own testimony and of her person again had two especially receptive listeners among the defendants: the one was Welte, who was brimming over with admiration and whom the president consequently took to be the girl's lover, and the other was that interesting, sinister young man, the next to the last on the prisoners' bench, who figuratively speaking opened his vizor during Sophia Moeller's testimony and showed his face, the face of an enraptured and entranced youth. And once he even smiled, with flashing teeth and flashing eyes, when the girl mentioned the well managed love scene in the "amusement park."

Finally, the president observed that his procedural sleight-of-hand by which the defendant Sauer had been by-passed after the girl had finished and the last in the alphabet had been called to give testimony, had been noted only on the prisoners' bench and had caused a certain depression, most clearly evidenced by Sophia Moeller who only a moment ago, standing at the sinners' table, had displayed a very self-assured, occasionally even triumphant attitude. And since she did not so much as raise her head while Welte spoke, the psychologist Behn revised his assumption of a more intimate relationship between her and the speaker.

The silver snuffbox clicks shut with a small, pert, and good-natured snap. Baron Freyberg is in high spirits; he leans over and in his nasal tone of voice says to the president: "Have a few questions to ask the two Wehrmacht men."

"So do I." Sturmbannführer Uhle speaks from the other side; but he means only Moeller, the invalid, who alone preoccupies him, deeply preoccupies him.

"The gentlemen of the Court shall have an opportunity to ask questions later," President Behn replies, and looks briefly at his youngest colleague whose face is no longer green and who now seems able to stand the strong tobacco.

"One of the master singers is still missing from the contest," Reichs Attorney Tischler observes pointedly; he has long since stopped taking notes, it is superfluous.

"And what about the noon recess?" Judge Schneidhammer inquires. He is the only one whose appetite is as healthy as ever.

"Not yet," President Behn answers curtly and rather impolitely.

He had seen very clearly that during the last hour the party magnate had been writing line upon line on his writing tablet under the calligraphed heading: "Fellow Germans!". Schneidhammer had written with a clumsy hand, breathing heavily from the exertion, and now he was hiding his scribbling under a blank page—outright rudeness; and Behn has his well-founded doubts about the value of this judicial collaboration. He almost suspects that the hidden notes are not so much concerned with the defendants as with the astonishing procedure.

"Suits me," says the dignitary, lifts the covering page a little, seems to derive joy from what he reads under it, and loses himself in pleasurably roaming thought.

2

President Behn speaks with a languid voice: "I now come to the person of the defendant Sauer Christopher."

He pauses. The next to last in the row stands up, not too fast and not too slowly, and turns toward the box gate at the right.

"Wait," the president says. Christopher stops. His friends' eyes are upon him, Sophia's eyes are upon him. President Behn contemplates the girl's face which is nothing now but a white receptacle for her eyes. Aha, he thinks, so that's the way it is . . . "You may remain seated," he says. Christopher sits down. The girl still looks over to the right where he has been standing. The others turn their faces to the judge's throne, and none of them conceals his agitation. He is a special case for them also, thinks Behn, who never before had his defendants so completely at his mercy. He is pleased with himself.

"I have excepted defendant Sauer from the procedure laid down for the other defendants," the president says with especially marked languidness and assuming an especially stiff posture, "because his peculiar behavior during his arrest and during the preliminary investigation demands a legal clarification. Mister Court Reporter, will you please read to us the report submitted by the authorities who carried out the arrest and the preliminary investigation?"

Judge Lucius has grown more calm, though not more collected. That inner confusion, coming from the heart, which he still felt and expressed when the principal defendant concluded his peroration, was suddenly resolved—one might even say it was dissolved by the gladdening appearance of the professor's wife. Yes, the confusion has been supplanted by something gladdening, and this feeling of gladness persisted and caused mental escapades which degenerated into rather serious aberrations.

It happened that a feeling stole into Judge Lucius' heart which in all honesty would have to be called a feeling of sympathy, sympathy with the professor's wife, the war invalid, his sister, the medical-corps man, and, alas, also with that which they told. What these people are and how they became what they are, and also their manner of telling it, is not only likable in itself, it coincides easily and without reservation with the moral sentiments of Walter Lucius, who is a decent man; it coincides, therefore, with the moral sentiments of all decent men. And thus it may be that Walter Lucius not only is multiplying himself, sitting there and sympathetically listening in the capacity of the whole of decent humanity, but also sees, behind the one who happens to be speaking at the sinners' table, the long row of those who became, and are, and must speak like the man or woman who at the time is their spokesman.

Now this is not the kind of revelation which the president had meant to impart to his judges by his procedural magic. It was simply a mental aberration and confusion.

Judge Lucius, thumbing through the file before him with confused fingers, twice misses the page on which the report begins, and finally reads in a mild, sober voice:

"Pursuant to the measures taken against Hennings and Associates on February 13, 1943, SD officers Roller and Müller went to the apartment of locomotive engineer Herman Hansemann at 45 Luisenstrasse at 23:10 o'clock, in order to arrest the law student Sauer Christopher who occupies a room in Hansemann's apartment.

"The officers found the said Sauer Christopher in the company of an elderly Catholic priest, who identified himself as Monsignor Ruhsilver, 60, Rector of Niederhall Parish, District Reichenhall, and uncle of Sauer Christopher. He presented a round-trip ticket to prove that he had arrived in Munich from Reichenhall on the same evening to discuss a family matter with his nephew. He testified that he had waited in his nephew's room since approximately 21:00 o'clock. Sauer Christopher, who even at the moment of their entrance gave the officers the impression of absent-mindedness and failed to answer to his name, had come in at 22:30 o'clock, according to Rector Ruhsilver's testimony. After giving his temporary Munich address, and having been given strict orders to keep himself at the disposal of the authorities for at least forty-eight hours, Rector Ruhsilver was dismissed as not involved in the case of Hennings and Associates . . ."

"One moment," President Behn interrupts, raising his head. "Defendant Sauer, do you wish to tell us what family matter your uncle came to discuss with you? You may remain seated."

Christopher does not answer at once, he makes two attempts, and as he speaks at last his voice is hoarse and his friends can hardly recognize it for its agitated animosity: "It was about my mother."

"To be more exact," President Behn comments, pointing his finger at him, "about your mother's arrest, is that correct?"

Christopher jumps up, although he is permitted to remain seated. He grips the railing of the prisoners' box as if he wanted to tear it loose, and yet all he can say is "yes" and he says it softly, almost whispering: "About her arrest, yes . . ."

His friends look up at him, aghast and unreservedly prepared to condone his isolation; for they feel the blow that has split him off from them. Sophia, however, who knows more about it, desires above all that he look at her now instead of standing there, solitary and forsaken. But Christopher stares at the judge, and his jawbone stamps his face with a hard line from chin to ear, so that his face appears as strange as his voice.

"I should add," President Behn addresses the judges, "that the date of this woman's arrest makes it abundantly clear that it does not concern the case of Hennings and Associates . . ."

"But it does concern me!" Christopher exclaims in the clear and incisive voice familiar to his friends.

"Sit down," the president says very calmly, waiting for Christopher to obey the command and for the defendants to turn their attention once more to the judges' tribune. Then he glances at his papers: "Rector Ruhsilver was examined by the Secret State Police yesterday. On the basis of his testimony the District Court at Reichenhall was called by telephone and requested to furnish information about the case. It was established that Ursula Sauer, 40, née Ruhsilver, widow of a hereditary peasant proprietor, had been arrested on February 12, and committed for trial on charges of violating the Treachery Act and of resisting the authorities. This by way of clarifying the so-called family matter. Mister Court Reporter, will you proceed?"

Judge Lucius reads:

"The officers now intended to carry out the arrest of the said Sauer Christopher and encountered the following difficulties in the process.

"First: the defendant could not be induced to acknowledge his name as required by law. He was standing motionless and with staring eyes in front of his bed, exactly as the officers had found him on entering the room, and did not react to the identification procedure nor to the farewell words spoken by the said Rector Ruhsilver.

"Second: the defendant could not be induced to read the order for his arrest, nor even to look at the official document.

"Third: the defendant could not be induced to abandon his position and follow the officers. He responded neither to gentle nor stern admonitions, nor to the mild slap in the face administered by SD man Müller, nor to the threat of the officers that they would handcuff him, nor to the application of the handcuffs to which he offered no active resistance, though he did resist passively; SD man Roller succeeded only with the assistance of SD man Müller in bringing the defendant's hands sufficiently close together to apply the handcuffs.

"Fourth: the defendant, forcibly removed from his position in front of the bed by SD man Müller, was unable or unwilling to use his legs and fell sideways, hitting the floor with his left shoulder first. In falling, his body did not bend and he uttered no sound.

"In view of this unusual behavior of the defendant and in view of the officers' inability to determine whether it was a question of resisting the authorities or of illness, SD man Roller went to the telephone and reported the circumstances to his superior officer. Thereupon the undersigned SD commissioner, after consultation with Commissioner Negele, in charge of the investigation of the case Hennings and Associates, ordered the defendant Sauer Christopher to be conducted to the Gestapohaus instead of being delivered immediately to Commissioner Negele at Police Headquarters, as originally intended.

"As the prisoner was still lying on the floor of the room, motionless, though with his eyes open, SD men Roller and Müller were compelled to carry him downstairs to the service car, and after arrival at the Gestapohaus, to carry him from the car to the office of the undersigned SD commissioner. While carrying the prisoner, the officers noticed that his body was entirely rigid and that also in the car he remained in a stiff and unnatural, half-reclining position.

"The undersigned SD commissioner received the prisoner in the same condition toward 24 o'clock, and, convinced of the impossibility of evoking any response on the part of the prisoner, ordered him submitted to the measures designed to break down passive resistance, though without success . . .

"Thank you," President Behn interrupts, and looks into space with narrowed eyes. Then he says: "Defendant Sauer, step to the table here."

Christopher rises and turns toward the box gate at the right. He does not graze his comrade Welte as he passes him, he does not look at him, and walks to the sinners' table, not slowly and not fast.

"Defendant," says the president, "is that which has been read about your arrest just now, new to you?"

"I do not understand the question," Christopher answers.

"Then I shall formulate it differently. Can you or can you not confirm the correctness of the report about your arrest?"

"I can confirm it."

"If you were not conscious at the time, or only half-conscious, you cannot confirm its correctness."

"I can confirm it."

"Then you were conscious."

"Yes."

"Was the blow administered to you by one of the two SD men a mild slap, as stated in the report?"

"No, he gave me two severe blows, in rapid succession, one with the palm, the other with the back of the hand, just like the blows old Herr Wolff got in his day."

"That is irrelevant and immaterial. After all, you did *not* ask: 'Why please?'" President Behn observes, showing a rare smile. He cannot keep from looking quickly to the right and left, to determine the success of his witticism. But the gentlemen of the judges' tribune look with fascination at the man standing before them, all save the worthless neighbor at the right who pursues his suspicious scribbling under the half-lifted cover page.

The president, somewhat annoyed, again addresses himself to Christopher: "You did not feel a mild slap, then, but two solid blows . . ."

"No."

"What do you mean?"

"I did not feel them."

"I thought you said you were conscious."

"Entirely."

"How then could you fail to feel the two blows you described so minutely?"

"Because I did not want to feel them."

"Just because you don't want to, you don't feel anything?"

"That is correct."

"How do you accomplish that?"

"Through will power."

"That is a metaphysical disposition. I am asking you to explain the physiological process."

"Through muscular contraction."

"Has the action of fright anything to do with it?"

"Controlled fright action."

"You mean that you can force fright to act in any manner you desire?"

"More or less."

"And fright action set in when the two SD men appeared in your room?"

"Only the effects of fright action."

"Do you mean that the appearance of the two officers was no surprise for you?"

"No great surprise."

"The authorities started their proceedings at the university around 22 o'clock. Had you already known about it?"

"The proceedings must have started after ten o'clock, since I myself left the university only after ten o'clock, unimpeded and unaware of any proceedings."

"How come then, that the appearance of the two officers in your room was no great surprise for you?"

"Because I was emotionally prepared for the worst. I have a gift for feeling the approach of catastrophes."

"You are gifted in many ways, it seems."

"Yes."

"But you speak of controlled fright action and at the same time you deny having been frightened by the appearance of the two officers and you call it merely the effect of a fright action—the effect of what fright action?"

"Of a preceding one."

"Rector Ruhsilver's news of the arrest of your mother, is that what you mean?"

"Yes."

"It would interest me to know if you discussed this matter with your uncle as a normal, though frightened, man."

"I don't think I said anything," Christopher answers softly.

"Did you take up your position in front of the bed only when the officers appeared?"

"I think I was already standing there . . ."

"How long?"

"I think I posted myself there as soon as I entered my room and saw Uncle Ruhsilver sitting at the table . . ."

"Didn't you shake hands with the Rector?"

"I don't think I shook hands with him . . ."

"Are you on good terms with your uncle?"

"Yes, I am on good terms with him, very good terms . . ."

"But your gift of foretelling catastrophes told you immediately, after a mere look at the Rector, that something had happened to your mother, and it paralyzed you."

Christopher nods.

"But this type of paralysis surely doesn't depend on your will?"

Christopher does not answer.

"Never mind," President Behn brushes it aside; "the family matter does not concern us. You controlled your paralysis, then, with the effects reported by the officers. You strongly emphasize that your action was conscious. There is a possibility, however, that you may have imputed consciousness to your action only later, after hearing the report—I mean only now and here. In order to get a clearer idea of the nature and extent of your passive resistance, I shall not let the Court Reporter continue with the reading of the report but shall ask you to speak for yourself and give us an account of events during your preliminary examination, in so far as you may have maintained or regained consciousness during the proceedings. Can you do it?"

"Yes," Christopher answers.

"Your unsuccessful subjection to measures designed to break passive resistance has already been read to us from the report. You need not go into these measures any further."

"I was not aware of any such measures," says Christopher, and it seems to the president that the defendant is suppressing a smile.

"Is that so?" Behn remarks somewhat uncertainly. "At any rate, begin with the following morning."

And now it cannot possibly be deception: the defendant is smiling faintly.

3

It is difficult, on occasion, to keep track of the time of day and to know that now night has passed and morning is beginning. For when it has come to this, that the body has hardened and turned into armor, it is an entirely different life, a turtle's or a snail's life deep in the citadel of the body, and not only the time of day but people, too, are beyond the enclosing armor, at a remote distance; and since the eyes look out as through the eye slits of a closed vizor, the field of vision is narrowed.

Christopher was put on his feet and looked into the mousy face of the SD commissioner who asked him a few questions and immediately began to shout when he received no reply. Christopher was lifted up and put in a small closet which resembled a telephone booth. There was a repulsively sweetish odor in it, Christopher could hardly breathe and his heart began to hammer. The mouse face was glued to the outside of the round, platelike window and asked in regular intervals: "Do you want to talk?" Christopher held his breath as long as possible and stared at the little mustache that sat like a black fly on the oversized upper lip of the commissioner, and at last he lost consciousness. Then he felt fresh air, smelled vinegar and saw the little fly of a mustache again. The commissioner stood in the open door of the closet and asked: "Do you want to talk? You have two minutes to say yes." He waited, watch in hand, and then closed the door again; his mousy face appeared at the window, grew smaller and smaller, a dot on the horizon . . . When Christopher regained consciousness he did not open his eyes; he let them unbutton his shirt, listen to his heart, put him on a stretcher and carry him to a room which was very cold. The mouse face with the fly on it bobbed up once more, this time above him, and asked: "Do you want to talk now or shall I have you beaten to a pulp?" He gave him two minutes again, watch in hand, let the two SD men march in with steel rods and then said unexpectedly: "Enough for today!" Christopher was not beaten; he was taken to a cell and left alone for a long time—it must have been for the rest of the night.

When it has come to this, that the body is hardened, then the violence which the outer world tries to inflict on it, and even the respite which it is granted, only serve to harden it all the more. When Christopher saw the mouse face again after the long intermission, the commissioner seemed to have realized that his question: 'Do you want to talk?' had been sufficiently answered, and continued the examination in the form of a soliloquy. It was as if he were reading to himself a long questionnaire, whose inexhaustible theme was the connection between the encrusted man and the crumpled onion skin of a leaflet. For Christopher it was almost a sort of silent amusement to sit in his snail shell and listen to the monotonous rain of questions pattering outside—and perhaps, perhaps he was thus also protecting his friends, whose names were not mentioned.

But then—and the course of the hours had become ever less perceptible and ever less important—the commissioner changed his tactics and did not ask any more questions, but himself gave answers—not to the questions he had asked the prisoner, but to questions which burned in Christopher like the fire in the core of the encrusted earth. The man outside, that remote and impotent enemy with the fly of a mustache, reported the arrests of his friends in inexorable sequence: Hans' and Welte's, the professor's, and then the arrests of the women, yes, of Frau Dora and Sophia, the revered one and the beloved—and to these two women was now joined the third, the dearest of all, his mother: How could it be forgivable? But the commissioner began to read the testimony of the comrades, in inexorable sequence—and perhaps the day had turned to night again . . .

It is a different life, that turtle's or snail's life deep in the citadel of the body, but there is something terrifying and uncontrollable in the increasing hardening: you are ultimately like a fist which cannot be opened, neither from without nor from within where you yourself are. You have become the prisoner behind the bastion of your body, and it is harder, much harder to liberate yourself from it than to push yourself into it or to let yourself be drawn into it, in deepest entwinement of will and impulse.

When Christopher felt that he wanted to talk, that he had to talk, he could not move his chin. When the commissioner read and submitted to him the prepared deposition—"I, the undersigned Christopher Sauer, herewith declare that, together with the defendants Karl and Dora von Hennings, Hans and Sophia Moeller and Alexander Welte, I have participated in the preparation and distribution of a leaflet inciting to treasonable action"—he could not sign. They took him back to the cell, put the deposition and pen and ink on the chair next to his cot and left the electric light burning.

It may be that they observed him and saw how the sweat ran down his forehead. It may be that they heard him moan; for he could hear himself moan. His effort to liberate himself was prodigious, and the will to accomplish it and not to let up, and his determination to overcome the choking fear that his body might be paralyzed, irrevocably, in the deepest sense of the irrevocable, created such a tumult in his heart and brain that his eyes saw red, whether he opened them or shut them. He opened and shut them incessantly; he feared that he had gone blind. No, he thought he had to fight for his eyesight, too. His effort at bracing himself made the veins protrude from his forehead; he could feel the veins plainly, they lay on his forehead like two very small hot fingers, and perhaps the keenness of his sense of feeling was so great because he had lost his sense of sight.

Now it was a twofold fear: not to see any more and not to be seen any more. His friends don't see him, he has disappeared— And what then, if five are there and one is not, if five see one another again as prisoners but not the sixth? Then the most terrible of all uncertainties must rage in the hearts of the five, also in Sophia's heart—and once already, only last summer, as they were walking in the Isar valley, and it was night, she had suddenly said: "You know, I am really always afraid of you," and laughingly he had asked: "Why?" and she had answered gravely: "Because I don't know of what you may be capable."

She will think me capable of it! Christopher thought, tore his eyes open wildly, put the red clouds to flight and saw the dirty grayish mortar of the cell's ceiling again. To sign the deposition he needed his eyes and his right hand. As he moved his body in short jerks onto its side and toward the chair, he also shook and jogged at his right hand, from within, as one would shake a rusted doorknob—and finally he could move his fingers. When he had signed the paper—perhaps night had already passed—he fell asleep, exhausted, dead tired and contented, and this sleep completely thawed out his body.

4

Christopher however says nothing about the night and about the struggle with his own body. He gives a short, concise, mildly arrogant account which makes the fruitless efforts of the SD commissioner appear somewhat ridiculous. He closes with the sentence: "In the night I then signed the deposition."

But President Behn is no easy opponent and immediately asks: "Why did you not make your deposition orally?"

"Because I did not want to talk."

"Because you did not want to talk or because you were not able to talk?"

"Because I did not want to talk."

"I could imagine that the muscular contraction which you mentioned might have made it impossible for you to talk."

"I could have released my muscles in order to talk."

"The SD commissioner reports that after the testimony of your accomplices was read to you, you gave the impression of wanting to talk, but of not being able to do so."

"Wrong."

"But you were sweating with exertion—that is right, isn't it?"

"Quite right. Muscular contraction is an exertion and this exertion finally made me sweat."

"And why didn't you sign the deposition when the commissioner submitted it to you?"

"Because I did not wish to abandon my pose in the presence of the commissioner."

"He is convinced, however, that you wanted to sign but were incapable of doing it, and he observed that you not only sweated during this futile attempt, but that the exertion made the veins protrude from your forehead."

"I call that a compliment for the persuasiveness of my performance," Christopher says with a cursory smile.

"It is a compliment," President Behn observes with remarkable patience. "But tell us now, just exactly when in the night did you sign—immediately after you were carried back to the cell?"

"No . . ." Christopher answers, and he is on his guard. "I was very tired . . ."

"You fell asleep at once?"

"Let us say, I passed out . . ."

"But with your eyes open. The observer reports very descriptively, if somewhat oddly, that you were lying there like a paralyzed woman in labor. I suppose that means you did not move but nevertheless gave the impression of having something like cramps. Toward two o'clock you started to move visibly. It took you an hour and ten minutes to turn from your back to your side. You put your signature to the paper shortly before four o'clock. Then, to be sure, you did pass out, and snoring at that."

"It is rather obvious," Christopher says softly, "that the light wasn't left burning in my cell merely for my comfort."

"You mean to say that you continued playing your act to the end because you were being watched?"

"Yes."

"But why should you have done that?"

Christopher shrugs his shoulders and does not answer.

"And when did you decide to return to normality?"

"This morning, when I heard that I would be brought before the People's Court."

"And at that time you already were in the same state in which you are now?"

"My limbs were heavy and my muscles ached."

"And you also talked?"

"I had no opportunity to talk."

The president raises his head: "Are the guards present who escorted the defendant to this court?"

"Present, Herr Präsident!" calls the SS tractor and pops up from his seat next to Christopher's empty place on the prisoners' bench.

"Did the defendant have an opportunity to speak?"

"Yes, Herr Präsident," the man answers, "since I had orders to ask him, as casually as possible, how he was feeling."

"He did not answer?"

"He acted as though he hadn't heard the question."

"What was his general behavior?"

"He behaved like a drunk who hasn't slept himself quite sober, Herr Präsident."

"How did he act when he saw his accomplices again?"

"At first he gave the impression of not seeing them. Then someone called to him and suddenly he was wide awake and talked, and immediately he also got stubborn again."

"Stubborn in what way?"

"He refused to walk another step unless his handcuffs were removed—and yet he hadn't made any fuss before, when they were put on him."

"Who called to him?"

"This girl here," said the man, pointing to Sophia.

"Defendant Sophia Moeller, what was it you called to defendant Sauer?"

"I can't remember," Sophia answers.

"She called, 'Please, look at me!'" says the SS tractor.

"Defendant Sophia Moeller, why, in your opinion, did Sauer not look at you?"

"I never asked myself that question," Sophia answers.

"Have you some sort of close relationship with Sauer?"

"Yes," Sophia answers after a brief hesitation.

"Have you ever observed him to behave abnormally?"

"No."

"Defendant Karl Hennings, what was your impression of Sauer when he entered and did not seem to see you?"

"He gave me the impression of a man," says Karl, "who has been subjected to measures designed to break down passive resistance."

"A false impression, then—or do you still persist in your view after Sauer's own statement?"

"Certainly; for I did not say that his passive resistance had actually been broken down by these measures."

"You believe, then, that his performance was deliberate?"

Karl does not answer at once, and Christopher at the sinners' table turns his face to him with a sudden movement. "I believe it firmly," Karl says softly.

"Defendant Sauer," President Behn turns to Christopher, "how do you explain the fact that you took no notice of your fellow prisoners until your friend called to you?"

"I was elsewhere with my thoughts," Christopher replies.

"In view of the circumstances it seems almost incomprehensible to me that you should have been elsewhere with your thoughts, in so far as you could have any thoughts at all and were not still more or less in a state of insensibility."

"In my thoughts I was with my mother, for whose fate I feel responsible."

"And what was your reaction to the words called out to you by your friend?"

"I apologized to her and to my other friends."

"What for? For not having noticed them?"

"For letting them wait for me. You see, I know what that means and how tormenting it is."

To his astonishment the president observes that at these words the defendant Sophia Moeller hides her face in her hands and the others lower their faces abashed, and he cannot understand it, psychologically and pragmatically experienced though he is. He gazes reflectively into the bony, stubbly face of the man at the sinners' table and suddenly says to himself, almost shuddering: how he hates me! He raises his head and asks in a languid tone of voice: "By the way, what was the cause of your father's death?"

"The consequences of an accident."

"What accident?"

"A fall from the threshing floor."

"Did he fall often?"

Christopher does not answer, and again his jawbone stamps his face with a hard line from chin to ear.

"Epileptic?" the president asks.

"Alcoholic," says Christopher, barely opening his lips.

"I ask you now in this connection, defendant, if your so-called muscular contraction is not a pathological phenomenon?"

"No."

"I ask you now, and this is a question of great significance for you, if you have ever before suffered from this or a similar illness? I emphasize: illness."

"No."

"You assert, then, that you are not ill and were never ill?"

"I assert it emphatically."

"Very well," says President Behn, leaning forward and scanning the courtroom. "Sergeant, call the expert witness Professor Ackermann."

5

Christopher is not sent back to his seat in the prisoners' box, he stands at the table, lowers his eyes and waits. If the president expected to strike a blow of surprise in calling the witness, he finds himself disappointed; the defendant is not frightened or at any rate gives no sign of being frightened.

Professor Ackermann steps up to the table and Christopher looks at him. He recognizes the lean, beardless, bespectacled face of the man to whom he owes so much. The face is again in his possession; for he had lost it, he had seen it only from afar through the vizor slit—no, he had seen it once again, close up, that time when he reported to his benefactor at the beginning of the winter semester 1940, and was recommended by him to Karl Hennings. And yet he had lost the psychiatrist's face, perhaps because he wanted to lose it. Ackermann does not look at him.

President Behn quickly and rather informally rushes through the prescribed identification and swearing in of the witness—the oath includes the solemn promise to maintain silence about everything the witness may see, hear and say in this court. Then the president turns to Christopher: "Defendant, do you know the witness?"

"Yes," Christopher answers.

"Where did you meet him?"

"In the psychiatric clinic."

"In what capacity do you know him?"

"As my attending physician."

"Why were you taken to the clinic?"

"For observation of my mental and physical condition."

"Do you happen to know the date on which you were taken to the clinic?"

"March 16, 1940."

"Is that correct?" President Behn asks the psychiatrist.

"To the day," says Professor Ackermann, looking through his papers. "Brought in by military ambulance from the induction center of the Bodies barracks."

"What was his condition when he was received at the clinic?"

"He was in a stupor-like condition."

"Don't you think it remarkable then, Professor, that the defendant can remember the date?"

"The date is probably recorded on his certificate of discharge from the clinic."

"You think it unlikely then, if not impossible, that the defendant would remember the date of his entry into the clinic because he was aware of it at the time?"

"I think it unlikely."

"Defendant, do you know the date from the documents, or because you remember it?"

"Because I remember it," Christopher answers.

Now the psychiatrist looks at him, with a questioning and searching look.

"Do you wish to comment on the defendant's answer, Herr Professor?" President Behn urges.

"His answer may have been given in good faith, even from my point of view," says Ackermann; "an unstable individual's mental reconstruction may become remembrance."

President Behn narrows his eyes. "How long did the defendant stay in the psychiatric clinic?"

Ackermann looks through his papers.

"Twenty-seven days," says Christopher.

"Yes," Ackermann confirms without looking up, "until April 11, 1940."

"Had his condition improved?" the president asks.

"Not materially. The observation of the patient was concluded and he was transferred to the Army Convalescence Home at Oberstdorf in Allgäu."

"The results of your observation led you to render an opinion which exempted the defendant from military service, is that correct?"

"Yes."

"Then his condition was not only stupor-like, but was a real stupor."

"I didn't say that, because certain symptoms typical of stupor were missing from the patient's pathological picture."

"Be that as it may, you speak of a pathological picture, of the undoubtedly pathological condition of the defendant."

"Naturally!"

"Naturally," the president stresses. "Otherwise, how could you have reached the weighty decision to order the defendant's release from military service!"

"Perhaps I misunderstood your last words, Herr Präsident," says Ackermann, agitatedly fussing with his spectacles; "but could it possibly be that the Court has the slightest doubt about my professional integrity?"

"Not the slightest doubt, Herr Professor," says President Behn; "the defendant asserts, however, that he is not ill and never was ill, although at the time of his arrest and during the preliminary examination he was in a state exactly corresponding to the pathological picture observed by you and described in your written opinion."

"And how does the defendant explain his condition?" Ackermann asks softly.

"As an act of will power."

"That is impossible!" Ackermann exclaims hurriedly.

"I have proved that it is possible," Christopher says sharply.

"Which case do you mean now, defendant," President Behn takes up, "that of yesterday or that of March, 1940?"

"Both cases."

"What do you mean by that, man?" the witness says, turning to him. Ackermann is very pale and lifts both his hands as if to shake Christopher's shoulders and to shout: Is this your thanks?

"I mean by that, Herr Professor, that in both cases I simulated the stupor or whatever you want to call it—the last time so as to avoid having to testify, or in other words to shield my friends, and the first time in order not to have to become a soldier."

"I, on the other hand," Ackermann speaks slowly, fighting to control his agitation, "believe that you are only simulating your simulation, Sauer, and I can see no other motive for your attitude here but again a pathological . . ."

"Jesus Christ!" Christopher whispers and closes his eyes for a long moment, and there is such despair in his face that Ackermann rues his words—after all, he doesn't know why Christopher acts as he does.

"Dr. Ackermann," says President Behn, "my estimate of the situation is quite like your own and I now come to the pivotal point, that is, to the question whether the defendant is or is not of a sound mind. It is the task of the People's Court to judge those who commit crimes against the existence and the security of the Reich, but it is not its business to judge the mentally ill. If you deny or doubt defendant Sauer's accountability, the Court will have to decide whether the trial of defendant Sauer should be continued, or whether it should be stopped and the man be turned over to the health authorities."

Is that it? Karl asks himself, and his throat aches from dryness. Is this the trap door through which the devils let the poor devil of a Judas disappear? His throat aches, and between his heart and his stomach there is an unbearable pressure—and only a short while ago, at Christopher's words about the pain he had caused his friends by letting them wait, he had begged his forgiveness from the bottom of his heart . . .

Judge Lucius leans over to the president's ear and whispers: "This man's head is as clear as yours or mine . . ."

"I know that," Behn whispers back unamiably; "but the fellow interests me and, incidentally, he also interests the chief of the SD. I want to press him further; I am not completely convinced that he doesn't want to be separated from the others . . ."

"What an error . . ." Lucius murmurs, shaking his head. Perhaps it was only a thought, since it would have been improper to say it. President Behn turns away abruptly and thinks: the old man is becoming impossible. And he now considers a substitute for Judge Lucius after all.

Professor Ackermann surveys Christopher's lowered face and again sees infinitesimal beads of sweat on his forehead; and again, as once before, when he sent the stretcher bearers out of the room, he feels affection—no, admiration—for this man. Christopher lifts his head under the doctor's gaze, looks at him briefly and imploringly, and then he turns around and walks toward the prisoners' box.

"Defendant!" the president calls, leaning forward, dumbfounded. "How can you dare leave your place?"

Christopher stops and looks at Sophia and Karl; he does not turn around, but speaks with a clear voice:

"I only wanted to show the witness where I belong, as a proof of my accountability!" Then he smiles to his friends, and his smile begs them for an answer, and they smile back, Sophia and Dora first, Karl last.

"You belong here in front! Come back to the table!" the president exclaims sharply. "Immediately!"

Christopher returns to the sinners' table, and his face is cheerful.

"Herr Präsident," Professor Ackermann speaks with deliberation, "you have put a question to me which decidely impugns my own responsibility as a physician and a German. As a physician it would be irresponsible of me to deny that even a pathologically inclined person may be accountable and thus also punishable. As a German it would be utterly irresponsible of me to let a criminal who endangers the security of the community escape unpunished."

President Behn puckers his eyebrows in annoyance. "Would you please express yourself in somewhat less general terms, Professor? Do you consider the defendant accountable, or don't you?"

"His behavior here, in so far as I could observe it, does not permit me to declare him unaccountable."

"But did you not state just a moment ago that his behavior here was pathological?"

"I am coming more and more to the realization, Herr Präsident, that in his case it is a question of a pathological determination—and precisely for this reason a formidable determination—to stand by his convictions."

"Indirectly you are admitting two things with this statement, Professor. First, that he was a simulant, and second, that you did not see through his act and consequently exempted a simulant from military service."

Ackermann shrugs his shoulders. "To err is human, Herr Präsident."

He observes the president writing a few words on his note pad, tearing off the page and passing it to the young SS officer who reads it and puts it in his breast pocket with a nod of approval. Professor Ackermann does not know what is written on that piece of paper, but he can imagine what it is. He remains calm, he is not timid by nature, and at this moment especially he is satisfied with himself.

Also President Behn receives a note, from the right, relayed through Judge Schneidhammer, and he reads: "Respectfully wish to report that as for accountability and also as for courage I feel definitely inferior to this devil of a fellow. Signed Freyberg." President Behn crumples up the note, looks up, and says languidly: "That is all, Dr. Ackermann, I thank you. Since the provisions of the penal code do not apply to procedure in the People's Court, you are not required to remain here, but are at liberty to go."

Professor Ackermann bows slightly and struggles with himself whether to throw one last glance at Christopher or not. He thinks of the note that has gone to the SS judge, and he looks at Christopher. But Christopher keeps his head turned away. Ackermann turns around and walks away, and he looks toward the prisoners' bench at Karl Hennings, his old friend. But Hennings keeps his head turned away. The doctor knows that they avoid looking at him in order not to incriminate him; but he is pained nevertheless, he feels excluded.

The police sergeant shuts the door of the hall behind the witness. President Behn asks: "Defendant, are you a conscientious objector on religious grounds?"

"No, on grounds of political conviction."

"Because you do not want to fight for the Germany of the Führer?"

"Yes."

"Your opposition to the Germany of the Führer, then, did not develop under the influence of defendant Hennings and his circle?"

"No, it did not develop at all; it is in me, as my heart is in me."

"That's just talk! At the time of the National Socialist revolution you were a boy of thirteen and under the influence of your environment, probably of your mother or of your cleric uncle."

"My mother did not influence me, I was with her so rarely," says Christopher, and he continues after a brief pause, "but she gave me the heart that is in me . . ."

Chapter Nine

THE LEGEND OF THE BASTARD

It came to pass that in her thirty-eighth year and after a clean, hard life, Ursula Sauer, hereditary peasant proprietress of Vogelöd, fell into ill repute as a whore.

She was a well-shaped woman, still beautiful and fiery, with that Mediterranean darkness of hair, skin and oblong eyes which one finds along the ancient Roman roads in the Tyrol, in Salzburg and in Upper Bavaria. She looked capable of committing what her people branded as the unpardonable sin. So far her life had been conformable to custom and tradition, she was a faithful daughter of the Roman Church and a worthy sister of the Reverend Rector Ruhsilver whose parish embraced the hamlet Vogelöd.

Each Sunday she went to early mass in the old, needle-spired village church at Unterhall, kneeling in the old ancestral pew of the Ruhsilver family, whose members one and all lived and died in the village and were buried in the graveyard behind the church, and each Sunday she went to confession and received the host from her brother.

Though burdened with work in her house and tavern and on her farm at Vogelöd, three miles away from Unterhall, she went to church even on weekdays when occasions of special devotion arose, for instance, in March when the Saint Joseph exercises were held, certainly on Maundy Thursday to pray at the Holy Sepulchre when a dark wooden Jesus with a mysteriously rapturous face lay beneath the main altar, surrounded by many-colored oil lamps, and the crosses were draped in purple and Rector Ruhsilver wore purple vestments. In May she attended the lovely novena for the Holy Virgin, at least on Saturday, which is the day of God's mother, and in June she went to the Sacred Heart devotions, of which one really shouldn't miss a single one.

People knew her as a pious and industrious woman, as she had to be, pitching in where the work was hardest; and they didn't hold it against her that she had born only one child to Tobias Sauer, the hereditary peasant proprietor, and for the rest had had only miscarriages, that God's blessing, therefore, did not seem to brighten her righteous life. People did not feel sorry for her, however; not only was her life the way it had to be, but she also had to accept her lot in humble resignation. And a part of her lot was that Tobias Sauer was a drunkard and an epileptic.

That was how Ursula's life looked from the outside, how her neighbors and kinfolk judged it—and, incidentally, there were only a few neighbors since Vogelöd consists of nothing but the big Sauer farm, three cottagers, and the weaver Weber, old Wendelin, whose name was Weber because he was a weaver, he and his fathers from old, and he was a respected ancient, deeply enmeshed in his own thoughts. Of kinfolk there were many, more or less the entire indigenous population of the parish seat Unterhall.

Ursula herself saw her life not much differently; she judged it in the same way people around her judged it, and like them she knew no other norms of life but conformity to the old established ways. She did conform, without any difficulty, and never asked herself whether her life was hard or easy. Nor could it be said that Tobias Sauer was a bad man; he was a handsome and a prodigal man, the richest peasant in the border district; he was a wild man and a sick one, and the wildness and sickness attained a strange mixture in him, frightening; to be sure, yet not repulsive—no, it could even turn into a frighteningly attractive ecstasy. And when he took to drink it was no ordinary craving for intoxication, but a means of stunning his tormenting fear of his own body. Thus it was that matters stood with him and not otherwise. It was God's will, not a trial, and Ursula did not ask herself if she was unhappy, she did not even ask herself if her husband was unhappy. She lived with the wild, sick, drunken man in holy wedlock, managed house and farm and tavern when Tobias was no longer able to do so, and went to confess to her brother when she found herself frighteningly fascinated by her husband's fits.

At all times of her life there was her brother, the Rector, her hold and her security. Strictly speaking he was her half-brother, twenty years older than she, a son of the first marriage of their father who had been blessed with many wives and children and had been sixty-five when she was born (though she was not to be the last of his children), and had died at ninety as if by mistake. But this very old man, whose seventieth birthday was her first childhood memory, was to her like a grandfather, and brother Rupert, who from inclination and family tradition had become a clergyman, occupied the position of father or, rather, educator; for their relationship was determined by the cassock he wore, and permitted only a spiritual intimacy, not the intimacy of brother and sister. She did not call him brother or Rupert, but Rector; and there wasn't a single particle of her life that he didn't know. By virtue of his office he saw to it that her life should be pleasing to God, and with all respect for him she felt that he loved her both as a brother and as a father. If there was anything in her life that she permitted herself to regard as a happy, divine ordinance, it was this blood relationship to piety.

And there was her son Christopher, her only child, a handsome and wild child, and, she hoped to God, not a sick child. The Rector, who was bound to know, called him a wide-awake boy, let him attend the village school at Unterhall for only three years, and then sent him to the famous monastery school at Ettal near Oberammergau. Thus, in a way, it had already been decided that Christopher was not to be a farmer, but a cleric—the only alternatives for fitting into the traditional way of life. And yet it was an unusual decision, because he was the only child and heir to the Sauer farm. But perhaps Rector Ruhsilver counted on Ursula having another successful pregnancy; perhaps he even believed that Christopher's early dedication to the priesthood might have a beneficial influence on God's blessing and on the matrimonial life of his parents.

Thus it came about that at nine years of age Christopher was separated from Ursula, and that from this time on she had to learn over and over again to know him. Not to love him, for love him she did, once and for all, and where there is love there can never be estrangement, but only and always a mother's readiness and capacity for understanding. Learning to know him and knowing him again was one and the same for Ursula. One look sufficed, and she understood Christopher, the rare visitor, as did no one else on earth.

It would be wrong to say that Rector Ruhsilver determined the political attitude of his parish; he was merely the voice of the Church, and it was only natural for the Church to back the party that served Catholicism, in other words to back the Bavarian People's Party. It was only natural for the Rector to remind his parishioners, before elections, of their duty to the community, their duty to cast their votes in support of the Church. And it was only natural for his deep voice to grow ever stronger and to use ever stronger words when the surge of National Socialism sharpened the electoral conflict and the Catholic party in Bavaria felt its dominance threatened. And after Hitler had won, or rather because he had won, Rector Ruhsilver had to fight on; though the Bavarian People's Party had disappeared, the Church was still there, and the Church knew that it had to fight for its life now, and that it had to fight cautiously and quietly—and the Rector fought cautiously and quietly, with the gentle and sad pastoral letters of his bishop and with quotations from the sermons of the great Cardinal Faulhaber of Munich.

It was only natural for Ursula to know who was the enemy of piety to which she was related by blood. But the enemy remained for her something like the devil, like the spirit of evil; for in 1933 there wasn't a Nazi in Vogelöd nor even in Unterhall.

When Christopher came home for the Easter holiday that year, he wore the becoming dress of the Catholic boy scouts. That was something new for Ursula, as were the boy's violent outbursts against the Hitler Youth, although this organization of the devil, according to Christopher's belligerent assertions, did not exist nor would ever exist in the Ettal monastery. In no time, however, she was again accustomed to her son, to his neat dress as well as to his eager talk; both were pleasing to God, in the estimation of the Rector and also in her own estimation; and if Christopher expressed it differently, wilder and more vividly, that was because he was the son of Tobias, who also used expressions different from those of his brother-in-law Ruhsilver and with frightening, drunken eloquence gave the Revelation of Saint John an anti-Hitlerite interpretation.

It went on like that for the next few years; Christopher came to Vogelöd once or twice a year, Ursula observed that he continued to grow, and talked ever more grown-up; she kept pace with his time as it were and she was sure of him, sure of his immutability as her son or of his fidelity to himself, and she was sure that he pleased God just as he was and as he developed. And that time, which harbored the spirit of evil and passed over the border district quietly and uneventfully, though uncannily, was exceedingly vivid in her son; he violently attacked it and at the same time enlightened her about it. Ursula learned from him that the spirit of evil had assumed a million incarnations throughout the land and had become omnipotent; that there was no longer any open struggle and no longer any handsome boy scout dress, but that there was a hidden resistance and a secret collaboration of the dissolved youth organizations under the leadership of intrepid young men of the clergy and the laity, who daily risked their lives.

Time jumped ahead, and Christopher told his mother that he had to live in Munich now, that the Chaplain himself wanted to keep him in the center of resistance, and that it was a great honor. Ursula understood that it was a great honor, even if she didn't know who "the Chaplain" was. But she did know that he was more than a man who pleased God, that he was a fighter for God, and she persuaded Rector Ruhsilver to let Christopher change schools—she did not have to persuade her husband, for Tobias no longer had any interest in such matters. Incidentally, she told the Rector only that the Chaplain wanted to take his pupil Christopher to Munich with him, and that it was a great honor. But she did not speak of the hidden resistance, of the secret collaboration and of the nameless chaplain's pious heroism. She did not regard this omission as a lie and did not feel compelled to confess it. The understanding between mother and son could contain no sin, not even a venial one.

It was on an evening in the late fall of 1936 that Christopher unexpectedly appeared at Vogelöd. He entered the rambling house not through the taproom nor through the side entrance, but from the rear through the stables, and he was not alone. He stuck his head in the lighted pantry where Ursula was fetching some wax candles for All Soul's day from one of the beautifully painted chests, and when he saw that his mother was alone, he entered, followed by a man of slight build wearing a coarse woolen cape and a sports cap. Ursula recognized the sports cap; it belonged to Christopher who was bareheaded; and it looked rather strange over the transparent, bespectacled face of the man, and the knapsack he carried also seemed out of place, like an insult to his narrow back.

Ursula did not express any astonishment at seeing Christopher at Vogelöd while school was in session, and so great was her understanding for her son and the strange man who wore her son's cap and on his face a shy smile reflecting his pious courage, that she didn't say anything at all, but went to close the door which the stranger had not dared close behind him. Christopher asked for something to eat and for a glass of milk for himself and for the gentleman. He said it thusly: "For the gentleman."

"I'll bring it here," said Ursula and stopped in front of the door, thinking. "But I have only smoked pork and cabbage, perhaps it'll make you thirsty later," she said.

"It will do," said Christopher.

"Or should I make some fried potatoes for the gentleman and for yourself?" Ursula asked. "That would also keep you and it won't make you thirsty."

"We haven't much time," Christopher answered.

Ursula left and returned with a loaded wooden tray covered with a linen cloth. In this way no one could see what she was carrying out of the kitchen. She put the tray on one of the chests; there was no table in the pantry.

"Your father is playing chess with old Wendelin in the taproom," Ursula said to her son.

"Yes," Christopher nodded, uncovering the food, "we'll have to move on at once."

"God bless you, Frau Sauer," said the stranger, the gentleman, opening his cape at the neck; and Ursula saw the low, white, upright collar and a bit of the black cassock worn by priests, and she quickly turned away.

"I hope the gentleman will enjoy the food," she said and left the room.

She went to the taproom, sat down with her darning basket and darned stockings. Her husband and Wendelin played chess and did not speak. The game as well as old man Weber, the weaver, had a quieting effect on Tobias; but they played only once a week, and Ursula called the chess evening "quiet Monday."

At another table sat the cottager Krumberger, who drank beer and likewise said nothing. Ursula started a conversation with him because the silence was too great for her and because she had to prevent Krumberger from leaving the place too soon. And she also had to keep an eye on the barmaid. The other servants already were asleep.

When the dogs barked outside—not her own dogs who knew Christopher, but the Krumberger dog and then the Schweninger dog and lastly the Weber dog—Ursula knew that her son and the gentleman were on their way again and she even knew which way they had gone. She knew the dogs by their barking, and immediately in back of old Weber's house starts the trail up the wooded mountain, named without much imagination the "Forest Mountain," along whose ridge ran the Austrian border. The border meant nothing to the youngsters of Vogelöd and when they went to pick blueberries in the summer they were not conscious of the fact that the berries on the northern slope grew in Bavaria, and those on the southern slope grew in Austria.

By March, 1938, Christopher had smuggled fourteen persons across the border, and the understanding between mother and son had grown into a collaboration so discreet that not even Ursula knew the identity of those whom Christopher led to safety. She saw only him alone, gave him the key to the pantry which contained all the necessary supplies, and assumed responsibility for providing safe passage. When she knocked at the door of the pantry, the nocturnal march to the "Forest Mountain" could begin; and after a while the neighbors' dogs didn't bark any more: Ursula would ask Krumberger, Schweninger and old Weber to lock up their dogs, so her husband's badly needed rest would not be disturbed, and the neighbors always complied with her request.

After March, 1938, however, the blueberries on the southern slope of the "Forest Mountain" grew in the Third Reich; Austria had been incorporated, the power of evil no longer knew any boundaries, Rector Ruhsilver grew more cautious yet, and Ursula knew that Christopher would bring no more fugitives.

He came at Easter time, alone, with his high-school graduation diploma—he was eighteen now. But he did not speak of his plans for the future, as young men out of school are expected to do. He was taciturn and distressed, despite having passed his examinations with flying colors, and when Rector Ruhsilver insisted that his nephew now enter the seminary at Freilassing, Ursula had to speak up and say: "Why don't you give him time!"

When he left to return to Munich, he said to his mother, "So far almost all has been in vain."

That was no news to Ursula; his face had already told her as much. She gave him time and wasn't quite sure what he did with his time. He stayed in Munich and Ursula heard little or nothing from him. And within two boisterous years the power of evil reached out not only over the Salzburg country whose snow-covered peaks Ursula could see from a spot on the road to Unterhall, but over the whole of Europe. And Ursula now saw none but very old or very young men or sick men like Tobias, and among her kinfolk in Unterhall there were already some war widows.

Ursula, however, began to rack her brains about an insoluble problem: how could it be conceivable for Christopher to become a soldier, to march into battle and to fight under the command and for the triumph of evil—and how could it *not* be conceivable?

After a long absence Christopher unexpectedly returned to Vogelöd in the early part of March, 1940. He said nothing about his doings—only his face told his mother that so far almost all had been in vain—and reported that he was to be inducted into the army on March 15. Ursula committed the grave error of not concealing the news from her husband. In those days Tobias lived in exhausting fear of his body and drank copiously. He did not sit on a chair, but on a thick mattress, lest he be surprised by his body and knocked about. With a pitiful and at the same time mysterious expression on his bloated face he waved to Christopher to come nearer, and the son sat down next to the father on the mattress.

"Chris has been drafted?" he asked as if he were not speaking with him but about him, and he looked into space.

"Yes, Father."

Tobias slowly shook his head and spoke—and by speaking in a very deep voice he indicated that he was not speaking his own words, but the words of the scripture: " 'Who is like unto the beast? and who is able to war with him?' "

Now this was from the thirteenth chapter of the Revelation of Saint John. Christopher knew it, and Ursula knew it by heart, her husband had quoted it so frequently, and she felt apprehensive.

"All must war with him," said Christopher.

"And war *for* him," Tobias said—and by speaking in a very clear voice he indicated that now he was interpreting the scripture; "war *for* him and carry his mark on their foreheads and on their sleeves and then, following the great voice of the third angel, they shall drink of the wine of the wrath of God and be tormented with fire and brimstone in the presence of the holy angels, and in the presence of the Lamb; and they shall have no rest day and night, in the smoke of their torment for ever and ever. Is this what Chris must do and what must befall him?"

"No," Christopher answered, "I shall not do it, Father, and it shall not befall me."

"Then Chris is not going to join the army?" Tobias asked and chuckled slyly.

"I must, Father."

"What is a 'must' in the face of the beast?" Tobias chuckled, and continued in a deep voice: " 'And there was given him a mouth speaking great things and blasphemies; and there was given to him authority to continue forty and two months . . .' " And in a clear voice: "Three and a half years the war will last and six months already have gone by and there is no 'must' when one knows that in thirty-six months . . ."

"Why do you figure it from the beginning of the war, Father, and not from 1933?"

"Because then it doesn't come out right!" Tobias shouted. "And it must come out right!" He raised his forefinger and spoke in a deep voice: " 'And he causes all, the small and the great, and the rich and the poor, and the free and the bond, that there be given them a mark on their right hand, or upon their forehead; and that no man should be able to buy or to sell, save he that hath the mark, even the name of the beast or the number of his name. Here is wisdom. He that hath understanding, let him count the number of the beast; for it is the number of a man: and his number is Six hundred and sixty and six . . . !' " And in a clear voice: "Here is wisdom! HITLER has six letters. That's the first six. H is the eighth letter, I is 9, T is 19, L is 11, E is 5, R is 14. That totals up to 66. And we have the number of the beast: Six sixty and six!"

"That's right!" Ursula exclaimed agitatedly; for she felt disaster approaching.

"That is not right," said Christopher, and he did not see his mother's imploring look, because he figured with his eyes closed; "R is 17, not 14."

"It must be right!" Tobias screamed and jumped up from the mattress.

"Of course it's right," Ursula tried to pacify him. "Christopher figured wrong."

But Tobias did not listen to her and wanted to be left alone, so he could figure. He figured through half the night and forgot to drink. At two o'clock Ursula saw that he had fallen asleep on his mattress; she pulled off his boots and covered him.

In the morning Tobias went to the threshing floor; his face was ashen, he was monosyllabic, but apparently quieted. Perhaps it was a mistake that Ursula did not follow him alone, but with Christopher. Tobias stood high up on the ladder and with his pitchfork stabbed at the pile of chaff which he needed for the stables. He turned his head, looked down to his son and said with a pathetic smile, "It doesn't come out right . . ."

Then it seemed as though he were listening for something, his face changed in a strange way, becoming at once transported and distorted—a blissful grimace.

"Toby!" Ursula screamed, running to the ladder. Tobias' body became slowly disjointed, as if he were a weight-lifting circus athlete; and his right arm with the pitchfork was stretched out backwards, stiffly and unnaturally. And then it was as though his body were blown up by a mine and torn to pieces by the explosion. His legs pushed away from the ladder with such force that they broke the rung on which they stood.

Ursula ducked so as not to be hit by the ladder and the falling body; she covered her face with her hands, but then she had to look after all. Tobias sprawled, impaled on the prongs of the pitchfork, and yet his body raged and danced, if only for a short time.

Christopher stood as if paralyzed, yes, paralyzed; he still stood there as the farm hands came rushing to the scene, and the maids and finally old Wendelin Weber who knew how to treat wounds and hurts, and who had a cure for every ill, though naturally not for death. Christopher stood like one tied to a post; and it was a great effort for him to get free, as if he had to break his chains. And this, too, Ursula had to witness.

The widow Ursula knew that her son was to report for military duty on March 15; but she did not believe it. A long time passed without any news from him and she believed less and less that he had been inducted. Late in the summer he returned to Vogelöd, emaciated despite the ruddy color of his face, no longer elastic, but moving with a strange caution, as if his body had undergone a change or as if he had lost his confidence in it. And he came in civilian clothes, as his mother had expected.

"You weren't inducted," said Ursula, not even as a question.

"I was inducted," Christopher countered, "but I was discharged again."

"Why?" Ursula asked softly and sadly, and the son saw that his mother had grown ten years older in these months.

"Because I simulated the sickness," Christopher answered.

"What does 'simulate' mean?" Ursula asked.

"I acted as if I had the sickness," said Christopher and didn't look at her.

"I guess it's no sin," Ursula whispered pensively.

"That I simulated?"

"That you are lying to yourself, Chris, or to me . . ."

"But I am not ill, mother!"

"Then maybe it isn't a lie, but good faith," said Ursula, and there were tears in her eyes.

To Ursula this happened rarely.

And this is what happened to her on Christmas Eve in the year 1941.

The Christmas tree was lighted, Ursula distributed presents to the help, now consisting only of maids except for the aged foreman, and the old horn gramophone—ordinarily reserved for the guests in the taproom and performing only upon the insertion of a ten-pfennig piece—bawled "Silent Night," the only available Christmas record, with "Oh, Thou Joyous Christmastide" on the reverse side. Ursula interrupted the presentation of gifts when the song had run out, turned the disc around and dropped another coin in the slot.

At this moment the door was opened, the front door to the taproom, and Christopher stood on the threshold, and Ursula forgot to set the needle to the disc, and it ran off without uttering a sound, for ten pfennigs.

Christopher did not stand alone on the threshold; holding on to his hand stood a little boy perhaps two years old, a lovely child in fine clothes, his eyes enraptured by the Christmas tree.

"This is Fridolin," Christopher introduced him smilingly, and he spoke more to the help than to his mother. And Ursula felt her heart beating and did not know why; for this time she did not know what was happening to her through her son, she only saw him miraculously cheerful, and his face proclaimed that no longer was all in vain, and she felt anxiety in her heart, though a sweet anxiety.

Fridolin tore loose and with small sounds of rapture tripped to the Christmas tree. Ursula picked him up and it was so blissful to carry a child in her arms, for the first time in twenty years, for the first time since she had carried Chris in her arms; and she lifted the child to the tree, as she had once done with Chris, so he could reach and pluck the silvered nuts, the little bells and the little wax angels. And the child was as happy in her arms as Chris had once been, and when she wanted to put him down on the floor he cried and clutched her.

So she kept him on her lap when the doughnut feast started. The foreman tended and paid the gramophone, alternating between "Silent Night" and "Oh, Thou Joyous Christmastide." The maids were delighted with Fridolin; he had black curls and moist doe eyes with long, silky lashes and an adorable, well-shaped, brownish little face, and the foreman, his tongue loosened by the Christmas punch, exclaimed: "Could be your own bastard for sure, missis!" At that, Christopher burst out in loud laughter, with flashing eyes and flashing teeth. Ursula also laughed, softly, although she had not touched any drink.

When she saw that Fridolin had fallen asleep on her lap, she rose cautiously and carried him out, her eyes fastened on his sleeping little face. Christopher followed her, and the servants looked at them, suddenly silent in their eagerness to broach the momentous question of who this little Christmas child might be. The foreman sacrificed another coin to the gramophone, so it would bawl while they talked.

Ursula carried the boy to her bedroom and laid him on the bed of Tobias, God rest his soul! The bed was always freshly made and she opened it every night to let the departed one know that his bedstead was prepared for him. Christopher entered the room after her, carrying a small suitcase. Ursula undressed the child. She examined his firm body and his round little belly. Christopher took a pair of diminutive pajamas of light blue flannel from the suitcase and handed them to her. She put them on the boy and covered him.

She looked at Christopher. "He's a Jew boy," she said.

"Yes," Christopher nodded, "I knew his parents well. I esteemed them highly, they were our confidential physicians."

"What does that mean?" asked Ursula.

"Both were physicians, Dr. Hans Blum and Dr. Alice Blum, and of course they were not allowed to practice or could have only Jewish patients and they offered their services to us; we needed doctors. Dr. Hans Blum was a surgeon and Alice, really a women's doctor, assisted him. It took courage to be our confidential doctors."

"Yes," Ursula nodded.

"They only married in November, 1938, although they had known each other a long time. Then all the Jews were sent to concentration camps, among them Dr. Blum; but he never got out, perhaps because it was discovered that he had been our confidential doctor. I suppose he isn't alive any more. And Fridolin was born in August, 1939, on August 7. I remember very well, because Alice was very happy that he was an August child, a lion."

"I am an August child, too, you know," Ursula smiled.

"I know," Christopher smiled. "I am a crab, a crustacean, and so is Alice—and she was deported to Poland; perhaps her shell will be hard enough, she believed in hardness, and she couldn't or wouldn't take Fridolin along, it would have been certain death for him—yes, she didn't want to take him along; she loves him very much. And she brought him to me, at the last minute."

"And you bring him to me," said Ursula.

"To whom else?" Christopher asked.

"To whom else . . ." Ursula repeated.

"You don't know it and you can't imagine it, Mother," Christopher said after a pause, "but it has even happened that a Jew or half-Jew in Germany dishonored his mother and made an adulteress of her with a non-Jew in order to slip through the net and please the race maniacs."

"That is a sin that cries out to Heaven," said Ursula.

"But what would you say, Mother," Christopher asked, "if this were again the time of the slaying of the children of Bethlehem, and a woman said to Herod's bailiffs, 'This is my child and not a child of Bethlehem,' and thus saved it by taking upon herself the shame of being an adulteress? Would this be a sin?"

"That is not a sin," said Ursula and unpacked the suitcase containing the boy's suits, coats, shoes and underthings. "What's this?" she asked, pulling out a yellow envelope.

"His birth and vaccination certificate," said Christopher.

"What shall I do with it?"

"Hide it."

Ursula put the envelope in the linen closet between some of Tobias' shirts which were no longer used. Then mother and son went back to the taproom, and the servants broke off their conversation.

"A pretty little boy!" the foreman shouted; for the gramophone was bawling "Holy Night," but stopped that very moment, and the inserted coin dropped into the coin box with a tinkle. "The very picture of the Christ child," the foreman said suggestively, "a very lovely child."

"No wonder," Ursula smiled.

"Haha!" Christopher laughed with flashing eyes and flashing teeth.

Then they all drove to Unterhall to attend midnight mass, all except Ursula who did not want to leave Fridolin untended. And thus Unterhall, too, heard the first whispering of rumor in the holy night.

After the holidays Christopher returned to Munich. Fridolin stayed, hung on to Ursula's apron strings, said mommy to her and slept in her room in the late Tobias' huge bed.

Rustic life, intimately entwined with teeming nature and dependent on the blessing of fructification, knows no narrow-minded morals in the relation between the sexes; the peasant lad is allowed to climb up the ladder to the maid's room at night, and the peasant maiden is allowed to receive him; the country is ruled by an unsentimental utilitarian principle, a sanctioned form of trying out love which wants to assure itself of physical compatibility and even of the blessing of fructification before plunging into matrimony. Matrimony, however, is a sacrament, indissoluble and irrevocable; and if rural custom does not accord equal rights to the sexes and closes an eye to a husband's infidelity, it has nothing but rigid and inexorable severity for a wife who has erred.

The mistress of the Sauer tavern has a bastard! In Vogelöd and Unterhall people started to figure. The bastard was in his third year and Tobias Sauer had been dead for a year and a half. This, however, was the simplest problem in arithmetic. Much more difficult adding and subtracting was called for to solve the two most important problems: when and where had Ursula Sauer conceived the bastard, and when and where had she given birth to him.

Whosoever calculates in the ledger of his neighbor's trespasses arrives at some result. Had not Ursula been in Reichenhall alone now and then, and even in Salzburg, toward the end of 1938, ostensibly to make purchases? Had she not met her lover there, or perhaps several lovers? Just toward the end of 1938, had she not had an especially sinful prettiness, fiery eyes and a voluptuous body—at thirty-five years of age, when any righteous peasant woman has long ceased to be coveted? And then the pregnancy? Haha, she only fooled us when we believed her to be an honest, virtuous wife, bravely bearing the cross of her husband's wretched condition! But she isn't fooling us now that we see the strange little fruit!

Is she not tall and erect, of powerful build, modestly dressed in many skirts uncertainly surrounding her stomach and broad hips? Had anyone been able to tell when she bore Christopher, Tobias' child—let's hope to God—and his three or four stillborn brothers and sisters? Three or four: you see, we don't even know exactly how many miscarriages she had. No, it was quite possible not to see that she was pregnant with the strange little fruit, although this or that cousin now remembered having said to her in just those summer months of 1939, "Lord, Ursula, but you're getting big!" They all remembered, however, that she had then gone to Salzburg for three days, ostensibly to buy Tyrolese wine—haha, Tyrolese wine! And with that the calculation came out right.

But the ledger of guilt was not closed with this, it was only opened. For now it was no longer Ursula who had born the cross of matrimony, but the late Tobias, God rest his soul, and perhaps his cross had been so heavy that he fell under it, again and again, until he fell on the pitchfork; and who had seen her cry then, the whore, who couldn't remember her tearless stare during the services for the departed one? And wasn't it easy now to imagine that it had not been Tobias who had held the pitchfork as he fell, but that bad woman who was standing close by? It must be said, however, that this thought occurred only to a few termagants and was rejected with horror by the others; what could be seen and figured out was sufficient—the bastard sufficed for Ursula's excommunication.

Ursula meanwhile went on living in her accustomed way and took her proscription with cheerful unconcern.

Every Sunday she drove to Unterhall to attend early mass, as always; confessed the petty trespasses of the week and received communion. But on one of the first Sundays of the new year Rector Ruhsilver did not give her absolution at once, with the customary penance of three Lord's prayers, but asked: "Have you nothing more to say to me, my daughter?"

"No, Rector," answered Ursula.

"Have you really nothing more to say to me, my daughter?"

"No, Rector," answered Ursula. Only then he absolved her, with three Lord's prayers.

In the early afternoon of the following day he bicycled to Vogelöd. The curtsying maid told him that the mistress was in the laundry, and wanted to go to call her. But the Rector asked her not to trouble herself, went to the laundry himself and found the door locked. Ursula's voice begged for patience, as she was just bathing Fridolin. The Rector could not understand why she had to lock the door when she bathed the child; but he said nothing and waited patiently.

When she opened the door, he saw the boy in a tiny bathrobe of red toweling. He had never seen a child dressed that way. Fridolin laughed to him, he was a friendly child, not afraid of people. Ursula knelt in front of him and put on his stockings.

"Yes," said Rupert Ruhsilver and stroked the child's curls, "I think we shall have to have a talk together, Ursula."

"Yes," Ursula nodded.

"What about this child, Ursula?"

"It's the way it is, Rector."

"It is as people say it is, Ursula?"

"I guess it must be so, Rector."

"What hurts and disappoints me as your brother, Ursula, is your obduracy."

"Oh, Rupert," she said, shrugging her shoulders, "I can't help that either."

It moved him strangely that she should call him by his Christian name, and he pretended more severity than he felt. "What disturbs me greatly as your spiritual adviser, Ursula, is the fear that you may have made a false confession."

She looked at him and shook her head, slowly and smilingly: "I did not make a false confession, Rupert."

"But what if my conscience doesn't allow me to give you absolution and Holy Communion in the future?"

"Then I shall have to go to the Capuchins in the monastery; it's only two miles farther."

Ruhsilver lowered his head, defeated. He pondered. Then he asked an unexpected question: "Where is Fridolin's baptismal certificate, Ursula?"

She started, and he saw it. "He has no baptismal certificate," she answered softly.

"Good Heavens!" the priest exclaimed, "hasn't he been baptized?"

"He hasn't been baptized, Rupert . . ."

"How can you let his little soul live in darkness, Ursula?"

"How can I do otherwise?" she whispered in distress.

"It will be a sin upon your soul, my daughter, if you don't bring the child to me and have me baptize him."

"But we have no right to do it, Rupert!" she exclaimed.

Ruhsilver looked at her. "Come, Ursula, speak out, have confidence in me. Perhaps I am beginning to suspect why you must lock yourself in when you bathe the child."

"I have confidence in you, Rupert, but I am also afraid for you . . ."

"Afraid?"

"If I tell it to you now, then you share the secret, Rupert, and you would not be protected by the secret of the confessional, and

I must be afraid for you, maybe even of you. I'm not going to tell it to you now, and not in this house."

She told it to him on the following Sunday before early mass, under the seal of confessional secrecy; and Rector Ruhsilver spoke: "*Absolve te!*" He said it in an unusually loud voice, as if he wanted the world outside the confessional box to hear it.

On the square in front of the church stood three women, Ursula's cousins, and as Ursula approached, quite stately in her Sunday dress of stiff, black taffeta, someone said quite loud enough for her to hear it: "Here comes the whore!" and Ursula passed them with a smile, the picture of sinful pride.

But there was one person in Vogelöd who did not believe in Ursula's sin, a respected ancient, deeply enmeshed in his thoughts: the weaver Wendelin. He had much time for thought, for his loom stood idle, by order of the wicked ruling power which confiscated even his home-grown hemp, calling itself "Hemp Authority" for this purpose, and turned over the war-essential material to war-essential industries. Neither Wendelin nor his loom was war-essential. But whoever thought that they felt themselves unimportant, useless and out of commission, misjudged the old man; and whoever regarded the cobwebs stretched athwart the dead loom from one end to the other as a manifestation of laziness or a symbol of work abandoned, did not possess the old man's insight into the mysterious weaving of creation.

For Wendelin was not idle, his loom was not dead, and the five garden spiders, which he nourished with flies and whose labors he observed with expert understanding, wove their delicate, tough creature weave in triumph over the Hemp Authority. All life is a weave and at the same time a weaving, finished and unfinished, an artful and joyfully emerging pattern; yet, to the expert it is not bewildering, and weaver Wendelin is on intimate terms not only with the spiders, but also with the Lord, the Almighty Weaver and Master Spinner, and nothing can disconcert him, neither time nor people. Be the evil of the times ever so sharp, with tyranny and war, like mighty shears cutting through the weave: weaver Wendelin knows that God weaves on, if only through the spiders. It keeps up his good spirits and his joy in his loom.

And when it comes to people, Wendelin knows much more still;

for everyone openly displays the weave of his face, the expert weaver only has to look at it to gauge the pattern and structure, the big and the little flaws of the weave, the manner in which the soul looks out from the web of life through the eyes: and he is not in doubt about the face and about the good or evil that lurks in back of it. He had known Ursula's face as long as she lived, he had looked at it many times, in her happy hours and her troubled ones, and it had always pleased his expert eyes; for the weave of that face was strong and true, clear and good. He looked at it now, bearing the heavy reproach as if it were lighter than air, and he saw that it had lost none of its firm truthfulness. And he looked long and intently at the little bastard, very long with his old weaver's eyes; and lo, the child was of another fabric. A wise man, however, is not a know-all and a tattler, and Wendelin's weaver-wisdom did not lend itself to the spreading of his knowledge. To be sure, the taciturn old man was highly respected in Vogelöd and Unterhall, although he was now rarely seen in the parish seat; he was reputed to possess unusual common sense and a profound knowledge of human nature, and his laconic judgments carried great weight. He did not take part in the neighbors' debates about Ursula; but at every occasion he said, always choosing the same words with equanimity, "You do her a great wrong." That made a certain impression, particularly on Ursula's foreman, who had been one of those primarily responsible for her proscription. But here was the wise weaver's word, after all no more than an old man's obstinate assertion, and there was the bastard, living proof to the contrary.

Perhaps Wendelin, too, relied on the force of habit, as did Rector Ruhsilver. People could not forever talk of Ursula's sin—the little fruit was there, innocent of his existence, conciliating by his very loveliness. By Easter the scandal had subsided, by Whitsuntide it wasn't worth another word. That was not to say that Ursula had been forgiven or that her proscription was revoked; but even shame can settle into habit, and it trailed Ursula only as an ugly name.

She bore it with ease, whether she was talked about or not, and this was not due to frivolity, but to peace of mind. She was well and she prospered, as a reward for her good deed; and Fridolin was a source of joy, he formed his words in Ursula's dialect and, like her, smelled of field and stable, as if he had grown out of this strong earth, a living part of the country. And often his infectious laughter rang out, for no apparent reason unless it was to praise life, and Ursula laughed with him; for she felt a similar joyfulness and she also sensed that there was joy in Christopher, her son and benefactor, the third confederate, even if he was far away and never wrote.

And then he came, in this bright, sunny, late summer of 1942, and he did not come alone; with him was a blonde girl whose name was Sophia and who was the joy of life. They stayed a week, and it was as if this golden August enclosed the four confederates, like a bell jar of happiness, as if what was outside Vogelöd lay outside happiness and did not concern them. And that was the last time that Ursula and Christopher were together.

In December he wrote that he couldn't come for Christmas and that he had good reasons for not coming—and in his letter he had underlined the "good" of his reasons. Ursula knew that he was doing well, although during the happy week in August it had come out that he was not studying divinity, but law, together with the blonde girl, and she knew that it must be such law as would please God, the law of justice—giving battle, no longer in vain, to injustice.

So she celebrated Christmas Eve cheerfully without him, together with her help and with Fridolin, the exultant admirer of the Christmas tree; and the horn gramophone kept bawling either "Silent Night" or "Oh, Thou Joyous Christmastide." Since it had become terribly difficult to obtain shirts and the foreman complained loudly and pointedly about his irreplaceable shirts falling apart, she presented him with six shirts that had belonged to her departed husband. And since she thought of her husband with great piety while she took out the shirts from the linen closet, and asked the blessed one if it was all right with him to give away some of his shirts, and heard him answer that it was quite all right because everything was right that pleased God—since for a fraction of a second she even saw the blessed one's face, and it was a blessed face, no longer frighteningly ecstatic and bloated, a mild and joyful face that was pleased with her—since she was thus momentarily transported into the world of the spirit, she never gave a thought to the yellow envelope stuck in one of the shirts, the fifth, to be exact.

Thus it came about that on Christmas Day the foreman, greatly agitated, went to see the weaver Wendelin. He had not told anyone of his discovery as yet; this was a case for a wise man and for him who had been right from the beginning. Wendelin read the birth certificate of Fridolin Israel Blum, Jew, son of the Jew Hans Israel Blum and of the Jewess Alice Sarah Blum, née Lilienthal, and he saw the mighty "J" even on the vaccination certificate and he said not one word.

"I found it in the fifth shirt," said the foreman. "If she had given me four shirts I wouldn't know anything."

"Why are you so anxious not to know anything?" Wendelin asked, knitting his thick brows.

"Because I don't know which is the lesser evil: to know it or not to know it."

"The greater evil," said Wendelin, "is that all of you did a great wrong to Ursula."

This was his judgment, and he was a righteous man, and the times must be monstrous in their malice that a righteous man who strives to see a pious deed get its just recognition should unloose injustice and that the good deed should reap vengeance on earth.

"Yes," the foreman nodded. "Should I show it to anyone else?"

The weaver thought a long time; then he said: "You have a loose tongue and no one believes you; I am an old man who doesn't like to talk and who sees no one. Show it to the head maid."

"Yes," the foreman nodded. "And what shall I do with the papers after that?"

"Return them."

"How can I return them without causing anguish to Ursula?"

"Give the fifth and the sixth shirts back to her and tell her that four are enough for you."

This the foreman did, after the head maid and, to make sure, also the stable maid had glanced at the documents. The two shirts went back to the linen closet, and in one of them was the yellow envelope, and Ursula hadn't noticed anything.

Nor did she notice the apologetic tone of the neighbors' greetings and conversation, and she overlooked the obvious attempts of her cousins at Unterhall to approach her again on the following Sundays. She merely felt, full of contempt and haughtier than ever, that she had once again become the center of interest, and she failed to observe the change in her favor.

Rector Ruhsilver, however, was horrified by the new gossip

which was the truth, the dangerous truth, and which took the sin away from Ursula only to replace it with the crime of the times. But gossip cannot be stopped; it does not stay only with those whom it concerns and who must right a wrong; as an odorous rumor, it flutters on to those others who do not care about wrong and sin, but only about the crime of the times. And the scripture says: "Wherever there is carrion, there will the vultures be gathered together."

It came to pass in the second week of February in the year 1943 at five o'clock in the morning that the black vultures swooped down on Vogelöd. They grabbed the foreman, who let them in, and closed his mouth with a fist when he wanted to scream; they grabbed the stable maid in the stables and the other maids in their rooms and examined them separately. But the leader, with three of his men, forced his way into Ursula's bedroom, and she was still in bed, and in Tobias' bed lay Fridolin. And she started with eyes black and big, and knew that it was a matter of life or death, of Fridolin's life or death; she threw herself on Tobias' bed, and the child's laughter pealed under her.

And the leader spoke: "Woman, who is the boy?"

And she exclaimed: "My child! 'Tis my child!"

The leader spoke: "Woman, speak the truth!"

Ursula screamed: " 'Tis my bastard!"

The leader spoke: "Woman, let me see if he is your bastard or a Jew!"

And he stepped to Tobias' bed, and the child was very quiet and cowered under Ursula.

The leader spoke: "Woman, I count up to three, then I use force."

He counted to three, and Ursula closed her eyes, flung her arms around the bed, dug her fingers into the mattress, and the child pressed its face against her armpit.

The leader used force; but Ursula was a strong woman and was not to be torn away from the child. So he called the men to help him, and they shook Ursula like a locked door and they set about to smash her like a door, and they broke her fingers, and she moaned, and now the child under her cried, and she would not release her grip.

A commotion arose outside the room, and the men let go of

Ursula. The foreman was dragged in, his face showed two bloody weals crossing each other, from two blows with the steel rod, his whole body was shaking, and he stammered: "In the linen closet . . ."

The closet was forced open in no time, and he stammered: "In the fifth shirt . . ." But the yellow envelope came flying out of the first shirt.

Ursula sprawled over the child as if crucified. As she was still holding on to it, with superhuman strength, the leader said: "Michael!" and motioned with his eyes. A man, powerful as a bull, stepped to the bed and struck the woman in the neck with the edge of his right hand. Then they pulled the child from under the prostrate woman and laughed at his tiny pajamas of light blue flannel. Fridolin screamed.

The maids heard him scream as he was carried out of the house. The cottagers Schweninger, Krumberger, even Unterholzner in his remote house, heard him scream, and all the dogs barked. Only old Wendelin Weber did not hear it; for he had grown quite deaf. And Ursula did not hear it; and when she regained consciousness, Fridolin was already gone. She dressed, obediently and hastily, and did not ask about Fridolin, she asked nothing and let herself be taken away, her face lifeless.

Chapter Ten

THE FATES

I

"My mother did not influence me, I was with her so rarely," says Christopher, and continues after a brief pause; "but she gave me the heart that is in me."

"I call that big-hearted of the lady," President Behn comments; "but your lyric begs my question: Who set you off on the road that led you to oppose, and ultimately to betray, the Germany of the Führer?"

"I think that is fairly clear," Christopher replies. "It was the Germany of the Führer that set me off on that road. After all, I grew up under the Third Reich."

"If you have profited by the impudences of your friends on the prisoners' bench—although I can assure you that the People's Court has profited much more from them—I shall now give you, too, an opportunity to describe your progress along that road, freely and without restraint."

"I have already told you that my life has been dominated by resistance to the prevailing system, and you know the reasons why I refused to become a soldier. That's enough."

"We only know the result and some of the circumstances of your so-called resistance, but we are very much interested in your rebellious development."

"I am not," says Christopher. "I am not interested in the exposition of my development."

"I must say that the other defendants were more cooperative, or should I say they had more courage?"

"When my fellow defendants gave an account of their lives they spoke about their friends who are sitting with them here on the prisoners' bench, or about our enemies or about people who are dead, like Judge Moeller. In my case it is different."

"I take this to mean that you refuse to speak in order not to jeopardize certain persons who were connected with your rebellious development."

"That is correct."

"Do you think we don't know that you were a member of the dissolved Catholic Youth Organization and a disciple of Chaplain Rossaint who meanwhile has been tried and convicted?"

"One more reason for me to say nothing about my development."

"But the two Moellers did not hesitate to speak about their father, did they . . ."

"No, but he is dead."

"Not any more so than the organization that brought you up."

"If you profit by it," Christopher says with a faint smile, "I am happy to correct you and to admit that I am not the last member of the Catholic Youth Organization who is not dead yet."

President Behn sees a note being shoved under his face; on it is written with clumsy letters and reproachful exclamation signs: 'NOON RECESS!!! signed Schneidhammer.'

President Behn raises his head: "Well, defendant, you are a profit to us, with or without *curriculum vitae*. You may sit down."

Christopher whispers hastily, as if prodded: "My mother did not influence me, but I influenced her . . ."

"The Court is adjourned for the noon recess," says the president, rising.

The judges and the prosecutor leave the tribune through the curtain leading to the judges' chamber in back of the president's chair. And they leave in disorder; for A. Schneidhammer steers the mass of his body so impetuously and inconsiderately into the clumsily demanded noon recess that the president is forced to step back and let him walk ahead. The others, with the exception of Baron Freyberg, are so disturbed by this tactlessness, that for several seconds none dares to walk through the curtain; the order of precedence is complicated anyway, and it is an unsettled question whether the Reichs Attorney should walk ahead of the honorary judges or not. Only Captain Freyberg waits disinterestedly until the reverential traffic jam is cleared, and gladly walks out last; he is never hungry.

The defendants are led from the courtroom in single file. It goes without saying that ahead of them and between them march the black guards. Only Dr. Langbein, the official defense attorney, remains at his little table, lets his head drop to his chest, and immediately drops off to sleep. This is his noon recess; his desire for sleep is great, he had a big breakfast and expects to eat a big dinner; and going to sleep is the simplest way of avoiding any professional demands that might possibly be made upon him during the noon recess.

The defendants are taken to the washroom one by one, and even nature is relieved under supervision; the two women enjoy the privilege of looking at the backs of their guards. Then they are locked up in six individual cells in order to give the guards an opportunity to go to the canteen and fortify themselves. There the black ones do not utter a word about the trial, because it is forbidden. Only the prize fighter, cutting six slices of bread from a loaf, says, "hack!" at each slice. It sounds silly and childish; but the others grin understandingly.

Through the peephole of his cell door each defendant receives a tin bowl of hot vegetable soup in which are even a few pieces of meat, plenty of bread and water. Each eats mechanically, and his head is emptier than his stomach. They all are exhausted. They have no cause to be displeased with themselves. They are six, they are six! But they don't think, they are in a dead calm, perhaps they can no longer bear any cessation of wind, of word, of fate, perhaps they can no longer bear any pause.

Also Christopher eats—from absent-mindedness, as it were; for he should know that he cannot eat anything yet, and he throws it up again. It is always this way after his body has thawed out; the stomach continues to be obstreperous for a while longer. Christopher drinks water, much water, lies down on the cot, takes deep breaths and falls asleep; it is like a plunge into sleep.

Each of the defendants, including Christopher, feels refreshed when his escort reappears and takes him back to the courtroom. Here they are out of the dead calm, and hoist the sails of their thoughts. Five of them ask themselves the same question: Are we going to learn who denounced us? But Christopher thinks: I am not even going to learn what they are doing to mother . . . Thus it happens that he does not feel how Sophia, already standing at her place on the prisoners' bench, caresses him with her eyes.

The tribune is still empty. The defendants and their guards must await the Court standing. Dr. Langbein also stands at his little table in front of them, refreshed by his little snooze; he breathes on his reading glasses and polishes them with a handkerchief—he breathes and polishes and thus conveniently has no time to look at his clients.

Then the gentlemen of the Court enter through the stage curtain: the president first (which is proper and fitting) and, last and somewhat tardily, Judge Schneidhammer, a toothpick between his lips (which is not proper or fitting).

2

President Behn speaks in a languid voice: "We now come to the second part of the testimony, in which we want to establish whether, and to what extent, Hennings and Associates constitute an objective danger to the State. Police Sergeant, call the witness Vierck."

He looks at the prisoners' bench and observes that the name of the witness makes no visible impression on the defendants. The six are staring at the eagle suns of the windows, and the SS professor, who appears in the courtroom, walks past the prisoners' bench and steps up to the judges' tribune, but has no more effect on their stares than a shadow.

Vierck, a slight and somewhat malproportioned man, stands so exaggeratedly rigid as he lifts his arm for the salute and offers his Heil Hitler that he appears to bend backwards. At other times, too, he gives the impression of being bent, and at the same time pulled together; it is due to a certain asymmetry of his body which can be sensed, even if it cannot be clearly discerned. In short, he looks and carries himself like one who wears a not quite successful corrective corset. He is so dark that his face seems stubbly, although it is smoothly shaved; he has a receding, but impressive forehead, a protruding nose, a receding chin. His ugly, intelligent, strangely envious head could be that of a hunchback; certainly it does not harmonize with the black SS officer's uniform which he wears with such assiduity that Karl Hennings once remarked that even in bed the penal lawyer must wear black, discreetly padded SS pajamas with all the required insignia and decorations.

"Witness, you are Gustav Adolf Vierck, J.D., Professor of Penal Law in the University of Munich, SS Obersturmbannführer, born on January 27, 1899, at Magdeburg."

"I am, Herr Präsident."

"Witness, raise your right hand and swear to God that you will tell nothing but the truth."

Vierck raises his hand; no, he raises his arm in the Hitler salute and speaks through his nose and solemnly: "I swear to God and my Führer that I shall tell the truth."

"Witness, how long have you known the defendant Hennings?"

"Since 1928, the year in which he was made a professor in the University of Munich and in which I, too, was admitted to membership in the faculty."

"What were your relations with him at that time?"

"He was one of the sponsors of my thesis which I submitted to qualify for membership in the faculty."

"Was that of any particular advantage to you, or did the faculty accept your thesis unanimously?"

"By no means. I had to suffer from the fact that my then teacher and predecessor as professor of penal law was a Marxist."

He turns his head sharply toward the prisoners' bench; for Karl is laughing loudly.

"Defendant, why do you laugh?" the president asks.

"Partly because of my sympathy with the Herr Obersturmbannführer's troubles in joining the faculty," Karl replies, "partly because of curiosity."

"Why curiosity?" the president asks.

"Because I must ask myself why it was that the Marxist and predecessor referred to by the witness defended his dissertation with the same fatherly interest with which he furthered and financed the witness' studies."

"Herr Präsident," says Vierck sharply, "do you allow this question by the defendant?"

"I do not allow it," the president decides mildly, "because it is not addressed to you, but to your predecessor in office."

"Herr Präsident," Vierck speaks even more nasally than before, "may I ask you to protect me against further insinuations by the defendant!"

"In so far as such insinuations are not considered by me to be pertinent and conducive to clarification of the issue to be decided," the president observes in a friendly tone and in fluently articulated complicatedness, "I shall protect you against them, witness. We were talking about the question whether the defendant's sponsorship of your thesis was of any particular advantage to you, and you admitted it. I am interested in this question because I have to determine to what extent the objectivity of your testimony might be prejudiced by a natural feeling of gratitude."

What a bloody cynic! Karl thinks and doesn't even smile.

"Gratitude?" Vierck says in astonishment. "But it should be obvious, Herr Präsident, that the defendant's sponsorship—leaving my personal academic qualifications out of consideration for the moment—was due to his solidarity with my predecessor!"

"Political solidarity?"

"My predecessor was interested in reforming the penal law; Hennings was active, to a much larger extent, in penal reform."

"If you regard that as political solidarity, then you imply that Hennings, too, is a Marxist. But the fact that he retained his academic chair after the National Socialist revolution speaks against this view."

"To describe him as a disguised Marxist would not quite do justice to the situation. To describe him as an enemy of authority would be more to the point."

"And what would hit the nail on the head?"

"To describe him as an enemy of the State, as an enemy of our State."

"Very well, we know that *now;* but when did *you* know it, when did you hit the nail on the head?"

"The answer to this question is not a simple one, Herr Präsident. It is the story of an observation carried on over a period of fifteen years, a veritable fugue of suspicion. I might say that as early as 1933, even 1928, I had already hit the nail on the head, though only in theory. For ten years now I have held the hammer in my hand—to stay with my metaphor; but it took me all of these ten years to spy out the nail I was to hit."

What a picture! thinks Karl. He has been holding the hammer in his hand for ten years . . .

The president observes with satisfaction that none of the defendants now stares at the windows, whose eagle suns are paling imperceptibly; each of them looks at the man who has been holding the hammer in his hand for ten years.

"The difficulty you encountered, witness, apparently lay in the defendant's ability to hide not only his feelings, but his actions as well."

"Quite right, Herr Präsident, and since I daresay it is no easy matter for one on whom I keep an eye to hide his actions, I would go further and contend that until well into the war years the defendant in his capacity as a university professor had no action to hide. He committed no punishable act and for all the world appeared to be a so-called non-political professor who was racially above suspicion and who, as early as 1933, manifested a certain loyalty by refusing a professorship at an American university. I, for one, naturally saw quite another motive in this refusal, it aroused my suspicion, and through all these years I was not deceived by the apparent integrity of the defendant's conduct."

"Herr Vierck, on what basis do you contend that as a teacher the defendant committed no acts he needed to hide, until after the outbreak of the war?"

"On the basis of exact knowledge, Herr Präsident. His lectures were watched."

"And his seminar?"

"Likewise, Herr Präsident. Until the outbreak of war, and even thereafter, it was relatively easy for any student to be admitted to the seminar, consequently also for students serving the Security Department. Later that was changed—and my method of observation was changed too."

"How did the defendant manage the prescribed salute to the Führer in his lectures?"

"Extremely sloppily. The 'Heil Hitler!' became something like 'Hi!' if he uttered the formula at all, and he used to make a motion with his hand which could be described as derogatory. Of course I did not use this to snare him; I was not interested in his omissions, but in his actions. Only much later, in the second year of war, I ordered a demonstration in this connection, for a certain purpose."

"What was the attitude of the students toward the defendant?"

"He was popular, very popular!"

"Perhaps because of his omissions and derogatory gestures?"

"I am not competent to answer this question, Herr Präsident."

"It is nevertheless an extremely important question, Herr Vierck, even if you can answer it only incompetently."

"I am not in a position to answer it at all, Herr Präsident."

"Perhaps you can answer it, defendant von Hennings?"

"It is my firm conviction," says Karl with a smile, "that the affection of my students would have assumed positively ecstatic proportions had I shouted 'Heil Hitler!' loudly and clearly and had raised my arm to the sky."

Those on the prisoners' bench smile, even Christopher. But someone chuckles, someone on the judges' tribune, the president indignantly looks to the right. Baron Freyberg shakes with chuckling, swallows the wrong way or swallows his peppermint tablet, pours himself some water, drinks, chuckles, and doesn't show the slightest embarrassment at having become, for one speechless moment, the center of the proceedings.

"Which he did!" Vierck exclaims.

"What do you mean?" asks President Behn, who has lost the thread of the discussion because of the honorary judge's chuckling.

"After the demonstration which I mentioned a moment ago, the defendant performed the required salute exactly as he described it hypothetically just now."

"And how did the student body react to it?"

"The students approved."

"They approved uproariously," Karl corrects.

"How did the students express their uproarious approval?" President Behn asks toward the prisoners' bench.

"By laughing and by stamping their feet," Karl replies.

"Herr Vierck, what sort of a demonstration was it and for what purpose did you order it?"

"I shall answer the second question first, Herr Präsident. Already at the end of 1940 I felt compelled to consider the possibility that the student body might be subversively influenced by the defendant. The demonstration, carried out by my confidential agents within the student body and directed against Hennings, was staged in order to ascertain with one stroke who would participate in it, who would not participate, and who might even go so far as to participate in a counterdemonstration. The demonstration consisted in calling 'Heil Hitler!' in answer to the silent and derogatory gesture with which the defendant used to enter the classroom."

"And did the demonstration achieve its purpose?"

"The call was immediately taken up by all the students in the classroom, the defendant stepped on the dais, himself now called 'Heil Hitler!' excessively loud and clearly, and kept his arm raised until the applause had subsided and he could begin his lecture."

"Then the demonstration did *not* achieve its purpose," the president comments.

"My confidential agents were of the opinion that it was completely successful in achieving its purpose—that is, to establish that Hennings' students were still healthy . . ."

"And laughed healthily," President Behn adds. "Or was the laughter of approval not reported to you, Herr Vierck?"

"I cannot recall."

"What is your opinion concerning the laughter now, witness?"

"If it should really have occurred, it must have been directed against the defendant."

"What is *your* opinion concerning the laughter, defendant?"

"I concur with the opinion of the Security Department," Karl answers. "It was a manifestation of health."

"Did you feel yourself laughed at?"

"Of course and quite rightly so," Karl asserts; "there could be no doubt but that I looked utterly ridiculous in the pose I assumed."

President Behn narrows his eyes and turns to Vierck: "I am not of the opinion, Herr Vierck, that your confidential agents hit the nail on the head in this case. On the contrary, I am of the opinion that even at that time the subversive influence of the defendant on his students had progressed much further than you thought."

Vierck stiffly bends backwards. "Am I to take this as a reproach, Herr Präsident?"

"I only expressed my opinion, Herr Vierck. Besides, you yourself said that already at the end of 1940 you had to take into account the defendant's subversive influence on the students. Surely you must have had your reasons."

"Only my old suspicions."

"Did you watch the classes given by the defendant at that time?"

"Through my confidential agents and through occasional examination of their notebooks."

"And neither the students of the Security Department nor their notebooks could substantiate your suspicion that Hennings' lectures contained subversive poison?"

"Not in the slightest. So far as I can remember, his lectures dealt in a purely academic way with the question of criminal symptoms."

"I am almost afraid, Herr Vierck, that your confidential agents simply did not have what it takes to hit the nail on the head."

"I fail to see the justification for this unfavorable criticism," says Vierck with dignity and malice; "but in my own and my agents' defense I should like to ask you in all humility, Herr Präsident, whose work was responsible for putting the traitor on the prisoners' bench behind me?"

"There are six traitors on the prisoners' bench behind you," the president speaks with force, observing the motionlessly listening defendants, "and it is impossible to see with the naked eye how many more traitors are in back of these six, as you can ascertain for yourself. It is my opinion that if the Hennings case had come up for trial at the beginning of the war or even at the end of 1940, we would have had to deal with a small number of individuals instead of having to deal with the higher powers of that number. My recognition of your merits, therefore, is clouded by the fact that you have held the hammer in your hand too long."

"Not one instant beyond the moment when I could strike the blow!" Vierck protests agitatedly; "but I am not in the habit of striking blindly . . ."

"Your suspicion was not blindness, Herr Vierck! The People's Court has the duty not only of eliminating dangers to the State, but also of preventing their fruition. In this respect it follows Hennings' criminal psychology after its own fashion. And suspicion is sufficient reason for preventive action against danger."

"I, however, contend that even today the danger may be averted," Vierck exclaims. "More than that, I contend that there is no danger. Is *one* traitor a danger to the State? Are his five vassals a danger to the State? For I am convinced, Herr Präsident, that behind these six there are exactly as many more traitors as you and I can see with the naked eye—that is, none!"

President Behn motions impatiently. "These questions are for the Court to decide. We had better stop this theoretical discussion and return to your testimony. Was the exclusion of your confidential agents from the seminar a result of the demonstration?"

"Not at all; a man of Hennings' type would not work so clumsily. In fact, no one was excluded. There was only one of my men who was a member of the seminar, and since he obtained his doctor's degree last year he automatically dropped out."

"And the doctor's candidate didn't report anything suspicious either?"

"He reported things that were most suspicious. He reported that the seminar's topic, which was called 'The Limits of Penal Rule' or something like that, was discussed in such a way that it might have been interpreted as synonymous with a criticism of National Socialist philosophy."

"And how did the other members of the seminar interpret it?"

"They discussed it with imperturbable objectivity and without the slightest trace of subversive polemics."

"Which you took to be a proof of their immunity,—correct, Herr Vierck?"

"Certainly, Herr Präsident."

"And how did you interpret these seminar discussions?"

"As a portent of things to come, things for which I had waited so long."

"A patient cat and mouse play," President Behn comments, shaking his head. "Well, go on. The doctor's candidate left the seminar."

"After that none of the members of the Security Department succeeded in gaining admission to the seminar, supposedly because their academic qualifications were insufficient. But this bitter pill was sweetened by the dissolution of the seminar at the beginning of this semester. Thereafter its members met merely for the purpose of preparing a new edition of Hennings' 'Criminal Psychology.' "

"Did the number of participants approximate the usual membership of the seminar?"

"The students who participated were pretty nearly the selfsame ones who had previously belonged to the seminar. There were about twelve of them, and they actually worked on the revision, as a window dressing, so to speak. The editorial committee, however, which we might also designate as the revolutionary committee, consisted of the very people who are now sitting on the prisoners' bench with Hennings."

"The defendant's wife is also sitting there."

"Certainly; she was a member of the editorial committee, although she was not present at all the meetings."

President Behn does not look at the witness, even while addressing the last questions to him. He looks at the prisoners' bench, he sees how the defendants become petrified, he sees how the six faces lose their natural distinctiveness and come to look alike as if they were so many doll faces. They are paralyzed by one and the same single thought behind their pallid foreheads. It is a heart-warming sight for the president and compensates him for some of the annoyance the defendants have caused him.

"How do you know all these details, Herr Vierck?"

"Through the new method of observation which I devised to meet the new situation arising at the beginning of the current semester."

"Would you mind telling us some more about this method of observation?"

"I think that will not be necessary, Herr Präsident. The method was applied with the approval and the support of the chief of the Security Department, who received the resultant incriminating evidence, used it as a basis for the arrest and preliminary examination of the defendants, and undoubtedly put it at the disposal of the People's Court."

President Behn smiles faintly. "I think I owe you an apology, Herr Vierck. I did not credit you, but the Security Department, with the preparation of the phonograph records."

"And quite rightly so, Herr Präsident," Vierck protests, bending forward, "I am only a small part of the Security Department and did not even operate the machinery . . ."

"But contented yourself with holding the good old hammer in your hand!" Behn adds.

"Excellent!" Vierck chuckles, and his chuckle is that of a hunchbacked gnome.

3

The police sergeant puts a medium-sized electric record player on the sinners' table and connects the cable with one of the outlets for the desk lamps on the tribune.

"I see we have quite a selection here," says President Behn, looking at the three thick albums of records deposited in front of him, "but fortunately you are just the man to choose the proper selection for us, Herr Vierck. Perhaps you could single out two or three decisive passages characterizing not only the defendants' personalities—since we have already gotten beyond that stage of the proceedings—but passages disclosing their subversive effectiveness which interests us enormously."

He pushes the albums across the judges' bench to the police sergeant who stacks them up next to the phonograph.

"I shall do my best," says Vierck, "though I should like to say in advance that it was precisely this question of subversive effectiveness which was the central problem of Hennings and Associates, and this question is not answered by the recorded conversations . . ." He leafs through the first album and examines the titles of the records through the circular cuts in the folders. "Incidentally, I personally inscribed each of the discs with the date of the recording and with a few key-words from the contents," he remarks as if to himself. "Here!" he exclaims. "Here is a 'Meeting of the Editorial Committee' which is definitely worth listening to, in my opinion . . ." He chuckles and pulls a few records from the album. "November 9!" he announces. "A significant date, day of the disgrace of 1918! But this is November 9, 1942, at half-past seven in the evening . . ."

He hands the records to the police sergeant who puts them in the machine.

"To simplify the identification of the speakers for the Court," the president declares, "the particular defendant whose words we are to hear is to rise and remain standing while listening to his voice."

The needle hums on the disc. A voice emerges, a strangely faraway and disembodied voice, a ghostlike voice. Karl does not recognize his voice, but his words. He rises.

Karl's voice: ". . . in our circle a new comrade, Alexander Welte, friend of our friend Hans, described and announced by him as one of us. Therefore he is our friend, too, and not a new one at that, but an old comrade. Now we are six."

Alexander's voice: "Thank you, Herr Professor. But six are not many."

Alexander rises somewhat tardily and must sit down again at

once; it was a short sentence. Karl meanwhile remains standing; he knows it is not worth while for him to sit down again.

Karl's voice: "We don't know how many six are. That sounds senseless, but it makes sense. Each one of us has come through the jungle of these years, not because he was miraculously saved, but because he found the road which man can walk. We are not the only people who have walked and will walk along that road. None of us would be where he is if he had believed himself to be the only one. Each of us knew or sensed that there were others along this road—yes, I daresay that we didn't find, but that we asked our way out of the jungle. Therefore let us not call ourselves six, but six units. And now it doesn't sound senseless any more when I say: we don't know how many there are in six units. Or do you think, Welte, that you with your most individually distributed tufts of hair are representing only yourself as member number six?"

Alexander's voice, laughing: "According to my calculation I represent six units of the Sixth Army at Stalingrad, Herr Professor, and Hans another six . . ."

Alexander jumps up, and because he hears himself laughing, he twists his mouth as if to synchronize it with his laughter.

Karl's voice: "God bless you and your calculation, Welte, and since my assistant Sauer makes similarly enthusiastic calculations with respect to the student body, you two might join together to form an optimists' club."

Alexander's voice: "Hans also believes that among the students there are already some units that are ready to march, Herr Professor."

Karl's voice: "I know there are units that are ready to listen. Perhaps none of you knows as well as I do, what it means to get the students to listen, what labor, what patience and tactical experience it takes. I am quite satisfied if they are ready to listen and I don't consider myself a skeptic if I doubt their readiness to march as yet."

Christopher's voice: "They will never march of themselves, they are not used to independent action, they have grown up and have lived much too long under communal terror and unquestioned command. Believe me, Herr Professor, they will never march of themselves, without prompting!"

Karl's voice: "I certainly do believe you, Sauer, but that is not the point at issue; it is a question of the tactics by which we can induce them to march. We now notice that listening silence among the students which I like to call the new academic silence. Our impetuous Christopher would launch the call to march into this silence, even now . . ."

Sophia's voice: "On the 9th of November! Today is the 9th of November! Christopher wanted to launch the anniversary of the revolution into the silence!"

Karl's voice: "The silence would have swallowed it up, this anniversary of the revolution of 1918 which was no revolution, and it would have grown even sadder and more silent. No, I knew why I rejected it. I know what sort of silence it is: the time of waiting for the silent ones and also for us."

Dora's voice: "But how much longer, Karl, how much longer yet? You know I am not impatient, I have learned to wait, to sieve and to sift. But now I myself have come to believe that there are enough ears to hear the appeal. We should not let them wait too long."

Karl's voice: "Who: we? Who are we, Dora? We are no archangels bringing a divine message! We don't belong to the forces of fate, but to those who would take the cross upon themselves. We are a part of those who have grown silent, who take thought and wait, wait for the moment when they must speak, be it only one rebellious word. We must wait for that word, the first word: only then do we have the right to speak for ourselves, or rather, for our units. Only then shall we have to speak in the name of the archangels of fate, and call upon our units to begin the crusade."

Christopher's voice: "But what if no rebellious word is spoken?"

Karl's voice: "It must be spoken. For are they not silent from rebelliousness? It is as if they were holding their breath, and they can't hold their breath very much longer."

Hans' voice: "It will be spoken very soon, as soon as the catastrophe of Stalingrad fills the air."

Sophia's voice: "Even if Goebbels doesn't fill the air with the catastrophe?"

Hans' voice: "When 350,000 men are sacrificed all at once to the vainglory of one man, even the air must wail and be filled with it!"

Karl stands through the whole record, his face quiet, his lips tightly shut, separated from his ghostlike voice, yet deeply eloquent. The others bob up and down, one after the other, marionettes on the strings of their voices. Now Hans who had remained standing between his two sentences, sits down; getting up and sitting down is painful and time-consuming labor for him. The record still hums on, empty, then it stops, with the audible click of the automatic disconnecting device. And only now Karl sits down. The room is pervaded by a ghostlike stillness, as if it were difficult for natural voices to assert themselves again.

"Worth listening to . . ." Vierck chuckles and thumbs through the albums. "Here is one!" he exclaims, looking at the label of one of the discs. "Here is some additional material which, to be sure, is not part of the sequence of my observations, but nevertheless amply deserves its place in this collection of poetry. This is—I quote—'Recording of speeches held in the auditorium of the University on the occasion of the Reichs Founding Celebration on January 18, 1943. Recorded for the University Archives and confiscated by the Secret State Police.' Do you consider it worth hearing, Herr Präsident?"

"Exceedingly worth hearing," President Behn emphasizes.

The needle hums.

A voice: "It gives me great pleasure to introduce our guest of honor, our highly esteemed Gauleiter, party comrade Giesler!"

"That was the president of the university who spoke," Vierck comments.

Gauleiter's voice: "Fellow Germans . . ."

"Stop!" commands President Behn, and the police sergeant turns off the machine. "Because of the undoubtedly very useful interjection by the witness it was impossible for me to hear if and how the students reacted to the announcement that the Gauleiter would be the principal speaker. But this is of great importance for the Court. Begin again, sergeant . . ."

"And make it as loud as you can," a fatty voice speaks.

President Behn indignantly looks to the right. Yes, indeed, it is Judge Schneidhammer who is butting in on the proceedings, awake and interested for the first time.

"The record seems to be very clear, Herr Standartenführer," Vierck says eagerly, "since this recording was made under conditions technically much more favorable than in the case of the seminar recordings . . ."

"Witness," President Behn interrupts angrily, "the official title of the members of this Court is: Herr Volksrichter . . ."

"Turn it up just the same," A. Schneidhammer interjects, greasy and imperturbable, and to make quite sure he would hear he cups his ear with his tremendous hand. For he is interested, on three counts: because the Gauleiter speaks, because the Gauleiter is his old friend and at the same time his intimate enemy—and his position is already silently shaking and silently undermined, therefore expected soon to give way to the onrushing intimates—and because he himself, Alois, has gotten on quite nicely with his future speech to fellow Germans, except for the end, and hopes to glean this or that phrase from the Gauleiter's speech to impart more forcefulness to his own.

Voice of the university president: "It gives me great pleasure to introduce our guest of honor, our highly esteemed Gauleiter, party comrade Giesler!"

Then silence, humming silence.

Gauleiter's voice: "Fellow . . ."

"Stop!" President Behn interrupts again, the police sergeant turns off the machine, Judge Schneidhammer takes his hand from his ear and lets it drop to the table with an ill-humored bang. "To judge by this record," says Behn, "the Gauleiter was received with complete silence. Or does the recording exclusively reproduce the voices of the speakers?"

"N-no . . ." Vierck replies hesitantly, "on the other hand it seems to me that the silence of the listeners is not very revealing . . . I mean to say that it is no longer quite as customary for the students to applaud the introduction of speakers."

"Have you had the same experience, defendant von Hennings?"

"No," Karl replies, "the preceding speakers were greeted with the customary stamping of feet."

"And how do you interpret the silence of the student body?"

"As very revealing," says Karl.

"And you, defendant Hans Moeller?"

"As an expression of contempt," says Hans.

"And you, defendant Sauer?"

"As a sign of unity," says Christopher.

"Let us proceed," President Behn speaks in the direction of the phonograph. A. Schneidhammer cups his ear with his hand.

Gauleiter's voice: ". . . low Germans! We have heard much learned talk here about the origin of Bismarck's Reich. We have also listened to the spanning of neat rhetorical bridges from the Iron Chancellor to our great leader, from the founder of the fifty-year Reich to the creator of the thousand-year Reich. But it is neither my intention nor my business to turn my gaze backward to historical contemplation, while we are making history, not for fifty, but for a thousand years. I readily confess that my philosophy of history is plain and simple. What was good and fit for survival in the First and Second Reich is contained also in the Third Reich; what was mediocre and bad and unfit for survival is dead and forgotten. It is the same with the great men of past epochs, with the iron-willed Bismarck, with the taciturn Moltke, with the iron-willed and taciturn King Frederic the Great: like tributaries, they have merged with the main stream, they are contained in the powerful, epochal person of the Führer whom divine Providence has given us.

"I do not look back to the glories of Versailles of 1871, nor to the disgrace of Versailles of 1919; I look into the present. I only see the Versailles, the France, the Europe of 1943, over which waves the swastika. What alone concerns me is the present and the future. And it is not my business to make speeches, but it is my duty to watch over the people's community with relentless and indefatigable energy, and to drive it on to do its duty for the present and for the future!

"We are living amidst a titanic struggle for the Führer's Greater Germany, for the Führer's New Order in Europe, for the Führer's new world order! I stand here before you in a momentous hour, to watch over you and to drive you on, German students, to do your bounden duty for this momentous hour. And when I think of the Führer's heroic army at Stalingrad, now writing in its own blood the new Nibelungen saga of National Socialism's death-defying courage—when I look about me in this hall and still see a great many young Germans who do not wear the honor dress of Army or Party, then I ask myself and I ask you: Are you doing enough for this momentous hour? Then I ask you: What are you doing here? . . ."

"What is this noise now, Herr Vierck?" President Behn asks.

"I don't know," Vierck replies, shrugging his shoulders, "perhaps it is a flaw in the recording."

"The students are shuffling," says Karl.

Voice of the university president: "I will not tolerate any expression of disapproval."

Gauleiter's voice: "And while German mothers are working in war plants, subordinating their home and children to the greater duty, I see here in this hall young German women who seem to think they are serving the Führer when they attend classes and call themselves students. But I do not ask these German girls: What are you doing here? I ask them: What business have you here? Why are you not working in war industries? And if, in your academic parasitism, you are not capable enough even for that, why don't you at least get pregnant and bear children, so that you will have some justification in the Führer's Germany . . ."

A clear, incisive voice: "Enough!"

Christopher stands up.

"Why do you stand up, defendant?" the president asks him.

"It is my voice," says Christopher.

Many voices: "Enough! Enough!"

Hans, Sophia and Alexander stand up. "Sit down!" the president commands irritatedly. "Stop these stupidities!"

"Enough! Enough! Enough!" an ever louder chorus streams from the phonograph, drowning out the Gauleiter's voice and the university president's barking appeals for order.

"Enough!" the president exclaims with a sharp gesture of his hand. The police sergeant turns off the machine.

"What's the matter, what's the matter!" A. Schneidhammer snorts, his hand still cupping his ear. "That fellow Giesler wasn't through with his speech!"

"The Gauleiter did not finish his speech, Herr Volksrichter," Vierck explains, "but left the auditorium, followed by the president of the university."

"Such things can go on?" A. Schneidhammer grumbles; "not to let the highest Party dignitary finish his speech, such stinking rotten business can go on here in Munich? Don't they know who the sons o' bitches were, outside of them over there?"

"Students," Behn says shortly and contemptuously toward Schneidhammer.

"And why isn't the whole gang of them in Dachau?"

"At the orders of the university president the university guard immediately went into action, Herr Volksrichter," says Vierck, "but it was unable to identify the instigators of the disturbance. When the command for the raid was given, the students had already dispersed. In my opinion, the incident was not at all of a subversive nature, but was simply an outbreak of war nerves evoked by an attack on academic honor—an attack which was perhaps excessively vehement and not quite well-founded. This opinion, incidentally, was confirmed by the order of the Ministry of Education not to pursue the matter any further, to deprive it of any publicity and to avoid any unrest among the students. That was the reason for not closing the university, as the university president had threatened to do."

"Not to let him finish . . ." Schneidhammer grumbles more softly, and his thoughts return to his own speech.

"I am of a different opinion," the president addresses Vierck, "and I would be interested in a rough estimate of the demonstration's intensity. To judge by the recording, the whole student body must have participated in it."

"I, on the other hand, would estimate that not more than 25 per cent of the students participated in the shouting, Herr Präsident."

"And why was there no counterdemonstration on the part of the loyal majority?"

"Because it was not a political demonstration but an academic protest against the misunderstood disparagement of the Alma Mater. In other words, it was an act of loyalty, yes, a demonstration of student patriotism."

"What was your view of the incident, defendant von Hennings?"

"I consider the formulation of the witness extraordinarily apt," Karl answers. "It was in actual fact the first patriotic demonstration by German students against the National Socialist Party."

"I protest, Herr Präsident!" comes from the judges' tribune in a voice shaking with rage. Behn tears his head and shoulder around to the left. "I protest," says Baldur Uhle somewhat more subdued, and his handsome face is green with pallor.

"Against what do you protest, Herr Kollege?" the president asks sharply.

"Against . . . against the way the defendant talks!" Uhle blurts out.

"Only against the way he talks? You will have to judge the defendant primarily by his acts, Herr Volksrichter."

"It is an infamous twisting of my words and of the facts, Herr Präsident!" Vierck explains, and his body is twisted from indignation.

"An infamous twisting of your words, witness, I know it," the president says in ill-humor. "And now please go on, let us hear the editorial committee meeting immediately following the Reichs Foundation Celebration. I am anxious to hear the internal comments about the demonstration in the auditorium."

"Strangely enough there are no comments," says Vierck and looks through the album for the record. The needle hums. Karl stands up, even before his ghostlike voice begins to speak. He seems to know it is his part.

Karl's voice: "The moment has come to lay down directions, directions for our conduct from now on. Each one of us is responsible for the other. We are all responsible for our action. Our action is revolutionary, therefore responsible to the future. If one of us is arrested he must act in a manner to permit the other five to continue their work. If five of us are arrested they must act in a manner to enable the sixth to carry on. If all six of us are arrested, then we must act as if we were not six, but sixty or sixty thousand or six million—then we must act as the spokesmen of a power which has sent us out ahead into the present and which loses in us only six voices, six out of six million, of six million, of six million . . ." The needle obstinately runs through the same groove of the disc, again and again.

"Shut it off!" the president shouts, surprisingly uncontrolled.

4

President Behn drinks water, for the first time during the trial. Karl is still standing.

"Why don't you sit down!" Behn shouts and waves impatiently with his hand. "When does the action itself appear, the handbill action as a topic of conversation on the records," he asks the witness.

"It doesn't appear at all, Herr Präsident. The last recordings reveal conversations dealing exclusively with the tragedy of Stalingrad, in the familiar style. On February 3, when the capitulation of the Sixth Army was announced and the Reichs Government ordered four days of mourning, Hennings said, 'I am already sewing our flag of mourning, but it is not black,' or something like it. That was the only allusion to some sort of action."

"Defendant von Hennings, was this caution inspired by some feeling of being watched in the seminar room?"

"No," Karl answers, "we could really not suspect that we were talking into invisible microphones. What you call caution was nothing but the time I needed for undisturbed reflection and which I begged my friends to grant me on the evening of January 18, when we were gathered in my house after the commotion in the auditorium—it was the long and painful deliberation to determine if and how I could make myself alone responsible for the action and thus protect my young comrades and my wife."

"In spite of the 'directions'?"

"Because of the directions."

"And where did you sew the flag of mourning which wasn't black— Or, expressed more simply: Where did you write the text of the handbill?"

"In my house. There, too, I finally reached the decision to accept the manual services of my friends in connection with the leaflet."

President Behn has to smile. "It has now been amply proved, however, that your friends consider the title of manual servant to be degrading—and rightly so. What interests me at the moment is that after January 18, or more specifically after February 2, you made your house the headquarters for the handbill action, and you did not do so because of any mistrust in the seminar room, but . . ."

"But to establish my responsibility," Karl finishes the sentence.

With an annoyed shrug of his shoulders President Behn turns to Vierck.

"And why did you not order the arrest of the group after the allusion of February 3, Herr Vierck, why not immediately after the 'directions'?"

"That is a question you will have to address to the chief of the Security Department, Herr Präsident, not to me. His answer would probably be that from the point of view of the punitive authorities it would have been a colossal mistake to save the suspects from the commission of their crime by arresting them too soon; that such premature arrest would have deprived the authorities of the opportunity to learn not only the nature of the crime, but also the identity of other participants in the conspiracy."

"From the point of view of the Reich's security even premature crime prevention naturally outranks all punitive advantages which might result—but in this case did not result—from the actual commission of the crime. Much to my regret I must conclude that while you did have the criminals under control, you were nevertheless unable to control the crime."

"Herr Präsident!" exclaims Vierck in vehement agitation. "Day before yesterday, shortly after ten o'clock in the evening, the head gatekeeper delivered to me, in my capacity as University Representative of the Security Department, some printed matter issued by the Party. The leaflets were inserted in this printed matter. Within ten minutes the SD went into action in the university, and with such admirable precision that despite the greatest possible effectiveness it did not cause any commotion, made no uproar. Yesterday the university presented a perfectly normal picture with not one of the students wasting a single word about the closed lecture room—I am in a position to know that—and today, on the third day, the six criminals stand before their judges. I think I have every right to claim that I did have the crime under control!"

"You would have had it under control, witness, if you had made it unnecessary for the police to go into action at the university, that is, if the distribution of the handbills had been prevented. One may hold the hammer in one's hand for ten years, witness, and yet strike the blow ten hours, one hour too late . . ."

"Too late?" Vierck cries excitedly, and points to the prisoners' bench with a grandiose gesture, like an impresario.

"You are confusing the heads of the defendants with the oft-mentioned head of the nail, witness," Behn comments, raising his hand to end the discussion. "One last question: How many handbills or printed matter with inserted handbills did you deliver to the Security Department?"

"Perhaps a dozen or more, Herr Präsident."

"That is all, witness, I thank you. Since the provisions of the penal code do not apply to procedure in the People's Court, you are not required to remain here, but are at liberty to go."

Vierck bends backwards, raising his arm and exacting a solemn exchange of Hitler salutes. Then he turns around and marches through the center aisle of the hall to the door, his gaze fixed, looking to neither side. Behn observes the prisoners' bench with some curiosity; for between the entrance and the exit of this witness something surprising and bewildering has happened to the six. They did not know that this was the man who had held the hammer in his hand for ten years, and now they have learned it and they should show it to him with their looks and with the expressions on their faces: it was you! It was you! But the six stare at the windows, at the eagles which are no longer suns, but dark spots, and the man of fate with vaguely twisted shoulders and spine does not disturb their stares as much as a shadow.

The door closes behind Vierck, the president leans back in his chair.

"Gentlemen of the Court," he speaks and does not look at the judges, but at the ceiling, "in connection with the last question which I put to the principal witness for the prosecution we come to a very important point. You will have observed, partly on the basis of my own critical comments, that both the witness and the Security Department are deliberately underestimating the defendants' subversive success and that they are handling the student body with kid gloves in conformity with the order directing that no uproar be made over the affair. The tactics of the defendants are the exact reverse: they exaggerate their significance with the refrain of 'six out of six million.' I shall not do them the favor of asking them now how many handbills were distributed; for they might conceivably answer: six million. And it is rather irrelevant whether the defendants distributed two hundred or five hundred or one thousand leaflets—it is unimportant in view of the astounding and frightening fact that only twenty-one, I repeat, exactly twenty-one leaflets were handed over to the Security Department, and that number includes the one dozen delivered by Vierck. If we deduct these twelve copies, discovered by the head gatekeeper and consequently not distributed, if we deduct them from twenty-one, we have as good as nothing left. This can only mean that the absorption of the handbills was complete. At the same time it provides the answer to the question: Do Hennings and Associates constitute an objective danger to the State?"

A plea! Reichs Attorney Tischler thinks bitterly. My plea! This all-devouring monster has now eaten away even my absorption argument!

President Behn speaks languidly: "By way of concluding the taking of evidence, I shall now ask the members of the Court to direct a few questions to the defendants. I must warn the defendants, however, that I shall not permit them to pose any more as the 'spokesmen of a power'; that sort of provocative routine can add nothing to the testimony and therefore is no longer of any interest to the Court."

He looks to the right. Baron von Freyberg raises his hand. The president nods.

"Have a few questions to ask the two Wehrmacht men," Freyberg says good-humoredly in a nasal tone and blinks at the prisoners' bench. "Would interest me to know if even at your time there were whisperings within the Sixth Army about differences between the Führer and General Paulus over Stalingrad's being turned into a hedgehog position."

"Plenty, and by no means only whisperings," Alexander announces sonorously.

"I fail to detect any connection between this question and the subject of the trial, Herr Volksrichter," President Behn intervenes.

"I thought Stalingrad was part of our discussion," Freyberg amusedly comments to the president. "Well, then, something else" —he speaks to the prisoners' bench—"would interest me immensely: In your opinion could the Sixth Army be bolshevized in captivity . . ."

"Herr Volksrichter," the president interrupts, "this question has not the slightest connection with the trial. I cannot admit it."

"Very well," Freyberg observes. "Although according to my limited understanding every danger threatening the Germany of the Führer has a connection with this trial."

"Have you any further questions, questions pertinent to the trial, Judge von Freyberg?"

"Yes, I have another question." Freyberg speaks slowly and gravely, and he surveys the prisoners' bench. "I should like to ask the war invalid— What is his name again?"

"Hans Moeller."

"Herr Moeller . . ." Freyberg begins hesitantly.

"Defendant Moeller," the president corrects.

"Herr Moeller," Freyberg repeats obstinately, "are you sure that you would be sitting here if you hadn't lost your leg?"

President Behn shakes his head, angrily and impatiently. What an utterly superfluous question! he thinks, and at that he is the most intelligent of my honorary judges . . .

"I am not sure that I know how to interpret your question, Judge," Hans says distrustfully. "If you mean the simplest connection between cause and effect, then of course I would not be sitting here if I hadn't lost my leg, but would have gone on eastward instead with my motorcycle, eastward to Stalingrad."

"No, that is not what I mean," says Freyberg, and his yellow face now gives the impression of great suffering. "I mean the blow which has struck your life through the partial destruction of life, and in this respect I speak somewhat from personal experience; I, too, returned from the first World War partially destroyed and had to deal with a desperate inclination to look at all life as being destroyed—yes, to desire its destruction . . ."

"But in my case it is exactly the reverse!" Hans exclaims, painfully reminded of Commissioner Negele's "artificial leg psychosis"; "I am sitting here because I believe in a new life and because I see the destruction of life not in myself, but in my accusers!"

"Just the same, the destruction of life *is* in you, Herr Moeller . . ."

"It *was* in me," Hans breaks in. "It raged in me as it raged in every other young German. I didn't keep it from you—and I am sitting here . . ."

"Rubbish," Freyberg interrupts venomously. "You are sitting here with an artificial leg, and that's what I mean. I for one cannot be convinced that cripples believe in a new life."

"Why not?"

"Good God, man! Because once you have lost a leg you can't expect a new one to grow!"

"I know that, that's why I wear an artificial leg!"

"That is a melancholy substitute and reminds you continuously of the destroyed part of your body."

"No!" Hans exclaims; "because it is not a photograph in memory of the dead leg, but it is my new leg!"

"And at night?" Freyberg asks deeply irritated. "You know it is at night that the destroyed part of life quivers in one's memory, and that hurts and makes a man hateful, and he hates what is destroyed in him, and when he hates himself, he hates life, all life, and there is no room left for faith in a new life, but only for faith in the power of destruction . . ."

"But I don't hate the leg that I no longer have!" Hans exclaims, and now he, too, is irritated. "And I love my new leg. I love it so much that lately I started wearing it also at night, so that I have two legs in bed now and no room left for the dead one . . ."

"You have succeeded in doing this lately?" Freyberg asks gloomily, putting his fingertips to his temples. "When could you . . . how long after the destruction was it that you succeeded?"

"Last night," says Hans.

Freyberg opens his mouth in amazement, and he smells his breath—the exchange of questions and answers has made him forget his peppermint tablets. With a disgusted face he opens his silver snuff-box.

What a frightfully foolish discussion this is! President Behn tells himself, and who is interested in it, anyway?

His eyes roam over the prisoners' bench, as has become their custom: and there is one who seems to be interested in the macabre dialogue more than the others who listen with grave and yet somewhat empty faces. It is again this Sauer who is different from his companions and who seems to be deeply concerned and strangely agitated by what the invalid next to him and the decadent hypochondriac on the judges' tribune have to tell each other about a cut off leg. And President Behn once again opens the file "Sauer Christopher" with its margin comment by the chief of the Security Department, underlined with red pencil: "Defendant possibly of interest to us!"

He should be drawn into the conversation, Behn thinks.

"That is all I wish to ask," Baron Freyberg says wearily and unclearly, the tablet on his tongue hindering his speech; he closes his silver snuffbox noiselessly.

"It would be interesting to learn," President Behn quickly adds, "whether this well-nigh indestructible faith of the defendant in a new life is shared by others, for instance by his sister."

"Why, of course!" Sophia replies, raising her hands in astonishment.

"Also by you, defendant Sauer?" the president asks languidly.

"Yes," Chrisopher answers heavily, not raising his agitated face in the least, "as a Catholic Christian I believe in a new life."

What a peculiar answer! How restrictive and at the same time isolating an answer! His friends on the bench quickly raise their faces, and yet they seem to be cowering, too, as if something dark and uncheerful were fluttering close over their heads.

"If I am not very much mistaken," President Behn comments with a shameless smile, "it seems to me that up to now we were talking about this world, not the hereafter . . ."

But Christopher does not respond to the challenge, he is silent. Also Baron Freyberg makes a resigned or disgusted gesture, although the president looks at him expectantly and even motions with his hand to call his attention to the strange necromancer among the defendants.

"Herr Präsident," the voice of the youngest of the judges comes from the other side, "I would also like to direct a question to Sergeant Moeller."

"Go ahead!" Behn nods. He is now deeply immersed in the question why this man Sauer who might be of interest to the Security Department has so far frustrated every attempt to isolate him from the others; why he does not seem able to share his friends' confidence in the present world, which must mean that he is more skeptical than they regarding the watchword of "six out of six million." Or is it his malady? Or is it simply fear, fear of death? Are his energy reserves, his "act of will power," consumed at the end, after all? Could one still throw the life-line to him, in the very last moment?

Baldur Uhle has risen, although it is entirely unbecoming for a judge to stand up in order to question a defendant. When the judges eventually do stand up, it will be the dramatic and final rising which introduces and at the same time honors the passing of sentence. Judge Uhle, however, does not know that he is making a mistake; he does not even know that he is standing, he is beside himself, and has been for some time. But since the president is lost in thought, since he has actually relaxed, lightly touching the back of his chair with his head and shoulders, his eyes steadfastly gazing straight ahead, there is no one to correct Judge Uhle's mistake.

"Sergeant Moeller, I should like to hear, precisely from you or only from you . . ."

Judge Uhle falters, as if frightened by his boldness. What is it he does not already know? Is it not enough and more than enough, this viscous, belching and stinking lava flood of calumny and deceit, this defilement and pesterous infection which has paraded past him much too long and much too close? Is it not enough, this horror and wrath at the stream of pus which could still break out of the body of a nation miraculously healed and radiant with the beauty of Siegfried? And if it is his, Judge Uhle's, heroic duty to guard the Rhinegold of the New Germany and to destroy rapacious enemies, why does he not destroy them, grim and silent as Hagen? Why does he still want to put a question to this one, not from wrath, but from the distress of his feelings—precisely to this one, only to this one, not to the other who is also in uniform and has gone through the same school, but who is ungainly and mangy-scalped and does not touch one's feelings like this young sinner and one-time brother . . .

"Precisely from you or just from you, I should like to hear if you could muster enough courage to repent . . ."

"What are you saying?" Hans flares up, not trusting his ear.

"You should have the courage to repent, Sergeant! You are a badly injured front fighter, you have the Iron Cross, first class, you belong to the youth of which the Führer's Germany is proud, you have erred, gravely erred. But National Socialist Germany fights for someone like you and does not want to lose you. If you repent, honestly repent, honestly do penance, there may be ways and means for the people's community to receive you once more."

"Herr Volksrichter," Hans says calmly, "I have received a similar offer during the preliminary investigation from a Gestapo agent named Negele. The gentleman called it: 'Rehiring,' which is somewhat coarser and clearer and suggests the stool-pigeon services I was to perform among the students as payment for my liberation. You will find the details of the proposed deal in the transcript, provided Herr Negele admitted his shamelessness and did not falsify the transcript."

"But I do not intend to bargain for your repentance, comrade Moeller," Judge Uhle speaks with a warm voice; "I don't want you to become a stool pigeon, but a member of the people's community. And the repentance I demand of you is the restoration of your honor . . ."

"I repent ten of the twenty-three years of my life," Hans speaks, his voice raised. "The first twelve years don't count; but the last year, the unrepented year, counts as much as my whole life. For this last unrepented year has made my life worth living."

"Thank you!" Judge Uhle says curtly and somewhat pointlessly. "I have no further questions."

He sits down and his fingers drum on the table top for a while. Hans, however, unable to detach himself from the handsome man's disappointed and offended face which already shows traces of hardening from studied pitilessness, thinks two thoughts at once. He thinks: you must be killed; and he thinks: susceptible to infection.

But why has the president left his youngest judge without support and direction in this moral dispute which is badly conducted and uncalled for? Because he is preoccupied with the arresting gesture performed by someone on the prisoners' bench—again the special case among the defendants. For when the question was put, not to him, but to the war invalid alone, the question about repentance, Christopher raised his fists as in anger or as in contrition, held them in the air for a moment, on a level with his temples, and then pressed them against his eyes—and in this sorrowfully contorted or even penitent position he remains, his face lowered, his fists on his eyes, his elbows on his knees.

Is the fellow weeping by any chance? Behn asks himself, extraordinarily curious.

But now, in the stillness following Judge Uhle's last word, Christopher lowers his hands, straightens up and shows a face which, though not tearful or tear-stained, is nevertheless marred and distorted by grief. Thus at least it appears to the observer Behn.

"Any further questions?" the president asks.

Judge Lucius folds his hands on the table top, looks at them and speaks with his pleasing theologian's voice: "I wish to ask not one, but all the defendants a question which has thus far been forgotten, but which is exceedingly significant for the Court as well as for the accused. Among many other things the defendants have also claimed to be patriotic, and the tenor of their handbill quite clearly strives to imbue the students with the emphatic feelings of the wars of liberation. My question, then, is addressed to the defendants' avowed patriotism; and when I ask them: what, precisely, according to your ideas, should become of Germany . . ."

"For God's sake, Herr Kollege, what sort of a discussion are you launching here?" President Behn interrupts him. "Do you want to hear Herr von Hennings' declaration of policy as Chancellor and criminal psychologist-in-chief of the Fourth Reich?"

"That is not what I want to hear, Herr Präsident," Judge Lucius says, keeping his hands folded and his eyes lowered. "And the question I wish to ask is of such eminent significance for the present that it is more likely to be answered by silence than by discussion, and I would take silence for an answer too. For Germany is at war. When there still were parties and party squabbles they had to be silenced in wartime. The defendants, however, deliberately chose wartime Germany for their alleged patriotic struggle of liberation. My question to the defendants draws the only possible conclusion from their otherwise absurd undertaking. I ask the defendants as patriots, and I do not even put the word in quotation marks: Do you want, then, do you really and truthfully want Germany to lose the war?"

Silence follows, for the length of a breath—as if an invisible conductor were lifting his baton to give the chorus its cue. Then two female and four male voices answer in one harmonious chord, "Yes!" Then silence again. Judge Lucius disentangles his hands and strokes his forehead with the left, the right rests on the table.

He is trembling! President Behn thinks, looking at his neighbor's aged head. "Are you satisfied with the answer?" he asks softly malicious. Judge Lucius nods wordlessly. "Further questions?" the president asks, turning his head to the other side.

"Communists," Judge Schneidhammer growls without looking up, diligently writing below the upturned covering page. That is not a question, but a greasy stupidity, thinks Behn.

The president looks across the bench at the Reichs attorney who seems to be shaking with amusement. But it is not amusement, it is something like grim humor that moves the prosecutor; for now also his war argument has been eaten away from him, even if it wasn't the all-devouring monster, but his alternate who did it.

"Very pretty, very pretty indeed, the things one learns here!" Reichs Attorney Tischler chuckles. "These dregs of humanity counted quite without shame on the hour when their dream wish would be fulfilled and a conquered, dishonored and mutilated Germany would eat the bread of charity from the hands of the Jewish-plutocratic-bolshevistic trinity of Roosevelt, Churchill and Stalin!"

That is not a question, either. Why doesn't the poor devil save this excellent mess of phrases for his final plea? Behn jeers at him mentally. Or was it actually meant and understood as a question? He sees that defendant von Hennings is rising.

"Also the salt of the earth is the dregs of the earth," Karl speaks with dignity; "and since this is a war of faiths, with the fighting lines cutting across all nations, it must also be a victory of faith, and defeat must be Germany's salvation, its liberation from the curse of having been the container of evil. And then Germany's own bread, and the bread of all the countries throughout the world, will be the bread of charity, by the newly won grace of God."

At that Christopher speaks, without standing up or looking up: "I cannot believe in this bread for Germany for a long time yet . . ."

"Most interesting!" President Behn exclaims, swooping down like a hawk into this exchange with his man. "I observe the first deviation from the soul-saving doctrine of the infallible principal defendant! Speak your mind freely, defendant Sauer."

Karl looks along the prisoners' bench perplexedly, also the other defendants look to the right. But Christopher forgets to stand up and does not raise his head. "I think, Herr Professor"—he dares to address a fellow defendant in the presence of the Court, or perhaps he does not realize his temerity at all, so quietly and sadly and with such compulsion does he speak—"I think, Herr Professor, that it will be difficult, very difficult, and that it will take a long time, a very long time, for Germany to find grace and mercy again . . . I believe there will be a long night for Germany . . ."

"Why?" Karl whispers almost inaudibly.

"How Christian and Catholic!" President Behn exclaims animatedly. "He believes in the life everlasting for himself, and in the long night for Germany!"

"It is in the night, dear Herr von Hennings," Christopher speaks, "that penance must be done; for without penance there is no grace and no mercy—and yet there will be no penance for Germany, not for a long time, because Germany does not recognize penance in the night . . ."

"A suggestion, Sauer," President Behn exclaims and raises his forefinger significantly. "Let us say 'penitence' instead of 'penance,' and let us recall the question or invitation of one of the judges which might better have been addressed to you than to your accomplice: could you, personally, not formulate it this way and say: 'I repent?' "

"For in that night Germany will be terribly aware, with groaning and convulsions, that it has destroyed and has been destroyed, and the German destruction of life makes Germany hateful, and it hates what has been destroyed, within and without, and when it hates itself it hates life, all life, and there is no room left for faith in a new life, but only for faith in the power of destruction—for a long, long time . . ."

Even President Behn looks around dumbfounded and twice opens his mouth before he is able to speak. "That is what I call . . . that is a simply outrageous way of quoting our excellent colleague von Freyberg!"

Baron Freyberg takes the monocle from his eye, leaning forward, and under his emaciated cheeks the muscles of his jaws move incessantly.

"Yes," Christopher speaks on, oblivious of the others, "that man spoke well and rightly for a destroyed German . . ."

"Christopher!" Karl exclaims agitatedly, and he too forgets his surroundings. "I certainly do not believe in the long night after so long a night, and it is dreadful for you that you should think such dark thoughts! Shall I remind you of something, Christopher?

Who was it who once said he did not want to die benighted, but between night and day, no sooner?"

"It was I who said it," Christopher says softly, "who hoped it . . ."

"Christopher!" Sophia whispers into space. "Why have you become so different?"

"Because now I am one of them after all!" he whispers back, and again raises his fists to his temples. "One of the destroyed destroyers of life!"

"Why don't you put an end to this humbug!" Captain Freyberg challenges the president with astonishing impoliteness, and his face is frighteningly yellow and pained.

"Yes. Enough of this infamous contacting by the defendants," President Behn remonstrates with sudden severity, and pounds the table with his hand. "Enough!" he shouts again, and quite without reason since already all is quiet. "Further questions?" he asks to the right and left; and he seems to be certain that no one is inclined to ask further questions because he continues in the same breath: "I herewith conclude the taking of evidence. The Reichs Attorney at the People's Court has the floor."

Behn pulls a gold watch from under his robe and puts it in front of him on the table. Now this is the customary, though always offensive gesture with which he introduces the prosecutor's plea and at the same time limits it, not only with respect to duration, but also with respect to its dimensions and functions in general. For while the watch cuts down the time, it also clips the wings of eloquence, dampens the unbearable trumpet of a voice which loves to try its strength—old-testament-fashion—on the walls of Jericho, and makes the clipped and dampened mimic appear as antiquated and superfluous as he is.

But Reichs Attorney Tischler, prosecutor by nature and oratorical passion, takes a special kind of revenge on the all-devouring monster. He shames the monster, perhaps from a want of arguments, perhaps from grim, deadly humor! His plea lasts one and one-half minutes. It reads:

"Gentlemen of the Court! There are deeds that cry out to Heaven, and there are, much more rarely, doers who cry out to Heaven. We owe it to the brilliant conduct of the trial, in which a sovereign magician's wand dissolved the venerable, though unfortunately inadequate trial form and made the defenders be their own judges—we owe it to this that the six defendants have cried out to Heaven and have tried themselves, all without exception, each and every one of them admitting his full measure of responsibility in the most convincing testimony possible. And they have answered the question of their guilt in unison with Yes, with the most monstrous Yes my ears have ever heard, with the apocalyptic Yes, that Germany may perish. There is nothing left for me to do but to pass on to you the sentence which they have already passed on themselves. The defendants Hennings and Associates are guilty of the crime of high treason according to Paragraph 83, Section 3, of the Penal Code. Gentlemen of the Court, I ask that Karl von Hennings, Dora von Hennings, Hans Moeller, Sophia Moeller, Christopher Sauer, and Alexander Welte suffer the penalty of death."

President Behn keenly watches the defendant Sauer; but as the word falls, the last word, Christopher's face budges as little as the faces of the others. The six look straight ahead, at the high windows that are now walls of glass with evening breaking behind them. Only the strong, white light of the chandeliers pervades the room, and perhaps this is why their faces have the hue of white plaster.

"Counsel for the defense has the floor," President Behn says, and he puts the gold watch back in his pocket again. For Dr. Langbein's plea never takes more than three minutes.

"May it please the Court," the little voice rises plaintively, "I would do violence to my most sacred feelings, if I should try to question the guilt of the defendants or even attempt to minimize the extent of their guilt. Any discussion of possibly mitigating circumstances, which as a rule the Court graciously permits, is vitiated not only by the weight of guilt the defendants have loaded upon themselves, but also by the clearly expressed desire of every one of my clients that I abstain from just such discussion of mitigating circumstances. In view of the tragic clearness of the situation—if I may use the expression—there is little that I can do except to point out that among the defendants are three very young men and two women. It is for the Court to determine whether this circumstance contains the possibility of invoking the mercy of the Führer for one or the other of the defendants."

President Behn: "Does the Reichs Attorney wish to reply to the remarks of the Counsel for the Defense?"

Reichs Attorney Tischler: "No, thank you."

President Behn, to the prisoners' bench: "What have you to add to the remarks of Counsel for the Defense?"

Karl: "Nothing."

Dora: "For myself, I reject the defense attorney's plea for mercy."

Hans: "So do I."

Sophia: "So do I."

Christopher: "So do I."

Alexander: "So do I."

President Behn: "The People's Court will now adjourn for deliberation."

5

This is the legally prescribed sequence for voting in the People's Court: first the Court Reporter casts his vote; then follow the votes of the honorary judges, according to age, beginning with the youngest; the president is the last to vote.

There is the question of guilt and there is the question of punishment. The decisions are supposedly made by an absolute majority of votes, but President Behn nevertheless demands a unanimous vote. No, not he, but the dignity and sovereignty of this People's Court responsible only to the Führer demand it.

"Our office which gives us power over life and death," says President Behn, "makes of us the bearers of the State myth, the Fates guarding the thread of the Reich's fate. And the fate which we impose upon those who trespass against the Reich must be conclusive and unconditional, clear and clean like the Fates' cut through the thread of life."

The first to cast his vote is the Court Reporter. Judge Lucius bears that title, however insignificant his reporting activity may have been, however infinitesimal particularly in contrast to the fateful report the Court has heard that day. Judge Lucius receives one final shock to frighten him on his way to the voting: the metaphor of the Fates. It is not only the horror of the Protestant theologian at the blasphemous presumption of playing Providence—no, it is that here the bull-necked president in his arrogance has issued the word as coin and has thrown it into the game of fate, as the coin of fate. And the coin of fate has rolled and tinkled through this decisive day, fatefully enough and elusively enough, as it had already drummed in Walter's heart this morning when he awakened. Had he not called it absurd, this annoying drumming? Now he no longer calls it absurd.

The question of guilt, the question of punishment! The defendant Karl von Hennings is a man grown out of the spirit of the same religion as he, Lucius, a professor who derives from *profiteri* and this means: to avow something, and this means: to stand for something, and that is the political postulate for the defense of a conviction and for the courage to defend it—and Luther derives from *profiteri*, Calvin derives from *profiteri*. What a deep and genuine protestantism is concealed in the doctrine of Crime as State and in the struggle of faith against this State! And what else is the meaning of any deep and genuine spiritual protest throughout history, but that it is the form and expression of Divine Providence?

The question of guilt, the question of punishment! Here is the defendant Dora von Hennings who has given strength to her husband, as the earth gave strength to Antaeus, and here and there, at mysteriously propitious times, she was his Norn and guided his destiny in the right direction; but always she was his wife, and so sure are these two people of each others' love, that Judge Lucius has never yet seen a happier and more beautiful smile on a woman's face than that which this wife held ready for her husband returning from the sinners' table.

The question of guilt, the question of punishment! Four young people stand for themselves and for the invisible phalanx of young people behind them: the defendants Hans Moeller and Alexander Welte for the Moellers and Weltes who are heretics and who fight for their new faith with the zeal of converts; the defendants Sophia Moeller and Christopher Sauer for the Sophias and the Christophers who have never been a part of it and who have now been let loose to struggle for their old faith. Is there, in the fateful march of these changed and unchangeable ones, an aspect that could be called ugly, reprehensible or repulsive, and that would not speak for the courage and decency of the young hearts? Is not even the most difficult among them, the one most foreign to the Protestant Lucius, that militant Catholic peasant who has something of the medieval sorcerer in him,—is not even he a beacon of that will power and self-purification which will assure the resurrection of Catholic youth?

The question of guilt! It is a judicially established fact, it is the ominous conclusion of the trial, that the leaflet of the defendants has been absorbed by the student body, soaked up like rain by arid earth. Why? Because it was so well written? It is rather mediocre writing—intentionally so, it must be presumed—for the professor's literary capacity knows stronger keys; it is written in the somewhat philistine, fiery style of that well-meaning, would-be-poet Theodore Körner, in the manner of the liberation pyrotechnics of 1813 which so extraordinarily irritated the Olympian Goethe, aulic councillor of universality and universal order. No, it is effective, not because it is well written, but because it is written; and if it has the effect of rain on arid earth, then it is Providence which knows the thirst of the earth and guides the cloud over the thirsty spot.

The question of punishment! The coin of fate rolls and tinkles through this day in court as through a soothsaying machine which is out of order and impatiently shaken by its users. For who is not acting the part of the Fates on this day? The People's Court holds the thread of fate of the six defendants in general; the witness Vierck, the crooked Providence with the hammer, holds Karl von Hennings' in particular. But the defendants hold the thread of Hitler Germany's fate, and therefore also of Hitler's People's Court. And the heart holds Walter Lucius' thread of fate. The heart? It is a part of Lucius, and Lucius is a part of the People's Court. What else is he, Judge Lucius? Does he derive from *profiteri*, does he avow something, does he live up to the political postulate and the religious imperative of standing up for his convictions?

His title is "Court Reporter," he did it honestly and yet he might still make the one great, cataclysmic report of the day. Instead he has done something else, something else in cowardice of conviction. He has put the question about Germany's defeat to the six spinners of fate on the prisoners' bench, the question which was to make him, the nationalistically-minded conservative, an honest judge again—and yet he bore the answer in his sick heart, with such distressing clarity that in trembling baseness he immediately begged the defendants preferably to give no answer at all. It was in vain, naturally it was in vain. The sixfold affirmation came in unison, affirmation of guilt and of extreme punishment. The heart accepts the verdict and will execute it on Judge Lucius, in its role of Atropos, the goddess of fate, cutting the thread of life cleanly and clearly. It must necessarily be thus; for it is the betrayal of the heart that must be atoned . . .

The Court Reporter, as the first, affirms the question of guilt in all six cases and votes for the death penalty.

"Aren't you feeling well, Herr Kollege?" President Behn asks and looks at him with narrowed eyes.

"It is distressing!" Judge Lucius exclaims with strange aggressiveness. Then, with a confused look, he reaches for the water pitcher. But he spills the water as he pours it.

President Behn writes the name "Hagner" on his note pad. It is the name of a youngish, ambitious district judge who has already sat with the People's Court as a substitute judge. He will be Lucius' successor.

The second to cast his vote is SS Sturmbannführer Baldur Uhle, youngest of the honorary judges. To him the "State myth" is neither an empty nor a presumptuous word. For his life was cradled in mythology, so to speak, and flowed straight from a childhood drenched in the Germanic folk myth, into the millennial Reich.

His father was a teacher of Germanic philology and bore a given name which set him into the world as a Nordic alliteration. He whose name is Ludegund Uhle must necessarily dedicate his life to the sagas of ancient Nordic gods and heroes, with the magnificent cultural-political task of tearing away as much of them as possible from the old Nordic countries and incorporating them in German mythology. Ludegund Uhle's life work, then, was the interpretation and Germanization of the "Edda." And since for him the very essence of life, a living undertaking, was to distil anew the German saga from the divine myth of the struggle of light against darkness and create anew the German soul in the image of light, he sought, and also found, a blonde girl whose name was Freia, even if her surname was Kunze. He made her his wife and with her sired the son who was as handsome as Baldur, from whom he received his Edda name, though he was not a figure of light, but was dark-haired and somewhat melancholy.

Baldur, an autumn child, quiet and willing by nature, but clothed in the purple of the light- and sun-god's name, had his father's "Edda" for his cradle song, escort, and early nourishment, and bore the mythology gravely and obediently through his young life.

When he was only twenty years old—in 1927, when it was still dangerous—he already wore the double rune SS, the rune of victory and the symbol of lightning, on his collar, and on his buckle the motto of the new Germanic life: "Fidelity is my honor." Baldur marched through the six years of struggle, grave and obedient in his and the Führer's mythical name, fighting and killing. He was an "old fighter" when victory was won, advanced through many ranks to the high rank of Sturmbannführer, was attached to various SS formations and finally to the Security Department where he worked in the two main divisions of "Enemy Exploration" and "Enemy Control." He explored, controlled, fought and killed enemies, outwardly an officer of prosecution, inwardly a myth bearer, a somewhat melancholy technician of destruction. When he had reached the minimum age, he was promoted to the position of People's Judge.

But today, when his face turned greenish with pallor, it was not nausea from the pus stream which he saw breaking out of the German figure of light, but it was his father's "Edda" which nauseatingly rose in him . . .

For Baldur, the god, is dead, the sun is dead, the summer is dead; and the Norn at the world ash tree already envisions the twilight of the gods. "Lightning time, sword time, clashing of shields, storm time and wolf time, the world must fall." Already the cocks that watch over all the world are waiting for the last day to break. And it comes because it must come, the last day and the twilight of the gods. "Now brothers strangle and murder each other, and kinsmen prepare the destruction of kin." And the two enemies rise up, the fire and the wolves, advancing against the world ash tree, the high seat of the gods. The fire comes from the West and consumes the world ash tree. The wolves, however, come on the ship of death, from the winterland of the East, and devour the gods of light. "The sun turns black, earth sinks in the sea, the gay stars plunge from the sky . . ."

And yet, as Judge Uhle in his deliberation of guilt and punishment comes to the one defendant whose given name could be Baldur and who rejected the fraternal appeal for penitence with such hostility, he stops once more. Now brothers strangle and murder each other . . . And who is Cain, who is Abel?

"Herr Präsident," Baldur Uhle asks softly, "could death by a firing squad possibly be considered, as an honoring exception?"

"No," President Behn answers with a searching look, "the manner of execution is prescribed by law and is consequently not a part of the question of punishment in general, which alone you are duty bound to decide."

Judge Uhle, as the second, affirms the question of guilt in all six cases and votes for the death penalty.

The third to cast his vote is Baron Maximilian von Freyberg, Captain in the War Clothing Office, Munich. The War Clothing Office delivers uniforms, boots, socks, underwear and trouser buttons to the base depots for Bavarian ground troops. Captain Freyberg is something like a uniformed floor manager, and the baronial clothing activity is as little attractive as the secretaries and seamstresses under his command. Since horse races and prize fights have ceased, except for a few very inferior ersatz performances, the honorary judgeship is the only pleasure left to him. That even this pleasure can be spoiled is proved by the course, or rather by the end, of this trial which began so stimulatingly and promised to be such an enjoyable affair.

It is a pleasure to sit in a theater box, to be titillated by the performance and to forget the stomach—all this reinforced by the feeling of judicial sublimity and by the additional, positively classical titillation of turning thumbs down at the end like an old Roman and sending the gladiator to Hades, without any further inconvenience or loss of distance. It is no pleasure to be dragged out of one's box into the arena, and to receive a blow in the pit of the stomach.

Who or what dragged me into it, anyhow? Freyberg asks himself deeply irritated. The whole thing started so excellently, most amusingly, eminently excitingly. Those six fellows in their open mahogany coffin—yes, the two women are fellows too, and the good-looking blonde belongs to that black devil of a fellow, of course—the six performed admirably, with unheard-of boldness, they charged in like old Marshal Blücher and gave the dear Nazis a piece of their minds—guts, lots of guts, one could have clapped one's hands, it was so amusing! And all through the fun there was never a doubt about the final attraction: thumbs down and finished!

Why the devil did he have to get foolhardy at the end and pick a quarrel with that war cripple, no, get chummy with him, drink the pledge of the brotherhood of cripples with him and try to talk him out of his faith in life? What did he want to accomplish by it: to make the end easier for the one-legged man, to make the end easier for himself, to know another besides himself, who has been bitten by death and wishes the bite of death for everyone else? Lonesome, aren't you, Herr Baron? Yearning for like-minded companions who don't give a damn about this pest-ridden life? Why then, as a good German does he not found the club of peppermint munchers, of those whose breath stinks from internal putrefaction? Why did he have to approach this one-legged Parsifal who looks as though he had a monopoly of clean breath?

The consequence was the kick in the stomach with the artificial leg to which Parsifal declared himself morganatically wedded. He loves his artificial leg. Do you love your stomach, Herr Baron? Parsifal believes in life, his one leg already buried in Russia, his other leg standing in the grave dug for him by the People's Court. That is crazy to the point of blasphemy, truly deserving of hate and of thumbs down. To Hades with the optimist, with the traitor to peppermint munchers! It's one and the same whether he believes in the new life for himself or for Germany's youth after the twilight of the Nazi gods.

Why does the one-legged fellow not confine himself to the decline of the world? That would be more fitting for him and the Baron could go along with it. The anxiety of the inquisitor Freyberg to learn something about the bolshevization of captured German troops, still belonged to the ticklish questions. For all sorts of things are brewing there, rumors are flying about copulations of an apocalyptic nature, about first-class names, not only equal in rank to the nobility of the Freybergs, but superior to it, riding through the air on Soviet brooms and wishing to lead the witches' Sabbath westward, to the classic German Walpurgis night. That would be something! That would make it worth dickering for a few more years with this Shylock of a stomach—if that were the great dissolution, the tremendous sulphur cloud as *spectaculum mundi!*

And if it is not the end that is coming from the East, but the beginning, and if it is somehow mysteriously connected with these six propagandists of life who are doomed to death, if the thread of the Fates connects them with all the beginnings in all the world, with six million sunrises, then even the long night of hate and penitence, brazenly stolen from the Baron's mouth by this devilish defendant Bitter or Sauer or whatever his name may be, will not be long enough to forestall the dawn of the young morning.

When the stomach is hit and twists like a poisonous dragon, then even the peppermint tablet is no protection against the breath. For does not the body breathe through the skin, too? What unmitigated impudence of this defendant Bitter or Sauer, this peasant lout, to call Judge von Freyberg a destroyed German!

The Baron looks disgusted. The two females! His life cannot boast much of women—that is why he calls them females, except for his late mother, a lady so formidable that her son was permitted to speak with her only in French, for the sake of its elegantly respectful phrases. *Je vous prie, chère maman.* Rightly seen, his life is not even frivolous; it has been devoid of females for the last twenty years, in view of the Baronial breath and other ponderables. He does not prize women, because it is comforting to despise what one cannot have. But now People's Judge Freyberg has to turn thumbs down and for the first time send two females to Hades. In other words: Baron Maximilian has to execute two women. *Je vous prie, chère maman!*

"Herr Präsident, two of the six are women."

"Well, what of it? They are as guilty as the men. The Court recognizes no distinction on account of sex."

"And if they were pregnant?"

"They aren't. Besides, the establishment of such a fact would be a matter for the executing authorities. The questions of guilt and punishment have nothing to do with gynecology, Herr Kollege."

Freyberg reflects briefly. Were he, in order to salve his gentleman's conscience, not to vote for the death penalty in the case of the two females, he would also have to deal accordingly with the question of guilt. How could he do that, and what labor, what fruitless labor? Doubtless he would be outvoted and only irritate the president. And does he really want to save lives, he, the destroyed destroyer of life? Who whispered the jumbled, stolen words? Freyberg shakes his head deeply annoyed. His face is frighteningly yellow and pained. Enough of this nonsense and thumbs down!

Judge von Freyberg, as the third, affirms the question of guilt in all six cases and votes for the death penalty.

The fouth to cast his vote is SA flag leader Alois Schneidhammer. The Party dignitary's judgeship is one of his many honorary offices and by no means his most important one. The State myth finds expansive materialization in himself, and the Fates don't concern him in the least, especially since he has never heard of them. His interest in the trial was divided in consequence of his manifold importance, and not of his overflowing flesh, as the president was inclined to believe. A. Schneidhammer has it in black and white, and at the same time in his by no means fat head, that he has made good use of the day. The speech he is to deliver a week from today at the national convention of the National Socialist Cattle Dealers' Union, N.S.C.U., is under control, so to speak. He has even already delivered it in spirit; for the court proceedings, with the exception of a few importunate moments, did not disturb the satisfying preview of his thoughts.

It may be that A. Schneidhammer, the individual, is a colossus of flesh. But you should see him on the speakers' platform, as flag leader and Cattle Dealers' Group Leader, surrounded by flags, the cattle dealers at his feet: then he is colossal, the picture of strength and of the Reich Food Estate, the incarnation of the leader principle. And where in the world is there a more blessed sight than the forest of arms held upward and outward in salute, the mass gesture pointing to him, the All-highest one's deputy for the N.S.C.U.? Yes, indeed, A. Schneidhammer is a sight to behold; and a voice to be heard. While his stature—it must be said in all due modesty—mightily overshadows the All-highest in every dimension, his voice is to the voice of the All-highest as a widely noted echo; and that is almost a miracle when one thinks of A. Schneidhammer's bulging neck and beery throat. But he achieves it with goiter and harshened voice; he has the same, the incomparable Bavarian twang, blended with stilted High German sounds when he says "Fellow Germans!" he has the same, the incomparable harshness and callousness at the start, but with the resonance of an inexhaustible reserve of hoarseness, with the ever redeemed promise of hoarse roaring.

Here stands the leader of Group South and there sits the National Socialist Cattle Dealers' Union. This is a war convention, fellow

Germans, this is no time to peal the bells of peace, but to sound the trumpets of war. And even if you should, after the fourth winter of war, want to cave in like the walls of Jericho, you can't do it, you are held together by the Union of your world view. For of the four letters on which you sit viewing the world (here the expected laughter sets in, roaring and yet militarily drilled, the speaker concedes five seconds to it because it is the first and the last outburst of laughter, then he cuts it off, and it lets itself be cut off like a soft sausage, with one cut)—of your four letters N.S.C.U., "C" is the least important. "C" stands for Cattle dealers. When it is left out, there remains the National Socialist Union, remember that. If there is no cattle to deal in, what need is there for cattle dealers? The existing cattle belong to the National Socialist State, even in the mother's womb, and the National Socialist State takes care of the cattle, from birth to the slaughter house. And so it is the duty of the staff directors of the Reich Food Estate to inform you officially that cattle dealers, even those united in the N.S.C.U., are forbidden to continue their occupation for the duration of the war. You are occupationally dead, fellow Germans; through the impact of the war, you, as cattle dealers, have fallen on the field of honor as it were and are now entering Valhalla, at least temporarily. As living fellow Germans, however, you will find the doors of war plants open to you. Don't let it be asked of you in four weeks: what are you doing? Are you doing enough for this momentous hour? (These are the only sentences which A. Schneidhammer has taken out of the recorded speech of the Gauleiter, produced in the trial.) But let those of you who bellyache, or if they don't bellyache, bootleg, let those of you be warned that the National Socialist State has the power to inflict other deaths than the occupational death which honors you as soldiers of the Third Reich. And if you do find it hard not to bellyache, not to bootleg, and to go to work in defense plants because you are occupationally dead, you still have the great consolation of possessing what no other people possesses: our wonderful Führer, the guarantor of victory. Let us then hold together, fellow Germans, in National Socialist Union, with joy in our responsibilities, with thankfulness and love, and let us exclaim in unison: "Our Führer, we thank thee! Siegheil!"

And how they jump up, how they shout in a militarily drilled chorus and let the forest of arms grow, these occupationally dead ones! And this is the speech by the leader of Group South, and it is not interrupted . . .

"Not to let him finish!" Judge Schneidhammer grumbles, solving the questions of guilt and punishment. He looks at the president, closes his mouth with his hand, as under the shock of an inspiration, frees his mouth again and blows out his breath like cigar smoke: "Mister, I've got it! Hang them! Six gallows in front of the university, in the middle of Ludwigstrasse! Let them swing for forty-eight hours! That'll guarantee a discouraging effect, Herr Präsident!"

"I have already stated," Behn counters with a cold look, "that the manner of execution is determined by law. You have to decide only the question of punishment in general, thus for instance: death."

Judge Schneidhammer, as the fourth, affirms, the question of guilt in all six cases and votes for the death penalty.

President Behn is the fifth and last, the most unemotional and imperturbable. To decide the question of a man's guilt or innocence is to decide the question of his dangerousness or innocuousness to the State. President Behn had no trouble in getting a 4:0 decision of his judges in favor of guilt and dangerousness to the State. It will be a 5:0 decision, then, as it should be. Behn's office of Fates for the control of the Reich's fate functions without friction, at least with respect to Hennings and Associates.

This limitation sounds illogical, since after all the case Hennings and Associates is the only business on the agenda, but it is not illogical when further consideration is given to the Associates. For there are more Associates than merely five; let us make no mistake about that, even if the refrain of the six million partly amuses, partly annoys us. There are other things, too, that annoy us, for instance Hennings' paraphrasing of the Fates' activities—as the noiseless punching machine stamping out the inevitable double sentence: death and oblivion.

As for death, it is single-edged, in the fullest sense of the word: all that is required is a telephonic order to the executing authorities to prepare the finale in Stadelheim prison. But as for oblivion, in this case at least it is double-edged. The six—or at any rate five of them—are no longer interesting. The three-line press notice of the execution can be issued in three days or three weeks or three months, according to the wishes of the Security Department. But those behind the six are interesting and must not be forgotten.

The Fates notoriously have the peculiarity or the duty not to forget, to forget no one. The policy of the authorities toward the students, the policy of burying their heads in the sand while digging up subversive dirt from the sand with their legs, is as absurd as it is dangerous. Not in vain has President Behn upbraided the witness Vierck. It is necessary to disquiet and deter subversive elements, though not necessarily with cymbals and with Schneidhammer's gallows in front of the university. The public may read the press notice sooner or later— What do we care about the public. But the student body must learn the single-edged news about Hennings and Associates from the mouth of the university's president, with special arrangements for catching disturbers and "Enough" shouters.

President Behn is well prepared now to deal with Hennings' followers—six for six, six times six, six to any desired power. He plans then, to have two telephone conversations in connection with the case: an official one with the executing authority, and a semi-official one with the chief of the Security Department about the disclosure to be made to the student body, not about the margin comment in the Sauer file—or perhaps also about the margin comment.

Who knows but that a wedge may not have been driven after all between the five impenitents and the one who shows signs of contrition . . .

6

The six sit on the prisoners' bench and wait. They seek a point of rest for their eyes. The judges' tribune is oppressively empty, except for the blood-red robe of the prosecutor who, with a reserved face, makes notes and collects his papers, as if he were closing out accounts. One might say the emptiness of the tribune is contrary to the program, it is like a stage on which no one performs—and yet the curtain is raised and the audience is seated in the orchestra, looking apprehensively. The empty, red judges' chairs do not let the eyes rest upon them, but chase them away, as scarecrows scare off the birds. And the blind windows do not permit themselves to be looked at, nor does the meager back of the official defense attorney, nor even do one's own restless hands. The six find no point of rest for their eyes.

What an insane suspense is this, which does not let the mind roam any longer, not to the neighbor, to wife, sister, lover, to husband, brother, friend, not to the sacred pairing of fates, no longer to the last, audacious, tragic discussion between Karl and Christopher, Sophia and Christopher? What breathless, restless, ruthless craving is this to learn what after all is no longer written in the stars, but in enormous letters all the way across this day and this hall? How great and self-centered is the force of life, that they sit there and wait wait wait . . .

The blood-red velvet curtain of the judges' chamber is rent apart. The members of the People's Court enter the tribune, in the proper order of ranks. The two blood-red robes are wearing their berets on their heads, the three honorary judges are wearing their gray, brown, black uniform caps; they look different and faceless. They stop in front of their chairs. The prosecutor on the side rises and puts on his beret. The official defense attorney rises and puts on his beret. The six defendants and their guards are standing. It is as if the noble hall, already too mighty for the few people, were growing in height and breadth.

The president speaks in a languid voice:

"In the name of the People! The defendants Karl von Hennings, Dora von Hennings, Hans Moeller, Sophia Moeller, Christopher Sauer, Alexander Welte are guilty of the crime of high treason and are to suffer death by the ax. The People's Court declines to invoke the Führer's mercy for the condemned men and women. The verdict of the People's Court is final and beyond appeal, and is to be executed without delay."

That is all.

Chapter Eleven

ADAM

I

The barber at Stadelheim prison is called Adam, and most people don't know if it is his given name or his surname. He is not an independent businessman, but a state employee with the title of Surgical Assistant and a certificate attesting to his competence. He lives in the prison. Until 1935 he lived in the same capacity in the surgical clinic, and shaved the hairy parts of bodies before they were submitted to the surgeon's knife. He is a master of his trade, but his trade has nothing in common with the gay, loquacious beautification work of a Figaro. For he does not shave faces. Adam is grave and taciturn and emaciated like a fakir. His office, his appearance and the late hour of the night at which he usually goes into action, spread terror, deadly terror. He is used to it and pays no attention to it. Sometimes it happens that his clients must be tied to their cots face down, or be put in strait-jackets. It is all the same to him; he can shave and cut hair in any position and has never yet nicked anyone. That is his pride.

"Adam, work!" the prison's executive secretary speaks over the house wire.

"Cell number," Adam requests.

"There are six."

"Six," says Adam. It is not an exclamation of astonishment, but only a repetition of the number. He hangs up, and dons his work coat. Every barber in the world wears a white jacket, Adam wears a black one. He is no worldly barber.

"Six at one stroke, Adam." The head-keeper receives him. "World record. Students and their . . ."

"Not interested," says Adam.

"Two women among them."

Adam disgustedly wrinkles his bony nose. "In that case give me some old newspapers," he requests.

"Newspaper?"

"For the hair," says Adam. "It hurts women to see their hair lying around."

"That makes me laugh," says the head-keeper; but he gives him the newspapers. Adam puts them in his black, flat, wooden case that holds his utensils and resembles a paintbox. They walk along the corridor.

"You should take a look at the bowling alley, Adam," the head-keeper suggests. "Novel."

The "bowling alley" is that courtyard in the prison area in which the executions take place.

"Not interested," says Adam; but he does look through the grated window in front of which the head-keeper stops. They are now in the wing containing the death cells and forming the western side of the rectangular "bowling alley." The other three sides of the large courtyard are sheer walls, as high as the building. Floodlights enter from four sides. In each of the four corners and in the middle of the northern and southern longitudinal walls stands an executioner's block.

"Each one has his own," the head-keeper observes. "And if you think it will be a mass bowling, you are mistaken, Adam. It will be neatly played in six individual games, with novel lighting effects."

"Not interested," says Adam; but he does look at the spruce scaffolds, with a circling motion of his head.

"And there are three of them," the head-keeper says.

"Six," Adam corrects, with a circling motion of his head.

"I mean, three bowlers," the head-keeper says. "The head bowler with two assistant bowlers and general staff especially enlarged for the occasion. A record turnout."

"Bowler" is the executioner.

"Not interested," says Adam and turns his back to the window.

"But we have six axes," the head-keeper says and walks on, "not by accident, but because regulations require it."

"Pshaw," says Adam and walks on, his paintbox clattering a little. "I have twelve razors."

Adam knows how his appearance affects the delinquents, and he pays no attention to it. His long experience, however, has yielded certain modifications. At first he had remained entirely silent and had to learn how the mere opening of his paintbox and the displaying of knives and shears could give rise to panic, even to scenes of wild screaming. Adam hates screaming. He can shave screaming people, too, being a master of his trade; but it is difficult for him not to let the screaming bother him. So instead of entering silently, he would introduce himself. While still in the doorway, he would say, "I am the haircutter." Since that term was too unusual to bring about immediate pacification, he later conformed to common usage and said, while still in the doorway, "I am the barber." That had a somewhat better after-effect, but did not sufficiently mitigate the terror of the moment. So Adam finally resolved to make one last and and extreme concession, to add and stress one little word of self-deprecation, and said, while still in the doorway, "I am *only* the barber." That is the way he always says it now.

Adam, the head-keeper and the keeper on duty enter the cell. Karl ceases walking back and forth and stops, for one short second, with his back to the door. His neck is bare, and over the baggy trousers of the suit in which he was arrested, he wears a peculiar, sacklike shirt of stiff, grayish white coarse linen with a deep slit in the back. He turns around with one sudden movement. The sack shirt is cut out also in front, though not so deeply. The wide sleeves barely reach over his elbows; Karl has very long arms. He presses them to his body. His eyes turn glassy.

"I am *only* the barber," says Adam.

"If you please," says Karl with glassy politeness.

Adam walks around him—he is a short little man—he walks around Karl as around a column, looking up. "It's really all right," he says.

"What is all right?" Karl asks.

"The haircut," says Adam.

"No," says Karl, stroking chin and cheek with his hand, "there is stubble."

"Yes," says Adam behind him, "that's only stubble. But if you wish . . ."

"If you please," says Karl with glassy politeness, sits down on the stool and turns his face up.

Adam opens his paintbox, pours a little water from the tin pitcher on the washstand into his shaving mug and whips up lather. "Bend your head forward," he says; for the face is none of his business.

Karl does not bend his head forward, but lifts his face toward the barber, with his eyes closed. "My beard would be three days old, tomorrow morning," he whispers absently and repeats, with a diminutive smile, "tomorrow morning . . ."

Perhaps it is this smile that induces Adam to do something which he has never yet done in his official capacity; he lathers the face, which is none of his business, and shaves it; then he lathers the back of the head and shaves it.

"Thank you," says Karl, drying his face and head with the paper towel given him by Adam. It is an automatic and meaningless thank you, a glassy thank you; for Karl is not aware of the mercy he has been granted.

Adam leaves the cell without a word, he always disappears without a word, there is no occasion for a concluding word, there isn't any word that would be appropriate. The iron door is locked and bolted from the outside, and there are ugly noises, even if they are not as breath-taking and paralyzing as those of opening the door.

Karl crouches on the stool and with his hand caresses the clean-shaved surfaces of his face. That is a familiar, a daily gesture which surveys the restored cleanness and smoothness of the skin and rejoices in it. It is a part of this gesture for the hand to sweep past the ear over the shaved back of the head, from the neck upward. But here, on the neck, it stops; a cold hand, and a cold shiver runs down Karl's spine.

The fear of death comes wild and impetuous, with physical violence. Karl twists forward, one hand on his neck, the other on his throat, and hears himself rattling, and there is nothing but him and his body and the unbelievable nearness of death, razor edged and misty moist over his neck—there is nothing else in the world at this moment. He bends his neck lower and lower, as if to escape the grasp of death, his face now rests on his arm, and his arm on his knees, it is dark before his eyes and he does not hear his breath any more, the selfish terror is gone. For he now sees other things in this world, he sees how Adam grasps Dora's hair. He takes his hand from his neck and straightens up.

No, the horrible image does not go further, he does not see his wife bald. His eye is still full of her, of the long look at her. They sat facing each other in the prison car on the way here. They boarded the car in the order of Hennings and Associates, established for all eternity, Karl first, followed by his black jailer who sat down next to him. Dora, however, with feminine presence of mind, did not sit down next to the black one, but on the bench along the opposite side, facing Karl, and the four others took their seats alternatingly on the left side and the right. Thus it was that on this last ride Karl, Hans and Christopher sat on one bench; Dora, Sophia and Alexander on the other, interspersed by black guards. An electric bulb glowed from the ceiling, turning brighter as the car moved faster. The ride lasted quite some time; for Stadelheim lies outside the city, in the State forest extending southward toward the mountains. The ride lasted as long as the look between man and wife.

They were entwined in this look, forgetful of all else; persisting in each other, they surrendered no fragment of this look, they had the right to be miserly with this look. And Dora smiled. And behind that smile which grew ever thinner, as thin as glass, as thin as a wisp, she aged. At first there were rings, then sacks, under her eyes, the skin wrinkled around the corners of her eyes, lines furrowed across her forehead and vertically between her eyes and from her nose to her chin, past the corners of her mouth, and one furrow crept along her jaw and bulged the flesh of the lower part of her cheek, and the neck, the beautiful neck withered.

But this was nothing strange to him and did not frighten him as on the night of his arrest, when he had imagined her thus, cut off from her and desperately clinging to the outermost fringe of their companionship. Now he saw her and lived with her, eye to eye: to grow old together is a gift of Heaven, and should he yet see her white-haired and wrinkled, a dainty old woman, then the ride would have been well worth while and the look hallowed through the fulfillment of life.

The ride was at an end, too soon, much too soon, the car came to a stop, the ceiling light grew dim and Dora indistinctly young again. And both stood up, still in the enchainment of their look. The passage was not wide between the benches. Their bodies touched, he smelled her hair and she whispered: "Courage . . ."

How must his face have been, that she said it to him, and how was her face, that he did not say it to her? Her eyes were eyes restrained from weeping, with the last measure of her strength. This he could still see. Then a jailer cut between them, and their hands had not yet found each other, in this infinitesimal, infinite second of being together. And then she was gone. Karl could see only the black back of a uniform.

When Karl alighted, the last one, he saw nothing of her. He only saw black shadows vanishing. One of the shadows was Dora.

Karl gets up from the stool and walks back and forth. He crosses his arms close to his chest and slips his hands in the wide sleeves of the shirt, to warm himself. The cell is heated; but he wears nothing under his linen sack except his thin, sleeveless cotton undershirt. He is calm again; the moment of terror, which Adam had left behind, is long overcome. Dora is stronger than Adam and stronger than her shadow. She is stronger than his separation from her—the separation without farewell. For she has shown that even a separation without farewell can be undone and that the reunion is not one of dead souls, beyond the river Styx, but that it is of this earth, a reunion of the living. What does this mean? Oh, it means much, it means that Dora has not yet vanished as a shadow, that he will see her again. He must see her again—the compulsion is as valid, as legally valid, as the execution of the sentence: after all, they must die together. How can it be terrible to die together, after such a life together, and how can even this executioners' state rob him of the gift of dying with her, if its People's Court so decrees?

There is a clanking outside the door and the noise of opening the door is more evil than that of closing it. But Karl, stopping and looking at the door, does not even detach his crossed arms and leaves his hands in the wide sleeves; he only grasps more firmly his bare upper arms. The prison chaplain enters and stops near the door, a stuffed out man, and he speaks stuffy words: "My son, I come to offer you the consolations of the Church."

"I am a Protestant," says Karl.

"Oh, I see," the prison chaplain says; "but there is . . . Well, there will be no time to advise my Protestant colleague, who does not reside here."

"Nor is it necessary," says Karl.

"But you permit me, my son, to pray for the salvation of your soul?"

"I beg you to do so, Father!"

The prison chaplain lowers his head over his hands which he puts together in front of his chest, flat against each other with crossed thumbs, and from his experienced mouth roll, round and hurried, the words of *De Profundis:* " 'Out of the depths have I cried unto thee, O Lord. Lord, hear my voice: let thine ears be attentive to the voice of my supplications . . .' " Then he rolls the words ever rounder, more hurried and incomprehensible, to the Amen. He straightens up and makes the sign of the cross over Karl who has not come nearer and who has forgotten his hands in his sleeves.

"Amen," says Karl, "and I thank you, Father."

"Have you another wish, my son?"

"I wish to say a word of farewell to my friends."

"This wish cannot be granted, my son, neither with respect to your friends, nor, unfortunately, with respect to your wife."

"I have spoken only of my friends, Father, and of my wife I speak now. I have the wish to be cremated, and my wife has the wish to be cremated, and we both have the wish that our ashes be put together in the same urn—what happens to them after that is of no concern to us."

"I shall ask your wife to confirm it," the prison chaplain says after a pause, and his voice has lost some of its stuffiness.

"Do let her confirm it, Father."

"And have you another word for her, my son? I shall deliver it faithfully."

"All my words are for her, Father, as long as I can still speak, and there is no need for intercession. For I speak with her and she with me—I speak in her and she in me, as long as we can still speak. Is that so unbelievable?"

"No," says the prison chaplain, again after a pause, "no, it is believable, it is believable. But I shall have to come back, my son, unless you wish to go alone."

"Alone?" Karl asks softly, and his hands slip from the sleeves.

"No, my son, you shall not go alone," the chaplain says deeply moved, nods to him and leaves the cell.

"Alone?" Karl asks into space.

"No," he hears Dora's answer, "I, too, have to go, and Hans and Sophia and Alexander—and Christopher."

"Why do you name him last, though the order of names is established for all eternity, and why did you take a deep breath, Dora, before you pronounced his name?"

"Do you still suspect him, Karl, still?"

"Why did he drape himself in the black cloth of penitence, at the end—only to differentiate himself from us? Or to make us weak and our death in vain?"

"Our death is his death. He has fought for it as none of us has and he is more deeply rooted in our people than any of us and suffers more than all of us if he can leave nothing for Germany but the black cloth of penitence."

"And why does he count himself among the destroyers of life?"

"Because, for Germany's sake, he destroyed the lives of his loved ones."

"And why does he call himself destroyed, while he still lives?"

"Because he is sick, sick as a German, sick as a lover and sick as the son of his epileptic father."

"And why did you take a deep breath, Dora, before you pronounced his name? Because you agree with him, and believe with him in the long night, the long night before us and after us?"

"Because I begged his forgiveness during the deep breath."

"That I suspected him . . ."

"That we suspected him."

"I shall ask his forgiveness," Karl whispers, "when I walk past him or he past me—no, when I walk past him; for I am the first . . ." Dora is silent. "Do you believe in the long night, Dora?"

"I believe in the new life."

"Have I destroyed your life, Dora?"

"Have I destroyed your life, Karl?"

"Now I should really laugh, Dora, but I can't any more . . ."

"Do you remember, Karl, do you remember Kiel, after your lecture on 'Nationalism and Political Murder,' when I barged into your office, brazenly and at the same time awed with respect? That was the first time you saw me, and you laughed and asked me: 'What is it you want to learn from me, my dear young lady, nationalism or political murder?' "

"Do you remember Marburg, Dora, how you broke in on me at an indecent hour and demanded a long overdue declaration of love, and I said to you: 'I am certain of one thing—that you will flunk your examination with flying colors, candidate Roemer; and I am also certain of another thing—that I am not going to get any gray hair about anything when we are married; now choose, little

Dora'—and then you laughed and kissed my bald pate first and only then my mouth."

Remember, Karl? Remember, Dora? There is so much laughter in their memories. Karl does not laugh, but he smiles in the exchange of memories, and time is suspended . . .

Then time breaks in again and busies itself outside, at the door. Karl knows it well by know, the noise of the door opening and the noise of the door closing. The one is more evil than the other, he knows it. The afterglow of the smile is still on his face, but he forgets it as many people enter, led by the prison chaplain.

"Here I am, my son," he says with his stuffed face, "and I believe you have the courage you will need anon."

He says "anon," instead of "now" or "soon"; Karl can hear it distinctly, although his ears are humming.

"Karl von Hennings, your time has come," says the prison warden.

"Karl von Hennings, your time has come," Karl repeats like an echo, and he does not hear his voice, because his ears are humming. He feels that someone is standing behind him, shackling his hands in back, slipping on the steel cuffs and snapping them shut with a very sure and rather gentle touch. He does not know how his hands came to be in back or where they had been, if they had been hiding, cross-armed, in the wide sleeves or hanging down at the sides, halfway to his back.

The corridor is empty, there are only the black jailers and they don't count, they have never counted. The corridor is empty because Dora is not there nor the friends—and he still has to ask Christopher's forgiveness. There is, for the span of two steps, something like a grudge in him, but only against Christopher, because he does not stand there letting himself be begged for forgiveness, in passing. But then Karl forgets his grudge as well as the word he owes Christopher. What is forgotten now, is forgotten forever. The way is short, an open door gapes to the right. The prison chaplain, walking beside Karl, lets round, hurried, indistinguishable words of prayer roll from his experienced mouth. With the cross which he carries in his hand he points the way through the door to the courtyard.

Karl closes his eyes for one moment and then tears them open.

The light cone of one single searchlight cuts a white path through the night. The beam is glaring—no, it is shrilling, it shrills into Karl's ears. The light-beam beats into the left corner of the courtyard and there stands an executioner's block, only one—spruce and shining with cleanness.

Along the edge of the light-path people stand waiting—but there are only men, though two women should be among them, Dora should be among them—Hans and Alexander and Christopher should be among them, and they could not look like these men in overcoats with hats on their heads. And behind the edge of men lies deep darkness, impenetrable and empty like a great void. And among the men there are some who wear stiff hats and others who wear soft hats, and one of them wears the cap and uniform of the SS. That may be the SS judge; Karl knows the law and he knows that two judges of the court which imposed the sentence must be present—the other judge may be the one with the stiff hat or the one with the felt hat, what does he care?

Someone in back holds him by his handcuffs. Karl stops. The Court Recorder reads the judgment formula. The humming ears receive the voice, words from far away and as if packed in cotton, and hear only one name: Karl von Hennings. And only one of them is there: Karl von Hennings. And there is only one executioner's block, there, in the light-beam.

In back of the executioner's block stand four men, among them one in a black suit with a white tie and white cotton gloves on his tremendous hands. No, Karl looks at the tremendous hands in white cotton gloves to which belong the man in the black suit with the white tie, and the ax.

Karl quickly looks to the right, beyond the Court Recorder, into the blackness. There is nothing and no one. He sees nothing and no one. Someone in back pushes against his handcuffs. Karl must go. He does not see Dora again.

"Tell my wife I greet her," he says with heavy tongue to the prison chaplain who blesses him, in the name of the Father, and the Son, and the Holy Ghost.

2

Adam says, still in the doorway, "I am *only* the barber."

Dora raises her shoulders, not understanding. The peculiar,

sacklike shirt she wears, of stiff, grayish white, coarse linen, is too big for her and falls over her shoulders. She does not adjust it, and looks at the emaciated little man who is only the barber. Adam opens his paintbox, takes some newspaper out of it and a pair of scissors with which he starts to clatter. Clattering is part of the trade, and Dora understands. She unloosens her hair and shakes it free, with a graceful movement of her head. Her hair reaches below her shoulders blades, before her nephritis it went down as far as her waist. Karl used to bring her all sorts of mixtures and lotions to keep her hair from thinning; he was very proud of her hair, although not envious, as he always used to add.

Dora sits down on the stool, arches her back and puts the fingertips of one hand between the knuckles of the other hand. This is what she does at the dentist's, too, ready to sink the fingernails into her flesh if the nerve of the tooth should be hit in drilling.

Adam very gently takes hold of the soft and fine hair below the nape, not touching her skin, and executes a quick, noiseless cut. Yes, it is a noiseless cut, the scissors cut without metallic sound, one cannot hear how the two blades are reunited after their work is done. But Dora jabs her fingernails into the troughs of her knuckles.

And now the scissors start clattering. It is an energetic and somewhat senseless whirl of clatter, they clatter when they rage through the hair, they clatter when only cutting through the air, and it goes with the rapidity of lightning. Now clippers noiselessly creep toward the skin with a cool metal surface, cutting a swath up as high as the ear and leaving the hair not longer than one millimeter—and Dora digs deeper with her nails, and suddenly there is much water in her mouth, and she swallows, and her throat is taut. Then soap lather, like a tepid balm, settles over her scalp which never before has been naked, and in gentle coolness the knife glides after it—one wouldn't believe that it is a knife.

Adam does not use any of his paper towels—he takes the red-checked towel hanging on the tin washstand, unused and in all human expectation useless, and gently presses it against the naked back of the head and gently winds it all around the head, and lo, in his magic hands it suddenly becomes a turban, firmly and warmly enclosing the shorn skull. This, now, is by no means a part of Adam's official duties, but he does it and disappears noiselessly.

Dora said no automatic "thank you"—for what would she have thanked him? For robbing her of the hair which Karl still loves, although it has grown shorter and thinner, with touches of silver in the chestnut gold? And she did not notice the mercy that was granted her in the form of a merciful turban.

She twists forward, her face now rests on her arm, and her arm on her knees. Whether she wants to or not, her ears listen to the door. By now she knows; her heart rears up when the door is unbolted, and calms down again when the door is bolted. That is how her heart behaves and her ears, and her reason says in vain: give it up, for what must come, will come! Now she is tired, as after a hot bath; but it is only lassitude and not sleepiness; the silly wakeful ears take care of that.

What is also silly, is to close the eyes; for there is no mirror here and nothing that mirrors. She has forgotten that she is wearing the merciful turban, although she can feel it firm and warm. And what does she see with her eyes closed? A female bald pate, not exactly hers—because it is difficult or because she has a violent fear of imagining herself hairless—but some indistinct, female bald pate. No, it is not her own and it costs little effort to look closer. She has seen so many things in her life! She has also seen a female bald pate—and here it is again, the shorn head of the Jewish girl of April 1, 1933, the brown-shirted, top-booted April fool's prank of the Jew boycott. The girl's face, pretty and haughty to the point of laughter, is remarkable, it is exemplary. Be haughty, Dora!

She raises her face hesitantly. Toward whom should she be haughty? Toward her own shorn hair? Cautiously she looks behind the stool. There is no hair on the worn brick floor.

An orderly man, Dora thinks and rises.

She crosses her arms close to her chest and slips her hands in the wide sleeves of the shirt, to rub her arms. The cell is heated; but the sackcloth makes the skin shudder. She wants to walk back and forth, but she stops and stares at the gray wall.

Karl looked like an old man. It was as if during the ride his stubble had grown into a gray, grayish white beard. At the end his face was almost unrecognizable; but then, when they stood together, very close together for that one infinitesimal, infinite second, she saw that it was not only the beard which made him an old man—then she saw that his head was shaking, and she could have cried. But how could she see it, with the electric bulb in the standing car getting dimmer and dimmer? Was it the light that was shaking? Was it her own head that was shaking?

She listens. Karl walks back and forth. He does not stand still, like herself, he walks back and forth. She holds her breath and listens. That is no senile step, that is the giant stride of the long-legged master of the house creaking along the gravel path to the little studio house. Thanks to the gravel, Dora cannot be taken unawares . . .

Alas, her ears correct her: it is not the gravel creaking, it is a clanking at the door. Dora whirls around and presses her crossed arms to her breast. That is how her heart behaves and her ears.

"Are you a Protestant, my daughter?" the prison chaplain asks, stopping near the door. Dora nods. "In the absence of a clergyman of your faith, do you permit me to pray for the salvation of your soul, my daughter?"

Dora nods, distinguishes the first words of *De Profundis* and then nothing more but the Amen. The stuffy voice speaks: "Your husband, a brave and upright man, has expressed the wish to be cremated and is convinced that you have the same wish for yourself, my daughter."

"A brave and upright man," Dora hears, straightens up, and nods.

"Your husband wishes that his ashes and yours be put in one and the same urn."

Dora nods. The prison chaplain looks at her; he looks not into her eyes, but at the turban, and then he looks higher still, into space, and speaks more softly: "He said something else besides, and because what he said was good and beautiful and because it will strengthen your heart and console you, my daughter, I shall not keep it from you, although he considered the message superfluous. He speaks with you and in you as long as he can still speak. Make use, then, of your time with him, my daughter, until I return."

Dora nods and he leaves. She still nods, and such a warmth pervades her breast, a good warmth and deep joy of possession, that her skin no longer shudders under the sackcloth and she loosens her arms.

How great is the selection from which they both can choose, Dora and Karl! She only has to open the door, when his step creaks over the gravel, she only has to look at the door—and he is there, a day is there, from the treasure of their nineteen years.

What is it that beclouds him? The new student, the "crazy fellow," who seems to him somewhat uncanny, because he seems uncanny to himself? To disperse clouds is one of Dora's tasks. She has come to know Christopher well, and his step on the gravel has become one of the most familiar. Christopher's step was the last familiar one, Karl, before the gravel creaked strangely in the black morning, under the strange double step. Our wild hunter has second sight, Karl, and he sensed the hour of the catch—and it really didn't take so much clairvoyance, if you think about it.

And Christopher said to Dora that she should hide somewhere. It was senseless and also offending; but he had to say it, driven by the Furies of gratitude. To Dora belonged his gratitude, to Sophia his love, and so he had been compelled to say it also to Sophia, or had meant to say it to her, with the kiss of his pale lips. And had his mother been there, his mother to whom belong both his love and his gratitude, he would have said it to his mother, too. All of a sudden, in chivalrous hysteria, he couldn't bear it that we should be involved, he thought the hour of the catch was an affair for men only, the dear boy.

Why does Dora take precisely this out of the treasure of the years? Is Karl's brow still clouded, when he thinks of Christopher? A brave and upright man sees clearly and sees when he has been in the wrong. And the good warmth pervading Karl and Dora is a selfish warmth. Happiness is our happiness, mine and yours, you and I, we are two, we won't let ourselves be disturbed any more. We must speak, as long as we can still speak, about you and me. We must make use of our time. How great is the selection from which we can choose!

Remember . . . ? Remember . . . ?

Now your hair is on fire, Dora . . .

Someone standing behind her ties her hands to her back and takes the towel from her head. The air touches her naked scalp. The feeling is so strange, so shameless, so terribly hateful, that she fears her heart will stop beating. Her head is bald. Strange, shameless, terribly hateful people talk at her bald head. That is not what horrifies her. When her heart is set in motion again, she will know what horrifies her.

Her legs are set in motion, and now another, a colder air strikes her naked head. She has no way of protecting herself save by a helplessly shackled movement with her shoulders. The shirt sack, much too wide for her, glides from her shoulder; that is all she achieves. But it is not her body that is freezing and at the same time burning, it is her head.

Not until the icy air of night beats against her—and Dora is nothing but a hairless skull—does she know what horrifies her. Alas, it is no mercy to die together with Karl when she is so disfigured at the last—it is a curse, reaching backward over their life together and destroying the beauty of that life!

Grant, God in Heaven, that Karl may not see Dora as she is, at the last, and that it may not make him shudder into his death, grant that she may die before him or after him, but not with him!

Thus Dora learns once more what she has already forgotten: to see and to search. The light cone of a single searchlight beats into the right corner of the courtyard. No human eye can see to the left; for there is the fierce fire of the source of light and blinds the eye. At the right, along the edge of the path of judgment, people stand waiting, men in overcoats, with hats on their heads—not Karl. Behind them is the black void. Dora knows Karl is not in the black void. Where the light-beam lands, there is an executioner's block, only one, spruce and shining with cleanness.

"Oh, God! Oh, God! I am the first!" Dora whispers and is grateful.

The prison chaplain prays: "Forgive me, God my Lord, that I did not give her the man's last greeting. For Thou alone knowest, God my Lord, why I could not bring myself to do it."

3

"I am *only* the barber."

"What's that? Oh, I see, well, all right . . ."

Hans makes an effort to rise from his cot; he has difficulties, the fright has struck his artificial leg, so to speak.

"You don't need to get up," says Adam, "just lean forward."

Hans obeys and props his head on his hand. Adam stands next to him and yet does not touch his shoulder as he puts the clippers to his neck. Hans shudders. Adam quickly withdraws the instrument, reaches for his scissors and clatters through the air with them, as if to quiet his victim. The door opens. Adam raises his head in annoyance. He hates to be disturbed. A police sergeant appears, with another condemned man dressed in an execution shirt.

"As a special favor to front soldiers," the police sergeant announces, "the warden has granted your request. Non-commissioned officer Welte may stay here and talk with you for ten minutes, in my presence, of course."

Hans does not look up.

"Hans!" Alexander calls.

Being a polite man, Adam did not clatter through the sergeant's words, nor does he wish to interfere with the conversation of the two friends, though he does want to perform his task. So he must exchange the scissors for the clippers again, which make less noise, but feel cold on the neck. He can't help it if the bent-over prisoner's blond neck hair stands on edge from terror; the circumstances must be blamed for that.

"Hans!" Alexander calls for the second time.

"Tell me a joke, Alex," Hans whispers.

"What?"

"A joke, Alex!" Hans moans and draws up his shoulders.

Alexander makes big eyes, keeps a straight face and says: "A barkeeper sees to his astonishment that one of his guests at the bar has a radish sticking in each of his ears. The bar is crowded, the impatient guest disappears before the barkeeper can serve him and ask him why he has radishes stuck in his ears. On the following day the man comes back, radishes in his ears, and again vanishes before the barkeeper can satisfy his curiosity. On the third day the man appears with a red beet in each of his ears. The barkeeper pounces on him: 'For the love of God, man, tell me why do you stick red beets in your ears?'—'Yes, yes, dreadful times,' the man replies gravely, 'there wasn't any radishes in the market today . . .' "

The head-keeper, the keeper on duty and the police sergeant at the door are laughing. Adam throws a reproving look at them; for one does not laugh here. When a joke is told here, it is not to make people laugh, but to help get over the shearing. The woman just before did it with her fingernails, everyone has his own ways and means, some do it with screaming and kicking. Adam values it highly that this blond fellow and the woman before him and that first one, who held his face up to be shaved, have found the quiet ways and means. The fourth one here, the visitor and understanding helper in need, who told his joke as soothingly as a lullaby, does not seem to be an exception. Adam works fast and with nimble hand, and now he has finished.

"Could take care of this one right here," he suggests, pointing to Alexander.

"All right," the head-keeper nods.

"But my working time is not part of the ten minutes," Adam demands.

"At your orders, Adam," says the police sergeant, saluting. He is a man with a sense of humor.

"And his name is Adam, too," Alexander whispers and sits down on the stool. He bends forward and props his head with his hands, as he has seen Hans do it.

"As for my mangy scalp, Mister Adam," Alexander elucidates, "it is not the mange, but . . ." He loses the thread, the clippers settle metallically cold on his neck, he seeks Hans with his eyes.

"Simply think of heresy number two," Hans suggests.

"Yes, indeed," says Alexander with a pleased look, "I say that the face has drooping shoulders, broad hips and a soft belly."

"And the dark impulse to cover up something," Hans prompts him.

"Haha!" Alexander laughs to himself, not very loudly. "Where is it the hands are safest?"

Adam is puzzled; that a fellow should laugh during the shearing is something new, though not as reprehensible as the laughter of outsiders. And why, after all, should there not be some who do it with laughter, instead of doing it with screaming and kicking.

"But the eyes!" Hans exclaims.

"Melodramatic blockade breakers," Alexander retorts. "And imagine the moment when they no longer stab into the masses, but into empty space . . ."

"That won't do," the police sergeant breaks in. "You will have to talk in a way that makes sense."

"I beg your pardon, Sergeant," Alexander politely addresses

him, "this is entirely harmless talk. But we can drop the subject, too."

Hans quickly covers his smile with his hand.

Adam has vanished. Alexander strokes his skull with his hand. "And that calls itself Adam!" he marvels, shaking his head.

"A pretty sight we make," Hans observes.

"I don't feel that I am any uglier this way," Alexander counters; "better to be bald than mangy. And in Rostov on the Don neither your haircut nor your hospital shirt was any more elegant, young man."

"And yet, old top, I would prefer to have my little sister sitting here in your place."

"I, too, would give you up for her, Hans, and, anyway, you sat facing her during the ride, I didn't."

"Console yourself, Alex, she didn't have much time for me, her eyes were chained to Christopher. Tell me, did Christopher look at my sister, too?"

"Why do you ask?" Alexander says somewhat hesitatingly.

"Because I couldn't see him, but you could, and because Sophia's eyes didn't look as if they were being looked at."

"He kept his eyes closed," Alexander says; "only toward the end he looked at her."

"How did he look at her?"

"With inexpressible fear."

"Do you understand that?" Hans asks softly.

"Yes!" Alexander exclaims impetuously. "I understand that! I thought that my heart would break, too, when I saw Sophia climbing into the Black Maria in the courtyard of the Palace of Justice."

"Oh, I see," says Hans after a short pause. "You mean his inexpressible fear for her."

"And for himself!"

"That's it, then," Hans whispers. "He has changed after all, then."

"No, Hans, it isn't that he is afraid of death! Remember the unbelievable struggle he fought today to regain his accountability, and kindly take your hat off to his fear!"

"Oh, God . . ." Hans whispers and sits very straight on the cot.

"And now you can say: That's it!"

"That's it . . ." Hans whispers.

"Stupor, or whatever you want to call it," Alexander says.

"Only three minutes more, gentlemen," the police sergeant warns, watch in hand.

The friends look at each other, and of the three minutes half a one passes in silence, so difficult is it suddenly to find a word.

"Well, and as for the fear . . ." Alexander finally speaks with an awkward chin.

"My dear fellow," Hans consoles him, "I have already had so much fear, East of the Don and West of it, that it really doesn't matter."

"Give me some sensible advice for the damned situation, Hans, when I am lying under my death and know exactly where it will strike. You should know, because you were under the flak truck once."

"Only my leg."

"And what did you think about in the last moment?"

"About my leg."

"But I *don't* want to think about my head!"

"Then don't think at all. Ways to avoid thinking: cursing, counting, praying, singing . . ."

"Singing!" Alexander exclaims. "What could I sing?"

"I don't know," says Hans. "Unfortunately we have no song of freedom . . ."

With that the three minutes have run out. But the prison chaplain appears and the separation of the friends is postponed a second time.

"What's this?" the chaplain asks the police sergeant. "Two together?"

"Special concession for front fighters, Father."

"Well, well," the chaplain nods and looks at the uniform trousers which are visible beneath the sack shirts, "and what about the religious affiliations of the two war buddies?"

"I am a Protestant," says Hans.

"I was born a Catholic," says Alexander.

"Do you mean by that, my son," the priest turns to him, "that you are no longer a Catholic?"

"I mean by it, Father, that in the Hitler Youth we had to forget all that."

The priest closes his eyes and opens them again, as a mildly impressive indication that he has not taken note of Alexander's answer. "But undoubtedly you will still be able to pray the 'Credo' or the 'Pater noster' or at least the 'Ave Maria' with me."

"In the Hitler Youth, Father, one prays only: 'We were born to die for Germany!' "

The priest lowers his head, clasps his hands in front of his chest and speaks with a strong voice: " 'Out of the depths have I cried unto thee, O Lord!' " Then he lowers his voice to an incomprehensible whispering, until the Amen.

"Amen," says Hans. "And I would like to express a wish, Father."

"That is what I am here for, my son."

"I have an artificial leg," says Hans. "I desire that it stay with my body, as my right leg. I ask you to take official note of it, here and now."

The chaplain looks at him and lowers his head and looks at him again. Out of his cassock he produces a notebook and a fountain pen. He clears his throat and asks: "You are?"

"Hans Moeller."

The prison chaplain writes standing up, with an expert and hasty hand. "At the same time we might take care of this, too," he suggests, looking up. "The law permits the delivery of the mortal remains to the next of kin for the purpose of interment or cremation, provided no ceremonies of any kind are held. In case next of kin live out of town, only cremation and transmittance of the urn can be considered. Have you any relatives, and where?"

"I shall still have my mother," Hans answers slowly. "She lives as a bombed-out refugee in Oldenburg. But I want to be buried."

"For religious reasons?"

"Because my right leg cannot be cremated."

The chaplain puts his pen to the notebook twice, then he writes on. "Read this and sign," he says and hands the notebook and pen to Hans. Hans reads and signs.

"Would you please countersign it, Father," he says. The priest looks at him and complies.

"I, too, wish to be buried," Alexander speaks up.

"I am glad of that, my son," the priest nods, "for a good Catholic there can be no cremation."

"My father," Alexander explains pitilessly, "is a veterinarian, much in demand and consequently pleased with God and the world, and such urns are professionally disturbing."

The chaplain closes his eyes and opens them again. "And now also I should like to express a wish," he says to Alexander; "I have to battle for your soul, my son. I wish to go to your cell with you now to administer the last sacrament to you, so that you may go before your God consoled and cleansed."

"I wish it too, Alex," Hans says softly.

"It is high time," the police sergeant warns, tapping the crystal of his watch with his finger.

The young man from Bremen is cool and reserved by nature and only grips his friend's shoulders and looks at him. The young man from Ulm is a warmer sort, born under a bluer sky, and he throws his arms around Hans' shoulders and strokes his shaved head. But both, as with one mouth, whisper: "Auf Wiedersehen . . ."

And yet their ways are parting now, however near they may be to each other and however short their time. Even the glaring galleries of light in which they end are not the same; for the one searchlight cuts out of the night the third of the courtyard's four corners, the northeastern one—the other, however, lights up the fourth, on the opposite side.

4

"Only! Only!" Sophia cries out, runs to the farthest corner of the cell, and shields her hair with her hands. That he is the barber is enough to make her feel the long threatened radical shearing. That he is *only* the barber mocks the fear of death and death itself.

Adam knows the effect of his appearance upon delinquents and usually disregards it. Had this very young girl screamed "No!" or "I don't want to!" or had she simply screamed and kicked, he would have directed the two keepers with one look to seize the shrew by her arms and put her into position for the treatment; whether standing, sitting or lying down, it is all the same to him. But that she was horrified not so much by himself as by the additional and emphasized little word of self-depreciation, gives him pause, and with a silent look he directs the two keepers not to go into action.

"Miss," says Adam, opening his paintbox and looking into it, "I have said the same thing to four others today; so you are not the first, but the fifth. But you are the first one to make a fuss."

Sophia lets her hands drop, comes out of her corner with small steps, and sits down on the stool, turning her back to Adam and to the men at the door.

Adam's scissors clatter soothingly. He does not like it that the girl holds on tightly to the stool with her hands, as if she were afraid of falling off. Adam knows he has not won yet. He stands behind her now, his scissors clattering through the air, nearer and nearer to her profuse hair, until they clatter into it, very lightly, so that according to his expert opinion she cannot notice the first locks falling. But she does notice it, and it hurts her, he can see it by the quiver of her shoulders; and since it is not one single quiver, but a continued up and down of little shocks, he knows that she is weeping, though soundlessly.

Adam stops clattering and says, "None of them cried."

He does not wait for the shoulders to be quieted, but mows through the blond thicket with deep and rapid cuts. By the time he has bared the nape, the shoulders stand firm and calm again.

The scissors, however, Adam knows, are only the enemy of the hair and do not touch the skin, they are not the enemy of man. If this girl wept even at the scissors, how will it be when she feels the clippers on her neck!

Adam puts the scissors away, reaches for the clippers and says: "One of them even laughed, the fourth."

Sophia releases her grip on the stool and puts her hands in her lap. Who is the fourth? She asks herself. For this is highly deserving of the question, since she was the fourth in the ironclad sequence and yet is the fourth no longer. Now she is the fifth in Christopher's place, their places are changed, God knows for what reasons, and if the fourth laughed during the shearing, then it was Christopher . . .

Even the metallic impact on the neck only touches the skin when the thoughts are elsewhere and thus do not heighten the terror into a portent of death. Sophia's thoughts are with Christopher who has laughed in such a moment. But how could he laugh when during the ride in the prison car his face was so full of a fear the significance of which only she, his beloved, comprehends; how could it be anything but the laughter of a despair which no longer knows the bliss of weeping?

"But *how* did he laugh?" Sophia asks in a very small voice.

Adam cannot remember that a person ever asked a question when being shorn by him, and at that a question about another person. "As a fellow laughs when he thinks of something funny," he answers.

"How beautiful!" Sophia whispers.

Adam marvels and does something unusual: he bends slightly forward and looks at the face of a person who, while being shorn, said: 'How beautiful!' It is not exactly a smile that he beholds, but only a softness around the mouth, which is as good as a smile, or better. Adam does something else still, which is not in the least a part of his duty: he is considerate of the young girl's exceedingly pretty face, he leaves short curls on the front part of her head, and they fall charmingly over her forehead. She could look into a mirror without fear, if there were a mirror here. She needs no merciful turban. Adam vanishes soundlessly. She notices neither his departure nor the mercy that has been granted her.

"Now we'll do nothing but laugh, for a whole week," Christopher had said in that lovable crisp voice of his, as they cycled from Salzburg to Reichenhall, last summer. Already the preceding day, the day of their arrival in Salzburg, had been beautiful, like any first day of vacation in a strange city, although it had not been without its shadow. For here it was again, what they did not want to see and hear: swastika, uniform, the Führer's likeness and the radio's Nazi gibberish. It marred their enjoyment of the good Tyrolese wine in the good, old Peterskeller, that timeless monastery inn facing the changing times with monkish indolence. Not until night, when they roamed through the quaint streets and the moon glittered over a baroque fountain, over a church portal, over the blissful stillness of the cathedral square, had the city regained its ducal bishop's features, and it smelled Catholic, as Sophia put it. Then they had gone to their little hotel on Mozartgasse. Christopher assured her solemnly that on his mother's place at Vogelöd there would be no swastika, no uniform, no Führer's likeness and no radio. He kissed her and went to his room. He never stayed with her, they are a strange pair of lovers; it is not Sophia's fault, the shadow comes from him.

Oh, the happiness of that week at Vogelöd! A happiness that fulfilled itself obediently in conformity to Christopher's decree. It consisted of the sun-drunk August days, Forest Mountain, meadow and yellow wheat field, of house, stables, milk warm from the cow, home-baked ryebread, eggs, butter and pork meat. Only four people shared in it: Christopher and Sophia, Frau Ursula and Fridolin.

There are mothers who are jealous of their sons, and peasant women who suspect every stranger from the city. But Frau Ursula did not rob Sophia of a single hour of her good time, not even for one minute did she survey and appraise her; she received her with motherly joy, and she radiated happiness, like the warm and wonderfully understanding August days over this enchanted corner of the earth. And there was much laughing, with flashing eyes and flashing teeth, as only Christopher could laugh and his mother and Fridolin. The child, especially, possessed as the gift and sound of life a pealing laugh which did not wait to be awakened by Christopher's handstands and bicycle tricks, but rang through the house every morning, like a blissful alarm clock, infectious throughout the day.

"That you never told me a word about this sweet little brother of yours!" Sophia wondered.

"From discretion!" Christopher laughed. "I only got him nine months ago, you know."

"But the boy is already three years old!" Sophia exclaimed.

"Don't start figuring, Sophia, it will lead to nothing!" Christopher laughed.

They were sitting on the ridge of Forest Mountain; Fridolin picked blueberries, ate them instead of gathering them in his tin bowl, and laughed.

"This is where the border used to run," Christopher said, "and over there was another country, and who was born here is a born smuggler, and the born smugglers were just the right ones to smuggle people who were in danger, who were hunted, or who had escaped, from here to there, out of the torture chamber into supposed liberty. Of course that went on only until March, 1938.

Since then the born smugglers have been complaining of bad business."

Christopher lay on his back and laughed to himself. He wore short leather pants and heavy, low shoes, nothing else. His brownish body was hairless like that of a boy and sinewy like that of an athlete. He looked younger still than he was, radiantly youthful, entirely without shadow. Sophia looked at him and kissed him. "That for the born smuggler," she laughed.

He held her fast. "When the boy was born," he said, "there was no border here any more, and so he became my sweet little brother —do you understand that?"

"No . . ."

"Then I shall tell you about my sweet big mother, Sophia . . ."

He told her. A woodpecker tapped affirmingly. Somewhere in the underbrush Fridolin laughed pealingly.

Could Sophia declare her love to the sweet big mother? It did not seem feasible. She could look and smile at Ursula, her eyes could follow her with great tenderness when she disappeared in the laundry with Fridolin, to bathe him behind locked doors. More could not be conceded, and it was not enough. It was not enough to shower the child with love, the little, unsuspecting, human contraband smuggled out of the wicked custom house of these times. And her love for the born smuggler who brought his beloved to his treasure cove and packed her heart full with unknown goods of happiness: is it enough for her overflowing heart?

And Sophia went to Christopher, one night. His room was opposite hers, the floor boards in the hallway did not creak under her naked feet, she only had to stretch out her hands in the dark and find his door which was not locked; no door was bolted in this house, save one now and again: the laundry door.

"It is I, Chris," she whispered and noiselessly pressed the door shut behind her; "you needn't turn on any light."

"Yes," he answered and did not move.

At this, she did not move either, and stayed where she was, standing near the door. Oh, it would have been better, had he turned on a light; for there is nothing so black and shadowy, as silence in the dark. And the shadow came from him, as always and ever, it had stepped out of him and shrouded him as never before, him and her.

"I am going again," she whispered at last, "and I have never been here at all, Chris, good night . . ."

"Sophia!" he exclaimed softly, to keep her from leaving, it seemed; but she was still standing there. "Look here, Sophia," he continued, and his voice was not even troubled, "I want you to know that I am not on very good terms with my body, I can subdue it, but it can subdue me too, I can initiate a convulsion, but I never know when my body will release me from it again. And that time when I let the stupor come over me so as not to become a soldier, it took weeks—and our week's vacation will be over soon, Sophia—it took weeks for me to find my way out of my . . . of my"—he groped for the word and finally found a rather peculiar and almost jocular one—"of my snail shell."

"Don't disturb me!" Sophia exclaims, forgetful of herself, without turning around. She has not yet finished with Christopher, who has laughed; she now knows the shadows that rushed in upon him, the shadows from the fate of his sweet big mother and of his sweet little brother and of his untouched beloved, she knows the shadows of the snail shell, she regrets her question, the last question she put to him: "Why have you become so different?" But she is unable to understand how he could laugh under the shears of the black jacket—she is unable to believe it, and yet would like so much to believe . . .

Sophia hears whispering behind her, turns her head and sees a priest standing in the cell, softly murmuring prayers. She jumps up, runs to the farthest corner of the cell and cries: "No! No! Not yet! Not yet!"

The priest speaks a gentle Amen and leaves his hands clasped in prayer in front of his chest. "I do not come to disturb you," he says cautiously. "Compose yourself, my daughter, look at me and see who I am, and let your young heart be consoled, even if you do not belong to the Church."

"Consoled . . ." Sophia whimpers the one word her ear has discerned, and she shakes her head.

"My dear child," he says soothingly, "you are not the first member of the Protestant Church, who today . . ."

"Oh, please . . ." she interrupts, trembling, "how many—oh, please . . ."

"I have already called upon three Protestants among your friends."

"No, no . . ." she says hastily and her hands are fluttering, "I mean, how many have you seen altogether . . . how many of my friends have you visited . . . Oh, please!"

"I have seen four; you are the fifth, my daughter," the priest answers, still puzzled.

Now she comes out of her corner and nearer, nearer than any of the four before her has come to the prison chaplain, and she touches the sleeve of his cassock and implores him: "Oh, Pastor . . . Reverend, how was . . . how has . . . how did the fourth bear up? Oh, please . . ."

"The fourth . . ." says the priest, and lo, he smiles, he smiles; "the fourth is a bold fellow and yet no lost son of the Church, the bold fellow . . ."

Strange and wonderful can be God's ways and means of giving consolation to a young heart, and great calm. As Sophia stands in the stream of light ending in the middle of the courtyard's northern longitudinal wall there is for her no right or left behind the curtain of night, but only the spruce, scrubbed thing straight ahead, and she is the first, perhaps because she is the youngest and a woman, too.

"He sends you his greeting, my daughter, he is of good cheer," says the prison chaplain, and then he prays: "Forgive me, God my Lord, that I gave the greeting to this one and not to that other to whom it was due. For Thou alone, God my Lord, knowest why it had to be thus and not otherwise."

5

Adam is shrewd. He takes a look at the sixth one, before he introduces himself.

There, in the middle of the cell, stands a fellow, tall and straight as a tree, and trembles.

"I am *only* the barber," says Adam somewhat crossly.

The man looks at him. It is a deeply troubled, but not a trembling look—yes, the distress comes from the depth and is not the receipt for Adam's appearance. One should not judge hastily,

Adam, and simply think: there stands a fellow, tall and straight as a tree, and trembles. For the man is not trembling, he is moving, or more precisely: he keeps himself in motion.

Everything about him is in motion, in infinitesimal movements: the eyelids, the face muscles, the shoulders, the arms, the fingers, the knees and even the top leather of the shoes in which the toes are stirring. One could think that a nervous itch prickled the body: but then he would scratch himself. One could think that he was freezing in the low-cut sack shirt on his bare body: but then he would hold together the heat of his body with his arms. His motions, however, are infinitesimal, continuous and uncannily necessary—perhaps to keep his blood in circulation. There is a cliché about the blood curdling. One should not use the phrase indiscriminately, Adam: perhaps his blood threatens to curdle in his veins.

"If you wish," says Adam, opening his paintbox, "you may continue keeping yourself in motion, standing or sitting, it doesn't bother me."

Christopher is not astonished at the stranger's offer. The stranger's? How could one say that! A stranger couldn't know that Christopher has to keep in motion.

"That is not enough," says Christopher, and his voice is like that of a man who hasn't spoken for a long time.

"What shall we do?" Adam meditates.

"I'll do it myself," says Christopher.

"Hardly possible," Adam muses; but he doesn't say no, he doesn't say that it is impossible, he meditates. "Put your hand in back of your head," he orders, "but loosely, very loosely!" Christopher complies. Adam shoves his right hand with the scissors under Christopher's hand. "Hold my hand now," he orders, "but loosely, very loosely!"

Christopher's hand rides on the hand which bares his neck and scalp. He handles the instrument indirectly, and that is enough to subdue it, instead of being subdued by scissors, clippers and razor.

"All right?" Adam asks.

"Quite all right," Christopher answers.

What ways and means! Adam marvels to himself.

"Thank you," says Christopher after Adam has already vanished, and he looks at his hand which had participated in the shearing. His fear of the shock had been great, and everything went off beautifully. But he must not permit himself to think back, he must not let his thoughts play with the danger he has overcome; for his body is gravely wrought up and challenged, perhaps it would be enough merely to think of the shock, of this stroke of lightning, crackling hot and cold through his spine, with heart-stopping lust: and the body closes itself like an iron curtain. Nor must he permit himself to think ahead, of the next danger he may have to face, or especially of the last danger, the extreme and unfathomable one. No, he must exercise great care and utilize his momentary advantage. Now why did it go so wonderfully well with the shearing?

Because his own hand did the violent thing to himself. Do violence to one's self?

What kind of answer is this, Christopher?

Again he sets his body in motion, infinitesimal movements, and then there is a clanking outside the door. A gentleman enters and with a gesture of his hand orders the keeper to wait outside. The gentleman wears a stiff black hat and a black overcoat with a velvet collar. Christopher does not know him.

He does not know him?

He stops moving. He forgets to keep in motion. He recognizes the gentleman.

"Sauer," President Behn speaks in a languid tone of voice, "it is not customary for the president of the People's Court personally to attend executions. This legally prescribed obligation usually falls to the two youngest members of the Court. That I am here nevertheless and contrary to custom has its reasons. I just wanted you to know that."

Christopher puts his hands behind his back, so that he can move them unseen.

"Secondly," says President Behn, "I also want you to know, or recall to your memory, that the law forbids the execution of the death sentence in the case of the mentally ill. Stupor, or whatever it may be, is regarded as a mental illness."

"I am not suffering from stupor," Christopher whispers and moves his fingers behind his back.

"I know," says President Behn; "but the said act of will power would suffice . . ."

"I won't . . ." Christopher whispers.

"The said act of will power, performed in this cell, perhaps during the next quarter hour and carried through with well-known expertness, would suffice to postpone execution indefinitely and to turn you over to the health authorities. And since the said act of will power would be proof to us of your readiness to do penance, a readiness we have noticed earlier, your stay in the care of the health authorities would, so to speak, represent only a transition to a new life . . ."

"Go!" Christopher shouts, and the shouting does him good, it puts his whole body in motion.

"Before I go," says President Behn, "I must tell you that personally I doubt your so-called act of will power. In other words: I think you are ill and I am fairly certain that you will have one of your notorious attacks on the way to the scaffold, a way peculiarly subject to attacks. I shall be close by and watch like a hawk. It so happens that we are interested in you and in your new life, because you are unlike or have become unlike the other five. As you will remember, I am not the only one to hold this opinion; and we consider ourselves capable of instilling the necessary contrition in you. And, watching you on your way to the scaffold, I shall be joined not only by the prison doctor, but also by an unprejudiced psychiatrist—not Professor Ackermann, of course, who, incidentally, may already have been taken to the concentration camp at Dachau. I don't think I have any more to say. I shall see you later, Sauer—or earlier. We still leave it open, generously."

President Behn leaves the cell. The door is still open, a priest enters, he wears a white surplice over his cassock and in his hands he holds a chalice, covered with a brocade cloth. He says softly, "Chris . . ."

Lost in thought, Christopher starts, then runs toward him: "Oh, God, Uncle Rupert . . ."

"I have received permission to visit you and to administer the sacraments to you, Chris," Rector Ruhsilver says, putting the chalice on the folding table attached to the wall.

Christopher is standing still. "Uncle Rupert," he asks, and his eyes are black with suspicion, "do you know who the gentleman is who was just here to see me?"

"No."

"And he didn't speak with you?"

"No. He did not even greet the chalice," Rector Ruhsilver says and puts his arm around Christopher's shoulder. "Is it hard, my dear lad?"

"Not any more," Christopher answers and swallows and asks: "What do you think will happen to mother?"

"Attorney Futterer thinks she will get off with six years in prison."

"Six years . . ." Christopher whispers and swallows.

"It won't last another six years," Uncle Rupert says under his breath. They walk to the cot and sit down close to each other.

"I am glad you are not the way you were that evening, Chris," says Rector Ruhsilver, "so speechless and motionless, I was afraid for you . . ."

"Yes," Christopher nods, "I am different now."

"Then let us hear Confession," says Uncle Rupert and he has his arm around Christopher's shoulder.

" 'I accuse myself before God Almighty and before you in God's place and I repent the following sins which I have committed,' " Christopher murmurs the Confession formula.

"That's all right, Chris. I give you absolution. You deserve it."

"No," Christopher whispers, "I have sent my mother to prison."

"You are not guilty of that, Chris, and if you do regard it as guilt, how dreadful then must be Peter's guilt in your eyes, when he thrice denied the Lord before the cock crew!"

"I feel guilt whenever I think of Fridolin, I can't help it . . ."

"I feel the same, Chris, and so does Our Lord, I think."

"I have it on my conscience that two women are sharing my fate, and one of them I love beyond all measure and yet I did not protect her from my fate . . ."

"Keep her on your conscience, Chris, it will do her good."

"I have it on my conscience that a physician and a good man was sent to the concentration camp because of me."

"I take it off your conscience, Chris, and put it on the scale of guilt which is so great, so great . . ."

"And who weighs it?"

"Not you, Chris, you lie on the other scale and weigh heavily."

"And who atones for it?" Christopher exclaims.

"Not you, but the rest of us."

Christopher shakes his head and speaks ever more softly. "But I know even at this moment that I shall not go all the way to the end with my five friends . . ."

Rector Ruhsilver looks at him and speaks: "*Absolvo te!*"

"The Church forgives too easily . . ." Christopher breathes.

Rector Ruhsilver rises and goes to the folding table to fetch the chalice. Christopher kneels down. The priest gives him the host.

They are sitting together again. "I have permission," Uncle Rupert says, "to stay with you until they come for you."

"How long will that be?"

"That I don't know."

"I must have ten minutes to myself, Uncle Rupert, at least ten minutes . . ."

Uncle Rupert stands up, without hesitating, and kisses him. He does not speak one word, he cannot speak any more.

But before the cell door he stops and speaks: "Knock for me, Chris, you see I must hold the chalice."

Christopher knocks for him, the door opens, Uncle Rupert walks out. The door is closed and bolted.

They have taken away his necktie and his trouser belt and even his shoe laces. He takes off his shirt—the sack shirt, the execution shirt, the shirt of death. He takes hold of it by the circular cut for the neck and tears it apart. The muscles of his arms swell from the mighty effort; oh, he is strong, the shirt tears along the seam on its side. With his strong teeth he bites a hole into the hem of the shirt and rips it into strips. He ties the strips together and twists them into a rope. He twists a rope for himself.

He ties the rope into a loop. He takes the mattress from the cot and puts it on the floor, below the grated window high up in the wall. He puts the stool on the mattress. He climbs up on the stool, fastens the rope to the bars of the window and tries it out, by pulling himself up three times, and the rope holds. He speaks to his friends: "Understand, it is the only sure way that leads to you." He knows that they do not hear him. He takes also this upon himself. He slips his head into the loop. He pushes the stool away. The stool noiselessly tumbles over on the mattress.

The light-beam cuts the middle of the courtyard's southern wall out of the night. There stands the spruce scaffold, the sixth of six or the first, it does not matter. The scaffold has been deserted. It has become a meaningless scaffold. Finally the searchlight realizes it and dies away. Then night prevails.

6

An announcement posted on the black bulletin board informed the students that they were to assemble in the auditorium of the university at ten o'clock of the following morning in order to receive a communication from the president of the university. The president then informed the student body of the crime committed by Hennings and Associates and of the punishment which overtook the evildoers without delay. Incisively he spoke the necessary words of indignation and of warning. The incident occurring in the course of his speech, however, did not come from the students, who listened attentively, with bated breath. The incident came from above. Through the air shafts of the auditorium leaflets came flying down, hundreds of leaflets printed on newsprint. At the same time hundreds of printed leaflets fluttered down into the street from the roof of the university. It was the leaflet.

The Security Department, prepared for every eventuality, succeeded in arresting the students active on the roof.

There were six of them.

